CODE NAME

SNOWBIRD

By

James H. Scott

© Copyright 2005 James H. Scott.
All rights reserved. No part of this publication may be reproduced, stored in a retrieval system, or transmitted, in any form or by any means, electronic, mechanical, photocopying, recording, or otherwise, without the written prior permission of the author.

Printed in Victoria, BC, Canada

Note for Librarians: a cataloguing record for this book that includes Dewey Decimal Classification and US Library of Congress numbers is available from the Library and Archives of Canada. The complete cataloguing record can be obtained from their online database at:
www.collectionscanada.ca/amicus/index-e.html
ISBN 1-4120-2645-8

TRAFFORD

This book was published *on-demand* in cooperation with Trafford Publishing. On-demand publishing is a unique process and service of making a book available for retail sale to the public taking advantage of on-demand manufacturing and Internet marketing. On-demand publishing includes promotions, retail sales, manufacturing, order fulfilment, accounting and collecting royalties on behalf of the author.

Offices in Canada, USA, UK, Ireland, and Spain
book sales for North America and international:
Trafford Publishing, 6E–2333 Government St.
Victoria, BC V8T 4P4 CANADA
phone 250 383 6864   toll-free 1 888 232 4444
fax 250 383 6804   email to orders@trafford.com
book sales in Europe:
Trafford Publishing (UK) Ltd., Enterprise House, Wistaston Road Business Centre
Crewe, Cheshire CW2 7RP UNITED KINGDOM
phone 01270 251 396   local rate 0845 230 9601
facsimile 01270 254 983   orders.uk@trafford.com
order online at:
www.trafford.com/robots/04-0473.html

10   9   8   7   6   5   4   3   2   1

ACKNOWLEDGEMENTS

Having received support from my family and friends during the writing of this book, I wish to express my thanks to my daughter Tina for giving me the idea in the first place and my wife Pat for giving me time and space to 'get on with it' and most recently to my Grand-daughter Alex for advice on computer technology.

I would like to take the opportunity to say thank you to Keith Robins for his wise guidance and encouragement in the early stages, to Norman and June Benneyworth for their reading and commenting on the first drafts and to any others whose ears I have 'bent' while trying to get it all together.

Most of all I wish to express my undying gratitude to Terri Last who most probably did not realise what she was letting herself in for when she 'volunteered' to Proof and Edit the final draft which had lain gathering dust a while. No easy task on its own but by skilfully using modern technology and giving me the occasional push, she completed the task in good time and at a distance - as she lives 130 miles away. Without her unfailing help I would not have got this far.

Well here we are folks we've made it, now look out for the other one it's on its way.

Thank you all.

Jim.

CODE NAME

SNOWBIRD

*For Betty
With Best Wishes
Jill*

To Avenge:-

To take revenge in return for a wrong or injury:

To retaliate:

To seek or take vengeance:

Prologue

7. p.m. Somewhere, in the Central Mountains of Colombia.

"Bloody Hell, I stink," I muttered, mopping the stinging sweat from my eyes. The jungle's stifling heat and the strenuous work of digging this 'hide' made me feel as if I was standing under a tepid shower. Worse still, every move wafted the acrid smell of sweat across my face; my head itched and my beard itched. I had a job to stop myself from scratching. If I did and opened the skin then infection would take over and that could be fatal.

Raging thirst was another thing I had to contend with. The heat of the day had given way to a clinging sultry humidity. Dying for a drink, but conscious of the need to preserve my small supply of water, all I could do was take small sips from my combat water bottle.

"Yuck. It's luke-bloody-warm." I almost shouted in despair.

Hey you .... Big mouth. You're supposed to be on a secret mission, a voice whispered urgently in my ear. Carry on like that and the whole of Colombia will know you're here. My training made me automatically look furtively around in the pitch darkness. There was no one there.

"Talking to yourself again," I cursed silently, while heeding the warning.

The need for caution was paramount; carelessness could give this hidden position and the whole operation away.

Code Name SNOWBIRD

My team were engaged on a dangerous mission; hence, my digging this deep hole in the jungle floor. It would be my 'home' over the next few long hours.

This covert operation demanded that my small team of volunteers and myself, all ex Special Forces members, be dropped by helicopter in a night landing on a very rough mountainside several kilometres away from our target area. Through the remainder of the long night and the following day, we had made our way slowly across the inhospitable and unforgiving terrain in a gruelling forced march. We could not just slash our way through the lush vines and clinging creepers, as this would declare our presence. Our only alternative was to follow animal tracks if possible, or push the soft growth aside. Moving cautiously, going to ground at any sign of danger, we approached our target. During the latter part of the move, small groups of the team had split off in different directions to reach their designated positions.

The risk element was high. Mine was increased by my part of the attack, requiring me to be alone for the duration - that is, accept for the *inner voice* that lone 'operators' learn to cultivate to preserve their sanity. So it was fortunate, while pushing my way through the thick jungle undergrowth, that only my pride was hurt when I took a bad tumble down a long steep slope, ending up in a stinking jungle swamp. Later, just to make sure I was really enjoying myself; Lady Luck threw in a very close call with a Big Cat. To be on the safe side, I'd followed rule number one in the 'Coward's Book of Rules,' and returned to the swamp to soak myself even more thoroughly. From past experience in the world of Special

Forces, this sort of discomfort was all 'par for the course,' but as I'd now been 'retired' for a few years, I didn't expect it on such a personal mission as this.

There's nothing you can do about the smell without a shower, my little voice counselled, as another wave of the sickening stink wafted past my face. Sipping some more of my precious water I said to myself, "A shower. Yeah, that would be great, but there's no chance of that. I've got to get this bloody hole dug."

Resuming my work, I couldn't help thinking that perhaps I really should be more grateful to Mother Nature for causing my tumble. After all, the soaking in the swamp had stained my face and other exposed skin with green slimy mud. This meant that here in enemy territory no flash of pale skin would alert any guards and my human scent would be masked to animals as well. The pungent muck, coupled with the heavy sweat pouring off me, was the reason for the smell so I could hardly complain.

"Get off you buggers," I cursed in a hushed voice as yet another squadron of huge, vicious flies came into the attack.

Flies? They're not flies. They're more like bloody sparrows, the little voice said in my ear.

Luckily, the persistence of these attacks had lessened as darkness fell. Now there was only a few of the more stubborn ones at the most, while the rest of the buzzing squadron had popped off home or wherever flies go. I'd never liked the damn filthy things. They carry disease and, to my discomfort, I knew that my acquired 'perfume' would attract them back in increasing numbers with the rising sun.

Being satisfied the area was safe on my arrival, I'd moved into this very carefully selected position, directly overlooking and in close range of the factory that was our 'secondary' target. Partly hidden by the thick jungle vegetation in the shallow valley below me was an isolated ramshackle set of large buildings. Mainly constructed from sheets of corrugated iron that were rusting rapidly in the damp atmosphere, they formed part of a long since abandoned coffee plantation now being used as an illegal drug factory.

During the past couple of hours, the other members of the team would have been busy, quietly establishing gun positions at various points surrounding the central area of this valley, which we intended to turn into a 'Killing Field.' Our 'primary' target had yet to arrive and <u>his</u> elimination would be my sole responsibility. By secretly listening to the local peasant labourers and buying information, we'd discovered that he was expected here the following day.

Known only as El Jefe, (The Boss), the Head of Colombia's largest and most vicious Drug Cartel was our main target. We knew from our informants that he would not be alone. Arriving at the site by helicopter, he would have an assistant and at least four heavily armed bodyguards plus the pilot with him.

If possible, we would try to avoid killing any of the local peasants who were used as forced labour so part of the plan was to allow the visit to proceed and then hit El Jefe as he departed. Part of my final briefing to the team had been to firmly inform them, 'It won't be a Shoot and Scoot operation. We stay until the job is finished. No-one must walk away.'

As I dug in the darkness at the base of this large fallen tree, I couldn't help reflecting that the survival skills I'd learnt with the Special Forces were now being put to a *very* personal use.

The jungle had been clinging onto the last vestiges of light when I first arrived and I was soon thoroughly investigated by several different species of animals. My activities, no matter how quiet, had drawn them in from all around. The monkeys were particularly curious as to what was going on. Generally, they had maintained a respectable distance as they sniffed the air, grunting or squeaking to each other. The variety of birds however behaved very differently. Having decided that my digging was a source of extra food, they'd soon overcome any shyness and cleared all worms and grubs from the soil I scattered during my digging.

"Get out of it you little buggers," I hissed, as I once again shooed away a group of young monkeys that were playing their favourite game of 'Fill the Hole' by throwing large lumps of earth back in as fast as I could put it out. Taking no notice of me whatsoever, they became bolder by the minute. It was this familiarity that could have been my own undoing as in my turn, I took no real notice of the increasingly agitated screams of the older monkeys who were dancing up and down in the trees, screaming at the top of their voices. Some even started throwing pieces of broken branches towards me.

Perhaps they thought I was hurting their young, some of whom had fled back to Mom.

An abrupt, strange silence descended on the area and a feeling that all was not quite right made me turn.

"Shit!" I exclaimed. There, a few feet from my face a huge Python had slithered its entire 20 foot length across the fallen tree towards me and was coiled ready to strike. Being in no mood to be 'cuddled' by such a creature, I reached for my machete. Too slow! With a lightning fast movement, it struck. A flash of sharp, backward pointing fangs and pink mouth filled my vision as the pale scaly head streaked past my shoulder, one edge of its thick brown body bumped heavily against me. A high-pitched scream rent the air; I turned and saw that it had grabbed a young monkey that was ineffectually wriggling and kicking in its writhing coils. With loud cries of alarm, the others scattered up into the trees to watch the unfortunate one being crushed to death and then slowly swallowed headfirst by the snake. A sudden icy cold feeling swept over me as I realised how close I had come to an unpleasant and lingering death.

They may not be poisonous, but your end comes in a painful, crushing death. This wisdom was whispered sagely in my ear.

During the next half hour or so, I kept one eye on the huge snake as it slowly devoured its meal before slithering by me on its way back to its normal habitat. This movement caused another period of noise as the parent monkeys vociferously renewed their scolding of their offspring. When the danger had passed, it became relatively quiet as the monkeys lost interest and moved higher up into the canopy for the night, giving just the odd half-hearted calls now and then as if to let me know they were still in the area. It was much later, when silence fell, that I became aware that I'd been subconsciously humming a silent tune while working.

"It must be job satisfaction," I thought, folding my combat shovel at last. Gently lowering all six feet of my 190-lb frame into the hole, I placed my water bottles and pack in the 'Kit Well' at the bottom. Satisfied that everything was OK, I settled onto the larger of the ledges I'd constructed. Though the heat of the sun had gone, the humidity stayed high. The pungent stink of rotting vegetation and cloying smell of damp earth hung so heavily in the air, it could almost be chewed.

"Home Sweet Home. Now, where's the tea and biscuits?" I muttered, carefully pulling a pre-woven camouflaged mat of small leafy branches across to form a type of lid. A gap had been left through which I could raise my head and my weapons were close to hand on an earthen ledge.

Though I'd arrived in the advancing twilight, I'd established that from here, though partially hidden under the massive tree trunk protecting my back, it was possible to observe the general area of our target without moving from the hide. It was also well within effective range of the various weapons I would be using. Anyone approaching from the front or sides would be seen. To help me stay awake during the tedious job of observing, I started running mental quizzes, as had long been my practice. Gradually, as on similar occasions in the past, an inner quiet settled on me.

This is Pay Back Time. ... Now let the bastards come, I thought, lifting the leather flap of my Nomex wristwatch to check the time and saw I was ahead of schedule.

"So, if all goes well, I may snatch a bit of sleep," I declared.

The 'hide' was situated about three metres in from the jungle's edge at the top of a rise which Nature was starting to reclaim. The spindly young trees surrounding me held little foliage, while the more established ones soared up into the sky to form a canopy with their evergreen leaves. The position also overlooked a long downward slope towards the wide clearing where I guessed the helicopter would land. The main buildings of the factory were partly hidden from my view by the jungle across to my right. Raising my head through the gap, I put my night vision goggles to my eyes to watch for patrolling guards and a faint hazy image swam before my eyes.

"Damn it. I can hardly see a bloody thing," I cursed to myself. Changing the battery I tried again but with the same result. "What the hell's wrong with these damn things? It must have been damaged when I fell."

Suddenly, the clearing below was illuminated by the soft glow of the moonlight while my position remained in darkness. "I don't bloody well believe it."

My curses were renewed as realization dawned. The night vision goggles idea had been blown to blazes by clouds and the close proximity of the trees around me, the branches of which were intertwined enough to cut out the natural light the image intensifiers relied on.

"Ah well. Adopt Plan 'B' and use the good old 'Mark One' eyeball," I moaned.

During the first hour of my lonely vigil, I'd been alerted several times by the sudden rustling of leaves, stirred maybe by an almost imperceptible breeze. This faint noise accompanied by the fast, flitting movement of shadows to my front set the adrenaline flowing and kept me alert. Relief flooded through me as after a few tense, nerve wrenching minutes, I'd realised it was the large unseen clouds scudding across the weak moonlight. Nevertheless, I still strained my eyes and ears and, thankful that it remained peaceful I relaxed onto my bench for a short doze.

This had all changed in the last few minutes when the hairs on the back of my neck suddenly stood up and an icy chill crept down my spine despite the humidity. My well proven *Early Warning System* had never failed and I snapped out of my half doze to slip my head up through the opening in the cover. My senses told me I was being watched. Was it imagination, or could I hear a strange sound approaching my position? No, something <u>was</u> moving out there. This new noise wasn't caused by any of the normal jungle animals or birds; it was something different, very different. Something I couldn't put my finger on.

There it was again. It was only a slight but unidentifiable sound, yet it set those warning shivers up my spine. My mind started to float as an adrenaline surge charged around my body giving me a hollow, churning feeling in the pit of my stomach.

"What is it?" Now fully alert, my ears strained for any identifying clue. ... Silence.

Years of military training told me to keep perfectly still while my taut, fraying nerves screamed at me to 'Take a bloody look.' My skin felt prickly and creepy, and a band of cold sweat broke on my brow to trickle down my nose.

"What the bloody hell is it?" I whispered.

Crack!

There, to my right. The faint sound of a twig breaking sounded like a rifle shot in the silence of the night. It signalled stealthy movement in the deep almost impenetrable blackness. The skin on my back felt cold and clammy and as if it was on the move. My stomach lurched into motion again.

Though I could see nothing, my sixth sense told me there <u>was</u> something out there. Suddenly, the sound of my heart beating and the blood rushing around my system cleared. My hearing became sharply focused and the soft rustle of undergrowth being moved aside, accompanied by a faint panting sound penetrated my brain.

"Oh shit," I gasped.

Was I imagining that a deep throaty rumble accompanied it? My brain started to feel funny. As if in a dream, I clearly heard myself years ago telling young recruits that the effectiveness of the human ear was not fully appreciated. When properly 'trained,' it was as effective and capable as any animals. It could collect the faintest of sounds. All the brain had to do was to identify it.

So let's keep calm and try to work this out, I silently ordered myself.

That was proving to be easier said than done. Wild thoughts and pictures of fierce, bloodthirsty animals with huge yellow teeth and vile smelling breath swirled around in my mind.

A clear example of my brain throwing a wobbly, I thought. I swear my ears are working properly, but my brain has nothing to match the sounds to.

With a feeling of total inadequacy that I'd never felt before, my imagination continued to try to take over in wild rushes. I knew if it was not checked, it would result in me going into panic mode or, worse still, I could 'lose my bottle.' Certain that I was well hidden from discovery by humans, I knew if it was an animal moving out there in the pitch black darkness, there was a high risk of it scenting the raw fear I was now transmitting. My mind flashed back to the earlier incident that had driven me back to soak in the swamp. The unearthly scream from that unidentified creature once again echoed in my ears.

"If this is a big cat, with its superb sense of smell and driven by hunger after a bad hunt," I murmured despondently, "then I don't stand a bloody chance."

I was already imagining the red-hot lances of pain as sharp claws raked me, and long teeth ripped at my flesh. My stomach heaved, accompanied by a further sensation of looseness in my bowels. My imagination even let me smell the rancid breath when its massive slavering jaws clamped over my head, for that was all there was of me above ground level.

Sitting as I was, surrounded by rotting vegetation that had collected over the years on the floor of this South American jungle, I had suffered enough indignities with worms, centipedes, beetles and lizards already.

These held no fear for me: even the chance snake slithering into the hole could be dealt with. Part of our training all those years ago as young soldiers had been specifically designed to cover such long exposure to nature's delights while observing the enemy; this was different.

I felt the 'buzz' as a fresh charge of adrenaline rushed around my system. The sound of my heartbeat once again drummed in my ears. My tongue was so dry, it stuck to my palate. A sudden sharp pain in my chest made me realise I had actually stopped breathing. I opened my mouth to gulp in air.... at last my heartbeat quietened.

I can put up a good defence against an animal, I tried to kid myself with a distinct lack of conviction, but <u>not</u> in the position I'm in now. Any sudden movement may trigger a panic attack by whatever it was out there.

Worse still, it may frighten the unknown animal away while leaving me exposed to any chance human watcher. The other members of the team were too far away to be of assistance and were acting under a strict radio silence - imposed by me. So I <u>had</u> to face this on my own.

I won't go without a fight. The unconvincing thought flashed across my mind. Careful not to make a noise, I slowly reached out my hand for the silenced automatic pistol on one of the earthen shelves nearby. Gripping it firmly, despite my sweaty palms, I eased the safety catch off as I slowly moved my body enough to give me a chance of bringing the weapon out from under the lid of the hide. The sounds drew nearer and I heard the little voice inside my head saying,

Ben Carson, what <u>are</u> you doing here?

Code Name SNOWBIRD

🕊 Code Name SNOWBIRD 🕊

Chapter 1.

<u>The Reason.</u>

My enjoyment of classical music playing on my CD player was not disturbed by the quiet purr of my silver-grey BMW saloon as it slipped effortlessly through the Cotswold countryside. My feeling of anticipation increased with every passing mile; it would not be long before I met the young lady who is the main passion in my life.

Today was the long awaited 18th birthday of my goddaughter Sophie. Mal, her father, is my best friend and he'd asked me to collect her from the pub where she was celebrating the event along with her friends from the school she attended in Cheltenham. My simple and pleasurable task was seeing her enjoying herself and then to see her safely home.

Just before eleven that warm summer evening, I turned into the crowded pub car park and became immediately aware of the sound of young people having fun. Locking my car, I paused for a few moments to savour the sweet heady scent of jasmine and honeysuckle that hung heavily in the warm evening air. Those lovely scents and that of orange blossom had always been my favourites. They invoked some fond memories of happy times spent in Cyprus, a place I love. With a last appreciative intake of the evocative bouquet, I approached the door marked Function Room. The solid oak door burst open with a crash just as I reached for the handle. Half a dozen excited young females rushed out, so intent on their own mission they seemed oblivious to my presence and almost flattened me. Foolishly, I tried again. This time it was a group of youths bearing trays of brimming glasses that I had to dodge.

"Hmm. It seems the party is still in progress and the hunt is on," I murmured, as the eager youths disappeared in the direction the girls had gone. Warily, I made another attempt to enter the building; this time with greater success. Inside, the smoke-laden air vibrated to the driving beat of overloud rock music played by a gyrating, prancing band. Groups of swivelling, flashing disco lights dazzled me as I peered into the smoky atmosphere and the throbbing music vibrated through my body. This, combined with the voices of over a hundred youngsters wriggling and jiggling on the dance floor, deafened me.

"No good trying to find her in this lot," I muttered. "They don't even know I exist."

Dodging several groups of groping couples, I made my way towards the bar where a decidedly underdressed and very attractive young woman waved at me from across the room. Sitting on a tall stool, her black ultra short dress was showing more leg and smooth creamy thigh than if she'd had a bikini on.

Quickly scanning the room and seeing no sign of Sophie, I was about to go to the next room when a hand grabbed my arm and a plumy voice, thickened with alcohol, said, "you *are* Sophie's Uncle Ben, *aren't* you?"

It was more a statement than a question, but that didn't matter to me as I found myself gazing into the blue eyes of the blonde girl in the short dress. Aged about 18, she was a beauty all right. The plain black velvet band around her long, slim neck enhanced the paleness of her skin and was a thing I had always found to be very sexy. Her thick, well-groomed blonde hair fell freely across her creamy white shoulders while her tongue traced her wet lips seductively as she waited for my answer.

"What? Oh, yes, that's right, I'm Ben Carson. Do I know you?" I asked, struggling to tear my eyes away from her almost see through and very skimpy top that was bursting with the firmest, shapeliest breasts I had ever seen.

A slow, sexy smile crept over her lovely face as she saw the effect she was having on me.

"We met at the riding stables a few years ago, don't you remember? You used to lift me onto my horse."

Memories of a precocious, well-developed thirteen-year-old girl, who took every opportunity to rub her upper torso against me, came flooding back.

"Yes... I remember now, but you've certainly changed a lot since then," I blurted. My instincts screamed out *be careful*. She moved closer to let someone pass; her firm breasts rubbed against my arm; my body reacted dangerously.

"She's sex mad," I thought. Desperate to escape, I gasped lamely, "Actually, I'm looking for Sophie; have you seen her lately?"

"Not for a while Ben, I *can* call you Ben .... can't I?" She whispered huskily as she rubbed her thigh against me. "After all, I *am* 18 now. Why don't you buy me a drink while you wait; we could go outside... and ...?" She paused; her tongue once again worked her lips suggestively as she eyed my well muscled six foot frame. "We can look for her later."

To my great relief, her attention was suddenly taken by the arrival of a very wobbly and equally underdressed young brunette whose dilated pupils made her look stoned.

"Lo, whoosh thish luvly man?" she slurred, leaning heavily against Blondie and draping her arm around her neck in a proprietorial fashion.

"This is Sophie's Uncle Ben. Have you seen her lately?" Blondie replied. It was then I realized I hadn't asked her name.

"Yeah. She wen' out the garden wiv that creep Soovius."

"Soovius. Who on earth is *he*?" Blondie demanded testily. It seemed that she resented her friend's intrusion.

"Soovius. You know, 'im wiv all the shpots on 'is face. C'm on lesh get anuver drink, eh," she giggled as she tried to pull Blondie away. "I dunno wha' she sees in 'im wiv all 'is shpots. He's prob'ly trying to screw 'er right now ... Yuck!" Her words caused my alarm bells to ring but, before I could react, Blondie cut in.

"Vesuvius. That's who she means," she gasped, clutching at my arm. Her eyes widened in alarm and a worried look came over her face. "I call him that because he's covered in erupting spots. God knows what she sees in him, but he's *real* trouble."

"When did they go out there, show me where it is will you," I demanded, grabbing their arms.

"Hey. Shteady on. All I know is he put sup'm in her drink and she wen' ou' side wiv 'im about twenty minutes ago," the brunette muttered sulkily.

"He did WHAT?" I exploded, jerking her round to face me. Both girls shied away at my sudden outburst. "You *saw* what he'd done… and did *nothing*?" I shouted at the brunette who was by now almost in tears. Sensing a drama, other people were gathering round and taking notice.

"What're your names? Quickly." Shaken, they both stammered their names and making a mental note of them, I headed a small crowd out through the door to the poorly lit car park.

"Sophie … Sophie." My shouts drew no reply. Suddenly, I heard the sound of running feet coming from behind a thick hedgerow.

"That's the Beer Garden," someone shouted and, as one, we moved quickly in that direction.

A motorbike started up in the distance. It moved rapidly away as soon as the engine caught. My professional training registered it as an old worn-out machine and its rider was in a hurry. Rounding the corner of the hedge, I saw we were in the top end of the Beer Garden adjacent to the car park and floating in the air under the only lamp that was on, I saw a cloud of blue smoke. "Two Stroke Oil." The seemingly insignificant thought crossed my mind. Then someone shouted.

"There she is." I saw her lying half concealed by tall shrubs, just discernible in the dim light. Dashing across the deserted area, shoving tables and chairs out of my way, I slid to a stop beside her. She lay on her side, curled in a foetal position; her clothing in disarray with her panties around one ankle. One arm clutched at her stomach while the other clawed feebly at the muddy flowerbed in which she lay. Turning her over gently, I saw her teeth had bitten deep into her lower lip. Blood and vomit ran from her mouth while her lovely face was contorted in pain. Yelling for someone to call an ambulance - though subconsciously I knew it was too late as I'd seen this sort of thing before - I cuddled her golden head to my chest while attempting to cover her modesty.

"Sophie." I sobbed helplessly. A slight movement drew my attention and I saw her eyes flick open.

"Uncle Ben," It was barely a whisper. "I'm sor...." Then she was gone; the bright young eighteen-year-old whom I had loved as my own daughter had died in my arms killed by an overdose of drugs. Her sightless eyes stared up at me.

"How the hell was I going to break this terrible news to her Mum and Dad? They're my best friends and, at their request, I had come here tonight to bring their only child home safely." I asked myself.

My mind was in turmoil. I was hardly aware of shrugging off the firm hands that tried to pull me away from her; neither did I take any notice of a more authoritative voice saying, "It's all right, Sir. We'll look after her now."

"I'll kill the Bastard." My anguished cry echoed around and around inside my head. "Whoever he is, wherever he is, I'll kill him."

The next few hours were hell. I'd never experienced anything like it. It wasn't death as such: we were no strangers. I'd seen it before in many forms during the years I'd spent working with the SAS. This was different. This was personal and even the SAS, with all its specialized and diverse training, or the many harrowing operations I'd been on, could not prepare me for this. The first and most difficult task I had to undertake was to break the news to Mal and his wife, Julie. I *wouldn't* let the police do it. Life had dealt them cruelly enough already, now this. Taking a stiff swig of the brandy the pub landlord had kindly produced, I accepted the offer of a lift in an unmarked police car to Mal's house on the outskirts of Bisley, high in the Cotswolds.

As we travelled the few miles to this heart-breaking appointment, my mind reflected on the couple that I was going to see. Malcolm Courtney - Mal to his friends, at 46 years of age, was eight years older than me and married to Julie who was devoted to him. Both of them had doted on their daughter Sophia, or Sophie as she had preferred being called. Now, accompanied by a police constable and a decidedly nervous WPC, I was on my way to give them the most devastating news ever. Hatred for her killer was building up like a knot in the pit of my stomach. I couldn't ignore it; it was making me sick. Besides, there was no way I was going to let this action rest in the hands of the police. Even if they caught the killer and the suppliers, the Courts would only mete out some trivial sentence. I had thought that when I left the Services, the killing would be over.... now I wanted revenge for the death of this young, innocent girl.

That revenge would be bloody.

Chapter 2.

<u>The Colombian Jungle. The Past Catches Up.</u>

Suddenly, memories of my best friend Mal came echoing out of the night to haunt me.... and of Sophie, his young daughter. Thoughts of her ran through my mind too. I'd watched her grow up; she was my goddaughter. To her, I was Uncle Ben.... even though we weren't related.

A choking feeling closed my throat. I tried to clear my head of the memories in an attempt to concentrate on the dangerous situation I was in. It was no good. I couldn't stop my thoughts. My brain was on overload due to the unidentified 'Thing' that was out there in the jungle; it was bringing past memories back to cover its panic. This could be the moment before death, when my life would supposedly flash before my eyes.

Sophie .... Her pretty young face floated in front of me. I could smell the freshness of her hair. How could such a terrible thing have happened, and why her .... she'd been so full of life ....

"Daddy, Daddy .... Uncle Ben." Her voice came echoing through the trees. "I've made it .... I've made it ...." Her voice telling us she'd been selected for a show jumping team seemed to reach out to me from the darkness ... across the oceans .... from beyond the grave.

"Bastards." The stark reality of this last thought brought a surge of grief and anger and the whispered curse slipped from my lips. "She was eighteen ... just eighteen ... for Christ's sake." I swore as more images came flooding out of the night to torment me.

Sophie as a baby, sparkling and funny with blue eyes that shone and lips so quick to break into a smile. Then, as a growing child, her soft blonde hair tucked neatly up under her riding hat as she proudly rode her very own pony for the first time. The lively honey-coloured pony with its blonde mane was a gift from her father and myself on her tenth birthday; how pleased she'd been; how full of joy.

"Thank you, Daddy," she'd cried as she trotted off. "Thank you, Uncle Ben. Oh, thank you both, so very much."....

"No. .... thank *you*, sweetheart." My whispered response was lost in the deep darkness.

I was silent for a while, listening, focusing my mind while frantically trying to identify the strange sounds that were coming from the jungle, but the past wouldn't leave me alone....

"I'm hit! .... I'm hit." Mal's voice came crashing out of the trees. Vivid memories of that terrible day in Northern Ireland came flooding back. A quiet village street at the end of a routine Patrol ... A loud explosion as the car bomb went off..... My ears, still hurting from the blast, seemed to muffle Mal's voice as he lay in a shattered and bloody heap on the road screaming at me. "I'm hit.... Oh God. Help me!" I'd given him a dose of morphine, tried to stem the flow of blood and to shield him from the sight of his mangled legs.

"You'll be OK, mate," I kept saying. .... "You'll be OK ...." I was relieved when he finally passed out.

"The cowardly, gutless bastards." The curse flew from my lips. "No guts to come out and have a fight, they have to resort to sneaky bomb attacks, or shoot and run tactics." My blood boiled at the vivid memory of the following months of waiting and hoping. ... The endless surgery that he'd endured was with me as clear as day. My God, what courage Mal had shown when they finally told him that he would never walk again. He'd accepted his fate with a shrug of his shoulders. Then, with the love and support from his wife, Julie, he'd begun a new career as a self-employed computer programmer who now ran a successful computer business from home.

Crack! ... My blood froze. The sound of a twig breaking in the inky blackness suddenly snapped me back to the present. There, in front of me, a darker patch of the blackness seemed to be growing bigger.

It must be coming closer. The little voice whispered in my ear. I was pleased to note it sounded just as scared as me. My hand gripped the butt of my pistol. An icy coolness swept over me; I felt calm and collected as I remembered my promise to both Mal and Julie as we stood at the side of their daughter's grave.

I <u>can't</u> let them down, I thought. I <u>have</u> to handle this situation and survive to carry out that promise. In a flash, those cruel, tense days following Sophie's death seemed to come alive again, as sharp and harsh as ever. "I've got to handle this and survive. I've *got* to keep that promise," I breathed in an almost silent whisper.

Still single and in my thirty-eighth year, I'd found it hard to form a relationship and settle down. It was not for the want of female companionship - I've had my fair share of willing admirers. My reluctance was mainly due to the demands of the Regiment, with the all too often long and dangerous separations, which were not fair to a wife and family.

Even Julie who had become more like a sister to me, had apparently started to worry about my single status. This became clear some time ago, when she'd caught up with me in the yard of their house the morning after a party that had been attended by several of her very attractive and single friends. Dressed in a herringbone riding jacket, cream moleskin jodhpurs and shiny knee length riding boots, she looked a picture as she approached me, surrounded by a flock of eager chickens and a couple of dogs. The chickens fussed around our feet as always to the point, she hooked her arm through mine and led me out of the yard.

"Ben darling, I'm worried about you. Its time you got married, settled down and raised a big family." She'd paused to see what reactions this statement would cause. Seeing none, she'd continued. "Oh, I know you have some lady friends, but none of them become permanent. I know some who would jump at the chance of marrying you." Looking me straight in the eyes, she'd nudged me in the ribs with her elbow as she passed this gem of information on.

Before I could react to this boldness, she'd earnestly continued. "You're a gentle, good looking man." She paused, standing in front of me to study me again. "Why don't you settle down?" Her voice was so full of genuine concern; I couldn't be angry and felt she deserved a reply.

"Julie, I know you mean well. I also know that you are aware of how I feel about having to leave a family so often,"…..

"But, you're not in that job ……..," Putting my finger to her lips to stop her interruption, I continued.

"Even though I'm no longer serving, my civilian employment creates the same type of restrictions, so it's no use even thinking about it," I explained quietly, while being economical with the truth to spare her. I couldn't just come out and tell her that my civvy job was no different from the service one. Besides, no matter how beautiful her friends were, they were all after one thing: money, a meal ticket. Call it what you like, the truth remained that they visited too many beds for my liking. A look of sudden understanding came across her lovely face, quickly followed by a look of despair.

"You're still doing…I'm sorry," she gasped as realisation dawned … I … I didn't know," turning, she hurried away scattering the chickens as she went.

A guilty feeling swept over me; I should have told her that attractive though her friends were, they were just not my type. I should also have told both her and Mal what my job was, but had decided against it. Mal, of course, knew better than to ask even though we'd been through a lot together.

Followed by the dogs, I walked out into the fields reflecting on our long-standing friendship. Mal and I, we're like brothers really; he's a dark haired version of myself and we're of similar build. He had married Julie, who was a communications and language technician that we met during an exercise at her place of work in a highly secret, Ministry of Defence establishment outside Cheltenham. I can still remember their meeting.

When he first saw her, he said with a gleam in his eye, "there's the girl I'm going to marry."

"Ha," I'd scoffed, "you won't stand a chance with that beauty mate." I was soon eating my words, for having been secretly watching Mal over the three days we were on the site, Julie readily accepted his invitation to dinner and I still swear I saw the sparks jumping between them.

They seemed well suited to each other. Julie was a few years younger than Mal and just a shade shorter than his 5'10." Her figure was slim and athletic and she possessed a bubbly personality.

After a brief courtship, they married in a simple ceremony in Julie's home village of Bisley in the hills near Gloucester. I'd been proud to be invited to be the best man. Returning from a short honeymoon, Mal and Julie had settled into a beautiful house - one of the many fashionable homes converted from a typical Cotswold stone barn. Surrounded by gently sloping hills, their new home overlooked several large woods in a peaceful winding valley with its wide, well-stocked stream. They'd completed the picture by the acquisition or rescue of a bevy of animals of various sorts.

'Stonehaven,' as it had been named, had in fact become just that. I, too, on my frequent visits had always felt at ease there with goats, pigs, chickens, ducks, cats and a couple of dogs for company. It was into this ideal setting that in due course Julie had presented Mal with baby Sophie.

That had all gone now with her recent, sudden and tragic death through an allergic reaction caused by an overdose of drugs, administered in the opinion of the coroner, 'by a person or persons unknown.' The cold verdict of accidental death was no consolation to either Mal or Julie, or indeed myself.

At the funeral, we stood with a group of Mal and Julie's friends on one side of the grave while a large crowd of Sophie's friends stood dejectedly on the other side. Standing in a loose group with heads bowed trying to hide our own thoughts; our dark clothes matched the sombre greyness of this appropriately dull day. Even the clouds were crying.

There should be no brightness here, I thought. We are gathered to say our goodbyes to Sophie. People dabbed at their eyes as the Vicar's voice droned on. Here and there, some hid their feelings under black umbrellas that shielded them from the persistent light rain.

You can cry if you wish. The thought crossed my mind as I glanced around at the colourful patch of flowers and wreaths. It was as if they could improve the event by flaunting their bright colours. The mellowed stone of the village church with its tall tower topped by a soaring spire, perched brooding and protective on this hillside overlooking the stone tiled roofs of the village. The ancient trees bent in towards us under the weight of moisture. They had seen it all before. Tears were no stranger here.

Standing with my hand on Mal's shoulder, we watched the coffin being lowered into the ground. Looking at my two friends, I could see they were completely devastated though trying to make a 'brave' show. A shiver ran down my back as a renewed fury welled up from deep within me, spreading ice-like through my veins. My blood pounded in my ears and my throat was choked as some primeval force seemed to take control of me. I'd felt this once before many years ago when I'd seen the mangled bodies of children who had been callously shot or mutilated by 'heroes' of some African revolution. We'd tracked and disposed of these 'heroes' without any feelings of guilt. <u>That's</u> what I knew I was going to have to do now, track down the culprit. I felt the wheelchair shaking with Mal's silent sobs. *'Ashes to ashes - Dust to dust.'* Strangely, the Vicar's words sounded distant and detached from us as if they were burying someone else.

Suddenly, a hand closed on my arm in a vice like grip. I looked down into Mal's grief filled eyes - I'd never seen him cry before - but now, as he tossed a small bunch of flowers onto the coffin, the tears flowed freely. Another smaller hand gripped mine as Julie came to stand beside us both. The depth of their grief could be clearly seen. Freeing myself, I placed comforting arms around their shoulders and felt the sobs wracking their bodies. Suddenly, I realised that between sobs, Mal was talking to me.

"I ... I want him dead, Ben." His once powerful body seemed shrunken in despair and his deep voice had sunk to an intense whisper. The sobbing made his breathing jerky and ragged. "Whoever ... did this ... I want ... him DEAD." There was so much pent-up feeling in the last word that he almost hissed it. His grip tightened on my arm. I nodded, not really grasping the full implication of his words, yet sharing the same feeling of despair.

"I don't care how; I don't even want to see a body; I just want him killed." The eyes that stared into mine were burning with a ferocity I had never seen before. His voice was so pleading that I realised he was deadly serious.

"You mean that, don't you, Mal," I said at last, making it a statement rather than an obvious question.

"Damned right I do," he hissed, thumping his useless legs in despair. "I *can't* do it myself, but I know *you* can. You're the *only* person I trust and I know you've got the skills. I'll pay *anything*; even sell 'Stonehaven' if I have to." He snatched a quick look at Julie when he made that statement. "Just *get* him and make him pay; I don't care how much or how long it takes, just tell me the bastard's dead," he almost shouted. With a supreme effort, he turned his chair round on the wet grass and pushed his way through the staring crowd. Julie held me back as I went to follow him.

"No, Ben," she'd whispered, "leave him a while; let him drive out this devil that's tormenting him. You know he can't tackle this himself and that's what is really frustrating him." I pulled her close, kissed her forehead and placed her arm in mine as we walked slowly away with heads hung low, away from their daughter's resting-place. The scraping of shovels seemed to follow us. Neither of us could stay to watch and my thoughts were with Mal, confined to a wheelchair and unable to take action himself.

Later, after a stiff brandy in The Bear Inn and a little talk in which Julie had convinced me that Mal was deadly serious, we made our way back to the church to look for him. We found him sitting under the old-fashioned lytch gate oblivious to the now steady rain. It was a shrunken, shell of a man who stared out across the stone roofs of Bisley village as he faced his personal torment unaware of the rest of the world. His wet hair was plastered to his head.

"Why?" we heard him sob. "Why did it have to be her? She had so much to look forward to." Suddenly, aware that he was not alone, he turned and wiped his eyes with a handkerchief that Julie offered him. "You know what gets me most of all about this, don't you?" he said, his voice still shaking with anger as he once again slapped his useless legs. "I can't do a bloody thing about it myself; that's what bloody well bugs me most."

I'd seen and heard more than enough; this was the first time in all these years that he'd mentioned any bitterness about his injuries. I knew that if he were allowed to continue like this, the grief and resentment would turn his mind.

Making a sudden decision, I stepped in front of them both, grasped their hands and said, "I loved Sophie too; you know, your loss is also my loss. Whoever it was that supplied those drugs <u>will</u> be punished."

Then, with my own voice choking I added, "no matter how long it takes, I personally guarantee it."

Mal looked up at me then, his eyes full of fresh tears as he grasped my hand in a crushing, painful grip.

"Good on you, mate. I *knew* I could rely on you." Another deep sob wracked his body. "Whatever it takes ... if I've got it ... you can have it." He shook my hand and Julie kissed me. Then, as an idea struck him he added, "Use the network. Yeah, that's it. The guys on the network will help us; I've got a couple of contacts, so I'll set it up, OK?"

It was so damned simple. The network he referred to didn't officially exist but it was there all right, made up of ex Special Forces members from various nations who were scattered all around the globe. They all kept in touch and even worked together when required: English SAS, American Green Berets and even Russian Spetznaz had worked with each other on occasions.

"Great, that's a brilliant idea, Mal. Set it up and put my 'mark' - my service nickname - on it."

Of course this would work; it was personal, so they would fall over each other to help if they could. Satisfied that something would be done, Mal gradually calmed down as I wheeled him down the drive to their car and took them both home. After a shower and a quick meal, I made my farewells and left them to grieve together. I now had a mission to fulfil.

Over the next few days, I tracked down and talked to Blondie and her brunette friend as well as some of the other girls who had attended the birthday disco with Sophie and had been at the inquest and the funeral. Based on what they told me and what evidence they gave at the inquest, it only took me a short while to trace the pimply faced young local man who had, unknown to her, fed Sophie the drugs.

Late one evening, I waited outside the Gloucester Youth Club he frequented. As he dismounted from his clapped out old two stroke motorbike, I stepped quickly out of the shadows and grabbed him roughly by the arm. Not giving him a chance to escape, I twisted it viciously up behind his back and slammed him hard against the rough stone wall. The coarse surface drew blood from his face as it came in contact with him.

"Hello, creep," I snarled, ramming my forearm across the side of his neck to hold him there. Putting my face close to his I hissed, "Is it you that feeds drugs to defenceless young girls?" Applying more pressure, I watched his face change colour as the question sank into his brain. "Is it you that lets them die in terrible agony?" Another jerk of my forearm to further emphasise the question caused more flesh to be scraped off. "Well. ... I'm waiting, or do I have to <u>really</u> hurt you?" I snapped.

My face was so close to his that I could see the numerous pimples and boils straining at his skin. The smell of bad breath and rotten teeth were overpowering. Moving my head away from near him, I eased the pressure a bit so that he could speak.

"Yeah, it was me ... I didn't mean to kill her, *honest*," he gasped weakly, struggling to get his breath. "All I wanted was to get her a bit loaded and take her outside for a bit of fun." He paused to catch his breath before continuing. "She was the same as all her mates, stuck up and not int'rested in the likes o' me," he mumbled. "They'd take the piss out o' me, an' call me Spotty and uver fings. The only way I'd get near 'em, wuz to slip 'em a 'Mickey' then take 'em outside ..." A look of horror crossed his face as he said, "I may have given her a mixed lot …!" His voice trailed off as the import of his words made me increase the pressure on his arm again.

"How many others have you fed drugs to?" I demanded, pushing his face harder against the wall.

Frightened by my attitude and bleeding freely from the many abrasions on his face, the youth gasped, "a few, but I don't supply any of the other kids at college. Honest! I just buy for me self from a guy called 'Rats.'"

Being normally an easygoing person and having now seen him and heard his story, I felt there was a bit of truth in what the youth claimed. So, relaxing the pressure, I looked at this pathetic individual while summing up what he'd said.

The ignorant toad was showing off to those floozies. That had been his main motivation, I mused. It makes no bloody difference; he committed a crime so punishment is due.

Glad to be rid of the stink of his cheap after-shave, which coupled with his unwashed armpits and bad breath, was becoming too much for my stomach.

I shoved him back towards his bike, adding with as much feeling as could be mustered, "get out of here filth and don't go thinking this is the last you've heard of me though; you'll be seeing me again, I promise." I paused to straighten my jacket before adding, "very soon."

Sobbing loudly and with a last frightened look back over his shoulder, the youth quickly got on his machine and hurriedly kick-started it, forgetting to don his helmet in his haste as he rode away.

I quickly got into my car and followed the cloud of oily smoke to discover where he lived. He'd stopped about half a mile from the club to put on his helmet before riding off erratically. Staying back a bit so that he wouldn't spot me, I followed the smoke haze from his bike through the housing estate and out of the city limits to pick up the main road into the countryside. Without any warning, he suddenly turned off after a few miles and disappeared down a narrow lane through some heavy woods which, according to the signpost led to 'Riverside Farm ONLY.'

"Ha. A dead-end road, that's convenient." Using just sidelights, I followed. Within a mile, the lane abruptly changed direction to the right, the hedge bordering the dense woods giving way to dry-stone walling on either side at the same time as it dropped down a short, but very steep slope to the flat land by the River Severn. In the distance below me, the brake lights of his bike showed he was slowing down as he approached a well-lit house.

"So, let's see what there is to see." My muttered comment was lost to the darkness as I switched my sidelights off and drove closer. The house he lived in was obviously that of either the farm manager or herdsman as the main farm was at the end of the road, a couple of hundred yards further on.

"Right, that's all I wanted to know. Now let's see where he can have an accident." Turning the car round quietly, I retraced my steps. An unmistakable smell came in through my open window.

"Silage, that's just the thing, that'll do the trick." Pulling the car into a clear space at the side of the road and climbing out, I followed my nose across the field to the silage pit that nestled in the lea of the wooded hillside.

"Judging by the tractor marks, it looks as if they carry this up the road as well." The beginning of a scheme was forming in my mind. A few minutes later, satisfied that everything would fit into my plan, I returned to my car and drove home.

As darkness fell the following evening, I left my car well hidden in the woods off the lane to Riverside Farm but close to the main road. Donning some new wellies that were part of a special shopping trip earlier that day, and carrying the other equipment that would be needed to put my plan into action, I made my way down to the silage pit to stash my tools. Cautiously - you never knew if a farmer was out with a gun after rabbits, neither did I want to start a dog barking - I moved to a spot near the youth's home. The ground was still wet from recent rain so the fact that my vigil was not too long made me very grateful. The front door of the house opened and, in the light from the hallway, I saw it was the pimply faced youth as he pulled on his helmet.

"OK. I'll be back in a couple of hours," he shouted in reply to some unheard comment from inside as he shut the door.

Then the distinctive noise of his machine starting up reached me and he came rattling past my position, oblivious to my existence. Judging by the fast way he drove his bike, he was confident there would be nothing else on the lane and very soon, he disappeared over the hill and out of sight.

"Right. That's it then." I began retracing my steps across the darkened fields to the silage pit to recover the garden fork, two large plastic buckets and heavy-duty rubber gloves.

"How *can* they work with this stuff?" I muttered. As I got to work, the stench of the overripe silage cloyed at my throat. Thankfully, it didn't take too long to fill the buckets, then careful not to get any on my clothes, I returned to the lane. Using the fork to drop lumps at intervals, I moved up the hill leaving a small but obvious trail along the tractor marks. Two trips were required to reach the point I'd previously selected on the hillside, then returning to the pit for the final supply, I located the sloppiest bits of silage. Carefully carrying them to the top of the hill where the tractor had turned into a field near the corner of the lane, I judged the spot carefully and began to spread the silage in a haphazard fashion on the road near the bend. Taking great care I ensured that a suitable mat of it was strategically positioned in the angle of the bend. Satisfied and now perspiring freely, I returned to the car and washed the tools and my rubber boots off with water from a large plastic barrel that I had wisely brought.

"Now, we wait, but I'll be bloody glad to get out of these wet clothes." I had a moan to myself as I settled down with my back to a tree in a pre-selected position in sight of the corner of the lane. Even the almost constant sound of passing traffic on the nearby main road didn't stop my eyelids from beginning to droop during the wait but it wasn't long before the high pitched sound of his approaching bike brought me back to the job in hand.

"He certainly pushes it," I said with a chuckle as he revved the machine down the lane. The weak beam of his headlight flitted across me as he came toward the corner.

"Any second now." My teeth clenched in anticipation. "God. I hope I've got it right."

The bike literally flew towards the corner with its engine straining. The rider knowing the lane intimately must have felt confident that he could handle the rapidly nearing corner. Unaware of the trap I had set for him and maintaining high revs, he judged his course precisely. His youthful bravado made him lean into the corner exactly where I had hoped. The engine screamed as he went past me. The rider screamed as the front wheel lost traction on the mat of silage and the bike careered recklessly onward.

"Aaaaaaaargh".... The long drawn out human sound was suddenly cut off to be replaced by the screeching sound of tortured metal as the machine slid along the road. Thump. It hit the shallow verge, catapulted its rider into the dry-stone wall where he landed with a sickening thud and the distinctive crack of breaking bone.

Better take a look and see what damage has been done, I thought, as I clambered over the wall. Petrol and oily engine smells hung heavily in the air; the ticking of a hot exhaust seemed to be extra loud. Then I noticed there was something else. A totally unexpected smell assailed my nostrils.

"Fish and chips!" I exclaimed, stepping carefully around the several packets whose contents were scattered all over the road and showed in the shielded glow of my penlight.

"Well, I'll be beggared. They'll have a long wait for their supper tonight." With a laugh, I stopped by the youth's body and gave him a quick check over.

"Still breathing but out cold," I murmured, automatically following through a well-drilled medical routine starting at his head then working down his body until I reached his legs both of which lay at funny angles. Broken. What a shame. This rather unsympathetic thought crossed my mind as I hurriedly straightened up, then careful not to tread on any of the fish and chips, turned to walk away. Faint shouts were drifting up to me from down at the house; it was time to make myself scarce.

A police car and an ambulance, both with all lights and horns going, shot past me on the main road as I drove back into Gloucester. I made one quick stop where the road went over the fast flowing River Severn, dropping the wellies, buckets and fork into the deep water before going home.

Two days later, I paid a surprise visit to the youth in his hospital bed.

"Remember me?" I snarled as I sat down beside him. It was very obvious he did by the way he tried to draw away from me, his eyes widening in fear. Leaning in close so as not be overheard - so close I could see the pus in his numerous pimples straining at his skin. "You know *why* your accident happened don't you?" My fierce whisper made him withdraw into the pillows, his eyes narrowed in puzzlement, only to fly wide open as realisation dawned. Fearfully, he looked around for help but we were alone in the ward.

"You got off light <u>this</u> time but if ever you slip drugs to anyone again, it'll be the *last* thing you ever do, got it?" I added, poking him in the chest with a rigid finger. "Now, what was it you were going to tell me about this guy called Rats?"

The smell of disinfectant and other hospital smells were not enough to cover the smell of his fear. Trapped by the apparatus holding his heavily plastered legs, he tried to shrink down into the bed away from me. He couldn't escape, so for the next few minutes, he stammered out details of his supplier.

"You'll find him outside the pub on Commercial Road most evenings an' I aint goin' to do it any more, promise," he spluttered. "Christ. I'm truly sorry about that girl; I didn't mean that to 'appen," he snivelled as tears ran down his face.

"If you do, I'll find you <u>wherever</u> you go so on your own head be it." My departing snarl caused him to whimper again.

That evening, dressed in a faded pair of washed out jeans and a lumberjack style shirt which sported several frayed holes, I found a quiet spot to park my car about 200 metres from the pub on Commercial Road and settled down to watch. After about half an hour had passed, a large dark coloured American Ford Taurus style car came down the road towards me, its mass of chrome glinting in the street lights. The soft purr of its engine reached me as it pulled up outside the pub. Within seconds, a young man came out of the shadows opposite, crossed to the driver's door and leaned down to the open window. All I could see from my vantage point were a few words spoken and what appeared to be a brief handshake and the youth moved quickly away. During the next few minutes more people visited the car. All of them casually touched hands with the driver before quickly moving off.

"So this is where the supplies are passed out," I thought. "Now it's my turn."

Mussing my hair slightly and loosening my shirtfront from my jeans, I quietly got out of the car, picked up an empty beer can that lay nearby and scuffed my way erratically towards the dealer's car. The driver, seeing me approach and not recognizing me, started his engine ready for a quick getaway. Anxious not to lose him now, I lurched drunkenly in front of his car effectively barring his escape.

Leaning towards the windscreen and deliberately speaking in a drunken slur, I said, "Dun go machey. I gotch a lorra dosh fur yuh." With this, I held up a thick bundle of £20 notes and waved them about. If all else failed, perhaps the sight of the money would tempt him to stay. It worked. Hastily sticking his head out of the window, the driver's urgent whisper reached my ears.

"Hey man. What you try 'n do to me? Stop wavin' that money roun'."

Now I'd really got his undivided attention, I lurched a bit nearer and leaned against the car door. Tapping the side of my nose in a mock conspiratorial manner, I mumbled in a stage whisper.

"I wan' sum Snow, an I've bin told you got it." Taking another pretend slurp from my empty can I slurred, "hic. I've got sixsunedquidfrit."

That amount of cash proved too much for the driver. Leaving the engine quietly running, he pushed his door open and climbed out. Instead of some sort of huge monster of a person, to my surprise, I found myself looking at a slim, young African-Caribbean man in his late twenties, with deep pock marks all over his face. His movements were jittery. His hair, done in the usual Rasta' fashion, was bundled up under a large brightly coloured knitted hat which, like his jeans, was badly in need of a wash. His bony fingers grabbed me by the arm, urging me towards the back door of the car, which he opened and pushed me in.

"Get in there man," he gasped, nervously looking around. "I ain't got enough Snow for that kin' money with me, so we gonna have t' take you with me." Slamming the door shut almost before I had crawled in, he jumped in behind the wheel, gunned the engine and drove off at speed. Sticking to the narrow winding back streets, we eventually arrived at a dilapidated tenement building in one of the streets backing onto the canal that runs through the city.

"Come with me, an' be quiet man," the dealer instructed as he locked the car. Clutching the bag, which I suspected contained drugs, he led the way up the dark smelly stairway of the tenement building; its damp streaked, prefabricated concrete sections showed signs of crumbling. The irrelevant fact that it wouldn't last much longer passed across my mind. Still maintaining my drunken act, I picked my way erratically around spilled garbage bags, empty milk and beer bottles, abandoned pushchairs and a myriad of other such obstacles. Deliberately staggering against him and loudly voicing my apologies, I drew a few desperate "Shhhhh's" from the dealer.

In spite of the poor lighting - most bulbs had been smashed or stolen; it was obvious we were in drug territory. Every corner was littered with heaps of discarded needles, Kit-Kat foil wraps showing the stained lines of burnt heroin lay scattered about. As if to display its use by prostitutes, I saw numerous discarded condoms here and there. The dungeon like design of the building made its dark secluded corners a haven for drug-pushers and street girls. The whole place smelt of urine and shit as we picked our way carefully around heaps of human faeces - I'd heard that a main line injection of pure drugs may cause the user to evacuate their bowels. Thankfully, this was the first time I'd seen the evidence.

Arriving at the top floor, the man used a bunch of keys to open several locks on a door that was covered in a sheet of steel. It was more like a strong room door than the front door to a flat. Pushing the heavy door open, he indicated for me to go in and then, taking a last furtive look around outside, he followed me, shutting and securing the door firmly behind him.

Gordon Bennett. This place hasn't had any fresh air through it in a hundred years, I thought as I breathed in a foul cloud of lung destroying, smoke laden air that was overlaid by the all pervading smell of damp and neglect. Pushing me into the lounge, 'Rats' made his way to the small cubby-hole that passed for a kitchen where he poured a cup of thick black coffee from a heavily stained percolator. Weaving his unsteady way across the room and slopping coffee as he did so, he slumped onto the filthy, well-worn settee. Handing me the coffee, he indicated that I should sit beside him.

"You need that if we goin' do bus'ness man, I want you sober," he said knocking the bag on the floor and spilling the contents. My guess had been right; the bag contained a dozen or so small packets of powder and a very large number of crumpled twenty-pound notes. Struggling to remove his jacket, he revealed the many scars on his thin arms that gave testament to him being a user as well as a dealer. My stomach was promising to rebel from the combination of polluted air and lukewarm coffee. All thoughts of acting drunk forgotten, I placed the cup on the floor and addressed the man.

"You <u>are</u> the man they call 'Rats' aren't you and you do sell drugs? I mean, I hope I've found the right person 'cause I want to buy some 'Coke' like I said .... "

"Who are you man? Where you come from?" 'Rats' must have noted the sudden change in my sobriety for his voice rose in pitch showing his alarm when he interrupted me. "You ask a lot of questions, let's see the colour of yo' money before we do the business!" he demanded. To calm his growing fears, I fanned the wad of notes for him to see, again noting the greedy glint in his eyes.

"OK. OK. 'Rats' is what they call me, I'm a Rastafarian and they call my Dreadlocks 'Rats Tails' see," he blurted with obvious relief. "I can supply any drugs you want." His boast was not lost on me. "For that sort of money, I can give you a couple of packs of good 'Coke,' but I don' want you muscling in on my patch, OK?" He puffed out his chest in what he thought was an intimidating way, but was more akin to a starling threatening a turkey. Warming to his theme and keeping his eyes on the wad of money in my hand, he continued. "I've got all the contacts and I supply all the kids 'roun here."

Seeing my nod of agreement, 'Rats' got up and went into another room shortly returning with a couple of larger plastic packs of white powder.

"Is that good stuff?" I queried in a worried voice as I slipped on a pair of thin surgical gloves I'd had in my pocket and picked up a pack. "I don't want to supply poor quality and cause anyone to die or anything."

"Yeah man, it's high grade, the best," he confirmed. Then with a couldn't care less shrug of his skinny shoulders, he added, "what if some of 'em do die man? Lose some and more will take their place, so don' worry, you'll <u>never</u> be short of business."

"No. No, it won't be right." Pretending to have second thoughts, I stood up and moved towards the door. "I heard an 18 year old girl died the other day."

"Where you goin' man?" 'Rats' clutched at my arm to stop me leaving. "Yeah well, she must have been given the wrong stuff," he sneered.

"I hear she died an agonizing death." The horror in my voice was real; I'd watched her die.

"So what, man?" 'Rats' cut in, eager to get the deal over and get back out on the street. "She ain't the first," he said, with no sign of any concern about the misery and suffering he caused. While he talked, I had been eyeing the packet of powder, a plan developing in my mind.

Shame, not to, I thought, using a saying for which I had been famous in the Services.

"No!" I snapped. Moving fast, I grabbed 'Rats' in a vicious headlock declaring angrily, "but, she will be the last whose death you cause." With one quick move, I burst the packet with my thumb and emptied a good quantity of the powder into his wide open mouth which I then clamped firmly closed with my hand. 'Rats' wildly twisted and turned, grabbing feebly at my arms in a desperate attempt to free his mouth and spit the powder out. No matter how much he struggled, his lack of physical strength meant he couldn't break my grip.

Judging the right moment, I transferred my grip from his mouth and squeezed his nose shut. Already panicking from the shortage of air, 'Rats' opened his mouth wide to drag in the much-needed oxygen, only to go into a choking fit as he inhaled a large portion of the powder instead.

"Enjoy it, man. It's high grade," I snarled in his ear while removing my hand from his nose but maintaining the headlock. "Nothing but the best quality for filth like you."

'Rats' started coughing and spluttering, his eyes widened in panic as he realized what I'd done. The arteries and veins now stood out like cords on his face and neck; I could see his pulse thumping away. Thick mucous started to dribble from his nose, and saliva bubbled from between his now firmly clenched teeth. Turning his head to me, he tried to form words as the saliva ran from his mouth and down his shirtfront. The drug was rapidly having an alarming effect.

"I knew you weren't ri ...gh," he whispered feebly as his eyes rolled upwards. Drawing his last remaining strength, he tried again. "too ... many ... ques....." His voice tailed off; the sentence would never be finished. His nostrils flared and his lips flailed in time with his breathing which came in fierce snorts. The struggles weakened as his muscles went into spasms. A large dark stain appeared and began spreading across the front of his trousers at the same time as an overpowering smell of urine assailed my nostrils. From the foul smell that filled the room, I knew he'd also emptied his bowels. A thin line of frothy, blood specked spittle bubbled from his mouth to join the other mess on his shirtfront. Jerking violently, he began to shudder and moan as the agonizing convulsions caused by the drug took hold. A long drawn-out whooshing sound alerted me as he threw up on the already filthy carpet.

"Good riddance to bad rubbish, man," I declared, letting him fall. His face hit the floor with a soggy sound like a rotten melon being dropped. He didn't even feel his nose break as it took the full impact. I left him there twitching and feebly clawing at the carpet.

    I made a rapid but thorough search amongst the man's filthy belongings - and of what passed as furniture in his room. My efforts were soon rewarded with the discovery of a tatty notebook full of names and phone numbers taped up under the bottom of a drawer unit. One page in particular was of great interest to me as it showed a London phone number at which, according to his scribbled notes, he'd leave a message for supplies. More interestingly, a Paris number with the name Marcel alongside it showed that he could buy direct from him if he wanted. I placed this unexpected *'treasure-trove'* safely in my jacket pocket.

    Hidden in the recess of the stained and smelly mattress, I also found a large roll of high denomination bank notes.

    "There must be at least a hundred and fifty grand there," I said to the empty room, pushing the money into my pocket and adding, "that will come in handy to fight against this evil."

    Emptying the dirty coffee cup in the sink, I wiped any surface I may have touched before I'd put the gloves on. Without a backward glance, I left 'Rats' still twitching on the floor in a growing pool of body fluids and closed the door firmly behind me.

    Checking that no one was watching I quietly left the building and made my way to a nearby phone box and dialled 999 to call the police. Giving them the information anonymously, I retraced my steps and hid in the deeper shadows between some derelict garages opposite the tenements and waited for the result of my anonymous tip off. With lights flashing the local police arrived quickly and a crowd of curious neighbours and passers-by soon built up.

Donning a woolly hat and glasses that I'd had in my pocket, I turned my coat collar up against the damp evening air coming off the canal and joined them to watch as the police removed several large plastic bags which I thought could possibly contain cocaine and heroin as well as other drugs from the premises. When at last the undertakers brought the body down, I moved away from the gawking crowd and slipped unseen into a dark corner close to the police cars where the senior officer was talking to the detectives.

"Right, chaps, on the face of it I don't think there's any more to this than it's a drug killing," he declared, "it seems to me that the dealer may have stepped on a rival gang's toes and was paid back for it." Turning towards his car he added, "I'm off home; call me if anything else comes up." He opened the car door....

"Sir. Sir." An urgent voice calling from the direction of the stairs stopped him. Caught with one foot inside the car, the senior officer hesitated as a young constable ran over to him.

"Sorry, Sir, but there is something that's a bit more than just coincidence here and I think you should know about it," the constable blurted as he tried to catch his breath. Urged on by the impatient look on his superior's face, he started to explain.

"I'd completed listing the drugs we've recovered and had started listing the victim's personal effects when

I noticed this in his shirt pocket," he said proudly holding out a small plastic evidence bag containing a visiting card.

"What of it, Mason?" the senior officer queried. He turned to face the constable, his obvious displeasure at this interruption showing on his face.

"Two nights ago," the constable continued, with obvious pride and confidence in his own ability, "I attended a serious motorcycle accident a couple of miles away. When handling the victim's property, I found a card that had been tucked into his helmet strap." He paused for effect. The others in the group were now eagerly listening and he was enjoying being the centre of attention.

"Now, tonight, I'm handling this victim's property and I find the same type of card with the same words on in his shirt pocket."

Taking the evidence bag and looking at the card, the Chief Inspector's past experience told him it was a 'special' calling card that had been deliberately left at the scene.

"Aah," he said, rubbing his chin. "I think we can ignore that, Mason," he added, in a more friendly fashion. "It looks pretty innocuous to me and probably has little or no bearing on the crime. Anyway, I've no doubt that scum in there got what he deserved and your motorbike victim was probably a user also. So why waste more of our valuable time, eh?" he concluded, patting the constable affably on the shoulder as he turned away.

"Well done anyway; I'll make sure this is noted in your records." He got into his car and was driven off before the constable could respond.

Left on his own, as the other policemen resumed their duties, I heard him say, "if it's a rival drug gang, then how come they didn't take all those drugs with them ... Sir?"

His remark hung in the air as he spun on his heel and stalked off. I couldn't help smiling at that deduction, but the constable obviously had a lot to learn about the workings of his superior's mind.

Satisfied with my evening's work, yet angry that I hadn't thought of flushing the drugs down the toilet, I mingled with the crowd and returned home for a well-earned drink. Though it was now getting on for 11 o'clock, I felt it best to bring Mal up to date on the action so far. Glass in hand, I picked up the phone and dialled his number hoping that Julie wouldn't answer.

"It had better be good at <u>this</u> time of night," Mal's sleepy voice said.

"It's me mate. You remember that contract you spoke to me about the other day?"

"What? ... Oh, that." Wide awake now as he recognised my voice, he sounded much keener. "Yes, I remember." I heard him shifting his position in his bed.

"I've some news about it that you will be interested in."

"Oh that's great". All signs of sleep gone, Mal was now fully alert.

"By the way, did you read about that poor young lad who was injured on his motor bike the other day?" I queried, knowing he would make the connection and understand what I meant. Such is the power of service training, use veiled speech long enough and it becomes a habit. Neither of us trusted the telephone lines anyway.

"Yeah. If he was doing what I think he was doing, I think he got off lightly," Mal stated with a hint of sarcasm in his voice.

"Well, Mal, in my judgement, he was an inexperienced rider, playing with a thing he didn't fully understand. This accident should serve as a lasting warning to him."

"OK. So his card is marked, but what else have you got?" In the background, I heard Julie whispering something to him.

"The other bit of news is that the guy who sold him the bike has had a very serious accident himself."

"How serious?" Mal's mounting interest sounded in his voice.

"Terminal, I'm afraid but I'm sure he won't be missed." I heard him chuckle at that news. "By the way, I sent him my card so we'll see what they say about it in the local press."

"Now what's this news you want to tell me?" He queried.

"Well, mate. I have some leads that will take me away for a while, probably overseas. I'll be in touch."

"Thanks a bunch, my friend; we will look forward to getting your postcards. Anything you need, you call me. OK?" His voice sounded more like the Mal I knew as he put the phone down. I had to admit to feeling a certain level of satisfaction myself. Finishing my drink, I got ready for bed.

According to the following day's newspaper reports on the death of the drug dealer, the police viewed it as a drug related killing. The reporters, not being satisfied with that, tried to make a mystery of the card, asking people to call in if they knew what it meant or who used them. With nothing positive to go on, they simply said, 'it shows a picture of a white bird in flight. The legend beneath says,

'HE MET THE 'SNOWBIRD' WHO SEEKS REVENGE.'

Two days later, the story was forgotten as news of a huge earthquake in Turkey came in. With that, I knew it was safe to continue my self-imposed mission. Having no personal ties to hold me back, I could take a long leave of absence without any worries. My mind was made up. I was off on the revenge trail and after making a phone-call to a number I found in the dealer's notes, I drove to London to confirm the address of the main importer. Passing this information on anonymously to the NDIU - the National Drug Intelligence Unit operated by the Metropolitan Police Drug Squad - I caught the Eurostar for Paris and an appointment with the European importers of drugs.

Chapter 3
<u>Paris. First contact.</u>

My train arrived in Paris late in the evening and to help establish my cover story, I booked into a cheap hotel on the Rue De Chalon. The colour brochures show spacious hotel rooms with views over Montmartre and bill Paris as *'The Romantic City of Dreams.'* The room I was given was small and cramped. One consolation was, however, that if I stood on tiptoe on a chair and looked out of the one and only window, I could see the lights of boats on the River Seine or enjoy the glorious view directly across the railway tracks leading into the Gare De Lyon main station.

"Ah well. Can't have it all, can we," I thought as I settled myself in.

Sleep eluded me that night. It wasn't fear that kept me awake; I'd been around too much to let things like that worry me. No, it was because I was entering into new unexplored territory by taking on the drug suppliers without the remotest idea of how they operated. The sum total of my knowledge was that they were well known to place little or no value on life. My mind kept wandering over the sketchy cover story that I'd thought up; I had to know it off by heart.

After breakfast the following day, I made my way to the public phone boxes in the main booking hall of the Gare De Lyon. Feeling as if everyone was watching me, I dialled the Paris number given in the dealer's notebook. The single ringing tone sounded about four times; my mouth suddenly felt dry and I was about to hang up when the phone was answered. "Comment vous appelez-vous?" a suspicious sounding voice demanded in my ear.

"Sorry, but I don't speak French," I lied.

"Who are you?" the unidentified voice on the phone demanded in heavily accented English.

"My name is Ben Crawford," I said, giving the assumed name that had been specifically chosen to match my initials, while keeping my own Christian name because we react to them more naturally. "I'm a seaman and I want to arrange a regular supply of drugs to sell." I paused to swallow. He must have heard the nervousness in my voice. "Can I speak to Marcel, please?"

"Who gave you this number?" the voice demanded gruffly.

"On my last visit home to Gloucester a few weeks ago, I met a guy called 'Rats,' he said you may be able to help me." Though this statement was a deliberate lie, there was not much chance they would be able to check it.

"Moment, sil'vous plaît." There was a pause while muffled voices muttered in the background. "There will be someone at a place called the 'The Cafe d'Or' at 7pm. this evening; you will find this in a back street near The Place De La Bastille," the voice said. "He will be sat in a booth, at the rear of the Bar. Identification will be made by him having an empty beer bottle lying on its side in front of him." With that, the phone went dead.

So, I thought. It seems I have made the right connection and have some time to spare. Let's have a wander around to get my bearings and learn the locality.

With this decision made, I slipped into the crowd of travellers that flowed like a constant stream through the huge hall.

You've chosen your cover story carefully, so that it can't easily be checked on. A soft voice seemed to whisper inside my head as I walked out into the comparative quiet of the street. I hope they'll accept you in your assumed role of a seaman desperate for extra cash.

Such a role was not going to present any problem really. Having done a bit of sailing and owned a power boat, plus I held a current Royal Yachting Association Offshore Certificate, I felt that this would give me enough knowledge of ships that could stand up to any questioning the Frenchman may apply.

Well before the agreed appointment time that evening, I moved into a good observation position in a side road off The Place De La Bastille. Using the deeper shadows on the opposite side of the poorly lit street to 'The Cafe d'Or,' I watched the few people entering and leaving. By adopting such basic surveillance procedures as this, I hoped it would stop me walking into a trap. The building, on which I focussed my attention, was set in the middle of a terrace of eight similar buildings and turned out to be a run down seedy looking place, four stories high with a dingy basement area. As if trying to compete with its more dilapidated neighbours, it, too, had large lumps of plaster missing out of the walls and the doors and windows hadn't seen paint in many years. Above the front door hung a sign on which the faded outline of its name could barely be read.

Seven people went in, but only four people came out. That should mean its three to one odds then, my little voice whispered gleefully in my ear. As the appointed time approached and more satisfied that no nasty surprises awaited me, I walked across the road and opened the door.

Good God. What a dump, I thought. If the outside hadn't impressed me what I found inside was even more disgusting. Some walls were covered with garish maroon and orange paint that had seen better times while from the others hung the remains of wallpaper stained with years of tobacco and grime. The air, if that's what it could be called, was thick with tobacco smoke and stale cooking smells - mainly cabbage. "What a dump," I repeated to myself.

All conversation ceased when I opened the door. With a sense of unease in the pit of my stomach but an outward show of nonchalance, I crossed the room to the Bar knowing that I was being closely studied. Through the haze of smoke I could see the only customers. One man sat on his own at the back - with a spilled beer bottle in front of him - and two other tough looking characters were on the right, both ardently adding to the smoke of the room while giving me the evil eye. There was also one very old man on the other side talking to the barman by what I assumed was the kitchen door.

"Oui, M'sieur? Cognac, Pernod?" The barman grunted in an offhand way as he wiped his hands on his already filthy apron; suspicion was written all over his face.

"Two bottles of Stella, please," I said in reply to his surly question.

"Ah. ... English!" This unsavoury man exclaimed loudly as if he had just worked out Einstein's theory, but most probably to announce me as the expected visitor.

Paying for the drinks and pocketing the change, I picked my way between the tables and approached the man in the back booth. He showed not even a glimmer of interest as I identified myself by saying, "it looks like you need a refill."

Placing the bottles on the table, I waited. With a quick wave of his hand he indicated me to sit opposite him.

"Salut," he grunted as he took one of the beers and tipped a large swig down his throat, the bobbing of his Adam's apple causing the gold chain and medallion around his neck to glint spasmodically in the dim light.

Taking a mouthful from my own bottle, I cautiously studied the man, sizing him up quickly - he spelt trouble with a capital T. Powerfully built, his thick black hair was well groomed and combined with his swarthy skin to give him a Mediterranean look. He wore what was obviously a very expensive short black leather jacket, a casual open neck shirt through which thick, wiry black hair showed. Heavy gold bracelets adorned one wrist while a very expensive gold watch glinted on the other. More for effect than use on a dark night I suspected, he also had a pair of Ray Ban chrome framed aviator sunglasses stuck into the top pocket of his jacket. He smelt as if he bathed in Cologne.

"Stand up, M'sieur," the Frenchman suddenly instructed, rising to his feet in a smooth fluid movement that showed no apparent effort. Then, with a surprisingly light touch and the moves of an expert, he searched me; checking all the usual places, as well as some more unusual ones, for any hidden weapon.

"No weapons, mon ami?" He gave a characteristic Gallic shrug. "In Paris, you should have at least a knife," he added, demonstrating a quaint but reasonable command of English. "Please, to follow me." With that he led the way out of the cafe.

I followed him, heaving a sigh of relief as my lungs drew in the fresh air. A small sound behind me made me look over my shoulder. We were not alone. The two other men who had been smoking in an adjacent booth had come out with us and now stood close at hand, silently studying me by the weak glow of a street lamp.

With no attempt at any introductions - part of the intimidation act I realised, the Frenchman said, "we are going to a place that you must never go into alone M'sieur; the locals," - with a wave of his hand, he indicated his two unsavoury friends - "do not take kindly to strangers." With that, he turned on his heels and led the way down a series of narrow, smelly, unlit passageways between gaunt, towering buildings. The only attempt to make conversation was when he asked me, "do you understand any French?"

"Only the usual phrases," I lied, with a shrug that went unseen in the darkness.

"Ha. Typical English," he responded sarcastically.

"Up yours," I said to myself. "Why should I let you know that I passed French at school and have a useful command of German and Spanish as well as a smattering of Italian?" I smiled at these thoughts; it had always been my maxim not to let the opposition know you can understand them. My stride lengthened in an effort to keep up with the Frenchman in the dark alleyways, tripping frequently on the uneven paving.

Some while later, we entered another dingy, smoky bar situated in the cellars of what appeared to be an equally depressing brothel. We were led to a table in a corner of the room by an over-painted and ancient female who eyed me as if I was something the dog had left behind. Drinks that no one had ordered were pushed in front of us by a half dressed girl. Glancing around, I noticed a full width mirror on the wall directly opposite me through the grime of which I could study my companions while watching the rest of the room.

At the same time as someone is sizing you up from behind the mirror no doubt, my little voice hissed secretively.

After a short while - as if in response to an unseen signal, the Frenchman leaned across the table and looking me straight in the eyes, announced, "I am called John Paul, and am what you English would call the Gang Leader." He paused theatrically to let this information sink in.

Not Marcel? Then that must have been a contact code, I thought, as I took a nervous sip of my drink to give myself time to gather my thoughts. John Paul studied me keenly and there was a new, distinct edge to his voice when he continued, "I wish to know exactly what you are willing to do, to get the cash *you say* you so desperately need." The emphasis he put on the words 'you say' made me think he doubted me.

"I ... I'm desperate ... I will do anything, anything to earn quick money"   There was no need for me to try and sound uneasy when I replied.

"Are you in trouble with the Law?" snapped John Paul.

"No. No, I'm not," my response was perhaps too hurried.

There was a long pause while the Frenchman combed his hair and adjusted the set of his shirt collar, never once taking his eyes from mine.

Once again, as if by a hidden signal, the tension eased and, giving me a long searching look, John Paul announced. "We have a job that you can do that will test your skill and reliability. You will take a special package to London for us." He paused to sip his drink before continuing. "But remember, if you are caught, you will go to prison for many years and we cannot help you." Then, with a dramatic flourish, he stood and indicated with a crook of his finger that I should once again follow him.

Leaving our drinks largely untouched, we left the bar by a back door. Passing across a greasy, foul smelling back yard, we climbed some well-worn steps to emerge in the lane at the side of the building. As if he had the eyes of a cat, John Paul led the way unerringly down the unlit lane. I bumped into his back when he stopped suddenly near a darker patch of blackness. Someone produced a hand torch that seemed to be on its last legs. Its weak, faltering light showed me that we were stood at what appeared to be the rear of a battered Citroen cargo van, the distinctive corrugated style sheeting giving it away.

John Paul threw open the rear doors with a deft movement of his hand and pointed inside. Instinctively, I moved forward to see what was there only to be grabbed roughly by unseen hands from the dark interior, at the same time as someone behind me threw a filthy, dusty, onion smelling sack over my head.

"Hey!" I shouted. "What the Bloody Hell! ...." A mouthful of the dust in the bottom of the sack cut off the rest of my exclamation. Coughing and spluttering and trying to regain my breath, I had little chance to fight. More hands grabbed me and I found myself being roughly bundled into the van, hitting my head and shoulder on the wheel arch as I was dragged unceremoniously across the corrugated floor. Any further protests would mean another mouthful of dust so I wisely shut up.

Unable to struggle because of what felt like at least two men sitting on me, there was no option but to stay still while they bound my hands behind my back.

Why bother tying me so tightly? I asked myself. I can't move with those two lumps sitting on me. The van doors slammed shut, the engine started and almost immediately the vehicle was driven off at speed, hurtling around corners with its tyres screeching,

"Merde.".... "Ach. Mein Got.".... "Bastardo.".... "Got in Himmel.".... My unseen and obviously international companions cursed in a mixture of languages as they were thrown around in the back. Being weighted down by the two who were using me as a seat meant my chest was pressed painfully hard against the rough corrugations of the floor and in just a few minutes, I was a mass of bruises.

At last, there was an easing of my punishment when both men finally got off me. We sped along the narrow winding streets for what seemed ages, bumping and swaying as we hurtled along. Unable to do anything else, I attempted to relax and concentrate on restricting my breathing as much as possible, while preparing myself mentally for whatever they had in store for me. Cautiously, under cover of the darkness and general noise, I tested my bindings. They proved to have been done by an expert.

He must have twigged me so now it's a firing squad or worse, I thought, desperately trying to think where I had made a mistake. Through the thick sacking, I could hear the more obvious sounds of the city fading as the vehicle, its well-tuned engine belying its condition, continued its wild, powerful dash. I felt, rather than heard, the surface of the road change, which indicated to me that we had left the city and had joined one of the main Auto Routes leading out into the countryside. The concrete raft formation of it gave an unmistakable 'Dap - Dap' sensation as we sped along.

Uncomfortable from being trussed like a chicken, it wasn't long before the heat building up inside the heavy sacking made my head ache. That, and the swaying motion of the van, made me feel terribly sick but I fought it rather than choke on my own vomit.

After what seemed like ages, the road surface changed again: this time to a slightly rougher surface from which I guessed we were on a minor road and therefore nearing our destination.

We slowed for a sharp right-hand corner and the van bounced its way across what could only be a single railway crossing; the boards between the lines rattled loosely at our passing. At what seemed breakneck speed, we climbed a long winding hill at the top of which, without warning or slowing down, the van changed course to the right into an obviously unmade road. We bumped and swerved down this track for well over a mile before coming to an abrupt halt. Like projectiles from a gun, my unseen and unwary travelling companions slid in a heap against the front bulkhead. Unable to stop myself, I slid painfully along the corrugated floor to join them.

"Bloody Hell." My exclamation was lost among the renewed mixture of French, Italian and German curses from the now indignant passengers as they kicked me away. The back doors of the van were thrown open, rough hands dragged me to my feet and pushed me out. Thankfully, I was held firmly on either side to stop me from falling. Battered and bruised by the journey, disorientated and nearly suffocated by the dirty sack over my head, I was thankful for the support offered by the two men who force marched me across a cobbled surface and through some sort of entranceway.

The sound of a heavy door slamming closed behind us with a solid 'thunk' as we passed through echoed briefly. Sounds like the condemned cell to me, that cheery little voice whispered in my ear as I stumbled blindly between my 'guides.'

"That's close enough." A muffled guttural command stopped us in our tracks.

"Remove the sack," another voice commanded. Was I mistaken or did it have what seemed to be a Latin American accent? Either way, anticipating such an event, I had employed an old trick learnt in the Services and closed my eyes tightly to save them from being damaged by sudden exposure to bright lights. There was no flood of bright light to show through my eyelids as the sack was removed so I slowly opened one to accustom it to whatever light there was.

Surprisingly, I found myself almost enclosed by semi-darkness that was broken occasionally by the weak beams of my captors' hand torches. Their dim light showed me that we were in the middle of what appeared to be the inside of a large barn. Opening both eyes, it became clear that I was stood alone in the centre of a group of about eight shadowy men whose faces deliberately remained in the deeper shadows.

Just like the Kangaroo Courts in Northern Ireland. The alarming thought flashed across my mind.

"Vhy are you so keen to join us?" My thoughts were scattered by this sudden loud demand. In front of me, I could dimly make out the shape of a very large man. He impatiently repeated his demand in a guttural German accent as he stepped forward.

"Answer me. Vhy are you so keen to join us?" My ears, used to picking up minor details for reference, told me that my questioner had a pronounced difficulty in forming the letter W more so than most Germans as he seemed to hiss the words. He also pronounced the word join as 'choin'.

"*I'm* desperate for money," I spluttered, my mouth and nose still blocked with the dust from the sacking.

"Why?" This single word was snapped by the Latin American voice that sharply interrupted from deep within the covering shadows. "Why are you so desperate and more importantly ... why should we believe you?" His expensive education was evident in the way he formed his words.

Thinking fast, while still trying hard to suppress the urge to cough, I gasped, "I gambled and lost and now I owe a very large sum of money to a London gang called 'The Carvers;' they want it - or my life." The lie, part of my cover story, slipped easily from my lips between rasping coughs.

"Ha! Joe Carver's gang," the Latino exclaimed when I'd fallen silent. "I've had dealings with them; they're a bad lot all right." He paused as if thinking. "But you. You are just another fool who thinks that easy money can be made from gambling." Again he waited for me to stop coughing before continuing. "It is far better to *work* for it than to *hope* for it, my friend. Work for me and you will be rewarded well." His final words sent a chilling shiver up my spine. "Cross me ... and you will die." Having issued that warning, the Latin American gave instructions for my hands to be untied.

Gratefully rubbing my hands together to regain the circulation as the rough rope bonds were cut free, I took a step toward the Latino as I'd nicknamed him, only to be immediately roughly pushed back by the shadowy, larger man.

Got it. Large man is bodyguard. South American is Boss.

"Can I have some water to wash the dirt out of my mouth and throat?" I pleaded as yet another fit of harsh coughing racked my body.

"Water? There is no water, but we have a good line in French wine," the Latin American replied with a sarcastic laugh. Then, as an afterthought, he added in an intolerant voice that indicated a swift change of temper, "there is a horse trough in the yard. Go. Wash the dust away with that!" he snapped impatiently.

Accompanied closely by two of the men, I made my way out into the yard to the horse trough where, as one of them operated the ancient pump, I gratefully washed the clinging dust from my face and head. The water tasted cool and sweet so I swilled my mouth out as best I could but its coldness could not wash away a niggling worry in the back of my mind. My instincts told me there was something not quite right about the place. Straightening up, in the guise of shaking excess water from my hair, I snatched a quick look around but could only just make out the looming shapes of the barns and the darker silhouette of a rather large farmhouse in the moonless night. Having spent much of my childhood in the countryside, plus many hours crouched in 'hides' on observation duties across the world, I knew there was something strange about the place. Something was not quite right; there was something missing that I couldn't put my finger on. Before I could give the matter any more thought or look any harder at my new surroundings, rough hands pushed me back toward the barn. Disappointed that I could gain no clue as to our whereabouts, I complied without fuss.

Returning with my escort to the group inside, a change of scene immediately became apparent. In our absence the others in the group had found and lit an old oil lamp, the glass of which was so black that very little light was given out. They had also placed some hay bales in a half circle for seats. I was directed to sit on my own in the middle at the front from where I could hear but not see the Latino and his henchman who remained strategically sat outside the loom of the flickering lamplight.

"How much money do you owe the 'Carvers'?" the Latino asked, in a pleasant, conversational manner.

"Over eight thousand pounds." My firm reply was meant to convey confidence, something that I was not feeling at that time. It seemed they still weren't sure of me.

"How long have you owed it?" Again, this was put pleasantly.

"Ever since I took off six months ago. Now they're threatening my mother," I added miserably. An involuntary shiver ran through me, as water dripped from my hair and ran down my back.

"Can you drive a car and do you know your vay around Europe?" the German demanded gruffly.

"Yes, I can and I have done a lot of driving over here." My reply was truthful.

As the questioning went on, I caught an occasional flash of what looked like gold rings and bracelets or a gold wrist watch that reflected the weak light as the Latino made expressive gestures with his hands.

Expensive tastes, I mused to myself, as well as expensive Cologne. Each wave of the man's hands sent clouds of perfumed air wafting towards me, the smell cutting through the dankness of the barn.

Of course! That's it. That little voice seemed to shout in my ear as realisation dawned. There's no SMELL. Come to think of it, there were no sounds either. Every farm I'd ever visited smelt of animals and if they were disturbed at night, they'd be in full voice by now. An uncharacteristic silence is what you noticed outside and there had been no lights on in the farmhouse either. Can't be many disused farms standing near a railway crossing, can there? The voice seemed proud of having made this discovery. No, you're right and this information could possibly be used to lead me back here later, I thought in return.

"Answer me." My private thoughts were suddenly shattered by the voice of the German demanding a reply to an unheard question. "Do you know the new customs' procedures at Dover docks and Heathrow airport? Vould you feel able to valk through the Green Channel vith a load of drugs in a case?" he reiterated impatiently.

"I... I've done a bit of small time smuggling in the past, when returning home from abroad." My nervous assertion totally failed to convey any pride in my fictitious achievements.

"Have you any family you vorry about, a girlfriend or vife perhaps?"

"No." This time my answer was truthful; there was no one.

"Can you use a gun and a knife? Vould you be villing to kill someone?"

"Yes, I can and I would kill if I had to." This too was the truth; it was precisely what I was here for after all.

For over an hour, they threw searching questions at me and then, with a wave of his hand, the Latino instructed one of his men to blindfold me again.

"For your own sake, Señor Ben." I noted the use of my Christian name; it seemed I was in. "It is best that you do not know this place," he explained with another expansive gesture. Then he was gone, melting into the shadows as silently as a cat. Outside, a car's doors slammed shut; a powerful engine started up and the vehicle raced away.

The blindfold was fitted. This time, thankfully, they used a cleaner piece of cloth. I was taken outside and helped into the back seat of a waiting car. Another person got in beside me and the vehicle bounced as someone else took their place in the front seat. The driver, who ever he was, showed total disregard for the state of the track or for the car as he gunned the engine and sped away.

"What happens now? Where are we going?" I demanded of the person beside me. "Who was the Latin man? Is he the Boss?"

My questions were totally ignored. I didn't know who my companions were as we travelled for over an hour during which time it was obvious that they were just driving around to confuse me. Eventually, we pulled up in what I could identify as a fairly busy street from the traffic sounds. A boat siren sounded mournfully in the distance on my left and I heard a train crossing a bridge close by.

So, we are back by the Seine by the sound of it, I thought. At least that means I am not going to be dumped in the countryside.

"Get out of the car," a now familiar voice said, as a hand removed my blindfold and pushed me toward the door. John Paul sat there with a pleased look on his face. As instructed, I opened the door and was half way out when a strong hand gripped my arm.

"We will be in touch with you soon. Those two in front are Henry and Paulo; they do not speak much English."

"I do not like you *'Rosbif,'*" the man called Paulo snarlled at me.

"Don't call me Roast beef .... " My words were cut off as the car roared away, almost taking me with it. "Bloody Frogs." I spat into the cloud of fast receding exhaust fumes.

"Well, well," I muttered, straightening myself up. "It seems that I have been accepted. I'm going to have to watch that Paulo though; he's a nasty piece of work."

John Paul) by slipping out of the hotel via the back door. Once on the street and in keeping with the traditions of the finest spies, I took a circuitous route to the nearby Metro station.

Purchasing a day ticket, I promptly allowed myself to get swallowed in the crowds of office workers and other travellers jostling with each other for the best position. Keeping my eyes open for any possible 'tail' and changing trains twice to cause further confusion, I eventually arrived at my destination station. Choosing to use the stairs in preference to the crowded escalator - another attempt to isolate anyone who was following me - I emerged onto the street called the Rue Molitor and waited for anyone else to come up out of the station. Five minutes went by, during which no one came out that way, so quickly getting my bearings; I set off to find the house with the number 22.

Used to the more drab back streets around my hotel, I soon became aware of the scent and colours from the various blossoms on the trees that lined this street. My eyes were continually drawn to these and the many brightly coloured flowerbeds that made the short walk to my objective that much more enjoyable. Even at this early hour, it was promising to be a warm day so I found it quite pleasant, passing from one patch of scented shade to the next. Arriving at last outside number 22, I paused to study the many names on the brass plates adorning the wall by the door.

Curious, I thought. It seems I have an appointment at the surgery of a large medical practice which now makes me wonder if I have to pass a medical.

Making mental notes of some of the names for future reference, I climbed the few steps from the street a few minutes before the supposed 'appointment' time.

Approaching the reception desk I was greeted with a cheery 'Bonjour' by a tall, well built and very pretty girl in her early twenties whose name, according to the tag on her ample breast, was Michelle. She gave me a very frank and appraising look, a wonderful smile and an equally wonderful view down the front of her very low cut blouse as she bent over to study her papers.

Well, if that's not a come on, what is, my little voice whispered in my ear.
Giving my name and half expecting to be asked to join the other waiting patients, I was surprised when her interest in me visibly heightened.

"Aaah. M'sieur Crawford," she said in perfect English. Like her blouse, her husky voice was low and very sexy. "We have a package for you." She leaned even further forward, deliberately improving my view of her creamy firm breasts. Reaching into the bottom drawer of her desk, she extracted a package the size of a small shoebox and came around the front to stand close beside me.

"Here is the special equipment you need, M'sieur. Full instructions are inside." She breathed huskily as she deliberately trailed her fingers slowly across the centre of my open palm while handing me the package. Turning to pick up a small card from the desk, she brushed her breasts against my arm as she offered it to me. My stomach flipped and I was left in no doubt that she definitely didn't need a bra. Then I realised she was still speaking to me.

"Should you have any need of any other *special* services, please call anytime, my number is at the top." With a sweet smile over her shoulder and a wiggle of her truly wonderful hips, she resumed her post behind the desk.

My arm seemed to burn from the touch of her body; my nostrils were full of the smell of her perfume and the emphasis she'd put on the word *special* seemed to sear my brain. In a daze, I tucked the box under my arm, took a last lingering look at her, gave a muttered "merci" and turned to leave the premises.

Wow. If you didn't have high blood pressure when you went in, you certainly had it when you came out. Why is it only French girls can be like that, my little voice asked as I tucked her card safely in my pocket. Pity I can't take up what she offered there, maybe another time though, I thought.

Regaining the street, I quickly walked the short distance to a small park just off the main road. Finding a quiet spot and again making sure no one else was close by, I removed the outer wrapping to find that it revealed yet another one that was well sealed with black duct tape. In between this and the outer one was a small padded envelope with just my first name on.

"Don't want me to see the contents do they?" I muttered ruefully. It was only then that I realised how light the packet was. Judging by the weight of it, it could be a few packets of drugs, I speculated, so I'd best be careful with this.

For some reason, my hands were slightly shaking as I opened the envelope to find that it only contained a small key on a numbered fob. Stuck to it with a piece of the duct tape was a ticket for a left luggage locker in the Musee du Louvre.

The mystery deepens, my little voice said in my ear.

"Indeed, it does." My muttered reply was lost in the sound of passing traffic as I pushed the key and the ticket deep into my pocket. Ensuring that nothing had been left behind and taking a quick glance at my watch, I made my way back to the Metro station, dropping the outer wrapping into the mobile litterbin being pushed by a municipal workman as he passed.

The Metro was reasonably quiet now that the early rush of workers had gone, the crush of silent, newspaper reading office workers having now been replaced by chattering housewives making their way to the markets and shops, etc.

After studying the plan of the routes, I nipped onto the next train just as the doors were closing. Suddenly, I became aware that several people had stopped talking and were watching me closely. What they were thinking I don't know but realised I had been clutching the packet to me as if it were the Crown Jewels or, in their minds, a bomb. Even though the air was reasonably cool, sweat was pouring off me.

As we arrived at the next station I fled from their questioning gaze, crossed the platform and slipped aboard another train going the same way but destination unknown. Forcing myself to relax, I seated myself in a corner seat so as to observe my fellow passengers who for reasons known only to them seemed to prefer the other end of the carriage to mine. Glancing idly around, my eye was drawn to the headlines on a discarded newspaper lying on the seat beside me.

Picking it up, I read that a big police raid had taken place in London during the early hours of the previous day. A police spokesperson was reported as saying that acting on information received - that made me chuckle to myself - over 14 ½ million pounds worth of hard drugs had been seized and several arrests had been made in lightning raids. Similar raids had taken place in the Bristol and Gloucester areas, each giving good positive results.

I was just getting into the story when I realised that the train was arriving at a station by the name of Rue De La Pompe. Wrong direction! Quickly dropping the paper back on the seat and holding the package close to me, I mingled with the small crowd of housewives and other travellers as they left the train. Once again, I took the few steps between platforms and waited for the next train on which to retrace my steps to the Rue De Rivoli. A twenty minute train ride later, I arrived at my destination. My cautious but quick look around proved that nobody seemed remotely interested in me, so I slipped into the long underpass that goes to the other side of the main road.

At the other end, as if a concession to the growing heat of the midday sun, I paused to slip my jacket off and furtively watch the few other people who preferred to use this route. Still nobody paid any undue attention to me so I slipped into a nearby emergency exit and made my way up the stairs to emerge outside the Palais Royal on the Rue De Rivoli.

Dodging the traffic - or I should say the wall of speeding steel - that hurtled at me down this very wide and busy main road, I started across. Hastily dodging speeding cars, their irate drivers sounding their horns in anger at this mere pedestrian who dared violate their territory, I reached the other side unscathed but gasping from the exhaust fumes.

Using the glass of an electronic advertising hoarding as a mirror to see behind me, I checked to see if anyone else had been stupid enough to likewise defy death in that fashion. No one else had appeared from the exit so I walked on, muttering to myself.

"Here I am, supposedly on trial for this drugs gang, carrying drugs across Paris for them, and no one is interested in me." It seemed I was feeling rather let down.

Why do they need to follow you, that voice asked in my ear. They do know where you are going, you know. This piece of logic did ring true. From my own past experience, I was aware that you can 'follow' someone while being in front of them. All you had to do was know their destination and watch their approach routes while they tried to spot you *behind* them.

"That Pink Panther fellow would have thought of that," I sighed.

From a previous visit to the Louvre museum a few years ago, my recollection was that the left luggage locker to which the key belonged was situated in the lower level. Joining a crowd of tourists heading in the same direction, I crossed the open paved space of the Cour Du Carrousel - or as the Parisian's call it, 'Napoléon's Courtyard' - to join the queue waiting at the official entrance in the huge glass pyramid that stands near the centre.

For the next twenty minutes or so, I suffered the growing heat that was magnified by the massive glass structure while containing my growing impatience as we slowly shuffled forwards. The worst part was not the waiting itself nor even the heat, but having to suffer an overbearing and very loud camera bedecked American, a few paces behind me. In the time-honoured fashion of all Americans everywhere, he shared <u>his</u> opinion about <u>everything</u> with <u>everyone,</u> no matter whether he was right or wrong.

"Le paquet, M'siuer." I became vaguely aware of a distant voice saying as if in a dream. "Le paquet, M'siuer."

"Come on, Buddy." The American shouted behind me. "We have a lot to do and see so we sure can't hang about here waiting for you."

"Le paquet, M'siuer!" the voice repeated officiously; this time it was louder.

"Eh. What?" I was suddenly snapped out of my daydream by the voice of a uniformed and, I noted, armed guard who was holding out his hand expectantly.

"Le paquet, M'siuer," he repeated, impatiently moving his fingers in a 'give it to me gesture.'

"Oh. Yes, sorry," I said, feeling very embarrassed. Then my heart almost stopped as I realised that it was my turn to go through the narrow doorway inside of which I could see a very thorough search was being made of all persons and of any baggage. The packet was taken from me by the guard, who passed it through an X-ray machine. My heart almost stopped.

Do drugs show on X-ray machines? The alarming thought flashed across my mind. I don't even know what's in there. Surely, they'll see that I'm now sweating profusely and think its nerves. How the hell do I get out of this?

Trapped by the press of people behind me, unable to back out now, I made an attempt to affect a calm disinterest - which I definitely did not feel - as another armed security guard waved an electronic wand over me. No alarms started screaming. No hands gripped me to drag me off for questioning. Still pushed unceremoniously by the person behind me, I moved forward as directed with an immense feeling of relief.

"Merci M'sieur." The first guard grunted as he thrust the packet back into my sweating hands and impatiently waved me away. Somewhere in the distance, I could hear an American voice berating the guard who was putting his cameras through the X-ray machine. My knees felt weak as I made my way onto the escalator that whisked visitors down into the welcoming cool depths of the museum. Suddenly, the quite unmistakable aroma of real coffee wafted past me. My stomach did a double back flip as I became aware of a growing hunger.

"Oh Christ," I mumbled looking at my watch, "I need a drink to steady my nerves." Reaching the bottom, I was relieved to see a coffee and snacks bar on the lower level - though this also sold alcohol, and a stiff Cognac would have been more welcome - I thought Coffee would be best for my near shattered nerves. Choosing a table I heard, rather than saw, the American go by into the marble surrounded depths of the Museum.

"Thank God for small mercies," I mumbled half aloud then set to ordering a double espresso and a chicken sandwich. With the American in mind and my own privacy, I'd chosen a seat at a table in a corner partly hidden by a large decorative palm tree in a tub. Gradually, my nerves and taut muscles started to relax as the caffeine and extra sugar did its job. Watching the crowds while eating my lunch, I again failed to identify anybody showing any undue interest in me.

Feeling slightly recovered after the food and another coffee - into which I'd piled extra sugar - I sought the left luggage room. Handing the ticket to the attendant, who I noticed gave me a long, suspicious look from under his very bushy eyebrows; I accepted the small overnight case that was roughly and unceremoniously thrust at me without a spoken word. Secured by a strong strap and a very professional looking combination lock, it proved to be of average weight for its size.

"Just as well complete the exercise," I muttered, grabbing the case and packet securely in my hands and making my way through the throng of people to the bank of small lockers. The key fitted the one at the nearest end of the first block. Opening it, I saw another envelope inside. Placing the case between my feet and looking around carefully, I removed the envelope and saw that my name was printed in large letters on the front. Opening it, I found a small piece of paper containing a simple message in the same large hand-scripted print as before.

'Well done, we like the way you move around. Bring the case and packet to me at 9 a.m. sharp, tomorrow.' The initials JP, which I took to be John Paul, followed this.

So, it had all been a test and not only have they been watching me all along but they have a copy of the key to this locker as well. I might have known these guys are professionals; they don't do things by half. I smiled at an elderly lady who gave me a few strange looks as she walked by. I was getting used to being stared at. It seemed the whole world was doing the 'Let's stare at Ben Carson thing.'

Feeling smug at having completed the 'test,' at the same time as being quite impressed by their organisational ability, I tucked the packet under my arm and holding the case firmly in one hand, joined the crowd as they made their way to the exit. Reaching the surface, I paused to think over the next move.

It's a nice day, my little voice said, and you have plenty of time to spare, so take a walk along the embankment.

"Good idea." My sudden loud exclamation caused a Japanese lady to jump back from me: her eyes widened in fright. With a little laugh, I moved to mingle with the crowds and listened to the excited chatter of the many groups of children out on a big 'adventure.' This, along with the warm sunshine and the magnificent scenery combined to relax me enough to enjoy the walk immensely. For a long time, I studied the huge, prominent buttresses and carvings of the Notré Dame cathedral, trying to imagine the poor old hunchback living high up there in that cold, draughty place. The passing water buses - les bateaux mouche - also drew my eye, their decks crowded with camera waving tourists.

Feeling a new and unexpected sense of freedom, I spent a few francs on an enormous ice cream and considerable time in eating it before looking at the numerous small stalls that offer an amazing variety of knickknacks, from antiques to paintings.

At one location I found a huge selection of second hand books, displayed on one long shelving system that was attached to the railings near a bridge. There must be well over a thousand books in a variety of languages here, I mused as I picked out a couple of English ones to read.

Though I had been there before, it wasn't until approaching my hotel later, that I began to appreciate why so many people find Paris intriguing. Walk in this carefree setting, amongst people speaking so many different languages while intent on enjoying themselves in this truly universal city. View its wonderful historic buildings, open-air markets, wide boulevards and tree lined squares that give no hint of its blood soaked history. Who wouldn't be impressed?

Even though I still had no idea what they contained, I didn't want the case or the packet left unattended for too long so, after a refreshing shower, I made a call to the reception desk and asked for a meal and a bottle of wine to be delivered to my room. A short while later, a quiet knock on the door announced the arrival of the waiter.

"Your dinner, M'siuer," the old man wheezed, thrusting the tray forwards.

"Here you are," I said, offering him five Francs as a tip. "Come back for the tray later; it will be outside the door as I don't want to be disturbed. Do you understand?"

"Oui, M'sieur. Merci. Très bien," the old man mumbled, pocketing the money as he backed out of the door.

Feeling relaxed and content, having finished my meal and most of the wine, I put the tray outside the door and prepared for bed, tucking both the case and the packet under the foot of the mattress for safety before climbing in. Tired, but feeling pleased with progress so far, I soon drifted off to sleep thinking of the young medical receptionist and what might have been. The last sound I heard was a faint voice in my ear saying, I bet you go back for another look.

Chapter 5

<u>My Introduction to the Drug Trade</u>

The noise of the trains entering and leaving the station woke me very early the following morning.

"Why do they have to sound their whistles as they pull away?" I moaned as I struggled into my trousers.

After a quick breakfast, I made my way along the embankment, crossing the river at the oldest bridge in Paris that is strangely named the Pont Neuf, The New Bridge. I found myself in the 7th Arrondissement. There was no time for sight seeing as I wanted to be at John Paul's office in the Rue Dauphine in good time. It wasn't nerves or anything, just that I was eager to rid myself of the case and packet as soon as possible.

"Ah. Bonjour, Ben!" he exclaimed as I entered. Rising from his seat through a cloud of cigar smoke, he reached out to shake my hand.

He's probably been here all night, I thought, as I placed the packet and case on his desk, noting that his first action was to inspect the lock and strap on the case with great care.

Then with a laugh, he turned to me saying, "I knew we could trust you, mon ami. My instincts are always right, but I must say that you covered your tracks very well yesterday. Where did you learn that?" He studied me with great interest.

"I did tell you I was trained in the army with three tours in Northern Ireland and have had to dodge the

London gangs quite a bit, remember?" I replied with a dismissive shrug.

"Ha," he declared, puffing another cloud of cigar smoke out at the same time. "Those gangs, they have nothing on us; you will learn more here with us, I think."

With that, he moved over to a small cabinet, poured a couple of inches of Scotch into each of two glasses and handing one to me he said with a wink, "you, now, are one of us. Look after us, and we will look after you." With a complete disregard for the way he treated the best quality Scotch, he tossed his drink back in one go and then unlocked the case with a key he had taken from his pocket.

"Open it, please," he told me as he stepped back out of the way.

Nervously - not being one for nasty surprises and not knowing quite what to expect - I eased the lid up very carefully. No nasty bangs or squirts of dye into my face, but I was astounded to see dozens of tightly tied bundles of very large denomination bank notes.

"My God," I gasped, suddenly realising the reason for John Paul's inspection of the lock. "How much is there?"

"That, my friend," John Paul boasted with an air of nonchalance, "is the equivalent to one and a half million of your English pounds, all in Italian Lira. Not bad for one day's work, eh?" He gave a deep resonant laugh that echoed around the room when he saw the expression on my face. "You acted as our collector and *that* is just one of the many ways we do our business." With a satisfied chuckle, he puffed on his cigar.

"But what if I'd been stopped and someone wanted me to open it?" I pressed. "What then?" It was too much for me, suddenly, weak at the knees I sat down and imitating him, disrespectfully tipped the rest of my drink down my throat. - I *needed* it; I was in shock.

"Ah. Yes. The Guards and their X-ray machine," John Paul smirked. "You should have seen your face when you realised what was going to happen." The last came as a splutter as tears of laughter ran down his face. "Shock! Mon dieu. Complete and utter shock, that's what you showed." He paused to let his laughter subside before continuing. "But I must say, you recovered quickly and kept your cool." He dabbed away at the tears with his handkerchief. "That American, he really bugged you, didn't he?"....

"You were there. You saw it?" I exploded. "You knew what was going to happen all the time, didn't you?" My accusation hung in the air.

"Certainly," he replied, trying to suppress another belly laugh. "What else would you expect? I control the biggest movement of drugs and money in Europe, surely......"

The insistent ringing of his phone interrupted him. He grabbed it and moved away a few paces. I had great difficulty in taking my eyes off the money so didn't catch much of his rapid French, but I did hear my name being mentioned in the conversation.

"Finish your drink, Ben; we are going for a ride," John Paul instructed; his now cold sober tone breaking into my dreamlike trance. Taking a fat roll of French money from his pocket, he peeled off several large denomination notes and thrust them into my hand as he told me, "you have done well and I am pleased; this is your pay." He turned away to put his coat on. "Oh! by the way, the small packet you collected from the Doctor's is a present for you. Open it later," he added, tossing it to me and beckoning me to follow him out to his car.

Casually throwing the case containing the money in the back, John Paul climbed into the driver's seat and started the engine. Still trying to pocket the money - which I noticed was equivalent to about two thousand pounds - I tossed the packet into the back and got into the passenger side. Leaning across me, John Paul opened the glove pocket and indicated a small handgun that was there.

"Carry that," he instructed curtly. "You are now acting as the bodyguard." Then, in typical French fashion and without another word, he launched the car into the heavy traffic.

He drove us back to the embankment where we joined the one-way stream of traffic. Then, regardless of speed limits and other road users, we flashed along the Quai D'Orsay passing the Eiffel Tower on our left. Without giving warning or indicating his intention and with total disregard for others whether they were on foot or in a vehicle, John Paul suddenly threw the car across the traffic lanes and into a road that I just recognised as being the Boulevard De Grenell, one of the wide main arterial roads that cross Paris. At the speed we were travelling, coupled with the fact that I was attempting to keep my bearings, there was no time to fully appreciate the grand buildings, their fronts dappled in patches of sunlight that filtered through the many trees.

Again, without regard for the law or other people's lives, John Paul cut across the oncoming traffic. With tyres screaming and car horns blaring - other cars, not ours - he turned into the Rue Du Commerce then right again down a narrow one way street by the name of the Rue Tiphaine. Squealing tyres signalled our arrival to all and sundry as he pulled in abruptly on the right. He'd switched the engine off, grabbed the case and left the car before I could even get my feet out of my door. With me following at a trot close behind, we passed through the front door of a large commercial office block. I noticed the doorman picked up his phone and pressed a button as we swept by him without word or pause. Taking the lift - which was conveniently waiting with its door open - we arrived at the fourth floor.

"Wait there." John Paul instructed brusquely after we had walked a few yards along a passage. He disappeared through a door marked, 'Private, Senior Male Staff Toilet.' I started to settle myself outside the door, my hand on the gun hidden in my pocket. Hardly had the door shut, than it swung open again and he came out with the case still in his hand. Without a word, he grabbed my arm and steered me firmly back towards the lift that again curiously stood with its door open waiting.

"That was a quick visit to the gents," I managed to say as the doors opened on the ground floor; to which John Paul just smiled as he led the way back out to the car. The whole visit had taken less than five minutes. Tossing the keys across the pavement to me, he got in the passenger seat and waiting until I'd set the car moving, he turned to me with a self satisfied smile.

"There it is, my friend. You have just seen a delivery as well." With a flourish that would have made a magician proud, he opened the case to show that it was now completely empty.

"What? ... How? ... I don't believe it," I managed to say as I dodged a large lorry coming out of a side turning. The surprise in my voice was quite genuine. "How? You'd only been in there less than half a minute. ....What did you do, just tip the money in the waste bin?" My questions tailed off in utter amazement and the need to concentrate on my driving.

"Ah. My friend, we have a network of drops like that all over the city," he explained proudly. "You will go there again eventually and will do the same as I did. Enter the same Men's Room, put the case down beside an identical one and come out with the other one." He paused to indicate that I should turn up a side street. "Simple as that. Make a switch. You will not see who the contact is. He is already in a cubicle, the porter warned him of our arrival," he explained. "By now, the money is already on its way into our account via several other such commercial firms." With a deep satisfied chuckle, he lit a cigar as he settled down into his seat. All I could do was to admit that this guy certainly knew his stuff.

Later, as I was leaving the office at the end of the day, I suddenly remembered the packet I had collected from the medical centre and guarded so zealously still had to be opened. Going to the basement garage and reclaiming it from the back seat of John Paul's car, I settled into the vehicle that had been selected for my use and carefully tore the outer wrapping off.

"Tea Bags. Bloody tea bags." My exclamation echoed around the cavern like basement. "I nursed a box of bloody tea bags all the way across Paris." The anger welled up in me. I was about to go back upstairs and confront him when the funny side of it caught me. I had fallen victim to John Paul's sense of humour. The packet that could have contained drugs and which had caused me to sweat with fear for the first time in my life was a box of the best English tea bags.

I wonder if they can be contaminated by X-rays, my little voice asked, as I drove up the ramp to the exit. The Security Guard at the gate gave me a strange look as I again burst into loud peals of laughter, and the nervous tension from my experiences seemed to drain away.

A few days later, following the success of this first task, I was told that I would soon be accompanying Paulo for the next couple of months and this time we would be receiving deliveries from various places around Europe. Hearing this news, Paulo showed his colours and angered John Paul by saying he did not trust me and would not work with me. The normally calm and collected 'Boss' as he was referred to, practically blew his top and had almost dragged him into his office. The result of this 'behind closed doors' chat was that I was saddled with an even more sullen Paulo who showed his dislike for me at every opportunity. He did his job of guarding me as I delivered supplies of drugs to a variety of addresses in and around Paris. Then in the agreed way, it would be my turn to act as 'escort' to him as he collected the money. Though we were really supposed to work closely as a 'team,' it soon became obvious that I was not going to be consulted nor even advised as to what he was going to do next. We could be waiting for a train on the Metro and without warning, he would spin round and dash to get on board one behind us at another platform. Or, his favourite trick would be to attempt to separate me from him by side stepping in dense crowds.

Losing my temper with him would have been no good; neither would it serve either of us well if I actually lost him and then he subsequently 'lost' the money. Our necks would have been wrung like chickens without a doubt. After a few days, his predictability made things easier for me. He was of below average intelligence and therefore prone to signalling his moves by his body language. I soon learnt to counter any of his stupidity and he realised he was wasting his time. However, my ability to stick close to him regardless only served to intensify his hatred and determination. What worried me was the fact that he took such risks with huge sums of money that did not belong to us. Our joint responsibility was to deliver, then collect, and the 'take' was normally well up in six figure sums. Our 'cut' was decided by the amount of money we collected; some trips that only lasted a few hours could still be worth a thousand pounds to me.

The climax of my problems came sooner than I expected, when early one morning a week later, we left Paris bound for Rotterdam with Paulo at the wheel of one of the gang's nondescript vans. As with my last and unforgettable experience with such a vehicle, it was obvious that though the bodywork was rough, the engine was in excellent condition. Prior to our departure, Claudio, the diminutive Italian mechanic who maintained the vehicles with loving care, couldn't contain his pride while showing me how to operate a special switch that would short the plug leads in some way making what was a supercharged old banger sound just like a rough old banger. This was meant to put the police off the scent if there was a need.

To say that we travelled in silence was wrong. Well, Paulo was silent; he never uttered a word during the entire 447 kilometre run to our overnight stop. Instead, he smoked foul smelling cheroots and played trashy music on the radio all the way. I simply contented myself with dozing or watching the scenery slip by as we followed first the A1 and then the A14 across France and Belgium and into Holland, which I reflected, meant we were crossing the greatest battle ground the world has ever known.

No stop was made for food or comfort so our arrival near Rotterdam over five hours later came as a blessing as well as a surprise. Paulo drove us into a place by the name of Rhoon, and then turned in through the gates of a small, neatly kept house; it was obvious he'd been here before. Breaking his self-imposed silence at last, he simply snarled, "This is where I'm staying *Rosbif.* You find your own lodging." With that, he turned the engine off, climbed out of the van and marched into the arms of the young woman who had come to greet us. Slinging my coat over my shoulder, I went round to the driver's door and removed the keys which he'd forgotten to take with him.

"No way is that sullen bastard going to leave here without me." My muttered curse was lost in the roar of a low flying aircraft as it circled above.

Sitting for so long had affected my legs and thighs more than I thought, so walking stiffly at first, I wandered off in search of suitable accommodation for the night. Our strict instructions were to make contact the following morning with a Canadian sailor from one of the huge bulk carriers that would be moored somewhere in the vast expanse of the Europort which is strategically located at the tip of the Hook of Holland. The size of the place and the amount of shipping it dealt with meant that it had become the main port of entry for the majority of drugs into Europe. Even I knew that policing the largest port in the world would be nigh impossible. That meeting was on tomorrow's schedule so I could relax this evening.

To my surprise, the small conurbation of Rhoon boasted a reasonable selection of hotels. Booking into one, I had a late and much needed meal in the restaurant then had a bath and slept for a couple of hours. Awaking, I felt curious to see what Europort was like and knowing that the best way to get an impression of the size of a place was to see it lit up at night, I decided to have a look. That evening, I took a taxi the few kilometres to the settlement by the name of Oostvoorne, which directly overlooks the main part of Europort.

Ships of all sizes lay alongside, while stork like cranes dipped and swayed as they lifted cargo containers off their decks. On the dockside, several of those curious four legged mobile cranes that lift containers and scuttle off to some predetermined location moved around as if in a dance. Other ships were connected by various types of conveyors that could handle either liquid or solid matter while hundreds of minuscule workmen and crew moved about like ants. The whole place seethed with activity of all kinds. Finding a small restaurant that commanded a good view of the docks, I sat on the veranda drinking a cool beer and enjoyed a decent meal.

In good time the following morning, I climbed aboard the van and sat and waited for Paulo to come out. Half an hour went by with no sign of life from the house and I wondered if he'd gone off looking for me. Suddenly, the front door of the house burst open and I was treated to a spectacular display of feminine flesh as he said goodbye to the almost naked woman. His hands kept pulling her short nightdress up over her ample buttocks as he kissed her farewell.

When he saw me sitting there, he gave me a look designed to frighten me to death so it was obvious that he knew I'd taken the keys. Returning his stare, I held them up between finger and thumb as he climbed on board. He snatched them from me, fumbled to get them into the ignition switch then furiously gunning the engine he reversed out of the gate without looking to see if anything was coming. We shot off down the road like a rocket, narrowly missing a dog that came out to see what all the noise was. By the time we had regained the main road; he had calmed down a bit, but still maintained his surly silence. He reached for the radio and turned it on.

No sound came from it. I held up the fuse for him to see then with a flick of the wrist, threw it out of the window.

"You bastard Englishman," he yelled, pounding the steering wheel furiously with his fists. "I hate you, you bastard."

"Oh. I know that," I replied. "What is it you are scared of, Paulo? Are you scared I will take your place in the gang?"

"Ha," he spat. "I hate all English pigs. They let my father and his comrades die in the war by running out on them at Dunkirk. So I hate you ALL." This final frenzied tirade seemed to wear him out and he slumped over the wheel in dejected silence again.

So. That's what it's all about eh? Once again the English are blamed for the inadequacies of the French. I kept this thought to myself, there seemed to be nothing to gain by putting the record straight. Too late anyway, as in a cloud of dust stirred up by his furious braking, we arrived at our destination.

As the dust settled, I saw that as had been arranged with our contact, we were in the car park of a grubby little cafe cum petrol station not far from the gates of the port. Paulo refuelled and parked the van, then after ordering coffee, we seated ourselves in a corner of the dingy room. It wasn't long before we were joined by a man in the uniform of an engineering officer from one of the large Canadian bulk carriers that regularly plied the seas. Placing his coffee mug on the table, he sat opposite me. From Paulo's rough greeting, I took it he knew the guy and soon realized there was no love lost between them either.

Bit like us really, I mused.

"Got the goods?" Paulo grunted, not even attempting to introduce us.

"Sure. .... Have I ever let you down?" The man replied confidently.

"We can't hang around here all day, *Canuck*; where is it?" Paulo demanded.

"Outside in my car. Cut the crap, I'm having a coffee first, OK?" The Canadian wasn't going to be bullied, I thought. To show solidarity with him, I ordered another coffee and was pleased to see the increased look of annoyance on Paulo's face.

Chatting to the sailor while we drank, I learned that relying on his intimate knowledge of his vessel as an engineer, he had successfully hidden a 20 kilogram pack of cocaine from the Customs 'rummage crew' when they searched the ship.

"Twenty kilo," I gasped in honest amazement. "That's a hell of a package; how'd they miss it?"

"Ha. They always send old men to do a 'rummage' in our ships; they can hardly manage the companionways let alone the steep ladders to the girders holding the decks up," he crowed.

Quickly explaining that I was also a sailor, I asked how they'd missed a package that size just left on a girder. "Surely they would have seen it?"

"No chance," the Canadian boasted. "I welded a couple of plates on during a refit a few years ago, so it all fits snugly in a box."

"Questions," Paulo snapped at me, banging the table with his fist and almost spilling our coffee. "Always questions ... and you," he said turning to push his face close to the Canadian's, "you talk too much."

"Hey hang on. If I get back to sea, I may be able to use the same sort of trick," I cut in, but my excuse sounded a bit lame to me. It was the only way to take the heat out of Paulo's growing suspicion of me.

"I'm going to have to be careful of him," I thought. Right from the start, we'd merely co-operated with each other as the job required. I didn't like Paulo's sullen, bullying attitude and him? Well, he just didn't like me. Simple as that really. Besides, I knew he was reporting back on me to John Paul and as the 'new boy,' I was still under constant surveillance by other members of the gang no matter where I was.

"Right. Come on, let's get the goods and get on the road," Paulo said, pushing roughly past me as he walked to the door; he was obviously upset by my show of friendship to this man. The Canadian gave me a conspiratorial wink. I responded with a shrug of the shoulders as we finished our coffee and went outside. Taking our time, we walked about 100 metres down the road and joined Paulo beside a rusty, salt encrusted old car. Seeing my questioning look, the Canadian explained with a smile.

"Deck cargo. I like my own wheels with me."

Opening the door, which hadn't been locked, he indicated a large, well wrapped package resting on the back seat.

"You didn't drive out the gate with drugs sat on the seat did you?" I gasped, turning to the Canadian in astonishment.

"Sure, why not? If the police see a package there in the open, they assume it's a bundle of dirty washing or something. They only look for hidden things," he laughed.

I was still shaking my head in surprise a few minutes later as Paulo paid him his money. Eager to get on with his life, he gave a quick wave of his hand, jumped into his car and sped off towards Rotterdam and a good boozing session, no doubt.

I placed the package in our van and was about to open the driver's door when I felt a sickening blow to my kidney and my face was rammed against the side of the van. I felt myself collapsing as a wave of blackness interspersed with flashing lights swept over me. Subconscious instinct and training saved me as I struggled to protect my head by rolling partly under the van.

Vicious blows continued to rain down and I heard a rough, gasping French voice saying, "you English bastard." Another kick emphasised the words. "Don't *ever* make me look a fool again." More kicks landed in my thighs and back before I could wriggle away to safety.

The attack stopped as suddenly as it had started. Carefully - I didn't trust this mad bastard of a Frenchman not to undertake another cowardly attack without warning - I crawled slowly out. Looking around, I could see no one, not even Paulo. Where was he? Was he hidden 'round the corner of the van waiting his chance for another sneak attack? These questions were answered by the sound of the driver's door slamming shut and the engine starting up. Thinking I was going to be left there, I struggled - not without some considerable discomfort - to the passenger's door and dragged it open. Painfully, I climbed into the seat; the door swung closed behind me with the momentum as Paulo let the clutch in and we roared off down the road.

Fighting the pain and trying to shake off the dizziness, I slumped into the corner of the seat. Sometime later as the pain dulled slightly, I reflected that this, my first trip to Europort had certainly opened my eyes and though I was keen to learn as much about the import/export methods as possible, I had to be very wary of Paulo. No more open questions, they alerted him too much. From now on I'd have to be content with just making mental notes of names and addresses etc. in case my room was searched. I had already learnt quite a lot by keeping my eyes and ears open, more especially in the vicinity of the senior and trusted gang members. I'd soon found that this would be the quickest way to learn about the operations they ran because when everything was going well, they celebrated by getting drunk. The drink loosened their tongues and it was then that they would openly boast about the amount of packages they had sent via such and such a port, how much money they had earned on such and such a deal.

As we drove on our return trip, my mind wandered over the amount of success I had already achieved in the information gathering department. Some time ago, by listening to this idle chatter - while pretending not to understand the mixture of languages - I'd first heard the name of the man in overall charge,

John Paul's Boss. He, it seemed, was a man whose very name was said in a reverent voice, always with a hint of fear. The name, José, spoken almost in a whisper, would cause the speaker to look over his shoulder in fear of being overheard. This was what I had been waiting to hear. Was this the Latino man in the barn all those months ago? I wondered. Was he in overall charge? Was he ultimately responsible for sending drugs to England and, by implication, responsible for the death of Sophie? All these questions crowded my brain. My excitement mounted as I realised that at long last I was getting somewhere.

Though the man José was rarely seen by the ordinary members of the gang, it became clear after a few days, that he was in fact the main point of contact between John Paul and the actual source of the cocaine and other drugs. By listening to their idle chatter over the next few weeks and by asking the odd question, I'd learnt that he was in fact the 30 year old son of a Colombian drug Baron. Originating from near Bogotá in central Colombia, he was the head of the European wide distribution network of the business and was reputed to be utterly ruthless.

On his frequent visits to Paris, José ran his organization from a large luxurious apartment overlooking the River Seine which, rumour had it, was 'staffed' by beautiful French and Oriental girls none of whom were over 20 years of age. Here, living like a King, he held 'Court' with great panache and is known to have several high ranking foreign ministers, diplomats and members of the legal profession among his regular house guests.

The mechanic, Claudio, had been very informative. Because of his love of all things to do with cars, he had been keen to tell me that Jose's car was driven by a highly skilled, professional driver and was fitted with everything you could wish for, from TV to cocktail cabinet and food cooler for the canapés he loved to indulge in. It was also very well protected with discreet, full body armour and bullet proof glass both of which could withstand machine gun fire. This was required because in the course of establishing his business on the continent, he had undoubtedly upset several other gang leaders. He had already survived a couple of 'reprisal' attacks, making the taking of such elaborate security precautions necessary. Such vital information went into my memory bank for future reference. José it seemed was also never without two permanently heavily armed bodyguards who took turn and turn about within a team of eight, thus ensuring two fresh and alert members on duty at all times. They even sat outside his bedroom all night. Not surprisingly, it appeared that the senior of the bodyguards was the giant I had seen in the barn during my 'interrogation.'

These then, would be the people that I was going to have to eliminate, but they could wait a while. In order to avoid alerting the cartel leaders that something was going on, I had decided to learn as much as I could about the operation at this end first. Then, start my campaign of revenge at the source where hopefully, when the news got through, it would make the others like José, nervous and angry. Quite simply in my experience, the angrier an opponent becomes, the more likely he is to make mistakes. So, for the time being, I would continue learning all I could at the same time as earning huge sums of money all of which were being paid into a secret account in another name and would eventually be used against the cartel and its minions when the time was right.

🕊 **Code Name SNOWBIRD** 🕊

Chapter 6
Time to move on?

During the following long months, as a warm autumn turned into a bitter cold winter, I continued my duties accompanied by the sullen Paulo. There were several occasions on which his temper flared into frenzied attacks on me. What sparked him off was always based on jealousy and the more we associated the worse he became

We were by now, kept busy delivering large quantities of drugs to various buyers in numerous locations all over northern Europe and into Scandinavia. It amazed me how simple it was. Border Posts were largely nonexistent, Police and Customs Officers were tied down by the high volume of commercial lorries so had little time or inclination to worry about private cars as they were no longer required to stop. At times, when on some of the minor roads we were even unaware that we had crossed into another country because of the driving rain or snow. Winter Paradise came to have a new and more sinister meaning for me.

The following spring saw us travelling across a Europe that was wide open to anyone and everyone. Though it became apparent that there were 'bent' officials even in the UK, our membership of the European Union actually acted in the favour of drug runners or smugglers. In a misguided attempt to save money, the Government had reduced levels of staffing at the Customs Check Points at sea and airports like Dover and Heathrow to a minimum. By timing things nicely, we simply drove through with large supplies of drugs.

I was only to well aware that by doing this work, I was aiding the people I had sworn to destroy, that would be no defence should anything go wrong. At the same time, my conscience was salved by the knowledge that I was also creating a long list of those corrupt officials who, in return for large sums of money, made sure we were not hindered in our trips across borders.

On one trip, I even eyeballed a two-man team of well-known terrorists driving off a ferry into the busy Port of Keil. They had crossed via Scandinavia and were possibly on the way to do a job. Needless to say, I anonymously passed this information on to the German Authorities and felt a great satisfaction when watching TV in my hotel room and the late evening News Channel gave details of a shoot-out between the GSD 9 - the German Anti Terrorist Unit - and two known terrorists, both of whom died.

It was during this period that feelings between Paulo and I finally hit rock bottom. Even John Paul had barely been tolerating him for some time now, and was showing an increasing inclination to avoid speaking to him. Paulo, of course, saw this as another reason for jealousy and now openly begrudged my increasing status within the gang, so one night under the influence of drink, he declared his intention to get rid of me. For my part I tried to avoid complicating things by annoying him.

The crunch came when we had returned to Paris from the job in Denmark and went for the inevitable drink. Over the next hour or two, Paulo - who had by then been mixing his drinks far too much - had become increasingly belligerent toward me. His resentment and open jealousy became too much for him when one of the girls whose job was to hang around any unattached male, made a play for me against his wishes. Stumbling drunkenly across the room he promptly started mouthing off at her, roughly grabbing her by the hair and slapping her viciously across the face.

"OK, there's no need for that," I said, stepping between them and firmly holding the now very tipsy Paulo back with ease - having only sipped my drink I was confident in my ability to handle him. Without warning, the situation suddenly changed. I could not mistake the flash of a knife that appeared as if by magic in his hand.

We were all caught by surprise at the speed with which he pushed the girl aside and turned toward me; the evil sneer on his face showing he meant business. Tossing the knife from hand to hand, he feinted a couple of times as he approached me.

"Fancy her do you?" he snarled, then with a totally unexpected and supple move he lunged toward the girl catching her off her guard, he slashed her across the cheek, opening it to the bone and causing blood to fly all over the place.

"Fancy her now do you, English Pig!" he sneered and spinning on one foot as lithe as a cat, he deftly lunged at me. By instinct I reacted in the way I had been trained. Taking a quick step back and slightly sideways, I caused Paulo to over reach himself. Caught off balance and unable to slow his forward motion, he stumbled forward and I simply delivered a hard chop across the back of his neck, at the same time as bringing my right knee hard up into his chest. The air exploded from Paulo's lungs with a rush.

"Sorry about that Old Man!" I uttered through clenched teeth, "but you really are a nasty piece of work."

He crashed down face first in a heap on the floor and stayed still. Blood was pouring down the hysterically sobbing girl's face, as she was ushered away without ceremony by the Landlord - who obviously didn't want the Police involved. Disgustedly throwing a few notes on the bar to pay for my drinks, I walked out the door leaving the unconscious Paulo for them to see to. The discordant donkey bray of a Police siren already sounded in the distance as I made my way back to my hotel.

The following day I reported to John Paul as usual. Though it was obvious he would have already been thoroughly briefed on the happenings of last night, I was not prepared for and pleasantly surprised by, the amount of concern he showed for me.

"I hear you and Paulo have had a fight," he remarked with a laugh. "I am sure that he will not be very happy with you my friend!"

"Let me worry about that!" I replied. "He asked for it and I can take care of myself." While confident in my own abilities, I could not be too sure how Paulo would choose to act. He may choose another direct approach, or he could choose a knife or bullet in the back. John Paul confirmed my thoughts.

"But Mon Ami, he can be very dangerous to you I think. He will not play by any rules and has killed many times!" His voice had a genuine touch of concern. "You have proved to be reliable; I do not want to lose you, but him I can do without!" Pausing to light a cigar he studied me through the smoke. Then, as if making up his mind, he slid an envelope across his desk to me.

"This is for you, you've earned it." Knowing it would contain my share of the profits for the last few weeks, I nodded my thanks as I slipped it into my pocket. Rising, he went towards the door.

"Just be careful. He will act as he thinks fit in this case and I can have no control over him, as it's personal. Perhaps you should take a little holiday, eh?" He threw this question over his shoulder as he left the room.

Later, I called into a Bank - chosen at random - and paid the money John Paul had given me into my account. Handing over the equivalent of £75,000 I couldn't help thinking, there's the reason why so many people push drugs. Easy money!

Returning to the office and gathering the things I would need, I left to continue with my routine.

No one saw Paulo during the next week or so. It seemed he had gone to ground for a few days, and the story on the streets was that his nose had been broken when he hit the floor of the Bar. Without him, I was now the collector as well as courier, so this meant my cut was bigger. More than content with this arrangement, because there would be less hassle and the now substantial sum in my Bank would go towards paying for the action yet to come.

I continued keeping a secret mental record of who, where and when the drugs were delivered to while still conducting the gang's business. This information was then written down and secretly posted, addressed to myself at a Post Office Box number in England that I had used for some years. The contents would remain safe until my return.

It was my intention to use the information later, to track down and punish these buyers and officials and send the Police the other details. In the meantime, should anything happen to stop me doing so, my Solicitors had a letter of authority to be opened on my suspected death. They would be alerted by my Bank; who would advise them if more than one month went by without a deposit or withdrawal of funds being made.

This letter contained two others; one being a letter of authority for the Post Office, to give all the mail in my name to my Solicitors and the other contained instructions for them in turn, to send all the envelopes unopened to the Scotland Yard Anti Drug Squad who would in turn alert Interpol of any Continental connections.

Since my brush with Paulo had altered his standing within the gang, it was now clearly time for me to change my plans. He was more than likely to lay ambush for me in revenge and I could not allow that to happen as it would delay, or even stop me from achieving my main objective. In bed that night, I let my mind wander over the whole issue.

Perhaps John Paul's idea of a holiday isn't so bad after all, I have enough background information on the

European network now, I counselled myself. With about three quarters of a million pounds hidden in a Bank, including the original money from 'Rats,' I definitely have more than enough funds gathered together. I'm also now aware of the names of some of the Cartel people and places in South America.

"So! I think I am ready for the next stage! It's time for me to make contact with the 'Vets' (Veteran's) organisation and get onto the network," I told the darkened room as I drifted off to sleep.

Late the following evening, when my fellow gang members were celebrating another large haul being moved safely through Europort and were well on the way to being drunk, I seized my opportunity. Leaning across the drink puddled table, I caught John Paul's eye, beckoning him closer.

"John Paul, I've been with you for well over a year now and like you suggested, I think it's time to take a break for a few weeks." Pausing to take a mouthful of my drink while watching his reaction, I continued. "So, if you don't have any other plans for me tomorrow, I will disappear for a while." .....

"Of course Mon Ami!" John Paul said after some thought. "I am happy with that and you have been working hard so a break will do you good, take as long as you like it won't hurt us, but where will you go, eh?" Dangerous question, innocently asked!

"Don't worry about me," I said with a wink.

"I have someone waiting for me; she has a place we can go to in Germany." I lied. There was a sudden silence amongst the others, as they realised what I had said. At least, those whose brains were still functioning had stopped what ever they were doing to leer at me drunkenly.

"Hey! Ben has found a woman!" one character declared to the room at large.

"What's she like?" asked his partner.

"Where's she hiding? Is she French?" Another one chipped in.

"Does she"... The questions accompanied by increasingly lewd gestures, came tumbling out.

"All right! All right that's enough!" I said, banging the table in mock anger and standing up. "Yes, I have found a woman! What's so strange in that eh? Anyway, she's too much of a Lady, so I'm dammed if I'd let her meet the likes of you drunken slobs!" This last remark brought the expected howls and ribald comments such as 'English Toff', all of which were well meant as they respected me for dealing with Paulo. I nodded to John Paul as he stood to shake hands. Waving a two-fingered salute to the others, I went to the door.

"Are you coming back?" called someone to my retreating back.

"Oh yes, I'll be back my friends!" I replied from the doorway, then as I stepped outside I said to myself with an inward chuckle, "but NOT how you are expecting!"

Returning to my hotel, I packed my few possessions quickly and just before 1 am slipped out of the back door without checking out - the Bill was always paid by John Paul anyway. Careful not to be seen, I made my way to one of the secret underground storage areas the gang owned near the river. Using a key copied some time earlier, I entered the dungeon-like edifice. By the light of a powerful flashlight, I made straight for a top of the range BMW saloon that I had selected the previous day.

This car was one of the several high powered cars stolen by the gang for their own use. Complete with a new coat of gleaming black paint and reregistered under a new number, I knew it was safe to use. As part of my plan, I had a new set of number plates that I'd purchased some time earlier in a town well away from Paris. Securing the building behind me, I drove to a local Filling Station that was also part of John Paul's business and where all the gang's vehicles were fuelled on an account.

With the car's petrol tank filled and knowing full well that my moves were still being reported to John Paul, I bought a map that covered Belgium and Holland as well as one for Northern Germany. The Cashier, recognizing me gave me the docket to sign and seeing the area covered by the map asked where I was off to this time.

"I'm taking a few weeks off. I've got a hot woman waiting for me up the road and we're heading for Dortmund, but we'll be stopping at her place in Brussels first. Bye!" I replied, pretending to study the map as I left the Kiosk.

"Now tell your master <u>that</u>," I muttered. Using an old trick I pretended to wipe the already gleaming windows of the car, while watching the reflection of the attendant in the Kiosk. As expected, he was busy on the phone.

"So far, so good," I whispered. "that's set part of the false trail." I had just employed a trick of the trade we used to teach recruits. 'Let people know where you're going, then go somewhere different!'

Confident that my plan was working so far, I got in and started the car. The tyres screeched as I drove out across the sparse traffic into the fast lane and floored the throttle pedal. Easing off after a mile or so down the road - I didn't want the attention of the Police - I kept the car moving steadily and slipped out of Paris unobserved in the dark of night.

Using my now considerable knowledge of the region to get out onto the A4 main Auto Route heading east where a while later, I pulled into the parking area of a filling station cum Restaurant. Choosing a secluded corner hidden in the shadows behind some of the huge intercontinental lorries parked there; I changed the vehicle's number plates and threw the old ones in a handy rubbish skip.

Satisfied that all was well, I resumed my journey. Keeping my speed to around 100 kph I let the soft hum of the tyres soothe me so that I felt the tensions of the past few days ease off. Staying with this main intercontinental route for the next three hours or so I took the turning to join the A31 south towards Metz and Nancy. Knowing that the best place to hide a car is in a large car park, I drove through Nancy and made for the large, long stay car park of the Metz-Nancy Airport.

"Time for a bite to eat and freshen up," I told myself, as I turned the car into one of the bays in a block that contained mainly black cars of all descriptions even at this early hour. I removed all signs of my use and taking my one small case and hand luggage from the boot, I locked the vehicle.

"It'll take some time for that to be traced I've no doubt, now for an early breakfast!" I muttered, making my way into the main building to find the Restaurant. In the main hallway, a conveniently placed cleaner's trolley solved the problem of what to do with the car key and I deliberately dropped it into an almost full rubbish bin.

Feeling more comfortable and relaxed after my meal, I went to the Gents Washroom and freshened up, then used one of the toilet cubicles in which to change into a more business like set of clothes. Donning a pair of horn rimmed glasses, I moved into the concourse, made a quick phone call from a booth before mingling with the few passengers arriving on an early domestic flight and then sought out the Hertz Car Rental Office.

Using a false Passport, which named me as a member of the American Diplomatic Corps, I hired a Mercedes Saloon. Driving out of the car lot, I regained the Auto Route and headed south with the other patchy early morning traffic on the A31 before turning off at Exit 11 onto the N74 towards Colombey-les-Belles.

Now on familiar ground, but even with well over 400 k between me and Paris I kept my speed down while continually checking the rear view mirror for a telltale flash of sun on the windscreen of a car the driver of which was professional enough to 'lay back' a bit.

Considering myself on *'active service'* so to speak, I could not afford to take chances so was automatically employing training that had served me so well in the past. Choosing my spot very carefully, I reversed the car into a convenient farm track that twisted away from the main road. Stopping where the high hedgerow was filled with some overgrown nut bushes, through which I could see anything passing on the main road without being seen myself, I settled down to wait. An hour passed during which the only traffic was a milk tanker and a bus. The turning I had deliberately taken was situated in a dip at the start of a long unbroken stretch of dual carriage way that could not be crossed, so, any 'tail' I may have missed, would have to travel well over 15 kilometres down the road before they realized their mistake and could turn around and come back.

Reasonably sure I was on my own but making no bones about it; the group of people I was cheating, while not trained professionals; were certainly clever enough not to be underestimated. Ample time had passed, so I moved back out onto the road and resumed my interrupted journey. Bypassing the larger town of Neufchâteau, I took a turning to the small market town of Liffol-le-Grand and my pre-planned destination.

An hour later, I drove straight through the market place where some stalls were already busy. Taking a little side turning that was squashed between a Cafe and a Boulangerie, I followed the road up a short hill at the top of which, I turned into a farmyard overlooking a valley of the river Meuse.

Getting out of the car and stretching to ease my cramped muscles, I heard the sound of running feet, a barking dog and a young female voice calling my name. Around the corner of the garden wall, a large, boisterous and fluffy Old English Sheep Dog came charging, closely followed by a very excited young lady of about sixteen years of age.

"Uncle Ben! Uncle Ben! It's so good to see you, I've been awake all night waiting for you to arrive and I am <u>not</u> going to go to school today!" She said in slightly accented English as she threw herself into my arms. Barely pausing for breath, she hugged me and planted a big wet kiss directly on my lips.

Placing her on the ground and holding her at arms length, I saw a very pretty girl with long blond hair and green sparkling eyes. The top of her head almost reached my shoulder; her figure was that of a young mature woman. I was amazed at the close likeness to Sophie - I shouldn't have been; this was her younger cousin and life long close friend Judith, whose father and mother had moved to this farm some ten years ago.

This young lady and Sophie had been brought up together and I was pleased to say, they had both shared a fondness for their 'Uncle' Ben. Excitedly taking me by the hand, she dragged me into the farmhouse, where it was obvious that my earlier phone call had been well received. There waiting for a chance to greet me, were David and Sheilagh Courtney; David being Mal's older brother. Their greetings were almost as enthusiastic as their daughter's who perched herself firmly on my lap as soon as I sat down.

"Mal has told us about what you are doing and we only wish we could help in some way," David said, as he handed me a mug of steaming coffee. Embarrassed, he paused to run his fingers through his thinning hair and then nervously continued. "I. ... I'm afraid Ben, that I know nothing of the world you move in, but if there is <u>anything</u>."...... I held my hand up to stop him.

"No problem David, don't let it worry you, your letting me stay here for a day or two is help enough! In fact I am in your debt entirely."

"Come on, you must be tired after your journey, let's get your luggage and I'll show you your room," Sheilagh said, taking my hand firmly in hers. With Judith hanging on my other arm, we moved out to the car. An idea flashed across my mind as I was taking my case out of the boot.

"David, there <u>is</u> one thing you could do for me and that is to take this car to a Hertz Agency some distance away and return it in the name shown on the documents. Then if you don't mind, perhaps you could pick up another car, from another Agency, in another name that I will give you".......

"I can help if you like Ben," interrupted Sheilagh and stepping quickly forward, she grabbed my arm. "I mean, if David takes this car back for you, perhaps it would be best if I rented another car in <u>my</u> name for you to use. That way, no one would dream it was you using the car, then they could not follow you could they!" she exclaimed with pride.

"That's a brilliant idea Sheilagh, I'm impressed, lets talk it over later eh!" I managed to say, as I felt a lump in my throat at this show of concern.

Grabbing my hand luggage, I slammed the boot of the car shut. We all trooped back to the house accompanied by the dog, which had caught the new sense of excitement in the air and continued to prance around barking like a mad thing.

Later, when I had rested, we sat on the patio overlooking the surrounding countryside, enjoying a light lunch and a bottle of excellent local wine and earnestly discussed the problems I would face.

Judith, sitting close to me and hanging on my every word suddenly said, "I want to do something also, I know I can't drive, but there *must* be something I can help with."

Hearing the despair in her voice and thinking quickly, I placed an arm around her shoulder saying, "there is something you can do and that is to help me find out if I have grown a 'tail.'"

"Do you mean, see if any drug smugglers or hired assassins are following you?" she said in a mock whisper.

Seeing her excited look, I continued,"If we go into the town separately, I will do a bit of shopping, while you," I said to Judith, "can watch my back to see if anyone is taking unusual interest in me!"

I had barely finished, when she shot out of her chair and ran into the house. Minutes later, to the amusement of her audience she reappeared wearing a long dark Mackintosh and Trilby type hat - belonging to her father - a wig and false beard, all of which only served to set the dog off into another paroxysm of barking.

"The wig and beard are part of a costume I'm making for a school play and I thought that it was a good joke," she said seeing our amazed looks. This drew a round of polite applause. Satisfied she had done something to cheer us, she removed the disguise and reclaimed her perch on my lap saying in a serious voice, "Uncle Ben, you know how close Sophie and I were, I will do anything I can to help you catch these awful drug dealers. So *please* tell me what I have to do."

Later that afternoon, when I had given Judith simple instructions on how to act, we all climbed into David's car and made the short journey into town.

"Stop here," I instructed David as we approached the end of the high street. Sheilagh, Judith and I got out and David drove off. I was wearing sunglasses and a hat and coat of local origin as I walked slowly arm in arm with Sheilagh along the street. Judith, hanging well back, watched as we, like any couple in town for the day, paused outside several shops and went inside some others.

Using the shop windows as mirrors in my usual fashion, I could see Judith doing the same thing further up on the other side of the street. Eventually, when we had purchased a few items that Sheilagh swore she was in need of and there were no more shops to look at, we entered an unpretentious Cafe near the end of the road. This was, as Judith had quite correctly explained, situated on a slight bend in the road as it entered the small town. Its large windows commanded a view of the street and more importantly, all who passed along it whether they were on foot or in a vehicle. We found David already seated at a table facing the window as planned, he gave an almost imperceptible shake of his head as Sheilagh and I entered thus indicating that he had seen nothing to alarm him as he watched our approach.

We sat at a separate table, ordering croissants and tea. I faced the window, so that I could watch the road as we talked in hushed voices. After a while David got up, paid his Bill and left without acknowledging us.

A few minutes later, he re entered the Cafe using the door to the Car Park at the rear and went unseen by the staff into the Gents Toilet, where I joined him a few moments later. I gave him my hat and coat - they were his anyway - I took his car keys and the hat he was wearing, placed it on my head and went out the back door. Walking with head bent slightly as if looking at my keys, I opened the car door and got in. As I started the car, a movement in the rear made me catch my breath, a hand gripped my shoulder and Judith said in an Inspector Clueso type voice, "nuzzing to report Mon Capitain!"

Laughing both with relief and at her mock French accent, I entered into the spirit of the game by replying in an upper crust, Jolly Hockey Sticks voice.

"Oh! Jolly Well Done Old Thing!" At this, Judith curled up in gales of laughter and she was still laughing when I pulled up in a back road to pick up her mother and father. It was some minutes later, that she had recovered enough to explain the joke to them. We all had a good chuckle, which eased the obvious tension that had built up in them over the past two hours or so.

My stay with the Courtneys lasted for a few more days, during which time Judith and I spent a lot of time on horseback, riding the various trails through the wooded countryside. I was feeling much more relaxed now, after having let her conduct another check in the small town - this time on her own - to see if there were any suspicious strangers staying in the small Hotel. I was reasonably content that if the alarm had been raised in Paris, interest had not been shown in this rural area.

On the fourth day, I took them all in my hire car over to visit the larger town of Epinal, some distance away. Over lunch, it was agreed that David would return the car to the local Agency in my assumed name. Meanwhile, using her own French Drivers License, Sheilagh would go to another Car Hire firm on the other side of town and hire a suitable car on a long-term basis.

Giving them both sufficient cash to settle the Bill for David and to act as advance rental for Sheilagh, we parted company. Judith and I made our way into the main shopping centre, where I took her to a Fashion Store.

"Choose any outfit you like," I told her, to her delight. A couple of hours and several fittings later, we left the store under the not too approving glare of an elderly lady. Armed with her parcels of underwear and dresses, Judith hung on my arm as we walked towards the main Bus Depot where we had agreed to meet her parents.

"She thinks we are lovers," she said, indicating the old lady who was behind us and still watching us disapprovingly. Acting the part, Judith put her arm round my neck and gave me a long lingering and I must say, very experienced kiss.

"There! What *will* she make of that," she giggled.

Later, sitting in a Cafe waiting for her parents and watching the world go by, she spoke just loud enough for me to hear. "I suppose you will leave us now, don't forget to come back will you." She sniffed and suddenly pushing her chair back she rushed off to the Ladies Room. I felt very guilty when I saw the tears in her eyes. We were all in a sombre mood during the short journey home in the car that Sheilagh had hired for me.

Code Name SNOWBIRD

Chapter 7

<u>The Route South.</u>

The following day, after a rather late breakfast at which conversation was noticeably subdued, I collected my bags and loaded them into the newly hired Estate car.

"This isn't going to be easy," I thought, as the family approached down the garden path. It was one of those occasions when everyone tries to hide their own embarrassment by self-consciously avoiding direct eye contact. For my part, I fixed my gaze on a small basket that Sheilagh was carrying and which she offered me with a tearful, tremulous smile.

"I made you some pasties and a few cakes for your journey Ben," she mumbled. Then with a sudden rush, she threw her arms around my neck, kissed me quickly on the cheek and with a final, "take care of yourself," she rushed back to the house.

David stepped forward and grasping my hand, shook it so firmly that I could feel the calluses on his hand rubbing my skin.

"Take this," he said thrusting a bulging brown envelope at me. "It may help you in this awful task." He was gone before I could react, so I stuffed it into my coat pocket and placed the coat onto the passenger seat of the car.

Knowing the hardest part was to come; I slowly straightened my back and turned to face Judith who was waiting behind me with her head hung low. I knew that words would be of no use here, so I just held out my arms to her. With a sob she rushed forward, throwing her arms around me.

"Uncle Ben," she sobbed. "Please be careful, I couldn't stand it if I lost my other best friend to those awful people." With unashamed tears running down her pretty face, she tried to smile as she put a small wallet into my top pocket. "That's for you to remember us by." With a quick hug and a kiss, she too turned and ran back to the house.

Not to be outdone, the normally boisterous dog - which had obviously sensed the occasion and remained silent for a change - slunk over to me. With a long low whimper, it sat and raised its paw for me to hold. Then with a quick lick of my hand it too, turned and silently padded back to the house, its head hanging low to the ground.

"God, how I hate this sort of good-bye," I muttered, dabbing at my own eyes as I slumped behind the wheel. "I must be going soft."

At just before midday, I turned the car towards the gate and taking a quick glance back at the house, drove out. They were all there, standing in a tight huddle by the front door. David with a protective arm around the shoulders of his wife and daughter and the dog sat in front of them. With a last quick wave, I bid good-bye to those wonderful people, wondering if we would ever meet again.

Driving down through the town, I made my way out onto the main road to Neufchâteau then picked up the D74 which took me south through some of the most beautiful countryside before rejoining the A31 Toll Road

- or Route to the Sun to give it its tourist name. It was a warm day and I had all the windows down while maintaining a respectable speed. Enjoying the fresh air laden with the sweet scent of wild flowers, I stopped once for a coffee and a snack as I drove down through Burgundy, passing Dijon and heading for the ancient city of Lyon which stands at the 'gateway' to that famous region of France called Provence.

    Some four hours later, I was enjoying the bright, clean sunshine as I approached Lyon and could see why it was listed as the third largest city in France. Situated where the peaceful River Saône joined the fast flowing and larger River Rhône, it spreads out across both sides of the valley with the buildings of the new city, seemingly marching up the hillside and off into the east. From past experience, I knew that this city boasted more Restaurants and Hotels than any other. Being a lover of good food and having had a romantic interlude here some years ago, I decided that it would be here that I would stay overnight. Heading for the Place des Terreaux, I drove around the central ornate monumental fountain and pulled up outside that grand edifice called the Hotel de Ville. This Hotel, like many others, commands an outstanding view of both rivers as it is perched on the long finger of land between the two. Registering under an assumed name, I was shown to a spacious room with a view across the River Rhone.

    Tipping the Porter generously, I asked, "Where would you advise the best place to eat, other than in the Hotel?"

Seeing the size of his tip, this man, eager to please replied, "ah, M'siuer. I would recommend that you go to *La Grille*, which stands on the Rue Sébastien-Gryphe. It is but a short taxi ride away," then as if in afterthought, he added, "but it may be best to make a reservation M'siuer. If you wish, I could do that for you?"

Did I detect a cunning look in his eyes, linked to perhaps another sizable tip? - Ah well. In for a penny, in for a Franc as they say.

"Yes, yes you make a reservation for me for 7.30 pm," I confirmed, handing him some more bank notes which, in the manner of all porters and waiters everywhere, were slipped out of sight without him seeming to move. When I had finished my unpacking, I remembered the packet that David had given me. Recovering it from my coat pocket, I opened it and was astounded to see that it contained a bundle of French bank notes that I quickly counted.

"That's over ten thousand quid," I gasped. "It must be all of his savings." A feeling of guilt swept over me when realization dawned that I had not found time to explain to David that there was no shortage of money for the campaign. I should have told him that my peculiar sense of poetic justice meant that the action was indeed self-financing. In other words, the drug trade was paying for its own demise.

"I will send it back to him in the morning. In the meantime that can go into the hotel safe for the night" I declared, tucking the money back into the envelope and making my way down to reception.

"Oh yes. What did Judith put in my pocket?" I muttered, on returning to my room. Grabbing my jacket, I was all fingers and thumbs as I drew the wallet out. It was a small pocket size photo album, inside of which there was a photo of Sophie and Judith as young kids, then a later one of the three of us at the seaside. Laying back on the bed I looked at them, my eyes blurred with tears not only from the memories they invoked, but the realization that Judith had secretly paid for copies to be made.

"I shall treasure that," I said, placing it open on the bedside table. My eyes were still fixed on it when I drifted off to sleep.

That evening, feeling refreshed and rested, I was determined to have a few hours of enjoyment to myself so took a taxi to the place called *La Grille*. As I entered this select establishment, my nose was assaulted by what can only be termed as a Gastronome's delight. The aroma of spicy meats mixed with the delicate smell of fresh baked rolls greeted me. Taking in a deep lung full of the air I thought, the smells that greet you are enough to dine off.

The Maître D,' at my request, seated me at a small table in a quiet corner from which I could see all of the room and anyone entering or leaving. This gave me the chance to eyeball the other patrons while I studied the menu at length. Seeing no one I recognized, nor anyone who caused any alarm bells to ring, I relaxed and gave the waiter my order for a dish of what I called 'dumplings with meat in,' which were in fact one of the local famous dishes called *Quenelles*. They were a favourite from my previous visit to the region. An excellent meal, accompanied by a fine local wine served to put me totally at my ease and encouraged me to be more adventurous.

"Now, let's find some of the famous night life that this city has to offer," I told myself as I was leaving the Restaurant. The haunting sound of saxophone music coming from an open window brought memories back to me. A week with a beautiful girl; during the evenings of which we used to sit and listen to our favourite music in a local Jazz Club. Hailing a taxi, I asked to be taken to the famous local Jazz Pub called *'The Albion'* that stands on the rue St-Catherine - *so* English a name it had come back to me with ease and it was but a short walk from my Hotel.

Officially named *'The Albion Public House,'* the place was no different than I remembered, well crowded with people of all ages, thick with cigarette smoke and most of all, noisy. The sound of people was at first overpowering, but I knew that would change. Music lovers all, they would immediately fall silent as the first note was heard.

Mingling with the crowd of drinkers, who made this their regular Saturday night venue; I was eventually able to order a drink at the Bar just as the first performance of the evening started. As there was no other space, I had to be content with propping myself up in a corner against the wall and simply let the excellent music wash over me.

Returning to my Hotel in the early hours I undressed and climbed naked into bed, soon to contentedly drift off to sleep. A few minutes later, or so it seemed, I was awakened by a polite but insistent knocking at the door. Hastily slipping a thin robe emblazoned with the Hotel monogram around me, I opened the door enough to look out and was amazed to see a beautiful young lady standing there with a trolley.

Here is your breakfast," she said giving me a long appraising look.

Realising how thin the robe was and that I had my back to the now sunlit window, I hastily stepped back allowing her to push the trolley into the room.

"Wow," I said to myself, "that was the quickest night's sleep I ever had." Picking up my watch, I saw that it was just past 7.30am and the night had indeed passed quickly.

Studying me all the time, the maid set out the table. A large silver cover was removed to reveal an equally large plate with a full English breakfast. A pot of tea, toast and marmalade stood to one side. Searching for my trousers, I grabbed a handful of loose change. Thrusting this in her hand I stepped aside and ushered her out of the door. My mistake. She deliberately brushed her hand across my crotch as she past me in the confined space. Delightful though it may have been, but not having time for such distractions, I shut the door firmly behind her and turned the key in the lock.

"Phew. What *is* it with these French women?" I asked the empty room. Getting no reply, I turned my attention to the table. Though I didn't *feel* hungry, to my surprise I cleaned the plate and most of the toast, enjoying a second cup of tea after washing. Having decided a few days ago that a beard would alter my appearance, I deliberately omitted to shave and now sported a rather piratical stubble. Breakfasted and packed I went down to the reception desk, settled my bill and reclaimed the sealed envelope containing David's money then checked out.

When I saw my car, I was surprised to see it had been washed and polished overnight, so another tip was due. Once again laying a false trail by using the old maxim of 'tell people where you're going, then go some place else,' I tipped the Carboy enough to make sure he remembered me and asked for directions east to Geneva. Once out of sight of the Hotel, I made my way into the town centre and located a Bank, where it took but a few minutes to deposit the money, in exchange for them sending a certified cheque to David. I would write him a letter of explanation later.

Leaving the city of Lyon behind me, I took the A7 South towards Marseilles. Two hours and some 200 km later, I pulled the car off the main road and took the turning for the medieval town of Orange. Driving in past the remains of the Roman Triumphal Arch and the Theatre - both built by Julius Caesar - I drove a short distance to the northwest and made straight for the municipal campsite. Pulling up outside the building with a sign saying Main Reception, I entered, quietly crept across the room and opened the door bearing a plaque with Alain Dupré, Proprietor written on it.

"Hello Alain," I said - pronouncing the name in the French way - to the man engrossed in working a computer. On hearing my voice he looked up with the surprise clear on his face.

"Mon Dieu. Am I seeing things, it cannot be you Ben," this man said, as he pushed his chair back and rushed toward me. Wrapping his long arms around me, he clasped me in a bear-like hug, kissing me on both cheeks in the French fashion.

"Come in. Come in. Marie will be as delighted to see you as I am my friend." Excitedly waving his arms around, he barely stopped to open the door at the back of the office

"Marie. Marie. Look who's here," he called, as he dragged me by the arm into a back room where a petite blonde lady in her mid forties was also busy at a computer. Seeing who her husband had brought in, she let out a delighted yelp, sending her chair flying and nearly knocking the computer on the floor she leapt up to do the same as he had done, but kissing me several times squarely on the lips rather than the cheeks. Such were the feelings between these old friends of mine.

"Where did you come from? Where are you going? How long are you here for?" All these questions and more poured from my two friends' lips in their excitement. Freeing myself very reluctantly from Marie's clinging embrace, I looked at them, noting yet again the vast physical differences in them. Though of similar age, she was small in build with a well-kept, full body and thick curly blond hair. He was tall and swarthy with a shiny, bald head and whose rather plain face was split by a massive black moustache and an equally wide grin. Yet I knew they were completely devoted to each other.

Alain gripped my hands again and Marie clung on tighter.

Struggling to retain my balance under the eager onslaught, I explained, "I am in need of a little help from you Alain," I said. Reluctantly releasing myself, I took the chair that Marie pushed my way and sat down.

"I will explain in simple terms, you can say yes, or no,"......

"Say no? To you who saved my life? Never!" Alain interrupted indignantly in a loud voice. "If it is in my power, you shall have it, no matter what you ask, you *know* that." Marie offered us each a cup of coffee into which she also poured a stiff measure of brandy.

"Celebration for old time's sake," she said, wrinkling her nose in a way that I loved. Once again, I found myself telling the tale of the death of Sophie and the results of my mission so far, while my friends listened in respectful silence.

"Oh MY. What can *this* poor soul do to help you in such a task?" Alain said when I had finished. Marie was busy dabbing at her eyes with a lace handkerchief. The two telephones in the next office were ringing insistently, but remained ignored.

"Well, first of all I need a safe place for about three days and a place to hide my hire car. Then about two weeks after I have left someone who can return it to a local Agency," I explained.

"Is that all!" exclaimed Alain indignantly. "It's not much is it, I can arrange for you to stay in one of our caravans here, as long as you wish. Marie can ask her brother who owns a Garage, to sort the car out for you".....

"Wait," I interrupted his rush of words, "that's not *quite* all. Are you still in touch with your old 'friends' in the shipping world? I need you to see if there is a ship leaving Marseilles for North America."

"But of course my friend, nothing would be simpler. I will make inquiries about a berth for you; in the meantime we will have a meal, yes?" Alain said as he picked up the phone and in a business like manner set about making the enquiries.

Shortly after the meal, their private phone started ringing as the answers came back and the appropriate decisions were promptly made. Alain's own huge touring type caravan that stood close behind their house was prepared for my use.

"You will of course take all meals with us," stated Marie as she explained the use of the cooker and an air conditioning unit control panel straight out of Star Trek.

Later that evening, her brother called and collected the car that he assured me would be put in the back of his Garage cum workshop. He would return it to the Agency himself, two weeks after I left. I gave him enough money to cover the cost and some for his trouble. Just then Alain was once again called to the phone, where he spent several minutes pouring out voluble French, most of which was in a local dialect that I could not grasp.

"That was my friend in Marseilles," he said with a satisfied grin on his face, as he rejoined us on the veranda. "He has promised that a Second Mates Ticket would be supplied for you, forged of course," he joked, "and a berth is arranged on a ship leaving for Boston in the USA in about four days time." He paused as he poured two glasses of Cognac, the bouquet of which drifted temptingly toward me.

Handing one glass to me he continued. "The Captain, who is also the owner, will ask no questions as he does a bit of gun running and smuggling for other 'friends' of ours," Alain said with a wink. "The Mates Ticket would be in an assumed name and you will sail on the ship departing from Marseilles, more details will be sent later." Raising his glass, he said, "here's to the success of your mission my friend and confusion to your enemies."

Asking no questions - for I would get no answers - I could do no more than enjoy the company of Alain and Marie over the next couple of days. Spending some time acting the tourist in the town, a place I had always liked, I selected and posted some presents to Judith and her Mum. After their day's work was over, Alain and I spent some pleasurable time walking his two dogs in the nearby woods. The evenings were spent in warm companionship sitting on the veranda and watching Marie swimming in their large private pool as we talked of our times together in different wars around the globe. Alain had been a Senior NCO in the French Foreign Legion, whose specialty was survival training. Over a beer or three, we reminisced how we had met.

"Mon Dieu. I can still feel that swamp sucking at me now," Alain sighed, as he recalled sinking up to his neck in a deep jungle swamp in Malaya; his companions having been wounded in a fire fight with the Communist insurgents could not help him.

"Yes!" I exclaimed, "and I can still remember the awful *smell* of it." The memories came flooding back. I was then a Sergeant in the British Army and my patrol had found them and with great difficulty had pulled him out. We then took them all out by 'chopper.' Since that day, he and I had been firm friends and had met up more often after I had passed selection for the SAS.

Once again, after a delightful few days with old friends and seeing no unusual interest being paid in me, I found myself saying good-bye. Lacking transport now, Alain insisted that he drive me to the city. We left early enough for him to make the one hour drive to Marseilles and drop me off near the docks in the Port Moderne where, armed with an address in the Rue de Forbin I would collect my Mates Ticket.

I felt more certain at that moment that the mission would all fall into place, especially as I could call on others like Alain, whose contacts could be counted on to 'grease the wheels'.

"Bon Chance my friend," Alain said as we shook hands for the last time. With a final, "take care," he drove off as I stood and watched until he faded into the distance. Wonder what the world has in store for me now, I thought, hoisting my bags and walking towards the harbour.

The road he had dropped me off on was on the northern side of the harbour, in the arrondissement - or administrative area - known as *Quartier du Panier*. The pervasive smell of seaweed and fuel oil was enough to tell it was a busy working port.

"Nothing will alter my opinion that this second most populated of French cities is nothing but a seedy, sprawling place, full of violence, corruption, and racism and is mostly lawless," I mumbled to myself while crossing the road. Marseilles, situated as it is on the beautiful Mediterranean coast, was of course an interesting place to visit.

"Most certainly not one I would choose to live in though," I said with finality. According to Alain, its only claim to fame was the fact that the French National Anthem took its name from a marching hymn, which had been sung by the Marsellaise revolutionaries in 1792 when they marched on Paris.

Following Alain's careful instructions, I soon found the office of the shipping line I was looking for. As I entered the dingy building a tatty, heavily over-painted lady who looked as if she had long seen better years told me curtly to fill in a form. Taking my completed registration from me, she looked at it and called a man in from the back room.

Seeing my name on the form - the one I had been given by Alain's friends - this equally rumpled character signed to me to enter his office. He shut the door and looked furtively out the window, then in true 'Allo, Allo' fashion and speaking just above a whisper, said, "I 'ave been careful not to let 'er out there know about this," he indicated the outer room, "she talks too much when she is drunk. She cannot be relied on, so please be careful"......

"Surely you can tell her to mind her own business, or you will sack her," I cut in.

Wringing his hands together, this pitiful man replied, "you do not understand, I cannot sack 'er, let alone tell 'er to mind 'er own business. She is my wife." He wailed.

Signing another form with a flourish, he took my Registration papers and stamped it with a large rubber stamp that sprayed excess ink all over the place. Pushing these across the littered desk he held his hand out palm upwards, moving his fingers in a beckoning gesture.

"Oh yes, the money," I said, feigning that I had suddenly realised what he wanted.

"Shhhhh. Not so loud. *She* will 'ear you," he gasped. Handing over the equivalent to £1000 in French notes, I watched as it promptly disappeared into the pocket of his filthy trousers.

"Be outside the ticket office for the Chateau d'If tourist boat at 2 o'clock, it is on the Quai des Belges," he instructed, as he pushed me unceremoniously towards the door. I was still shuffling awkwardly backwards as we entered the outer office and he knocked some papers off the desk as we went by. Theatrically prodding me in the chest, the man pushed me out of the open door as he declared in loud authoritative tones, "don't come back 'ere with your stories again." With that bit of Pantomime he promptly slammed the door shut in my face.

The crafty old sod, I thought. She won't know he's now richer by his share of my £1000. Probably going to escape from her, when he has enough money saved.

With a laugh, I made my way around the harbour to a stall that was selling seafood and drinks. Buying some crab meat with pomme frits and a plastic cup of tea, I sat on a bollard and watched the numerous small boats moving about in the harbour. Out to sea, the glint of sunshine reflected off the windows of a distant passenger ferry approaching the off shore island called *Le Chateau d' If.*

I could remember taking a speed boat out there many years ago and could still recall the feeling of pity I had for the numerous prisoners who had died in that grim forbidding fortress of a place. I also remembered being at a cinema some years later, watching the film the Count of Monte Cristo and how shocked I had been when I recognised the Count's castle as being that evil fortress off Marseilles.

Throwing most of my now cold food into the oily water, I stood and watched the ever present and voracious seagulls fight over the scraps. Tossing the cartons onto an already overflowing rubbish bin, I made my way along the road towards a Ships Chandlers and purchased a small, but powerful pair of German Ziess binoculars and a hand held compass in a leather case, that could be fixed to a belt or worn around the neck. Next I entered a second hand clothing shop where I purchased enough suitable clothing for the time I would be at sea.

"Better get along to the meeting place," I said to myself as I saw the time was approaching 2 o'clock.

I quickened my pace and made for the Ticket Office on the Quai des Belges as instructed. No sooner had I stopped at the small queue by the office door, than I heard a quiet voice behind me say in English, "are you looking for me Mister?"

Turning round quickly I saw a small, but smartly dressed man wearing the uniform cap and jacket of a Ship's Captain.

"I presume so Captain," I replied respectfully. Shaking my hand and introducing himself as John Smith, the Captain took my elbow and guided me away from the growing queue.

"That really is my name just in case you don't believe me," he said with a wink. "Now my friend, what is it I can do for you?" This was said in a kindly voice, which made me think I would like the man.

"Well, Captain, I'm in need of a discreet passage to North America and I believe from my information, you are going to Boston, yes?"

Captain Smith nodded and then looking me straight in the eye, he said, "I am willing to take you, but as you have paid for your passage, you will not be required to work except for appearance sake when we depart, or arrive in port. This is purely for the benefit of any watchers my friend," he touched the side of his nose in a conspiratorial way.

With that, he led the way towards a ship's launch that lay alongside the harbour wall, its engine quietly turning over; the exhaust making a contented burbling sound at the stern. Captain Smith and I both sat in the stern sheets, as the Cox'n let go the bow line and expertly steered the boat out into the fairway.

About fifteen minutes later, after dodging Water Buses and Lighters, we were moored up to the side of an ocean going cargo vessel, on the stern of which was painted the name *'Grey Gull,'* above the port of registration of Liverpool. I noted that as per tradition, she was flying the British Flag, as well as the French courtesy Flag. It was also obvious that this was a 'tight' ship, as she was well maintained and freshly painted. Smartly turned out like her skipper, I thought.

Seeing my appraising glances, Captain Smith said as he followed me up the ladder, "she is 15 years old and as I am part owner, I like to make sure she is looked after. Now let me show you around."

I was impressed with everything I saw, the smartness was all embracing, every piece of equipment was well maintained and the crew were well turned out and obviously happy. Over a cup of coffee in his Cabin, Captain Smith suddenly threw a question at me.

"Are you outside the law Ben?"

"No. No, I'm not." I replied without hesitation.

Seeming content with the emphasis in my prompt but negative reply, he showed me to an adjoining cabin and invited me to get myself settled in. About an hour later, just as I finished changing into 'working' clothes, a knock on my cabin door heralded the arrival of a young deck hand.

"Sorry to disturb you," he said apologetically. "We are about to cast off, and the Captain has instructed me to show you to the Bow station."

Donning my Mates Cap and wearing the seaman's jersey and trousers I had purchased, I followed this young man to the Bows, where I was amused to be advised in a conspiratorial whisper, that I should make it look as if I was giving orders and supervising the removal of the huge rope that moored the boat to the dockside.

As there was nobody else about in the bow area, I thought I'd find out how much this chap knew.

"What has the Captain told you about me?" I asked.

"Eh? Oh. I see what you mean," he said, taken aback. "Nothing really, but I suppose you'd best know, my name's Jack." He stuck his hand out, "Jack Smith, I'm the Captain's son and believe it or not, the <u>other</u> part owner of this vessel." Noting my surprise, he laughed as we shook hands.

Well, I thought, that really is handy; I've been passed to a very competent pair.

Over the next fifteen minutes I was kept busy helping Jack with the various chores involved in controlling the machinery used to wind in the huge rope and then tidying up the area ready for sea. His quiet ability was very impressive.

A sudden ear piercing noise made me duck, as the *'Grey Gull'* hooted farewell to the attendant tugs, which had pulled and pushed her out of the harbour area, then fussed over her as she was turned to face the Buoyed channel. I felt the deck heaving gently as she stood out to sea.

Leaving the foredeck I followed Jack up the ladders to the Bridge, where we joined Captain Smith and a man he introduced as the duty Quartermaster.

Stepping out on to the Bridge wing, I looked back at the splendid view of Marseilles that appeared to be constantly changing as we slid across the azure waters. The angle of our direction of travel caused the sunlight and shadows on the buildings to move, thus making it seem as if they were growing or shrinking. It struck me again that you could but admire the situation of this city, spreading up the slopes of the bare limestone hills from the coast. The panorama was dominated by the semi-Byzantine church of Notre-Dame-de-la-Garde, standing in all its glory on the highest point

"A cup of coffee suit you, Ben?" I was dragged from my daydream by the voice of Captain Smith.

"Sorry, yes, coffee would be fine." I followed him back into the enclosed area of the Bridge. Aware of faint vibrations from the engines through the deck plates, I was struck by the lack of noise. Other than the radio messages from Port Control and soft orders to the Quartermaster, there was none of the expected sounds.

"Something wrong Ben?" the Captain queried.

"No, not really, this is my first time on the Bridge of a big ship; I was expecting a lot more noise than this."

"Ah. I see. But you must understand that the engines are not at full power yet," Captain Smith said, indicating a large dial marked Engine Room Repeater. He explained that this showed the engines were at one-third power. With obvious pride he gave me a quick rundown on the intricacies of the controls, answering my questions as if I had every right to know.

I watched with interest and admiration as he calmly took this big ship out through the narrow channel, at all times aware of the myriad of small craft - mainly pleasure cruisers and private speed boats - that seemed to disappear out of sight under the massive bow. On several occasions, as one disappeared out of sight under the high flared Bow, I found myself waiting for the crunch and the call of Man Over Board, but in reality I knew that they rode the bow wave away to the side.

"Half Ahead Together." The quiet instruction sounded across the Bridge, to be repeated by the Quartermaster and speedily followed by the ringing of the engine room telegraph. I stepped out onto the Starboard Bridge Wing and felt the extra power being pushed out as we hit the first swell of the open blue waters of the Mediterranean Sea. The clean salt air was a treat to smell after being cramped up in the fume congested confines of Paris and the like.

"I'm going to enjoy this trip," I told myself.

"Well Ben, Boston next stop, eh?" The Captain's voice once again brought me back to reality. "You're leaving Europe on some sort of adventure in North America and I'll not ask where or why, but I wish you all the best," he said, raising his cup in salute.

Yes, I thought, but my final destination will be Colombia, South America. Quite when or how I was going to get there, I could not say.

Code Name SNOWBIRD

Chapter 8

Boston, USA. & The journey South

We were due to dock in the North African Port of Oran to offload and on load cargo en route, which according to Captain Smith, would mean we would be at sea for about three weeks. Being in no set hurry, I felt the time could be well spent building up a tan and generally relaxing. Mother Nature intended otherwise. The 1500k Mediterranean crossing was beautiful, but as we cleared the Straits of Gibraltar and broached the Atlantic swell, I knew something was different. The Captain advised me that we were on the edge of one of those unpredictable Atlantic Storm Systems; it could leave us alone or suddenly veer round and literally attack us. The sea built up into 20 foot swells as we cleared land, then for the next two days they got steeper.

During the third night, I was unceremoniously tossed from my bunk when the ship lurched as a terrific wave hit her on the Bow Port Quarter. *'Grey Gull'* staggered under a wall of water before righting herself and plunging down into the next trough. I struggled into my outer clothing and was tipped on my ass as she fought to climb the next steep wave. Vibrating madly as the screws came clear of the water, she dropped her bow and seemed to race down the other side, crashing into the trough and throwing me hard against the cabin wall.

Even my limited sailing experience told me the engines were struggling to keep her moving, so it was no surprise when we started corkscrewing as the helm was put over to turn us to run before the savage seas.

Finally managing to button up my clothes, I made my way to the Bridge where I was greeted by chaos. Anything loose was rolling around on the deck, charts and other items had shot out of their storage spaces and the Quartermaster and the Captain were grimly hanging on to the wheel.

The view screens (those rotating discs on the Bridge windows which were supposed to maintain clear vision) were totally overwhelmed by the torrents of water that were hitting us. I couldn't tell if it was rain, spray or wave. Whatever, it was threatening to break the armoured glass and flood the Bridge. It would be suicide to attempt to go out on the deck, so I started securing the loose items on the Bridge decking.

"Hold on tight Ben, we are about to broach," Captain Smith yelled.

No argument, I clung to a roof stanchion as if it were the last thing I would do. It probably would be, for broaching means we are turning across the wave system and we would be in a most perilous position. If the next wave was big enough it would squash us down into the sea with little effort. Deep down below us, the engines struggled to maintain sufficient power. As we came broadside on, we began a rock and roll motion that had my insides churning. One minute I was looking down at the Port Wing door, the next I was looking UP at it. It got so bad I wondered if I could hold on any longer; my grip was gradually loosing its strength.

The tender care and good maintenance she had received paid off as *'Grey Gull'* gallantly struggled round and slowly changed her motion to one of up and down; Bow to Stern; which indicated to my great relief, that she had won her latest battle for survival.

Trembling from the effort of holding the stanchion, I helped the Captain release the straps that he and the QM had tied themselves to the wheel with. Engaging the Auto Steering System they both collapsed into the Watch Chairs, which I noticed were firmly bolted to the deck.

The motion of the ship eased as we ran before the storm, but still maintaining a high engine speed to avoid that other danger of the sea crashing down on the stern and sinking us anyway. We ran for two hours before Captain Smith considered it safe enough to reduce revolutions and ease the strain off the ship. The Steward made several cans of hot sweet coffee, which I, along with the others gulped down gratefully.

As daylight broke, I could see the storm raging way behind us. The Captain decided to continue on our present course to the south for at least another two hours.

"That storm has pushed us about 150k south of our intended course and we will have to run west for several hundred kilometres to get round behind it. Then, if we are lucky and it doesn't reverse its path, we will turn north to regain our course towards Boston," he said and I was surprised he even had the energy to smile while he did so.

"You'd best turn in Ben," he added, "you look rather ill."

It was only then that I became aware of how ill I did feel and just managed a grunt in acknowledgement of his statement before I dashed out onto the Bridge Wing and said goodbye to all that coffee and life itself; or so it felt.

I went to Hell and back almost continuously during the following two weeks, in which we seemed to be storm tossed most of the time. We'd been forced to run before more storms; although not as fierce as the first, they did nothing to improve my condition.

Fresh air was my only friend as staying below made me feel worse. So it was that I was on deck 'duty' as the *'Grey Gull'* slipped without fuss into Boston Inner Harbour on a cold wet evening and I was able to watch as the bright lights of the Logan International Airport slide by on our right. On our left, as we drew closer to the shore, I could see the more traditional buildings dwarfed by the many Skyscrapers fronting the Atlantic Avenue. According to the Guidebook the Skipper had loaned me, this was the heart of Boston that stretched from the North End District right down to the Financial District of central Boston.

I was really looking forward to being on 'dry' land again and after the vast, grey emptiness of the open sea, the colourful reflection of the millions of lights from advertising neon's and windows dancing on the wave tops were like a welcome to me.

Through the growing darkness, I could make out the lights of hundreds of cars, each one followed by its own plume of spray as they swept along the Expressway. This multi lane highway follows the line of the bay and is interrupted by several huge junctions, each of which I thought would make the Birmingham Spaghetti Junction look small.

Being listed as a 'Passage Only' crewman, I signed 'off' when the ship was docked and all my 'duties' were finished. I then sought out the Captain and his son, both of whom had shown me very considerable compassion during the numerous times I had 'died' while suffering the terrible storm that had torn at us all across the Atlantic.

"I've no doubt you'll be remembering this trip for a very long time my friend," Captain Smith said as we shook hands. "While I wish you well in what you do, I also offer you the chance of a homeward bound trip should you ever need it." Patting me on the shoulder, he moved off to greet the Customs Officers who had appeared on the Bridge.

"Well Jack," I said turning to his son, "I can't say it was a pleasure in all the true sense of the word, the trip I mean, but I am pleased to have met both you and your father."

"It was good to have you around Ben," Jack replied, as he helped carry my kit to the dockside. He firmly gripped my hand as he added, "what Dad said is true, we would be pleased to help you get home if in need." With a wave he left me. That last remark of Jack's made me wonder if they knew what I had planned.

"I wish the bloody road would stay still," I cursed, while attempting to walk along the dockside; my legs were still telling me we were at sea. It was only then that

I realised how the continual seasickness had weakened me.

"Oh well. Got to get on with it," I voiced aloud as I made my way out through the Customs and Immigration checkpoint.

"I'll be 'laying over' for a couple of weeks, before finding another berth," I replied to the Immigration Officers questions, then armed with an Entry Stamp in my Passport I made my way out into the Boston night. Ominous noises started to come from my stomach and a dull ache became noticeable.

Food, I thought. Can I really be interested? Then I recalled young Jack Smith's earlier advice. 'Get some food inside you, Ben, otherwise your stomach will cramp up.'

"He should know I suppose," I told myself. "So I'd better get some." Following the simple directions Jack had given me, finding the Seaman's Mission was easy. Rather than stay there, I asked for a copy of a Bed and Breakfast list they held and armed with this information, I moved off into the darkness. It wasn't long before an old awareness alerted me; my instincts were giving me a feeling of being watched. Using some well practiced, but not obvious ploys to check behind me, I could see there was no one there. Nevertheless, the feeling would not leave me and only a fool would ignore such warnings as this.

"My old sixth sense has never played tricks on me before," I muttered, using the darkened window of a shop as a mirror. "So let's make sure."

I walked for a further five hundred metres, then rounding a slight bend dodged silently across the road and into an alley where I melted into the darker shadows and waited. Nobody came past or into the alley. I'd have been in a fix if they had, for as luck would have it, it was a dead end anyway.

"You have all the time in the world, so wait a bit longer," I told myself. "A follower can't afford to wait too long in case his quarry gives him the slip." On that premise I let a quarter of an hour pass, but still nobody came near me.

"Must be getting jittery," I chided myself, then altering my appearance a bit by donning a donkey jacket and seaman's cap, I dumped my kit bag - from which I had removed all traces of ownership - in a trash bin and retraced my steps. Walking more briskly as a proper sense of balance returned, I made my tortuous way into the centre of the city while still keeping a wary eye on the few people who were about.

"Really getting hungry now," I said, as I felt the obvious pangs in my stomach. "My bloody feet are tired too."

An impulse made me visit an all night Burger Bar where I enjoyed the rest, if not the Burger. Tearing a map of the district out of a phone book that hung in a passageway at the rear of the Bar, I was able to plan my next move and decided to pass the night in an anonymous Church Hostel, a couple of blocks away.

For the grand sum of 1 Dollar 50 cents I enjoyed the bowl of thick vegetable soup and bread they offered.

"Take this up to Room 20 on the top floor," the tired looking, careworn night Manager sullenly instructed, as he took two dollars for a couple of blankets and a stained thin mattress on which to sleep. It was obvious that with my well-worn clothing and full, untrimmed beard, he had accepted me as another vagrant in need. Feeling better for the meal and now in need of rest on a bed that didn't keep trying to tip me out, I made my way to the large room that served as a dormitory, chose a bunk, but stayed fully dressed - you'd 'lose' any clothing you took off - and was soon asleep.

Rising early the following morning, I soon realised that Jack's words of wisdom had been correct. My stomach had settled during the night, so I joined the queue for breakfast. Later, but apparently long before the majority of the other 'residents' of the Hostel, I left. Keeping a wary eye open for any possible tail - couldn't shake the habit - I walked a few hundred yards from the Hostel before hailing a lone Taxi.

"Can you tell me where to get some sensible working clothes, friend?" I asked the cabby.

"Work clothes? Casual clothes? You'll get the best choice at the big CEA store in the centre," advised this friendly fellow.

"OK. That's where you can drop me then and thanks for the advice."

I paid the man a two dollar tip on arrival outside the largest store I'd seen for years. The doors had not been open for very long when I entered, so without the usual crowds I had a quiet look around, taking my time selecting and trying my choices. They had started to get busy as I was leaving the store an hour or more later.

Now fully kitted with a bundle containing a decent change of clothes that were suitable for the local climate, I chose to take the underground railway - the 'T' as it is referred to by Bostonians - to the district known as South End, where I had selected a B&B for myself. Buying an 85 cent token at the Station Kiosk, I went down into the brightly lit and well maintained subway. Despite the thousands of people who use it every day, the 'T' is fast, clean and efficient to use and within minutes I was at my destination station.

On regaining the surface, those old habits took over and I jumped on a bus that was just pulling away. Looking back at the Subway entrance where there was a small crowd, I failed to identify anyone as being interested in me.

Still edgy aren't we, my little voice murmured. If there was someone on your tail, they would have to be clairvoyant to know where you were and where you were going.

Realizing that I was being asked for my fare, I handed over a dollar bill and said I would get off at the next stop. Pocketing my change, while standing on the platform waiting for the bus to pull in, I caught sight of myself in the large Conductor's Mirror and realised how unkempt I was.

My God. I can't go looking like a tramp any longer, I thought.

Leaving the bus, I found a small Barbers shop and had my hair washed and beard tidied up. Feeling a lot better for that, I crossed the road to read an almost overgrown street name sign in a flower border. According to this, I was on Shawmut Avenue, which showed on the map I had taken from the Burger Bar phone book, as not being far from the Rutland St. address of the B&B. Getting my bearings at the next junction I started off in the right direction, seemingly passing back into time as the buildings changed from modern blocks of flats, to the 'old Boston' style for which the place is renowned.

  The address I had chosen turned out to be in a row of charming bow fronted houses, with neat balustrades and colourful window boxes, all of which were complimented by highly decorative wrought iron fences. Just as I climbed the six steps up to the front door, it was opened by an attractive, middle aged woman with a basket in her hand.

  "Oh," she said, with a slight gasp as if she had not expected to see me there. "You startled me, can I help you?"

  "Do forgive me," I said, putting on my best English accent. "I'm looking for temporary accommodation and was about to ring your bell." Hurriedly fumbling in my pocket for the list of addresses, I offered it to her as proof of my intentions. "I found your details in a list the Seaman's Mission gave me, here it is."

  "Well, if *they* sent you, I suppose it is all right," she said, trying to regain her composure. "You see, we normally only take in Students from the University Medical Centre over the way, but they're on holiday at the moment." She waved her hand in a vague indication of that establishment's location. "Dear me, now I'm forgetting my manners," she said in a flustered voice. "Please come in, I have a single room free at the moment, how long will you be staying?" She stood back for me to pass through the open door.

"I would like to book for one week, but it may be longer and I can pay in advance." Though I didn't have any set plan worked out as yet, I had to play it safe. Satisfied by this, she introduced herself.

"My name is Wardell, Mrs Miriam Wardell," she said holding out her hand. "You are?"

"Um. Yes, sorry, I'm Ben Lihou," I lied, still concerned about covering my tracks. "I'm a sailor from the island of Guernsey," I added shaking her hand.

"Oh yes, I've heard of Guernsey, I've never been there though," Mrs Wardell said handing me a visitor's book to sign. "I've never been abroad," she added almost wistfully, as she took the money I offered as a week in advance. With all other formalities dealt with, she showed me upstairs into a very comfortably furnished second floor room overlooking the front of the building.

"I was on my way out to the shops, but I will put a pot of tea on if you wish."

"Thank you that would be wonderful," I confirmed.

A decent cup of tea would be great, I thought. "I'll just unpack my things."

"Good. That's settled, it will be ready in the Lounge in about five minutes and I'll ring a bell," she said, as she left the room.

I thought I'd detected a note of relief in her voice, when handing the money to her - though I couldn't be sure. The moment she closed the door, I moved quickly to the window. Staying perfectly still and not disturbing the net curtains, I watched both of the approaches to the front of the house that I could see. As the house stood in a tree-lined boulevard, I could not see the entire street. Satisfied there were no obvious watchers I started to unpack.

"Stop being overcautious you fool," I muttered to myself, "there is no need for it." Against my instincts, I decided that perhaps I was being a bit paranoid. I can't afford to take chances, these are dangerous people I'm dealing with, so ....

The sound of a bell interrupted my thoughts, so I went down for tea. My unpacking could be finished later.

"Ah, that was good timing," Mrs. Wardell said, as she carried a laden tray into the lounge. "Now please help yourself, and I shall join you if I may."

While we enjoyed our tea we chatted about Boston, with me asking questions that any first time visitor would ask. Having lived there all her life, she proved to be a fund of information giving me several pieces that I logged in my memory for later reference.

"Perhaps this would be of use to you," she said, sliding a good quality street plan over to me. "You may borrow it if you wish."

I was pleased with her generosity, because the map showed me other things I wanted to know. Things which she would perhaps have been curious about, had I asked.

"Now, I really must get to the shops," she said, rising. "If you wish, as I am not too busy at this moment, I could get your evening meals for you."

"That would be absolutely splendid," I replied enthusiastically, putting on my English accent which made her twitter. "Just tell me how much money you will need as I can let you have that in advance also, if it will help." I added, thinking, what a Godsend this woman is. I won't need to go outside too much.

"Well that would be acceptable and I thank you for your thoughtfulness," she said, with a small sigh of relief. Yes, there was definitely a note of relief in her voice when she knew the money was up front. Taking out my wallet, I handed her two hundred dollars which she accepted willingly. "Now I really must fly," she gasped, and went out with the tray.

Over the next couple of days, I stayed in my room during the daytime, making good use of the comfortable bed; resting as much as I could and studying maps of the USA and South America as I slowly unwound and planned a couple of routes. At night I enjoyed the truly excellent meals supplied by Mrs. Wardell and went on some of the walks she recommended, seeing both old and new Boston lit up and watching the aircraft coming and going at the airport across the bay.

On the third day, leaving my 'digs' and taking my usual precautions - I would not drop the habit of checking for watchers - I collected some extra funds from the Automatic Teller Machine at one of the Banks - or Hole in the Wall as I call them. Then using the Gents Washroom facility of a nearby Subway Station, I changed my clothes and donned a hat and heavy rimmed glasses. Making my way on the 'T' to the South Station, where the Amtrak lines between Boston, New York, Philadelphia and Washington as well as other major cities terminated, I studied the timetables.

During the next few days, I spent some time making arrangements and preparing for the next move. Then, late one evening after Mrs. Wardell had gone to bed. I left my temporary 'digs' dressed in typical Canadian style clothing - lumber jacket and jeans, with typical warm hat.

Thinking how lucky I'd been in my choice of B and B, as my Landlady was a pleasant, hardworking woman, who it turned out was a widow struggling to support an ailing father. Content that I paid my rent in advance and did not come in drunk every night, she welcomed the extra bit of cash I paid for meals, but most of all she was not prone to asking questions.

To assuage my feeling of guilt in not giving notice and saying goodbye properly, I had left an envelope containing a few extra week's rent and a note telling her not to hold the room, as I had gone back to England.

With a positive need to 'lose' myself and all clues to my whereabouts, I deliberately kept to the busy main streets, which were crowded with people leaving Theatres, Restaurants or Clubs. Choosing a twisting route across the central part of the city I moved quickly into a Subway Station and regardless of its destination caught the next train in. After a short journey and acting on impulse, I got out at the next stop, ran across the platform and to the amazement of the people already on board, leaped through the doors of a train on the other side, just as they were closing. I continued on this train until it was pulling into a very busy platform, the crowd being thick enough for me to disappear into. Rather extreme precautions, but I was dealing with extremely dangerous people whose power reached across the globe. So precautions were the order of the day if I had any chance of succeeding with my mission.

After two more changes I eventually found my way to the Left Luggage office at the South Station where I had deposited some items purchased on earlier visits.

"I'd like these bags please," I said, handing my ticket to the attendant.

"That'll be five dollars Sir," the man said, pushing the bags across the counter and paying me no further attention. Making my way to a Gents Toilets, I changed my outer clothes for a more respectable 'office' style suit and overcoat. Then once again manufactured my 'disappearance' by unexpectedly - and I hoped unobserved - throwing my bags onto a train that was just pulling out and jumping on after them.

"Nearly missed it; didn't have time to get a ticket," I said to the pleasant mannered Ticket Inspector when he came to see who was invading his train.

"Lots of people do that, where you travelling to, Sir?" he asked.

"Montreal please."

"Mmmm .... Montreal, eh? We're not going to Montreal Sir; I think you chased the wrong train," he said, trying to hide his amusement. "We will be stopping in about two hours though; I suggest you sit tight 'till then."

"Well in that case, I had better get off at the next stop," I declared. I was going to anyway as I'd simply used that train to make my getaway on. As for having to wait for two hours, well that didn't matter either. My final destination in this great land was still over 1500 miles away and Montreal was in the wrong direction anyway.

I paid the Ticket Inspector for the journey west to a town called Springfield, which lay at the foot of the Appalachian Mountains. Just before we arrived there, I went through the now familiar routine of changing my clothes in the toilet. At the station, I also changed my direction by hitching a lift on a lumber lorry heading south to Newark.

There was now a need to set-up a few contacts in advance of my arrival, whenever that would be, so I stayed in Newark for the next couple of days, during which time I found a public phone and made one of my infrequent calls to Mal. This time I would be asking for his help.

"Mal? How are you Bro'?" I asked when I heard the welcome sound of his voice. "I'm sorry I've not been in touch, but the project is keeping me very busy. Can you call me back in about an hour on this number?" I asked, giving him the number of the phone in the room at my digs.

"Ben? Hi. How are things with you? Yes of course I'll call back. By the way, I called and spoke to David the other day, he said you had dropped in and to say thank you for the cheque. We understand you are making good progress with lots of 'sales' old buddy."

"Yeah. I am very happy with things so far, but there are some things you can do for me." The frantic beeping signal for more coins interrupted me, so saying our goodbyes we both hung up

I knew from past experience that without question, he would go out of the house and call me from a phone on 'neutral' ground to avoid any possible eavesdroppers.

On my way back to my 'digs' I had stopped off for a Chinese Take-Away and had just put the cartons in my waste bin and was wiping my fingers when the phone rang.

"C & C's World Tours, Reservations can I help you?" I announced, referring to our surnames Courtney & Carson, which we had jokingly nicknamed ourselves when we were sent off round the world at Her Majesty's expense. Tucking the handset to my ear I settled down on the bed.

"Jeeze mate. It's a long time since I heard those words," Mal said, his laugh echoing across the world. "Tell me, is everything going OK? Without asking him where he was phoning from - there was no need, we trusted each other - I gave him a complete rundown on the action so far. He waited until I had finished without interruption, before he started throwing questions at me.

"What is it you want me to do? D'you need any money or other help? ....."

"Hey hang on mate," I cut in. "To answer your questions yes, I do need some help, but I don't need any money, the 'trade' is financing itself at this time and we are showing good returns." I knew he would understand even when phrased so cryptically.

"I thought you would enjoy your 'holiday'," Mal said. "I only regret not being able to be there with you." I heard the sadness creep into his voice when he said that.

"Right, let's get down to the nitty gritty then," I declared rather sharply, in an attempt to stop him getting morose. "Can you give me any contact in Miami?"

"Indeed I can, hang on I've got his number here." I heard the rustle of paper as he searched his ever-present diary. "Here we are, his name is Brewster and he's a good man, Ex Delta Force. Write down this number, but I can't promise he'll be available as he's still an active Merc," Mal said, indicating that this man belonged to the American equivalent to our Special Forces and was now a Mercenary. I noted the details anyway.

"Got that," I confirmed. "Now I am in need of the usual supplies - shooters etc. - can you help there?"

"Well, if Brewster is at home I'm sure he can, but there is bound to be someone from the 'clan' in that city," Mal said, alluding to the world wide family of the Special Forces.

"OK. That's fine; give my love to Julie and you keep smiling my friend. I am enjoying myself and have decided to spread my wings further south, where I am told, I will find lots to interest me. I'll be in touch."

"We were only saying the other day, that we thought you may go further south, that's Bandit territory down there, so be careful." On hearing the chuckle at the other end as we said our farewells, I felt a bit better about Mal.

The following morning I checked out of my 'digs,' hoisted my bags and set off toward the station. It was my intention that from now on, I'd stay away from main tourist type routes and go over land.

From Newark, I once again headed south by doing my 'Hobo' impression by riding a combination of freight trains and hitching lifts on trucks. I made sure of keeping well away from the Eastern Seaboard ports also.

It had taken me six hard days to find my way down country on various modes of transport via Baltimore, into Virginia. Then it seemed that my luck had run out as I'd sat on the side of Highway 81 for almost two hours, watching the trucks go by without any offer of a lift. In the end, getting hungrier by the minute, I walked across the dry countryside to a small township where I booked into a Motel.

Feeling better after a good night's sleep and some good home cooking, I tried again. The local Sheriff, who was on the way to the bigger town of Roanoke, offered to drop me on the 81 near a Diner, which he said would be full of truckers. Good as his word, no sooner had he set me down than the driver of a huge refrigerated Road Train offered to take me with him.

Still unable to shake the warnings my sixth sense was giving me, I always omitted to reveal my ultimate destination to these drivers. What they didn't know, they couldn't tell. I'd told them all, including the Sheriff, that I was bumming around with no real destination in mind. Now, seven days after leaving Boston, here I was watching the endless mass of the Appalachian Mountains slip by on my right, while on the left; the famous Blue Ridge Mountains of Virginia came ever closer as I imagined the lovely Doris Day singing her well known song.

As we approached Knoxville Tennessee, my driver said he was taking the turn off onto Highway 75 towards Atlanta, Georgia and as this was on my route I agreed to stay with him. He also advised me that he would be stopping overnight and pushing on to the southern city of Orlando in Florida.

"Great!" I exclaimed; my excitement at this news was hard to suppress. "It seems I'm going to be chauffeured nearly all the way." Our stopover in Atlanta was just long enough for him to have some goods off loaded, then we went to a Motel where I insisted on paying his bill and giving him a dinner. He in turn, insisted on refilling my glass. The following morning, I was feeling very much worse for wear when my newfound friend loaded my bags and then me, into the cab. Within minutes of setting off, I was asleep. Some time later, I heard a voice calling me.

"Hey Ben. Wake up goddamit." A hand shook my shoulder; another slapped my face.

"Here we are pal. This is Orlando and I have to turn off here," the voice said.

"Uh. Wha....samatter?" I mumbled incoherently. Another shaking; this time with an added dig in the ribs.

"Ben, you've got to get out here, it's the end of the line pal."

I woke slowly, my head thumping like a big base drum. My mouth tasted like the bottom of a bird cage. Suddenly, the door against which I was slumped was dragged open. I nearly fell out into the driver's arms and he had to support me until my legs found out if they were still attached. Leaning me against a nearby fence, he returned to the truck for my bags.

"Here y'are Ben. Sorry about the head and all, but that Snake Eye is mighty powerful stuff y'know." He sounded sympathetic, but he had too wide a grin for any sincerity.

"Now you tell me," I managed to get out; my tongue was still glued up. "Hey, many thanks for the lift. Sorry I wasn't much company for the last couple of hours," I said as I struggled to get my bags together. "There's a bottle of best Bourbon in the rack for you."

"Well, that's mighty kind of you," the trucker said with a wave. "It's nice to have company sometimes. You take care d'you hear." With that, he climbed into the cab, shoved the engine into gear and drove off leaving me in a dust cloud.

"Well here I am, Orlando, Florida," I said, reading the large sign that declared the name of the huge jumble of buildings I could see a short distance away. "Now lets get some clothes more appropriate to the temperatures down here and some decent 'digs' for the night," I mumbled as I trudged into the city limits.

After a short walk, I found myself a comfortable night's lodging with a family by the name of Nbigo, whose ancestors came from Africa. This was the first time I'd had any close dealings with any Negroes and I found them to be totally different to what I'd been expecting. There was a happy go lucky atmosphere in the whole house. While not rich by any means, they lived a contented life which I'm sure was due to the good wholesome food that was placed before us. Accepting me without question, their whole attitude to life was simplistic; they were grateful for every day that dawned and I had never been made so welcome in my life.

The eldest of the six children was a boy called Matthew, who volunteered to take me to the local stores the next day so that I could buy my change of clothing.

Forty-eight hours later, feeling decidedly overfed but happy, I took my leave of these lovely people and hitched a lift for Miami.

Chapter 9

<u>Miami Florida.</u>

This time, Lady Luck really deserted me as I squatted beside my bags at the edge of Route 4 out of Orlando. Cars just sped by as if I didn't exist while trucks already seemed to have extra passengers in their cabs.

Some time later, as I was dozing in the mind sapping heat, a furious honking of a horn and the frantic bellowing of cattle brought me back to life as a gruff voice demanded, "d'you want a ride or not fella?"

"Oh, Christ almighty, can't I do better than that?" I gasped, as I opened my eyes with difficulty. After having travelled for almost 1600 miles in reasonable comfort, it seems that the last sixty would be in the cramped cab of a dirty, smelly old cattle truck. Oh I know cattle are dirty things, but the driver of this heap had not hosed his wagon down for years. The acrid smell of dung and urine was made worse by the swarms of buzzing, biting flies it attracted in the oven like heat.

Beggars can't be choosers, a glib voice chided in my ear. I felt like strangling it and with my stomach threatening me, I climbed on board and slumped down on the well worn seat, only to immediately jump up again as a broken spring clamped itself firmly onto my left buttock.

"Ha. That ol' spring catches everyone." The unsympathetic driver chortled heartily. "Must have had a piece of at least fifty asses in the last year."

Extricating myself from the jaws of the spring, I massaged my rump, then spread my topcoat over the seat and surveyed my surroundings. The wagon turned out to be a real old bone-shaker; choking exhaust fumes crept up through the floor boards and steam emitted from the bonnet. I couldn't suffer this for too long and was relieved when after about twenty miles had passed, I saw that we were coming to the faster main Route 27 that runs down the centre of this part of Florida. I told the old man to stop.

"Hey, what's the problem buddy? I was just getting to know you," he asked, as he brought the vehicle to a grinding halt. Wordlessly I opened the door, dropped my bags out and climbed down. I saw the man's mouth working as he drove away, but the noise of the engine and the calling of the cattle drowned him out.

The cattle were probably pleading for you to take them with you, that little voice whispered gleefully. " Oh, shut up," I yelled in frustration.

Hardly had I got myself sorted out, than I managed to flag down a heavy truck which stopped in a cloud of dust with its exhaust crackling to proudly announce its supercharged status. Chewing on the dust, I clambered up into the cab to be greeted by a large, jolly character straight out of 'Smoky and The Bandit.'

"Where you headin' friend?" the driver said, lifting his large cowboy hat with one hand, while wiping the sweat off his forehead with what had once been a bright red bandanna that matched the one round his neck.

"Anywhere in the Miami area." My reply was lost in the throaty roar of the engine as without waiting for me to settle, the trucker engaged his gears and the mighty machine leapt forward, throwing me off balance again as I struggled to place my kit on the bunk behind the seats.

"Well, pal. This is surely your lucky day. I'm taking this little Baby all the way down Route 27 and onto the Palmetto Expressway." My new-found friend informed me as he lovingly patted the flag bedecked dash of his vehicle, apparently unaware of my predicament.

"That'll suit me fine," I said with relief, finally managing to get things stowed away. If my memory served me correctly, this meant that we would be cutting through the vast uninviting expanse of the Everglades and circling round Lake Okeechobee. The heat had got at me so much that I relaxed into an exhausted doze only to be awoken in alarm when we were stopped by the Highway Patrol, who gave me a cursory check. It became apparent they were just checking vehicle paperwork, so I slipped off into another fitful sleep.

I wasn't feeling much better when some two and a half hours later, the trucker dropped me off at the intersection with Federal Route 41. With a wave of his hand and a blast on the ear piercing horns, the truck moved off down the road, seeming to disappear in the shimmering heat wave coming off the tarmac. Clambering down the steep grass embankment to the road into Miami and hoisting my few belongings onto my shoulder, I started walking eastward, passing a sign informing me that I was on the Tamiami Trail.

The sparse traffic passed me by, totally ignoring my raised thumb as I trudged along accompanied by the ever-present scream of jet engines as numerous passenger and cargo planes passed overhead on the approach to the mighty spread of the Miami International Airport. It wasn't long though, before the wilting heat and an ever- increasing thirst began to tell on me.

"Blow this for a game of soldiers," I gasped, my tongue feeling like lambs wool in my mouth. "Wonder if I'll ever get a lift down this road?"

The heat of the day was at its peak, the tarmac was hot and the road seemed never ending as it disappeared into the distant haze. The sound of a vehicle approaching from behind me made me swing round. There, coming towards me and seemingly floating on the air, was a car with a large white sign on its roof. As it closed on me, the mirage effect faded away and I identified it as an answer to my prayer.

"Taxi," I called, stepping out into the road as it cruised towards me. Dammed if I know why we shout at them, the driver can't have *that* good a hearing, I chided myself as it slid to a halt beside me.

"Down Town please," I said, thankfully entering the air conditioned, spearmint scented interior. Knowing that Miami would be a busy place at this time of year with Americans intent on enjoyment, flocking to its beaches and other lavish attractions in their hundreds, I had decided to go directly to the centre of this sprawling city.

"Hey, you're a Limey ain't ya?" The voice of the gum chewing driver cut into my thoughts. "I'll give you the best rundown on this city you'll ever get." He spat the gum out of his window. "On your right we have the resting place of Elvis, King of Rock-n-Roll." Thinking that this Englishman was a tourist, he'd launched into his tour guide act.

"Oh, great," I said, unable to stop myself from looking in the direction he indicated. According to the signs, we were indeed just passing the ornate gateway to the heavily guarded Graceland Memorial Park where Elvis was laid to rest.

"Over there,".... the driver continued.

"Look pal. I'm English, not a Limey. I'm also not a tourist so I'm *not* interested in the grand tour. OK?" I curtly informed him.

Leaning back and shutting my eyes, I endured the sullen silence that reigned for the rest of the trip - that is if you discount the chewing noise as the driver sullenly refilled his mouth with fresh gum. After a few miles, the cab pulled into the kerb and the man grumpily held his hand out. "That's five dollars Man." Handing him the right money I got out and found myself surrounded by Police cars.

"Humph. I suppose this is his idea of a joke," I said to myself as I stood looking at the massive building that housed the Miami Police Head Quarters. "Just like it is on Telly."

Looking around, I spotted what I was looking for; just up the road at the next intersection a sign declared another large building to be the Miami Post Office. Entering the cool marble interior of this lofty edifice, and making my way to the usual row of public phone booths, I inserted a quarter, dialled Brewster's number which Mal had given me and waited. After listening to the ringing tone for a long time I gave up, thinking the man was obviously out.

"Damn. I hope he's not away from home. Mal got his name from the 'Vets' organisation, so he could be on a job," I muttered, recovering my quarter from the phone.

Not many people are aware of the world wide unofficial organisation of ex. Special Forces personnel. They are occasionally used by Governments - deniably of course - what's more it was an indisputable fact, if you were on their recommended list, then you were good.

"Ah well. Fall back to plan B," I mumbled as I picked up my bag. From my earlier study of the street plan, I'd seen that this sprawling city was laid out like a giant grid. Which must mean, that if I walked east I would eventually come to the docks. Off I trudged, the paving seeming to burn right through the soles of my shoes.

"Wow. Would you look at that. Huge chunks of money floating on the water," I declared after walking about a mile. I was looking at the Port of Miami across the green expanse of what a large sign proclaimed to be Bayfront Park and the other side seemed to be wall to wall with huge white Luxury Cruisers of all shapes and sizes.

Jealousy will get you nowhere. Just think of them as being a mirage, I heard the voice saying inside my head.

"Yeah. Good idea," I agreed, dragging myself away from the view to ask a passer-by for directions to the small Seaman's hotel that stood on East Flagler St. Booking in for a period of two nights initially, I settled down for a rest and to think over what to do if my 'contact' was not available.

That evening I tried the number again. No joy. I rang again early the following morning, hoping to catch him before he went out. Several unsuccessful attempts later made me certain he was away so I decided on a change of plans. Mal always knew when my plans had to be changed, I'd start pulling the lobe of my ear - or as he had called it *'Feeling for the switch.'*

"I'll have to make my own arrangements if I can," I said pensively. "No matter what happens now, I'm on my own it seems."

Later that day, while moving with the crowds of shoppers and holiday makers as they made their way north along Biscayne Boulevard, I had a very distinct feeling of being watched. The hairs on my neck stood up and I 'felt' unseen eyes on me. A trickle of ice cold water seemed to run down my back. I froze.

"Bloody Hell. It can't be. No way can anyone know I'm here." I cursed as I stopped moving and must have spoken out loud, because a group of people gave me strange looks. No doubt about it though, the sensation in the nape of my neck according to my past experience told me I was *definitely* under observation.

"It's never let me down before, so it won't be ignored now," I uttered, and automatically started evasive moves to shake any watcher.

"But how?" I asked myself, while dodging in and out of the growing crowds. "How the bloody hell can anyone know where I am, I've twisted and turned, doubled back, even watched the following crowds myself. Nothing. So how come I keep getting this feeling?" There was no simple answer. "Just as well ask an Egyptian how many grains of sand in the Sahara. Damn." So certain was I of being followed, I decided to take action that would flush out this watcher.

Throwing my jacket over my shoulder and imperceptibly slowing my pace while stopping now and again to use shop windows as mirrors. Or even doubling back to look into some windows a few times - this way I would isolate anyone close on my heels. Nothing. There was no-one for me to see unless I was up against a real pro of course.

Eventually, somewhere in the Buena Vista area, I found the type of place that would interest me - the inevitable American Army Surplus Store. The huge sign above it declared proudly that they could sell you anything from clothing to tanks.

Great. Just what you want anyway, so just as well take a look while we're here, my internal voice said in my ear. Entering its darker interior, I immediately dodged behind a rack containing used Combat Suits and waited. No one came in but I stayed put.

"Is it the Law, or a woman you're hiding from friend?" An unexpected voice from close behind me made me jump. Dropping into a semi-defensive crouch, I turned quickly but could see no one.

"I'm down here friend," the voice said in a Southern Drawl. A movement in between the racks of clothing caught my eye. Then, in the semi-darkness I made out the shape of a man in a wheel chair.

"Neither," I replied sharply, all thoughts of my 'tail' forgotten for the moment. "What is it to you anyway?"

With sudden supple movement of his hands the man propelled the chair forward, effectively forcing me backwards and pinning me painfully against the door by my legs.

"In MY store, I ask the questions O.K," he said fiercely, and it was then that I saw the gun - which had somehow appeared in his hand - this meant further argument would be useless.

"OK. OK. I'm sorry, but you made me jump. I didn't mean to be rude," I said, making placating movements with my hands. As my eyes became accustomed to the dim light, I could see that he was dressed in the traditional style of the US Army Vet's and that he had no legs below the knees. However, his upper body was extremely powerful and he had proved he could look after himself already.

"You own the store?" I queried, rubbing my shins as he eased his chair off me.

"That's what I said friend," he paused as if in thought. "But hey. You're a Brit aren't you?" A note of excitement had entered his voice. "How about a coffee and you can tell me all about why you're playing hide and seek, huh?"

With deft movements the gun vanished and he spun the chair, disappearing silently into the darker recesses of the shop. I followed, taking a few glances over my shoulder to check if anyone else had come in. I caught him up in what served as his office just as he was pouring two cups of hot, strong coffee. Pushing one cup towards me, the man indicated for me to sit on a wooden packing crate.

"Well?" he said questioningly. Since this man was a Vet, I felt he could be told some of my story in case he could help me - he had the kit I would require anyway. So I sat opposite him and as we drank our coffee, I told him the part of my cover story about being on the run from the London gang. When I'd finished, he sat sipping his coffee and studying me for a time over the top of his cup, his face was deadpan.

"Bullshit!" he suddenly exclaimed, lending emphasis to his oath by banging his empty cup down on the table. "That's the biggest load of bull I ever heard. You, my friend, are ex SAS and you people don't run from *nobody*."

"How?"... Astounded I could only splutter the one word.

"Do you think I'm blind as well as stupid?" With a sudden movement, he'd propelled his chair across the intervening space and grabbed my left arm, pulled me closer. "What is that?" he demanded, indicating a small, faded tattoo of a winged dagger on my forearm.

"Damn." It was my turn to curse. "I ought to wear a plaster on it."

"Yes, you're right," my admission was reluctant. "I'm on an unofficial mission and think I'm being followed. I don't know for sure, or who by. It's just a feeling." The man nodded his head as he listened to me.

"My name's Ben," I volunteered. "Let me explain." I took another quick look out into the store while choosing my words very carefully and started to give him a brief explanation, glossing over the full details without giving away my real reason for being in the USA. Again I expressed my concern about being followed.

"They call me Rick," the man said when I had finished. "I would like to help you." He held his hand out as he made that simple statement and we shook before he continued. "I want to help, not only because of your problem, but because I owe one of your guys my life. Don't ask me who he was, all I know he was in the Brit' Special Forces." He paused, deep in thought before continuing.

"I was a Lt. in the US. Marine Corp., my patrol had been shot up pretty bad in the Gulf and when I took cover I ran into a mine field. Bang. Lower legs blasted and I'm left to die being the only one who got out of our vehicle"

He shifted his position in his wheelchair to ease his circulation.

"I applied tourniquets using my webbing straps. Didn't think I had a chance, being miles away from base and the radio went up with the vehicle. So I settled back to die, couldn't walk so what else could I do?" he declared fiercely, his voice filling with pent-up emotion.

Opening his jacket, he took out a pack of cigarettes, offering them to me.

"No, thanks," I said. Rick lit one and drawing heavily on it, he recalled the painful scene.

"The pain was starting to get me by then and my Morphine was in the remains of the Humvee. Then I heard the sound of movement behind me, this is it I thought, the bastards have come to cut my throat. A hand touched my shoulder and instead of a knife there was the sweetest sound I ever heard.

"A quiet Brit' voice said, 'Have you out of there in a minute mate, don't move.' He also said he was going to give me some Morphine and he was sorry if he hurt me while he moved me."

Rick's voice went husky at this stage, so I offered to refill his coffee cup. With a sheepish grin, he continued.

"All I know is that one of your guys who were on deep insertion had broken his cover and at great risk to himself dragged me out of the mine field and called in a chopper." He paused for another mouthful of coffee and dabbed his eyes with his sleeve.

"It was dark so I never saw his face; we never spoke to each other as he dragged me along. I kept passing out, and then I felt him dressing my legs. As he gave me a shot of Morphine he said, 'It's OK Yank, you're on a ticket for home now.' That's all, other than what I heard him say on his radio".......

"Which was?" I demanded a bit too roughly.

"He said," Rick continued, 'Strike, this is Delta One, Hot Extraction, Medivac.' Then I remember he was giving the coordinates as I passed out. I came to as the chopper came in fast and low. They were Brit's as well, in and out so fast the dust never settled while they were there. We drew fire as they took off and I always wonder if he made it out whoever he was; I never saw him again. Tried to get information, but your people are tighter than a Duck's Ass on that, but I would love to know even now." He sobbed. "I *owe* him."

By the time Rick had finished his story, the tears ran freely down his cheeks and his voice had cracked up, so I poured another coffee each.

Knowing that Delta was one of the SAS Troops and Delta One was the radio code name for its leader, I turned to Rick and said, "he made it OK. We lost some others out there, but not from Delta. In fact, I'm pretty sure I can put him in touch with you if you like." I took Rick's increasingly emotional state to signify that he *would like*.

When he had recovered his composure, Rick shook me by the hand and said he would find out if anyone had been following me. Picking up a phone, he asked the person at the other end to take a walk out and see if anyone was watching the shop.

In answer to my unspoken question, he said, "my son, he's upstairs and he'll go out the back way and have a look around." After a bit more talk about our experiences in the Services, Rick then invited me to stay with them for a few days. Having taken a liking to this broken, but gutsy man I happily accepted.

We were interrupted by a customer, so I took the chance to look around the store, which was typical of that sort of place. Military equipment of all descriptions stood in piles on the floor; the shelves bursting with almost everything you could wish for. Clothing and webbing being the main interest to me, I took my time in trying some pieces on for size, eventually assembling a special type of webbing harness to my own specifications. I took my compilation to Rick, who introduced the tall, fit looking young man he was then talking to.

"Hey Ben. This is my son Paul; he is keen to meet you."

"Hi Paul, pleased to meet you," I said, sincerely returning his firm handshake. The young man's grip was strong and from the confident way he held himself, I guessed he was also trained in the martial arts. .

"Going out on a job are we?" he said with a grin, as he spotted the webbing I had constructed. "By the way, there was no one taking any interest in this place, either in front, or behind in the alley." Seeing my obvious relief, he continued. "Pa has told me you know the guy who rescued him, it would be great if he could get in contact with us sometime."

"Hey. From the looks of that kit you had best come clean; we may even be able to help you with other stuff," Rick interrupted.

Taking a look over my shoulder to ensure no one else could hear and breaking my own rule, I quickly outlined the true reason for my mission and my destination. When I had finished, both Rick and his son sat quietly for a few minutes. Then without a word, they both nodded their heads at each other.

"OK. Ben," Rick said firmly, "you buy what you want from my store at cost price and whatever else I can get for you. No argument." He held his hand up to stop my protests.

"If you want this stuff shipped to Panama, I can do it and shipment won't cost you a red cent. We would sure like to help you; I have the contacts for kit and ready to use weapons of all sorts. It'll only take a few days to get it together, so give me a list." I thought for just a short moment before agreeing with this generous offer by shaking hands with both of them.

"Now all I have to do is deal with this 'tail' that has been following me".......

"That's a piece of cake." Paul butted in; he looked at his Dad who simply said, "go for it boy."

We spent the next few minutes listening to Paul's plan, which was so simple that I had to laugh while nodding my agreement.

Code Name SNOWBIRD

Chapter 10

<u>The 'Tail' stops wagging.</u>

A short while later, still acting the tourist, I walked out of the shop with a small parcel in my hand and made for the open park area close by. This time though I *knew* there was a shadow. As part of the plan, Paul had left the rear of the shop - as he had done earlier - and would come around the end of the block and wait until he saw me move off, then watch to see who, if anyone followed. Now moving at my normal pace I walked steadily along the pavement, avoiding the odd group of people intent on their holiday enjoyment.

Crossing the busy main road - remembering at the last moment to look left before right - I dodged a large car with its horn blaring and made it to the other side. Strolling casually across the grass area to a bench overlooking the sea, I sat down. The warm, clean sea breeze was suddenly replaced by an appetizing and it seemed an irresistibly unique American aroma that drifted across the open space to me - the smell of coffee and hot doughnuts.

That's a better way to pass the time, I thought and joined the queue at a stall further down the slope. With my Polystyrene cup gripped carefully in one hand and a delicious, sugar-coated hot doughnut and parcel in the other, I went and sat on a wall in the shade of some trees. As I sipped my drink and munched my 'dunker,' I watched the many small boats dashing about the surface of the clear glittering water that was seemingly trapped between the mainland and the two spectacular causeways - John F. Kennedy on my left and the Julie Tuttle on my right. Across the water to my front, I could see the long sprawl of the world famous Miami Beach. Built on many small islands linked by bridges; with many skyscraper blocks of luxury apartments reaching for the sky as they fought for supremacy in a very limited space Luckily, some wisdom must have existed in the Planning Department for they had not allowed these to block the views of the sea, but had strategically placed luxury hotels with their own pristine gardens in between.

No wonder this place is so popular, I found myself thinking. Wouldn't mind a chunk of it myself.

The unmistakable whirring sound of a skateboard on concrete brought me back to reality. The young man on it appeared to be a beginner as he kept falling off. Twice he made false starts as he came down the slope, then against advice shouted at him by wary passersby he unwisely decided to attempt the ride down the long steeply sloping path towards me.

Wobbling precariously, scattering pedestrians and those people queuing for coffee, he began to pick up speed, frightening a small dog and sending it into a yelping fit. Then, disaster! Hitting a rough patch in the path the skateboard abruptly stopped and the rider took a tumble, falling forward and rolling head over heels almost to my feet. Dropping my nearly empty cup, I reached down and helped him to get up.

"One man. White sports top and sunglasses, dark grey slacks. Sat at the top of the slope, he has followed every move you made. I'm ready if you are," Paul whispered in my ear as he put his arm around my shoulder as if for support.

"Let's go then, we don't want him to get sunburn sitting there do we?" I joked, brushing the dust off of Paul, at the same time unobtrusively scanning the area to locate the watcher.

"Better get that knee seen to as soon as you can and be more careful next time," I called loudly as Paul picked up his skateboard and limped away down the path.

Under the pretext of putting my coffee cup in a bin, I ensured that the watcher saw me move off along the tree line. A path turned into the trees a few hundred metres along on the left, just as Paul said there would be.

Just the job, I thought and checking out of the corner of my eye to see that my 'tail' was still following; I turned into the pathway and followed its several twists and turns through thick bushes as it led me into the tree belt.

Rounding another corner, I was confronted by the high, wire fence and low walling that formed a secure compound for the Park Keeper's hut. As if caught by surprise, I sharply reversed my direction back round the first bend. There, a few yards in front of me was the watcher. A look of shock registered on his face, as he'd been totally unprepared for my sudden reappearance. He could only stand still as I approached him. His body language was subtly changing as he warily shifted his position - a move noted by me as preparing to fight – and a sudden scraping sound behind him added to his confusion. Looking over his shoulder he saw Paul rolling to an expert stop on his skateboard a few feet away. Realization that he had been tricked dawned on his face, more importantly; he realized that he was now effectively trapped between Paul and myself.

Positioning myself firmly in front of him- while remaining outside his reach - I demanded, "who are you and why are you following me?"

"Foll.... I'm not following you," the man gulped. "I'm just taking a walk, like you."

Taking advantage of his confusion, I suddenly reached forward and grabbed him by his shirtfront, pulling him off balance.

"Pervert or spy, which ever you are we'll soon know," I said, hitting him hard on the side of his chin. His head snapped back, spittle flew out of his mouth and his knees sagged under him. Lowering the now unconscious man to the ground amongst the fallen leaves, I deftly searched his pockets. In his inside jacket pocket, I found a wallet containing several high denomination dollar bills, a plastic Gold Credit Card and some small family photos. More interestingly, another pocket contained a small high power radio and an ID card. The crest emblazoned on the card was like a physical blow to my head.

"CIA," I gasped. "How the Hell did *they* get on to me." I was so angry my stomach was doing flips.

"Give me a hand," I asked Paul. Between us we lifted the man onto the low wall forming part of the entrance to the compound. I completed my search and was not surprised to find a small .38 pistol in a shoulder holster. When the man started to come round a few minutes later, it was to find himself looking at the barrel of his own gun. He groaned and tried to sit up only to find that Paul held him firmly by the shoulders while I leaned onto his chest.

"Spit it out Mr. CIA, no tricks no lies and maybe, just *maybe*, you go home with a sore chin and nothing else," I snarled, waving his ID. Card in his face.

"OK. OK," the man spluttered with difficulty through his now swelling mouth. "We've been following you at the request of our London Station who wants the same information you are after. We had to make sure you continued without interruption." He hesitated slightly as he tenderly wiped his lips. "Our orders are to take out any interference, just the same as they did in Paris.".......

"Paris? What do you mean?" My interruption was sharp enough to startle Paul. "What did they do in Paris?" I angrily grabbed the man's shirtfront again and shook him.

Here I was, in the South of America; God only knows how many miles from Paris, confronted by a total stranger who knew what had happened there. On top of that, he was CIA. I was furious. Where had I gone wrong?

"I don't know the full facts," the man gasped, "all I know is that men from our Paris Station took out someone who had been after you." Relaxing my grip while signing for Paul to let the man sit up, I held up my hand to silence them both. I had to think. My mind was in a whirl trying to make sense of what I had just been told. There was only one way to find out what was going on.

. "Right," I snapped, whirling round on him unexpectedly and making him flinch. "I need to know exactly what happened, so <u>you</u> my friend," I poked him in the chest for emphasis, "can arrange for your boss to find out what, when and where it happened."

As he thought about this demand, I paced up and down, angrily rubbing my hand through my hair.

Turning sharply, causing him to jump again, I snarled, "you *must* get this information as soon as you can, d'you understand?" He nodded his head vigorously, almost eagerly, so I pressed home my advantage. "I can be contacted through Paul and his father in the Surplus Store, it's vital that I know. Understood?"

Rising but keeping a wary eye on me, the CIA man again nodded his head as he dusted himself off. I tossed his gun back to him and the feel of the weapon in his hand seemed to restore his courage. He puffed his chest out and lost the crestfallen look.

"We'll be in touch soon," he said, trying to sound officious. Then turning to Paul, he added with grudging admiration.

"You aren't really as dumb on that skateboard as you make out are you, kid?"

With a laugh, Paul showed him a badge on the pocket of his sports shirt that proudly named him Skateboard Champion of Florida County.

"What d'<u>you</u> think?" he said, with a wide grin.

"Maybe not, but it was a good cover and it fooled me," Mr. CIA said over his shoulder as he hurried off.

"That, my boy was nothing short of brilliant. If ever you want a job I'm sure the CIA will take you on," I said, clasping Paul's hand.

I liked this ingenious boy; he was very quick on the uptake and game for anything. Laughing together and with an arm around each other's shoulders, we made our way back to the shop to tell Rick the story.

The following morning saw me up bright and early. I checked out of my hotel and after sending Mal a letter explaining about Rick and Paul, I moved my stuff over to Rick's place, then went for a walk along the sea front. It did not take me long to identify the 'tail' that the CIA were obviously still maintaining. Though I didn't feel comfortable about it, I had to admit to myself that I could at least relax a bit and enjoy the sights of Miami.

Finding a Car Hire Centre and choosing a small open sports car I set off to explore, aided by the excellent folding wallet of large scale street maps in the glove compartment. I drove off across the McArthur Causeway towards the area of South Miami Beach, my 'tail' in a similar car behind me.

Parking the car near Flamingo Park, I strolled casually along the walkway, stopping to look at shops and dodging the crowds. On impulse, I turned into a street called Española Way which runs east - west from the sea, so was hidden between the backs of 14th and 15th Streets.

"Magic. Just the sort of place I need," I gasped, when I saw dozens of very colourful shops, including some that sold a great variety of unusual antiques. I spent the next two hours browsing; going from one to the other; before spotting the sort of thing I had been looking for.

"How much is that?" I asked the shopkeeper, pointing to an unusual and very attractive South American Indian bracelet.

"That's hand crafted in gold and silver Sir and comes at $1500," the shopkeeper told me.

"I'm sure Judith would like this," I said to myself as I counted out the money.

"Wrap it ready for mailing to the UK for me please," I requested.

With my package under my arm, I took it to a nearby Post Office, completed the Customs Form and sent it in an assumed name to an accommodation address in England. Mal would collect it from there at some stage and post it onwards.

The rest of the morning was spent driving and exploring the length of Miami Beach, and enjoying a very unhurried lunch in a Restaurant overlooking the pounding surf. Retracing my steps, I did a thorough exploration of the Docks and admired the masses of expensive looking Power Cruisers and Yachts in the huge Marinas.

"I'll bet you don't get any change from a quarter of a million dollars for any of these beauties," I muttered, when looking at some smaller ones. Green with envy I tore myself away. A couple of the massive luxury liners that regularly left Miami on cruises around the Caribbean were moored out in the harbour and small ferries were scuttling to and fro between them and the Docks.

Code Name SNOWBIRD

After a last drive around, I returned the car, popped into a Bank to get Rick's money then casually made my way on foot back to his place.

"Hey man," Rick called when he saw me walk in. "All your stuff is ready in the back store room, I'm just going to lock up and I'll join you," he said, indicating a small door at the back of his office. Going through into the large storeroom, I was impressed to see all the kit and weaponry I had asked for waiting there for my inspection.

"Here you are Ben, everything's in working order," Paul said, handing me a checklist that clearly itemised everything. "You check them off as I call them." We set to work; there was no real need to check the working parts of the weapons as Paul had already done that. The list was impressive:

4 x Browning Heavy Machine guns (belt fed)

12 x Heckler & Koch 9 mm MP5 submachine guns.

2 x Heckler & Koch G3SG 7.62mm Sniper rifles

4 x Winchester and Remington Pump Action shotguns.

40 x Fragmentation Grenades

2 x Man portable Rocket launchers & 2 spare rockets.

12 x Browning HP. 9mm high power pistols.

12 x M16A2 American Colt Armalite Assault Rifles

12 x Night Vision sets

12 x Hand held Satellite Navigation packs.

12 x Webbing sets as designed by myself and Kevlar Body Armour.

Eventually satisfied that everything was there and accompanied by the correct ammunition, we all retired to the living accommodation for our evening meal.

"Paul will pack everything ready for shipping," Rick said, as we ate. He threw some more clam chowder into his mouth, then added between chewing, "the bill for the goods can be settled in cash or cheque, the freight will be complimentary."

"That's great Rick, how long will it take to arrive there?" I queried.

"Don't you go worrying yourself over that my friend, it'll all be there waiting for you when you arrive. It'll be sent as a priority load via a 'friend' of mine," he assured me.

"D'you know something, Rick?" I asked. "I think the CIA did me a favour when one of their tame gorillas drove me into your place." He nearly choked with laughter at that, we had to pat him on his back to clear his throat. When he had fully recovered, I handed him the thick wad of thousand dollar bills.

That night I climbed into my bed feeling very pleased with the way things were working out and drifted contentedly off to sleep. This time, there was no need for me to worry about 'tails' as we now knew who they were.

The incessant scream of seagulls woke me early the following morning. I showered and dressed, then went down to find Paul had breakfast already for me.

"Hi. Ben. Heard you moving around and thought you may need breakfast," he said, as I walked into the kitchen.

"Morning Paul thanks, it smells good." I poured coffee for us both and sat down. Paul slid a large plate of bacon, eggs and the inevitable hash browns in front of me. In recognition of my hunger, I tucked in.

"Where you going today?" he asked.

"Not sure really, but I'd just as well do a bit more sight seeing while I've got the chance. Oh, yes," I added gleefully, "I mustn't forget that the CIA goon will have to be exercised as well must I?" There was a spluttering sound as Paul nearly choked at that comment.

"Take a ride on the Rapid Transit Train if you like scenery," Paul advised.

"May well do that, thanks," I said, cleaning my plate off with a piece of bread. "That was great, I enjoyed it."

Paul pushed the plates into the dishwasher and we went down to the store. He explained that he would open up while his dad got himself dressed. I left him pushing shutters up and made my way along the road. A glance in a window showed me that early though it was, I had already picked up a 'tail.' I was beginning to accept that there was a definite 'feel good' factor on me, so I decided to take Paul's advice and joined with the crowd of holiday makers walking down North Miami Avenue.

Crossing 11th Street, I became aware of the noise from the overhead rail system so decided to investigate. Studying a nearby Information Board, I found that it was the Rapid Transit Train - an above ground rail system - that runs for 21 miles from South Miami to a place called Hialeah in the north. A descriptive leaflet informed me that in the course of its journey, the Metrorail would take the traveller past some spectacular views of the city and all this for $1.

Making sure that my 'tail' would still follow; I climbed the steps and waited five minutes for the next train to arrive at the stop. The journey, though relatively short in duration, was definitely not short on scenery. Passing above all the traffic at a height that let passengers have views across rooftops to the stretches of golden beach and ever present blue ocean. Having been a TV addict in past years, I recognised some of the spectacular landscape as being used in so many of the inevitable American films that are based on Miami.

Arriving at the Hialeah Terminus I made my way to a Cafe/Bar, where I enjoyed an Espresso coffee and doughnut. A casual glance around showed me that my CIA 'companion' had settled himself in at a similar establishment, on the other side of the road. While eating my food, I studied an information leaflet on something called the Metromover. From this, it was easy to plan the rest of the day, as well as the route back to Rick's place. A loudspeaker announced that the train was ready to roll so finishing my coffee I made for the nearest carriage.

Feeling pleasantly relaxed, yet still retaining an awareness, I got off the train at Government Centre when we arrived back in Miami and joined the queue for the Metromover - or as the locals called it, the 'People Mover' - which the leaflet told me was - an over head Disney type Electric Train that travels a 26 Block area of downtown Miami.

Joining the other passengers whom it seemed were mainly grandparents with grandchildren, I settled in to enjoy the spectacular and at times dramatic views of the city from this fun ride. During the journey, the train passed such places as Fort Dallas Park, The World Trade Centre in its enormous building and the colourful Bayfront Park on Biscayne Boulevard that was a mass of flowers and flags.

"That's by far the best way to see the sights, from above the crowded streets and traffic congestion," I said to an elderly lady as we waited to get off at the Government building.

"Yes dear," she replied. "It's better than the normal buses."

Cheaper too at a dollar a time, I thought, when I realised she must use it as public transport for shopping.

A late lunch and a glass of wine was followed by a little more walking and window shopping, then a brisk walk back along the water front towards Rick's place. As I now sported a neatly trimmed full beard, it pleased me to notice that I attracted quite a few glances from some of the scantily clad young ladies in passing. Fighting hard to resist temptation by keeping my mind on the business in hand, I let my tired and aching feet carry me back to the dark and cooler interior of Rick's Store. Sitting on a seat in the office waiting for me was my old friend Mr 'CIA' as we still referred to him. This man, with ill concealed sarcasm, let me know that he had me tabbed at all times by saying in his Southern drawl.

"Enjoy your walks and train rides? Our poor man has blisters on his feet."

"You should issue them a good pair of walking shoes, or even a skateboard then," I snapped. Any reply to this retort was drowned by both Rick and Paul, as they went into fits of laughter.

"Now, what have you got for me?" I said impatiently, taking a seat and kicking off my shoes, then putting my feet up on a box beside him.

"OK," said an embarrassed Mr CIA. "We have asked our people in Paris for details. They tell us that our London Station have been trying to get someone on the 'inside' of this gang for a long time, and not been having much luck I might add. Then you happen along and they thought it would be best if a 'trained outsider' did the donkey work for them."

He paused to see what reaction the 'trained outsider' barb might cause. Seeing none, he continued.

"You have done pretty well so far and in answer to your question about Paris, all they came back with is a name that means nothing to us over here." Pausing, he looked at me as if trying to read my mind.

"Well. What was the name?" I snapped rather harshly. "I can't tell you if it means anything to me if you don't tell me who it was."

"Paulo," he stated. "D'you know any one of that name?" He'd obviously got the point as he started fidgeting uncomfortably. In a flash it all fell into place in my mind.

"Know him!" I exclaimed. "Yes, I know him all right and I'm not surprised." Pausing to collect my thoughts that his news had effectively scattered, I spoke aloud as the ramifications came clear. "I wonder. ... he could have been after me for revenge ... or was he acting on orders from John Paul who'd discovered how I'd tricked him. ... If that is the case, then he would have been acting on orders from Jose. ... If he was, then I am going to have to be more careful because that means they are on to me."..........

"Hey. Hey. Stop talking to yourself will ya," Mr CIA interrupted. "According to our man in Paris, this Paulo guy said he wanted to get even with you, that's why he had broken into your hotel room less than an hour after you left. Besides, I don't think they are on your tail, since leaving them you've twisted and turned and covered your tracks very well and even our experienced Agents had trouble keeping tabs on you." This was said with just a hint of admiration. I felt a distinct feeling of relief when I realised that Paulo had just been after getting his own back for the broken nose and humiliation he had suffered.

"All right, that's good news at least, but just how long are you going to be able to keep protecting my back?" I asked. Before he could answer I continued.

"The next stage of my plan is almost in being; much against my better instincts I'm going by sea to Panama, if I can get a berth that is. No problem when I get there as my contacts will be able to get me into the target area in Colombia." I'd crossed my fingers behind my back as I told that little white lie. I didn't even know who the contacts were, let alone how good they'd be.

Mr CIA drew himself up to his full height and looking me straight in the eye, he announced in a semi-officious manner.

"We can help you get there no problem, but we will stay on the shore here. This will be where our responsibility ends. The moment you step on a boat, finito. Is that understood?" The final declaration was made with obvious relish. Remembering the CIA's past involvement in Colombian affairs, this had to be accepted and I assured him of my gratitude for their interest so far.

"That's OK. All I ask is that you don't let our involvement become public knowledge, and by the way, we'll let you know about a berth as soon as possible." We shook hands and I walked him to the door. As he was about to leave, I asked the one question that had been niggling in the back of my mind for some time...

"Tell me, how did you get on my tail so quickly?" His face lit up with sheer pleasure at being given the chance to even the score.

"Well, as you know, our Paris Office had eyeballed you at an early stage. They had been informed by the London Head of Station. All they did was to use the massive resources available to us across the world. The moment you ducked out in Paris, we put out an all points alert, complete with picture." Pausing to light a cigarette, he teased me a bit more, knowing I was wriggling. A couple of deep drags later, he continued.

"A snitch who runs an office in Marseille booked you a passage to Boston; we had to pay him for that information. The rest was easy, sit back and wait for your ship to come in then tail you." Pausing again, he gave me a nudge on the arm as he added, "you caused a few 'old hands' to break sweat though. They lost you a few times, so we had to use the Highway Patrol and Local Sheriff's across the country."

He chuckled as he turned and walked out the door, then he swung round and nearly floored me when he said, "you really don't like being called a Limey do you?" With a wave of his hand, he stepped into the waiting car and sped off into the traffic.

"Well I'll be buggered," I cursed. "First they had me followed all the time in Paris, then I'm shopped by that old French Fart, who sold me my Mates Ticket. Then the Highway Patrols and Sheriff's confirm my direction of travel and I'm conveniently given a lift by the CIA disguised as a Taxi driver."

"Hey Man," Rick said as he joined me on the doorstep. "Don't let it bug you. You did well for him to admit that the biggest Security organisation in the world lost you, that's something to have a drink on." We did. In fact we had quite a few.

After a couple of more days enjoying the 'scenery' and helping Rick in the store, I received a message from Mr CIA. In it he said that they had managed to find the not too fussy Skipper of a rusty old Coaster, willing to sign me on as a crewman onboard his ship bound for Panama City.

Humph, I thought, I wonder what hold they have on him.

However, this suited me no end as Panama lay over 1100 miles away on the other side of the Gulf of Mexico and we would have to pass through the Panama Canal to get there. I would at last be able to completely relax my vigilance during the time it would take to make the crossing. I started packing.

"Well, you guys," I said to Rick and Paul as I prepared to leave in the early hours of the following day. "It's been a real pleasure meeting you both and I shall never forget what you've done."

"Gee man. It's nothing. Only wish we could come with you, but," Rick said smacking his useless legs in a deprecating gesture. "Anyway, it was great to meet you and to see our great CIA put in their place."

"Bye Ben," Paul said shaking my hand with a grip so firm for a young man. "Have a good war, my friend and come see us again." I didn't look back as the Taxi drove me away. I wanted to remember those two guys as they were.

I was genuinely sad at leaving the lively bustle of Miami; memories of this place and some of its people would stay with me for a long time. The Taxi drove along Bayfront Park towards the docks and there, sticking up through the early morning mist I saw the impressive but sombre John F. Kennedy Torch of Friendship.

"Sophie," I exclaimed in a whisper. It was as if it was her hand holding a torch to light my way onward. "I'm getting there, Sophie," I whispered, my eyes still drawn to that edifice as we drove past.

Chapter 11

<u>The 'Tequila Sunrise' and Panama</u>

Masquerading as a sailor didn't make me a real judge of ships. Neither did my assumed role help me form a very good impression of the one I had to report to. Ships, by tradition are normally referred to as *She*, but I refused to besmirch the female gender by naming the discoloured abomination that lay before me so.

Lying very low in the water - which *should* mean the hold was full of cargo, or if not it was in danger of sinking at the quay side - it was so rusty that any self respecting scrap yard dealer would have rejected it. The hull was dented from numerous collisions with unforgiving harbour walls. In some places, great gouges had been taken out of the wooden capping on the bulwarks and never repaired. Topside was no better; there was hardly a patch of good paint to be seen on any surface. Everything seemed to be covered in oily black soot from the colander that passed as a funnel. I thought it looked as if it had just been raised from the bottom of the ocean and doubted it would make the 2600 k trip.

My heart was in my mouth as I climbed the steep and perilous gangway to board the *'Tequila Sunrise'* as the faded name on the stern declared and the thought crossed my mind - you won't see many more sunrises, I bet!

Apparently, they had been waiting for me to arrive; for the moment my feet touched the deck the gangway was hauled in by a clattering, complaining winch, clouds of filthy black smoke belched from the funnel as we left the berth.

The inside of the ship was worse than the outside. The accommodation a sullen crew member showed me into was as dark as a cave, with a grease laden table bolted to the floor in the middle and decking that was so greasy my shoes stuck to it. The euphemistically named sleeping accommodation was arranged round the Mess and consisted of six rickety bunks, which were covered in dirty smelly blankets. I also found that the Off Watch crew members used the bunks, while those On Watch sat on the only bench there was for their meals, etc.

Without doubt, the worst thing for me was the all pervading smell of fuel oil and bilge water; which mixed with a most unsanitary smell emanating from the blackened, filth encrusted bowl of the 'Heads' behind a curtain in one corner. These combined to make the air thick and sickly, drawn in with every breath, chewed with any food eaten and swallowed with any drink. Too late to change my mind now though, because from the pitching and rolling that I could feel, I guessed we were well on our way out to sea.

Stowing my kit in my locker, I realised that the smell and filth had now become an inescapable part of life. As if to add insult to injury, I later discovered that the electric lighting in the Mess did not work, consequently the only lighting was from an ancient oil lamp that exuded thick tarry smoke as it gyrated crazily from the ceiling.

So, I thought, this is Mr CIA's way of getting his own back and I'm going to have to grin and bear it!

Luckily for me though, apart from the excessive 'duties' I was called on to do; mainly as the other crew sat around playing cards - the accommodation was the only thing I had to suffer. The weather was reasonably kind as this tired old tub beat its way southwards, the only exception being a short, but heavy squall as we passed through the Yucatan Channel between Cuba and the coast of Mexico. To my great relief, as I expected the old tub to sink at any moment, this meant I didn't have to stay below in the filthy cramped and smelly confines. During the time it took to get across the Gulf, the vastly overweight and constantly drunken Captain, kept me very busy.

"Hey! English," he'd yell. "this deck needs scrubbing!" I had to agree with him, it had not been scrubbed since it was laid!

Or the call would come, "Hey! English, this rust needs removing!"

He would shout with glee, knowing full well that we were short of good wire brushes with which to clean up the rusting deck gear. During any off duty time - normally when the Captain was in a drunken sleep - I took the chance to work on getting my body into trim, doing press-ups, etc.

The sullen, unfit Mexican crew considered this activity strange, but it also meant that none of them pushed their luck with me and I was left alone. They were content to nickname me "El Nort Americano" - The North American.

Over the next ten days, with the help of the tropical sea breeze, I soon built up a healthy tan. It also served to acclimatize me to the unexpected and increasing humidity as we drew nearer to the Equator.

Having previously only heard of the Panama Canal in lessons at school, I was keen to at last have a chance to see it. So, on the day we finally sighted the port of Colon on the Panamanian coast of the Caribbean Sea I kept myself busy on deck as under leaden skies, we approached the buoyed channel to the eastern start of the Canal proper.

Making good use of my Ziess binoculars during the time we had to 'standoff' and await our pre-booked turn to enter the first gigantic Sea Lock, I watched the other shipping as it moved into, or out of the Canal. My childhood impression of De-Lesep's engineering feat had been a huge ditch, dug from one coast of Panama to the other. I was amazed that we couldn't just 'drive' in and go through. This must have registered with our German First Mate, for being in a more friendly mood than usual and noticing the interest I showed in what was going on, he came to lean on the ship's rail next to me and immediately started to complete my sadly lacking education - for which I would always be grateful.

"An amazing thing isn't it," he said, indicating the first of the gigantic lock gates. "That lock is 1000 ft long and 110 ft wide. There are three pairs of them in all at either end of 'The Big Ditch' as we call it." He paused long enough to light one of his foul smelling cheroots. Blowing out a cloud of smoke, he continued with his display of knowledge.

"These locks will lift us up to 85 feet above sea level and in the next 6 hours, we will follow the Canal for

44 miles across the Darien Peninsula, through the locks on the other side and out into the Pacific. Mind you, we won't be in a Canal all the time!" He added with an air of mystery. Another puff of cigar smoke hit me in the face.

"You see, the ships use Lake Gatun for a great part of the journey. We follow a buoyed channel through the many islands and don't be surprised if you see divers in the water there. Not many people know that through that stretch of the Canal, you will be passing over the top of 14 submerged villages. Down there are the massive dredgers and excavators that were used to widen and deepen the channels. They were too big to dismantle, so remain there."

Seeing my disbelief at such wanton waste, he laughed and prodded me in the chest as he added, "don't you know its cheaper and easier to dump machinery of those huge sizes?"

He thought for a moment then as his memory cleared, he gave me another triumphant poke, saying with pride, "like the huge boring machine that dug your Channel Tunnel! That was buried in a side tunnel it had dug for the purpose. Dug its own grave, Ja?" His laugh at this his own joke rolled out across the water.

When he had calmed down, he cleared his throat and tapping his finger to his nose as if imparting a secret, he advised, "that is not all though. There are hundreds of dumped cars and railroad stock, a huge Railroad Marshalling yard complete with its workshops!" He paused again, this time to hawk over the rail, then drawing on his cigar he continued. "All of these were left in place, or dumped there when the area was flooded to create the lake. After passing that area, we rejoin the final part of the Canal just after passing the town of Gamboa."

"There, my friend," he expounded with feeling, "you will see as good a feat of engineering as I have ever seen and all done with native labour!" This was said with genuine admiration. "What's more, during the journey we will be among up to forty other ships that will make the journey either way each day." As if that had exhausted his knowledge he turned and without another word he walked away, his head seemingly followed by a stream of evil smelling smoke.

Even with this information, I was not prepared for what I was about to see. The sheer size of some of the ocean going ships that were coming through the Canal amazed me, but the fact that it was indeed a two way system, controlled by traffic lights in some sectors, was really out of this world.

Another surprise lay in store; one that no one had perhaps deliberately thought to warn me of. Although partially prepared for the clinging, sauna like heat of Panama, there was one thing that I neither expected, nor enjoyed. This was the continual invasion of my person, by what seemed like millions of flies and mosquitoes that swarmed out of the swamps surrounding the area as the ship passed through.

To my discomfort they were, it seemed, all determined to make a deliberate attack on me personally! They plagued me without mercy, much to the amusement of the old toothless Chinese man who acted as Mess Steward to the crew.

Taking a callous sort of pity on me, this character laughingly informed me, "Mista! Your soft skin is heaven to the blood suckers. If you want keep them away, you rub urine over yourself as a deterrent." The imparting of this advice, the wisdom of which I chose to ignore, resulted in his breaking into a high cackling laugh, which ended in a consumptive coughing that wracked his whole flimsy body.

Just like the ship you live on my friend, your days are numbered! My little voice murmured in my ear as I walked away. Unaware if his advice would have worked or not, I chose to douse my self with water from the Sea Pump on the premise that wet skin would work anyway and it did!

I was never more relieved than when we passed under the soaring bridge that carries the Pan American Highway over the Canal, as this meant we were approaching the last set of locks at the end of the journey. Here, we would emerge into the port of Balboa on the Bay of Panama and the cooler sea breeze would keep the mosquitoes away. As the ship finally came alongside the pier in this busy port, I was again put to work with a vengeance, hauling the heavy, unresponsive mooring lines that were stiff with old age and filth.

In response to the demands placed on it, my body chose to erupt in fountains of perspiration, which when combined with the humidity of the place, only made matters worse. Partially blinded by the sweat running into my eyes, I struggled to maintain my grip on the rope as well as retaining my balance on a deck that was getting wetter all the time.

Code Name SNOWBIRD

At last, amid the curses of the Mate and the oaths uttered by myself, the lines were hauled tight and the ship secured.

Making a dash for the fire hydrant - the valve of which I had coaxed into working order again during the voyage - to the amusement of the rest of the crew, I again tipped buckets of water over myself. Freshly soaped and scrubbed and with the last of my clean clothing on, I grabbed my kit and without even looking back, thankfully walked off the ship.

Chapter 12

<u>Panama City. The house of Miguel</u>

"I'll never go to sea again, unless it's as a fare paying passenger!" I declared to myself as I cleared the Customs formalities. The oppressive conditions on board the 'Tequila Sunrise' had been more than enough for me. Every thought of my short stay on that boat made me shudder. There was no doubt in my mind; that sea passage had been the worst experience of my life.

Eager to put it all behind me, I hailed a Taxi and headed for the main Panama City Post Office. A short dusty journey brought me to my destination where I paid the driver and loaded with my few possessions, sought a phone booth. After queuing for a few minutes, I managed to make a booking for a call to England and was told I would have to wait for just over half an hour.

Taking this opportunity to visit a Bank I was pleased to find my US dollars did not have to changed into Balboa - the local currency - as American dollars were accepted everywhere. To pass the other twenty minutes before my call would be connected; I drank what passed as tea in a small Cafe next door to the Bank. While sipping my drink, I cast my mind back over the preceding months and thought over what had been achieved, but more importantly, I sketch planned the next stage of the operation.

I enquired about temporary lodgings in anticipation of my stay being for at least a week. Then leaving my now cold tea, I returned to the Post Office, where after a short wait, my name was called and a clerk directed me to a cubicle where I could talk in some semblance of privacy.

Mal was delighted to hear from me and though the connection was not too good; using guarded speech he supplied me with the address of a contact in Panama City, who he said was already expecting me to call on him.

"He's OK! He's been written up in *'The Drop'* a couple of times," he added, referring to the magazine of the American Special Forces Association.

Good reliable old Mal! I thought. Still able to plan ahead across the world and he sure does pick 'em!

"He's an ex Ranger (American Special Forces) who has worked with me on previous occasions," he informed me. "He will help in any way he can and he is very reliable."

We spent some time talking about other needs and aspects of the job in hand, then sending my love and best wishes to Julie I signed off. After paying for the call at the counter, I found a Taxi to take me the ten miles to the sprawling suburb of San Miguelito, and the home of Mal's Mexican-American contact.

From the alarming noises made by the rusty, tired old Ford that served as a Taxi, I wondered if we would make the journey. Followed by a cloud of oily smoke and dust, we eventually arrived in an area outside the town where the Spanish Hacienda style houses stood in palm lined roads. Standing amidst shady, blossom covered trees, the balconied white walls and red pan tile roofs of these large mansions was a direct contrast to the slums we had passed through earlier. Each was of a size that showed the owners had plenty of money. Reaching my destination, the car pulled up in a cloud of steam accompanied by squeals of protest from somewhere under the bonnet.

I found myself outside a very large house standing in its own walled grounds. As the Taxi pulled away, I admired the building and its well-kept gardens through the wrought iron gates and had to admit that with its clean cool appearance, the style appealed to me.

"This is Mega Bucks!" I said aloud. Shaking myself from my dreamy state, I picked up my bags, opened the gate and walked slowly up the path. As I approached the steps to the verandah I became aware of a noise coming from within the bushes to one side of the door. The closer I got the more it became obvious that an unseen dog was snarling at me.

"Oh, great!" I exclaimed. "That's all I need." With one eye on the bush and hoping the dog could not sense my fear; I cautiously climbed the steps and rang the bell. As if reacting to the sound of the bell, a huge Doberman immediately came out of the bushes, barking and straining at the seemingly flimsy chain holding him. Too interested in keeping an eye on the dog, I didn't hear the door swing open behind me on silent, well-oiled hinges.

"Si Señor?" a soft, faintly amused female voice said, from behind me. Caught unawares, I swung round quickly to be greeted by the sight of a very beautiful lady, with long, jet black hair and coffee coloured skin. Dressed in expensive slacks and blouse, both of which only served to compliment her trim voluptuous figure, she had an amused smile on her face as she looked me over. Giving her an equally appreciative look and guessing her age to be about forty, I introduced myself.

"My name is Ben Carson!" I mumbled. All of my carefully rehearsed Spanish was forgotten at the sight of this dark beauty.

"Ah! Yes, Señor Carson. My husband and I have been expecting you," she said, with just a hint of the smile in her voice. She signalled to the dog which, while still regarding me warily had subsided into a deep, low growl when the door opened. Now, in immediate response to her signal, it silently disappeared under its bush again. I also noticed she let go of a pull cord by the door as I stepped inside the expensively marbled hallway.

"What was the pull cord for?" I queried, placing my bags on the floor.

"Oh, that! Well, if you had intended any mischief, one pull on the cord and the pin holding the dog's chain to the wall would be released and you,".... she paused to let her words sink in, "would have been attacked without further question," she explained with a light, musical laugh. "We have to be very careful in this area you see."

"Well, that sure beats the cake!" I said with sincerity, but I was pleased to note, that her laugh also reached her eyes.

"Oh, but Señor Carson, that is not all. It also releases three other dogs, two of which can get into the house in case of trouble!" This was said with such a teasing smile that I decided not to push the point.

"Please forgive me, I am Marguerite Lopez," she murmured, holding out her hand. I took it and felt a tingling sensation run through me at the touch of her cool skin. Savouring the moment while looking into her dark sensuous eyes, and unable to resist the urge, I planted a light kiss on the back of her hand.

She turned abruptly - was it my imagination, or did I see a glimmer of interest there - to lead me down a long cool passage which in turn, opened out onto a very beautifully laid out internal Spanish style courtyard. I couldn't fail to notice that the greater part of this area enjoyed the added benefit of the cool shade of a huge Tamborilla tree in full and beautiful blossom.

Seated in the centre of the courtyard, feeding fish in a large pond was a man of average height who looked very fit. On hearing our approach, he stood up, hastily pulling on a casual shirt. My appraisal of him was correct; he was obviously very fit. Though approaching middle age, his muscles rippled with every movement under his light coffee coloured skin; he really looked as if he could handle himself.

"Señor Carson, this is my husband Miguel," Marguerite said in a husky voice as she moved some magazines from an easy chair to the table.

"May I call you Ben?" the man said, as he took my hand in the firmest handshake I'd ever felt. Studying him, I could see that his 5'5" frame packed a lot of power; there was an air of confidence about him which I identified as being the self-assurance that came to a man in the Special Forces. He, I decided, would be a good man to have beside you in a scrap; furthermore, he spoke excellent English, as did his wife.

"Of course, please do!" I replied. "I have heard a lot about you from Mal and I am very pleased to meet you at last."

"My love," Miguel said, turning to his wife, "I'm sure Ben could do with some refreshment after his journey. Would you organize some cold drinks for us please?"

Turning back to me, he added, "we will have them out here in the shade, I think it's a pity to waste such a beautiful spot, don't you agree Ben?" Indicating that I should sit in an easy chair in the shade of the tree, he resumed his seat by the pond and threw the last of the fish food in. Wiping his hands on a small cloth, he turned to me with a serious look on his face.

"OK. Ben, I'll come straight to the point. Two months or more ago, I had a letter from Mal in which he told me what happened to his daughter. It is a thing that we both feel very sad about. Mal also told me that you were coming this way and what you are going to attempt to achieve." Rubbing his chin with his hand, he studied me for a moment, then as if making up his mind, continued.

"Don't get me wrong! The horrible death of his daughter should not be allowed to go un-revenged Ben, but I have to admit I am worried," he said, with a sincere note of anxiety in his voice. "While I understand from Mal that you are a very capable man, I feel I *must* warn you that you are *not* facing a simple task. These people," he made an exasperated gesture with his hands, "they are *very* well protected. You will have to choose the time and place with great care in order to be able to withdraw after the hit!".......

"I appreciate your concern, Miguel," I voiced, holding up my hand to stop him. "Perhaps you should know that I operate what I refer to as the 'KISS' principle on any job." Seeing his puzzled look I hastened to explain.

"Sorry! Of course, you may not have heard that expression before. It's one I use that means, Keep It Safe and Simple!"

"Ah! I understand and I heartily agree!" Miguel said, taking my point with an amused chuckle. "Don't worry my friend, having been warned of the task you have set yourself and knowing you will need some help, I have taken the liberty of having already sent out a call to some good men. One of them comes from the city of Medellin where this *El Jefe* lives; his name is Ramon. They have all been Rangers and I would expect reports within a day or two."

My reply was interrupted by the return of Marguerite, who was accompanied by a beautiful dark haired girl of about 20 years of age carrying a tray of drinks. I couldn't take my eyes off her. Marguerite seeing my interest told me her name was Juanita.

"Ben, I hope you will accept our hospitality," she said with a smile at her husband. "We have a room you may use during your stay here".....

"Of course he will," Miguel cut in. "He can stay here as long as he wishes, both before and after completing his operation."

So it seems, I thought, that once again, everything is being taken care of. I took a long draw at my drink, then making up my mind I turned to my host and hostess.

"No matter what happens, even if you can't find the right sort of men, I shall have to rethink the idea and do it alone. My promise to Mal and Julie must be kept!" I said, knowing my feelings were exposed in my voice.

"We will not let you down," Miguel said, rising and placing his hand on my shoulder, "and my friend, I shall be going with you!" This unexpected statement made Marguerite gasp and fighting to hold back a tear, she turned to her husband.

"You are saying that for the memory of our son, aren't you?" she said, with a catch in her voice.

"Yes, I am," muttered Miguel, his lips trembling. In a flash of understanding, I knew that they too had suffered a loss the same way as Mal, Julie and I had. To cover my embarrassment, I asked to be shown my room as I needed to take a bath.

"Lo Siento!" exclaimed Marguerite. "I am sorry, I should have mentioned that earlier, please follow me, your bags are already in your room." I was about to follow Marguerite, when Miguel held up his hand.

"By the way, I forgot to tell you Ben. In our workshop, we have two very large and very heavy packing cases for you. They are labelled Mining Machinery and arrived from Miami ten days ago on a plane belonging to one of my many 'cousins'," he said with a grin.

"That's great! That must be the weapons and kit I ordered, but what about the Customs?" I asked anxiously.

"No problems!" replied Miguel with a laugh. "It's really surprising what a few hundred US dollars and a few more 'cousins' can do, isn't it!"

Shaking my head in disbelief, but feeling very relieved to hear the news, I followed Marguerite out of the room. As we walked down the cool passageway, I savoured the delicate perfume she was wearing, it seemed to be one of the most exotic ones I had ever smelt and was undoubtedly expensive. As she gracefully led the way up a wide, curving marble staircase, I took the opportunity to admire her lovely, well-kept figure.

"This is a very grand house," my remark, though sincere, was an attempt to stop my thoughts. Pausing a couple of steps above me, she turned to face me; the movement of her breasts under the sheer silk blouse did not help me in any way!

"What a splendid staircase!" I gulped, indicating its wide sweep and the view of the large crystal chandelier hanging above the hallway.

"Yes, it once belonged to a senior member of the Government. We bought it ten years ago when our Fishing and Cargo fleet started making good," Marguerite explained with obvious pride as she resumed the climb. "It was originally the home of Spanish Royalty many years ago." This information was nearly lost on me as once again, I became mesmerized by the movement of her firm buttocks.

A short distance down a deeply carpeted passageway, she showed me into a very spacious and comfortable room. Protected from the heat of the sun by internal shutters and delicate lace curtains, the cool air was stirred by a large fan revolving soundlessly in the ceiling. This gave the effect of a soft, gentle breeze that carried the sweet scent of Jasmine and Honeysuckle with it. Against the centre of the main wall stood the biggest bed that I had ever seen. I tested it carefully and was amazed to find that it was in fact a waterbed.

"Do you not like it?" my hostess asked, again with a gentle smile on her lips.

"I shall be lost in it I think!" My reply prompted another of her delightful chuckles. "I have never *seen* such a big bed, let alone had the chance to sleep in one!"

Marguerite opened a door on one side of the bed that led off the back of the room and said, "Well, perhaps you had better see the bathroom then, before you make any other judgments!" Stepping back to allow me to walk past her she murmured, "I will leave you to have fun and you can take your time, as I have arranged dinner for eight o'clock. Oh yes, if you put out any clothes you wish to have cleaned, Juanita will see to them while you bathe."

With that she was gone, leaving me in a bathroom almost the size of the bedroom. Occupying the place of honour in the centre; stood a huge Jacuzzi that large enough for a whole family. Against the right hand wall, a double size shower unit was enclosed in highly decorative glass screens. Beyond that was the largest and most ornate bath that I could imagine, it seemed to compete in size with the Jacuzzi.

"Talk about luxury," I said to myself as I turned the taps to fill the bath. There was something about the taps; they had an unusual feel about them. Placing my hands on them again, a tingle ran down my spine with the sudden realization that all of the bathroom fittings were gold plated.

Returning to the bedroom, I hurried to unpack while the water was running; leaving a pile of clothing for the maid to collect later I relaxed in the bath. The soothing warmth of the water soon made the spring like tension of my muscles unwind. I hadn't realized just how much the physical effort over the past few days had tightened them up.

The therapeutic effect of the water made me loose all track of time. Lying there, cocooned in the warmth, I reflected on how fortunate I was to have such good contacts who were helping me towards the successful conclusion of my task.

My movements across the world had been covered by the CIA, so there was no way that Jose and his gang could have any idea of my present location. Undoubtedly, I had been lucky so far and it seemed that with the help of Miguel and his friends that luck would continue.

On rising from the water, I stepped into the shower cabinet, turned the tap onto full at the cold setting. After one minute of the pin sharp, ice-cold spray, I got out and started to dry myself. With my skin tingling from the vigorous rubbing, I stood in front of the full-length mirror flexing my muscles, drawing myself up to my full 6 ft height.

Gazing back at me was a tall, well-muscled man with flashing blue eyes and a neatly trimmed beard that gave him a sort of 'Devil May Care' appearance. I was pleased to see, that apart from the usual small area where my swim trunks had been, I had gained a very reasonable tan in the days at sea, and had also worked off all the small areas of fat, leaving my body looking lean and hard with the muscles rippling under the brown skin. A light knocking on the open door startled me and the young serving maid walked in; how long she had been there I didn't know.

"Señor Carson," she said quite unabashed, her eyes roved all over my naked body. "I have taken your clothes to the laundry room and your clean clothes are on the bed."

"Th...thank you!" I stammered in surprise. She stood behind me, staring at my reflection in the full-length mirror, her wide brown eyes were now fixed firmly on my groin. It was then that I realized I had become aroused! Feeling embarrassed, I turned to grab a towel to wrap around me, then walked quickly into the bedroom where I took a $5 note from my trouser pocket and thrust it at her.

"Will this cover it?"

"Gracias Señor, but there is no need to cover it!" she quipped with a laugh as she went out.

"Phew!" I gasped. "Must be getting old when a young lady puts you into a panic like that!" Secretly amused, I started to dress. Wearing loose casual clothes I made my way down to the lounge just before eight o'clock for a pre-dinner drink.

In my estimation, the dinner was nothing short of splendid. We started with *Sancocho de Gallina* - a thick chicken and vegetable soup. The main course was a chicken and rice dish, which Marguerite told me was called *Arroz con Pollo,* which was in turn, complimented by a wonderful salad. This was the best meal I had tasted in a long time and it was also spiced up by the extra attention I was receiving from the pretty young maid.

"I feel Ben, that you have gained an admirer!" Marguerite said teasingly.

"So it seems," I replied. "I apologize if it embarrasses you!"

"There is no need to apologize, it just shows that Juanita has good taste!" she replied, letting me down gently.

"Come!" Miguel cut in. "Don't you think it's time we got down to some real serious thinking now." He rose from the table, took me by the arm and guided me to a comfortable seat on the terrace overlooking the courtyard. There was a cool scented evening breeze of the type that can only be experienced in hot climates. Somewhere in the background a Marimba Band was playing. Miguel lit a small cigarillo and offering me one, we settled down to drink the very sweet black, strong Colombian Coffee - or **tinto** to give it its proper name - as Miguel informed me. When Marguerite joined us a short while later, they asked me to outline my plan and to tell them what I knew about the Cartel leaders already.

"Well as you already know," I said. "It started with the tragic death of Sophie ...." Over the next half-hour, I gave them a quick outline of my actions to date. They listened without interruption, both of them remaining solemn while I told my story.

" .... so here I am with you, almost at the point where I can mount the actual attack!"

My closing words rang loud in my ears. Yes, I had come a long way since making my promise. When I had finished, Miguel rang the bell for the servant girl to bring us some *Aguardiente*; a popular local rum. Again, during the time she spent serving us, I noticed that she kept looking at me as often as she could. To the amusement of both Marguerite and Miguel, she gave me a long, lingering look over her shoulder as she left the room.

"My friend," Miguel said, bringing my wandering mind back to reality. "I have heard what you say and if you agree, I can start certain enquiries going tonight. I have a contact who lives in Bogotá, he will locate the family home of this Drug Baron for us."

Noting his use of the word us, I could only nod my head in agreement, while attempting to recover from too long a swig of my fiery drink. Miguel picked up a nearby phone, dialled a number and almost immediately was firing off a long stream of very rapid Spanish, the tone of which made me feel he was issuing instructions and not asking favours. Pausing now and again to listen, he completed his call and replaced the receiver.

"There!" he said dramatically. "It is done, we are in luck because my man knows of these people already. He will go out there tonight and find out what he can and will report to me tomorrow or the next day at the latest, he will also contact another of our men."

"Though we don't have a target as yet, I think we start the planning now," he added, as he spread a large detailed map of the region we would be going into onto the table.

"By the look of those contour lines, it looks as if it's going to be hard work," I said, scanning the lines that showed it to be mainly steep mountain sides, very nearly vertical in fact.

"Ah! But the factory will *not* be in the real mountains!" Marguerite interrupted, leaning her body close to mine as she studied the map. "There are no proper roads, so it will be in this area near the plains," she indicated an area with her long slim finger and I could feel the heat of her breast pressing against my arm.

"I agree, but it would not be too far from the production area which is here," Miguel added, circling a large part of the mountain region with a red marker pen.

No doubt about it, her show of knowledge and common sense was beginning to impress me. Gradually, even though we really had insufficient facts, we established a complete plan of action along with a list of equipment required and against which we compared what kit and weapons were in the packing cases.

"There is a problem that you will not have anticipated though Ben," Miguel announced, as he pointed to the marshy land between Panama and the Colombian border. "Because of check points at the border, I'm afraid a crossing of the Darien Gap is out of the question for us. We can't even go overland as it is completely swampy with no discreet road transport at all, so you have to rely on the Indians with their boats. A crossing that way would take up to two weeks according to the state of the rivers. Besides," he added with an eloquent shrug. "I feel we *must* go by air!" he stated firmly. "I can arrange the use of two aircraft, one for us and one for the stores." Pausing to ensure that I agreed, he emptied his glass before continuing. "The only way we can do this is to land at night, on a private landing strip belonging to a friend, which is near the marshy area not far from the border. We can be met there by the other ex Rangers, who would have a truck available for all the stores."

Taking advantage of a short pause, Marguerite passed the bottle of *Aguardiente* around and we each lit another cigarillo. Between sips of our drinks and puffs on the cigars, it was generally agreed that after loading the truck, we should make our way across the Pan American Highway, which runs between the sea and the mountains. We would have to find a quiet place to ford the wide, and possibly deep Atrato River and go to a 'Safe House' in the small town called Quibdo.

"Where's this Quibdo place?" I asked Miguel.

"It is just about eighty miles from Manizales and on the second of the mountain ranges we have to cross," he said, jabbing his finger at an area of the map, which according to the contour lines, seemed to be all cliffs. "We rest there for a day, during which time the weapons would be made ready. Then moving only at night, we go by truck up into the mountains picking up a local guide for the final part of the trek." Pausing, his face split into a big grin as he added for my benefit. "Which is all on foot and the mountains are hard!"

"Well that's about it then!" I exclaimed. It seemed we had covered everything and everyone was happy. "From what I have seen here tonight Miguel, I am sure that it would have been impossible for me to have made it across those mountains alone. I'm damned glad that Mal has you as a friend.

"Ha! Yes," he responded. "And now *you* have me for a friend!" Laughing, we refilled our glasses and toasted the success of the mission, then sat talking well into the early hours of the morning. It was Marguerite who called the time to our attention.

"Hey hombres, you have four hours until breakfast!" Tired, but happy with progress so far, I wished them a good night and went to my room. On opening the door, I noticed a faint hint of a musky perfume that I could not identify. Too sleepy to worry about it, I lay on the bed without undressing and immediately fell into a deep sleep.

I slept soundly, blissfully unaware that Miguel's friends whom I had yet to meet were either setting out, or were already at work in two different locations on my behalf. It would not have surprised me though, because such cooperation even on a worldwide scale is typical of the type of people I now found myself working with.

Code Name SNOWBIRD

Chapter 13
<u>Bogotá, Capital City of Colombia.</u>

<u>The town house of El Jefe</u>

At about the same time as I was going to sleep, a man dressed all in black from head to toe stood in the darkest shadows opposite a grand mansion in the Candelaria Quarter of Bogotá. His almost invisible silhouette was only broken by the outline of the black satchel strapped to his back.

Acting on the telephoned instructions from his old friend Miguel, his intention was to find a way of gaining entry to the large house opposite. Although he knew this to be the town house of the much-feared Cartel Leader known as *El Jefe*, he had no fear of making entry. Confident in his own abilities as an active and very skilled burglar not to be caught, he knew that, as is the case with all rich people; they always have a country home to which they go to escape the summer heat. At this time of year, the owner would use the town house for business visits only. On gaining entry, part of this man's task was to seek evidence of the owner's involvement in the drug trade and the many murders connected to it.

This Spanish Colonial style mansion stood aloof in a large garden, that the watcher was pleased to note, boasted a great number of mature trees, their heavy foliage creating many convenient shadowy areas. Situated facing onto one of the narrow streets that made up the Barrio de Los Principes - the Princes' District -

where between 1550 and 1810 the Spanish Nobility had lived, this property was of singular grandeur.

During an earlier casual daylight inspection using his excellent eye for detail, the man had noted among other things; that the elaborate double wrought iron gates - so common in this neighbourhood - still held the intricate heraldic design that marked the property as being the home of one of the ruling class. This meant little to him at the moment; he was more concerned with establishing if any one was home. During the last two hours or so, he had remained motionless as he watched from his hiding place for signs of occupation. Now that he was completely satisfied that nobody was in residence and that no guards patrolled - or guard dogs wandered around loose, he prepared to move.

Moving as silently as a cat from shadow to shadow, pausing to listen and observe now and then, he worked his way along the road until he was opposite a pre-selected spot at the corner of the external wall, just where it turned to go up the side of the property. Suddenly, his internal 'alarm bells' began to ring as his acute hearing alerted him to a faint noise in the distance. He froze! In a flash, his brain searched his memory banks for stored identification of this noise. In a micro-second, it had clearly identified the sound and flashed the warning. Danger!

It was the unmistakable sound of an approaching Jeep in low gear that echoed up the road. That could mean only one thing! The Police were checking on the area and he had no wish to tangle with them, as they would shoot without question or warning. Caught as he was with nowhere to hide, not even a low bush, his heart rate quickened as he tried to estimate how much time he had. Caught in the open, with little choice, he decided that he had just enough time to make one swift dash across the intervening space of the unlit road. Experience in these things had shown him that if he moved parallel with the sweep of the headlights as the vehicle swept round the distant corner, he *should* remain unseen. Dressed all in black and masked by a dark night, he would rely on the occupants of the vehicle doing the natural thing and letting their eyes follow the beam of the headlights. His decision made, he drew breath at the same moment the approaching vehicle's headlights swept slowly around the far corner and ran.

Reaching the other side without pausing and in one fluid motion that belied his 37 years; he launched himself up into the air, grasping the top of the wall. With one quick movement, he pulled the rest of his body up and over, while reversing but retaining his hold, he hung on the other side in order to see what his landing would be. Content that he would not raise the alarm by crashing through the roof of a glasshouse, he dropped silently to the ground. He stayed motionless, then his stomach did a flip as dark shadows suddenly dashed across the open space of the lawn toward him and his heart missed a beat! They sped past him and with a sigh of relief, he realized the shadows were those of the trees, moving as the beam from a searchlight swept the wall and crossed the main gate!

He waited with eyes screwed tight for the beam of light to pass before crouching low and moving slowly forward, while looking for any indication of trip wires, heat sensors or any other such security measures. He found none, which on reflection caused him to wonder why. But of course! The owner of this property was a Drug Baron well known in the area as an utterly ruthless person. Only a *fool* would want to break into this property!

"That's what you are, Manuel Gonzales. A fool!" the man said to himself!

"Besides," he reasoned, "when the house was in use he would have all of his usual hard men around him, so it stands to reason that the only security system there was would be on the house itself!"

Crossing the grass to avoid making noise on the gravel drive and footpaths, he worked his way around to the rear of the main building. In his quite considerable experience - he had become a very successful burglar since leaving the Services - he had found that it was usual for all ground floor doors and windows to be alarmed, while the upper floor windows would not be. The reason being, unless you had air-conditioning going all night and were fearful of intruders also, you would catch the cool night breeze by leaving upstairs windows open in the summer! In the case of this property it was safe to bet that during any periods it was occupied, guards would be on patrol all night, possibly dogs as well, so the upper windows could safely be left open.

Si, this would do nicely, he thought, when he found a vertical sewage pipe, which conveniently branched off to run almost horizontal where it serviced two or more bathrooms at the level of the upper floor.

Above his head, he could see what appeared to be a wide, double window of a bathroom, next to which was a smaller single window, presumably for the toilet. This pattern was repeated again within a few feet so he was spoilt for choice. Now all he needed was a window that could easily be opened!

Taking a quick look around to make sure no one was about, he donned a pair of thin gloves, then grasping the pipe firmly at head height and leaning back at an angle he started to walk up the wall in a well-practised manner. All he was worried about now was that no one should come looking, because his dark clothing stood out against the pale colour of the wall. Reaching the first floor level, he transferred his grip from the main pipe to a smaller waste water pipe and using all his energy he swung himself up until he could stand on the horizontal section. Moving carefully, with good footing but little handholds, he worked his way along, testing the windows as he came to them. He was despairing that he was going to be out of luck when he found the first two secure and pressing himself hard against the building he inched his way along to the last one. Luck was on his side; there was a small gap in the top fanlight.

"Madre de Dios! Thank you for short members of staff who cannot reach high windows!" he jokingly said to himself.

Reaching up and carefully easing the window open, he took a grip of the frame and swung himself lithely up onto the sill. Then with head and shoulder inside, he reached down and unlatched the larger window in front of him. Pausing only to extract a pencil torch from his clothing and careful not to knock anything over, he stepped inside. A quick, guarded flash of the light showed him the layout and avoiding the many colourful jars of bath salts and shampoo's, he stepped down onto the bidet, then to the floor and reached up to pull both the windows closed behind him.

Crossing the room, he paused to listen with his ear to the door, then turned the handle slowly and opened it. Silently, he lowered himself to floor level and inched his head forward until he could see both ways down the corridor. All was still and in darkness and he noted the place even had a 'closed up' smell, so with a bit of luck he may get on with the job in hand undisturbed.

Making good use of the thick heavy carpets in this corridor and safe in the knowledge that in common with all the 'big houses,' the marble flooring throughout such a place would mean no creaking floorboards to give him away, he moved towards the staircase.

Ever cautious, he paused at each bedroom door long enough to listen for any night sounds as he made his way to the head of the central staircase. Here he stopped and with the help of what moonlight there was, inspected the layout of the hallway below. He could see the darker shapes of the doors to various rooms and the solid black recess of a passageway to the rear of the ground floor. Making his way cautiously down while listening all the time, he could hear nothing but the muffled ticking of a large clock that seemed to echo the beat of his heart!

Reaching the ground floor and immediately making his way to the door to the right of the main door, he tried the ornate handle; turning it until it was free. He inched the heavy door open enough to see inside what appeared from the easy furniture to be a lounge. Wrong room! Next he tried the door adjoining that. Dining room! Pausing to consider this, he thought that if function rooms were this side of the house, then personal rooms such as studies would be on the other!

He turned to cross the hall just as a brilliant beam of light caught him. He immediately froze and his heart leaped into his mouth! With a pounding in his ears that seemed to deafen him to all other sounds, he stood stock still awaiting the inevitable challenge.

Nothing!

The light slowly moved away and he drew a huge sigh of relief as he realized it was the searchlight on the Police vehicle shining through the glass panel by the front door as they checked the front of the house from the road.

"Had they seen me, were they suspicious?" he thought. "No, if they had seen me they would have been in here searching by now! All they were doing was earning the undoubted bribe they were paid."

The light moved on. Remaining immobile, he spent a few moments trying to stabilize his heart rate. Satisfied that he could hear normally again, he moved purposefully towards the door of the room facing the front lawn. Trying the door he found it locked.

"Bingo!" he exclaimed silently, reverting to the use of an American expression learnt in the Marines and Rangers. "This has to be the big man's private den, otherwise why lock it?"

🕊 Code Name SNOWBIRD 🕊

With his gloved right hand, he made a careful inspection with sensitive fingers of the door surround to find any internal security device. Discovering no obvious evidence of such, he next made a minute inspection of the door edges with the aid of his penlight. Finding no 'tell tales' that would alert the owner to an illegal entry having been made; he turned his intention to the lock itself. Again using his light, he looked inside the keyhole for any hidden electrical contacts that would trigger alarms.

"Caramba!" There! On the opening on the inside of the lock was a metal ring shaped to take the end of a key. This in turn was backed by what looked like a plastic insulating ring. Attached to the inside of the metal ring he could just see a small electric wire. Having made this discovery he now paused to think it out. Then, with the aid of his light and a small slim tool like a long plastic nail file, he returned to investigate the leading edge of the door itself again. Gently, oh so gently he slid the 'file' down the gap ensuring that all pressure was on the door frame side.

"Aha! There it was. Just as I thought," he mused. "The crafty fox has installed a fail safe that would shoot bolts into the frame work if the wrong key was tried."

Undeterred by this discovery, he checked the lower part of the framework to confirm his thoughts.

"Well, well! It seems he has not heard of Manuel Gonzales who can open **any** door, **anywhere!**" he silently boasted. Then in afterthought he added, "but I don't think I will leave my visiting card!"

He stole a quick look at his watch, after all that had happened since he had first come over the wall; he was amazed to see that only thirty minutes had elapsed. Taking a small wallet from his pocket, he selected the slim picklock he required purely by the feel of it - a skill he had gained over years of experience. Before inserting the picklock, he crossed himself and muttered a short prayer. Shining his penlight into the narrow lock aperture, he carefully fed the tool into the small space he could see. Resting his hand against the timber of the door to steady it, he gradually turned it until the patterned end was by the wards of the lock mechanism. Using careful and precise movements he gradually increased the twisting pressure, until he felt the well-serviced lock softly click into the open position.

Wiping sweat from his eyes, he stood up and slowly turned the handle of the door. Holding his breath, he gradually inched it open at the same time he ran his eyes around the edges to make sure there were no other surprises in store for him.

Leaving the door open just enough for him to pass through, while avoiding stepping on the small mat inside in case it had a pressure alarm under it, he found himself in total darkness. A quick inspection with his torch showed that the windows were sealed by solid internal shutters, which were in turn held closed by metal bars.

"Ha!" he thought. He's put in such heavy security that he *must* have something to hide behind all this!

By the light of his torch, he made his way across the marble floor avoiding treading on the numerous scatter rugs that lay around, as these were regarded as uncharted territory. Approaching the huge desk in the centre of the room, he inspected the small reading lamp on it. Pulling his hood far enough over his head to hide his face from any camera activated by the lamp he switched it on, confident enough that the shutters would not leak any light outside. While keeping one eye closed to retain his night vision, he took a quick look around the room. One wall was covered in a gigantic glass fronted bookcase and as it backed onto the wall of the hall he discounted it in his search for a safe or hidden doorway to a strong room. The other walls also appeared to be party walls to other rooms.

"So that only leaves the floor!" he said to himself, as he switched the lamp off. Going down on hands and knees, he shone his torch across the uncovered parts of the floor, nothing! Carefully, he lifted the edges of each of the scatter rugs. Again, nothing! Seeing no sign of a trap door or anything unusual anywhere, he decided to inspect the desk itself in case that gave any information. With a soft, almost caressing touch he ran his fingers around all the edges and ledges. Nothing! Getting anxious now, he ducked his head into the leg recess and shone his light around.

"Bingo!" There, above his head, right within reach of the person sat at the desk, was a bell push.

"Alarm bell to summon his guards," he muttered quietly. "Wait! What's that then?" Right beside the alarm bell, nestling in a neatly hidden recess in the thick wood, he could see a small switch. Closer inspection revealed no connecting wires leading from it, but he noticed the desk was firmly fixed to the floor by discreet brackets and so was the swivel chair! Curious now, he decided to inspect the floor around the desk, but he could see no reason for it to be fixed to the floor. He was about to give up when he noticed that there was a microscopic line like a fine scratch in the marble. A long straight scratch in otherwise unblemished marble! This aroused his curiosity even more, so he followed it and was amazed when it made a complete right-angled turn that maintained an equal distance from the desk. Realization dawned! He was looking at a separate section of the marble floor. But why was it there? Puzzled by his findings, he frantically sought the answer. A desk and chair fixed to a separate section of a fine Italian marble floor, not your everyday discovery, so it had to have been done for a purpose. The answer lay in the switch, he was sure of that.

"I think I will sit in the chair and operate this," he decided. Rising from his crouched position, he sat on the big leather swivel chair and with heart in his mouth flipped the switch.

The ground literally opened up beneath him! With a soft click and the quiet hum of well oiled machinery, the section of floor with the desk and chair on sank steadily into the depths of the earth! The sudden and total blackness almost made him panic, but common sense and training told him to stay still while the movement continued! A light suddenly came on and the motion slowed, then it stopped with hardly a jolt.

"That light had to have been automatically triggered by the floor's descent," he reasoned. Gingerly stepping off the section of the floor to look around, he found himself in an underground room about five metres square, in the centre of which was the desk and chair he'd travelled down with. The walls were lined with shelves and numerous small locked cupboards, which reminded him of Bank Deposit boxes.

"Madre de Dios," he said aloud, forgetting himself. "This is amazing! The chair and desk are on a section of the floor, which is in fact a lift operated by a huge hydraulic ram underneath it! I am inside the best Safe I have ever seen!" He crossed himself several times.

"What's more, El Jefe doesn't need two desks to work at; he brings one down here with him! What workmanship!" he added, full of genuine admiration for the Craftsmen who had made all this possible. Yet he knew in his heart, that whoever they were, they would not have gone home to enjoy their pay for this job. No! They would not have been allowed to boast of *this* secret. He crossed himself, then gathering his thoughts, he walked over to what looked like a writing bureau set into the shelving system. Rolling the lid back, he rifled through the papers he found, carefully leaving them in the same order and position. He soon found some lists of names with sums of money marked beside them. There were also separate lists with dates, times and the names of some small towns he knew of including Chiquinquira, Zipiquira, Puerto Berrio, Simitiand and Gamarca.

"Just what Miguel will want," he mused, taking a small compact camera from his jacket pocket. With great care to get the right focus, he took several shots of each piece of paper. He did the same with an invoice for aviation fuel; that clearly showed an aircraft was being fuelled very regularly in the region of the town of Chiquinquira. Several other piles of paper revealed nothing of interest and then behind a pile of books he found a small black ledger containing more invoices. These made continual reference to a place called La Hacienda Los Palmos, which, from the telephone number and postal district on the invoice, was in the area of the town of Amalfi. While he had never been there, he knew Amalfi was a favoured mountain retreat for the well-to-do and it lay a few miles N.N. east of Medellin. That then, could be the place he was seeking and again he took snaps of each invoice. A further search revealed nothing else of interest.

"Under different circumstances those locked boxes would be open by now," he thought to himself as he prepared to leave.

Well aware of the need to conceal the fact that he had been in the house, let alone down in this room, he resisted the temptation to steal anything. Removing the black satchel from his back, he rummaged inside it and then hid it behind a pile of sealed boxes in a corner, where no one would readily find it. Seating himself on the leather chair, he pressed the switch. A few seconds later a motor purred, the lift section rose and the light went out!

"Magic!" His admiration was genuine, as he found himself once again seated at the desk in the shuttered study. "Time to make my exit I think"

With that, he checked that nothing was disturbed and switched off the light before leaving the room. Carefully locking up behind him and leaving no sign of entry, he left the house the way he had come in. Agilely using the stack pipe again and leaving the bathroom window as it was before, he made his escape across the lawn and climbed to the top of the wall. Laying flat for several minutes, he waited to ensure that all was quiet; looking for signs of watchers before slipping silently to the ground. He departed as he had come, a shadow in the total darkness, a creature of the night.

Chapter 14

<u>Hacienda Los Palmos, Amalfi.</u>

<u>The country house of El Jefe</u>

That same morning, any casual observer would have noticed about a dozen cars parked in a semi circle around the spacious courtyard of the two-storied house which boasted the name of *'La Hacienda Los Palmos.'* This handsome building, standing secure within a walled courtyard, was a prime example of the Spanish Hacienda style. With many balconies and ornate pillars; boasting well-established vines and unobtrusively placed hanging baskets that were in themselves, a riot of glorious colour.

Well sited and shaded from the heat of the sun by many tall, flourishing palm trees, it had at least twenty rooms and was surrounded by well-maintained lawns and formal gardens. It also boasted an Olympic size swimming pool and two tennis courts, while standing away to one side of the main building, there was a large stable block and an equally large stock yard for the cattle that grazed in the lush valley beyond. The Hacienda's own fleet of four limousines and two off road vehicles - necessary because of the distance from town and the rough terrain - were housed in a spacious old building at the rear. The whole picture was of a cool, comfortable, but very expensive family home of which the owner could be justifiably proud.

On this occasion, any observer could not fail to notice that the splendid picture created by the devoted

hands of the gardeners and other staff was enhanced by the strategic placing of groups of gaily coloured party balloons and bunting all around the place. These colourful additions to the scene served to signify that there was a birthday party going on. Proof of this was printed in contrasting colours on the balloons and streamers where the words
Happy Birthday Maria could easily be seen.

    The task of inflating these balloons and creating the decorative clusters had been that of a young man in the employ of their manufacturer. His name was Rico whose father Felipe, was the balloon manufacturer and who in turn acted on the request of his good friend Miguel. The young Rico understood that the report he would take home with him, plus the result of some of his 'extra' duties this day, would be used to harden the plan of action being formed by someone named Ben, an English friend of Miguel's.

    This place was the country home of the man known as El Jefe, his guests whose cars were lined up and waiting were all senior members of the Cartel run by him. They, along with their ladies and children, were being entertained to a party piece by the youngest daughter of the house. Just seven today, Maria Cordoba was the apple of her father's eyes. Dressed in a pretty pink party frock, with frills and bows to match in her abundant dark curly hair, along with her sparkling smile made a pretty picture as she recited the latest poem she had learnt in a loud, clear and confident voice.

    She had invited some of her friends from the exclusive residential school they all attended in Bogotá.

In turn, they had all been tasked with entertaining the adults with recitals, mime and song. This they had done in splendid form and now the grand finale being presented by Maria herself; would signify the breaking up of the party into groups. The children would go off to play or ride some of the numerous ponies, while the ladies would inspect the gardens and grounds, play tennis or take a swim.

More important to young Rico however, was the grouping of the men with El Jefe. For they, he had overheard, were to hold a very important meeting about the movement of the biggest load of cocaine to date that was currently being prepared for distribution.

Rico as a legitimate employee of his father's firm had been to several of the other big houses in the area from time to time. He was popular with the children and known to the adults, so his presence would not be remarked upon. On this occasion though, he had some other more special duties to perform - not for the customer however. These little 'extras' had been detailed him by his father and were by far the most dangerous of tasks. He was to find a way to plant a couple of electronic devices in El Jefe's study and two more in the smoking room where it seemed the meeting would be held.

Arriving at the house deliberately early in order to take advantage of the fact that El Jefe would not rise until gone 10 am and his ever present bodyguard would be stationed near to him, Rico hoped this would mean the two rooms he was interested in would not be attended until later. As it was to be a special day, the servants would have too much on their minds to worry about him

- all that is with the exception of one beautiful young maid with whom he was very friendly and flirted with outrageously - they had been lovers for some time now. Her name was Juanita Arroyo and she had been recruited from a local village where the majority of El Jefe's 'workers' came from. Part of her duties was to clean and tidy her master's study and the room where the men would sit and smoke. She did not demur when Rico offered to do a bit of dusting in the high places she could not reach while he waited.

    Accordingly and unnoticed by her, he had, within a short while, skilfully placed all his electronic bugs. Now all he had to do was to wait until the party was over, collect the tools of his trade and leave, but not before activating the devices by remote control.

    All day he was kept busy, inflating and setting up the groups of balloons and he was also able to 'volunteer' to help the maid collect some bottles of wine from the wine cellar deep under the house, stealing a long lingering kiss for his trouble. She was too busy to notice that on one trip, he brought down with him a bulky satchel similar to the one he carried his balloons and tools in, but did not bring it out again.

    When the children's party started at 3 pm, he started to do the rounds checking that no balloons were going down and he also had to keep a steady supply ready for the children to play their various games with. Finally, with the heat and excitement nearly over - for the youngsters at least - he was, at last, able to slip into the kitchen and ask his young girlfriend if he could have a cold drink.

🕊 Code Name SNOWBIRD 🕊

"Yes you can, but you will have to wait until I have served Señor Cordoba and his guests," she said, quite firmly.

Nodding his agreement, he squeezed her bottom and slipped out of the door as she laughingly told him to stop it. He sat outside for a few minutes and followed her as she took her tray loaded with jugs of cold fruit drink and glasses across the patio to the French window leading into the smoking room.

"That's where they meet then!" he said to himself, as he went to his toolbox and withdrew a spanner for the Compressed Air Cylinder standing beside it. Pretending to be busily engaged in pressurizing some more balloons, he had in fact placed himself ready to observe the start of the meeting. He did not have long to wait; the men strolled in, in groups of two or three. When El Jefe himself arrived, one of his bodyguards roughly told Rico to move away, then along with his companion, positioned himself outside the closed door.

Rico obediently gathered his kit and moved off, at the same time, his fingers located and pressed a small button hidden in a recess under the bottom of the toolbox. This sent a signal activating the power supply to the first recording device in the room. Small but powerful, each of them could identify and record all voices within 30 feet of its location

With a keen interest and skill in electronics, he had developed and constructed these miniature bugs himself some time previously. Powered by lithium batteries, the actual recording mechanism was activated by sound. Linked in pairs, they would lie dormant during times of silence; on sensing voices the primary one of each pair would quietly activate itself and eavesdrop on all the conversations in the room.

Constantly monitoring its own battery state, if after four hours it was low, it would automatically send a signal to its duplicate to switch on. Between them they could record any and all conversation in that room for several hours. Utilizing the latest in computer technology, all the information would be stored in a microchip no bigger than a man's thumbnail. Then, responding to an external remote command they would transmit their stored knowledge in a split second burst of sound, which would be recorded by another device he'd already concealed in the hills over looking the house.

Finally, when all information had been gathered, that receiver would wait to receive the remote command to switch to transmit and in a similar fashion, send its information in a high powered burst of energy to a receiver in an airplane as it passed overhead. On board that plane would be his father's friend, Miguel and the mysterious Señor Carson.

With his mission complete and the party now over, Rico gathered his belongings and equipment and sought out the young maid to say farewell in the way that any twenty three year old man would want to do.

Chapter 15

<u>Panama City to Colombia.</u>

<u>First sight of the Target.</u>

The following morning, Miguel arrived in my room with a pot of coffee and two cups as the pretext for waking me. Tired though I was I could see he was in an agitated state.

"G'mornin!" I mumbled sleepily. "What's biting you? You look like the cat that got the cream!"

"Eh? What?" he replied - the English saying was lost on him.

"I said, what is exciting you so early this morning?" I repeated, taking the tray from him before he dropped it all over me. An unwise move as it turned out because forgetting that it was a waterbed, he plonked himself heavily down on the side of it, causing me to immediately bob up and down like a cork in a storm while trying to do a balancing act with the tray at the same time.

"I have had a phone call from my man in Bogotá," Miguel stated, seemingly unaware of the mini tidal wave he'd created.

"Hang on a minute will you!" I said in desperation. He paused to let our violent bobbing motions subside and then continued as I gingerly placed the tray on the bedside table.

"Manuel, that's the man I told you about," he explained, waving his hands excitedly, "was given the task of gaining entry to El Jefe's town house. The building was empty, so he's been inside!" He paused to wipe spittle from his lips. "He's been into his Safe!" Miguel was so excited now he could hardly speak properly. I poured a cup of coffee and gave it to him; he gulped it down in one quick movement.

"Well? I said. "What did he find?"

"Find?" Miguel gasped. "He found papers with names, dates and places on!" Having cleared this off his chest, he subsided into silence. Taking the now empty cup from him, I encouraged him to continue as I poured my own coffee.

"That's great news, but what has he done with them, he didn't remove them I hope?" My fear of discovery before we started was real.

"Took photo's of those that mattered and replaced them all so that nobody will suspect they have been tampered with!" This last statement came out in a calmer manner as his excitement cooled. I slipped off the bed, removed my crumpled outer clothes and went to the bathroom for a shower and to tidy up my beard. Miguel followed me asking what we should do now.

"Well that's great news; these papers may help us identify the target. Can we get copies of the film very quickly?" I asked above the sound of the water.

"They are being brought here as soon as possible and should be with us by tomorrow!" His shouted reply echoed around the room. "I will see you when you come down." I heard him say as he went out.

Now fully awake, I could feel the excitement and tension building up in me as I trimmed my beard.

Obtaining such vital information so soon was totally unexpected, it meant that at last we would have some good firm evidence to use. Even though I knew it was no good making plans until we saw the films, my mind repeatedly went over the new options that we now had. Humming to myself, I dressed and went down for breakfast.

There was a tangible note of excitement in Miguel's voice when I joined him on the patio. Typical of the Latin persona, I could see he was having great difficulty in containing his feelings.

"OK! OK!" I said throwing my hands in the air in mock desperation. "What's got into you *now*?"

"Ben, my friend!" he declared, clapping me on the shoulder. "It is wonderful; everything is now working out better than we could ever hope for!" He was nearly dancing with excitement so I realized he had something else to tell me.

"Right then! Why don't you sit down, have another cup of coffee - I indicated the waiting coffee pot - or a stronger drink and tell me all about it?" I chided, in as humorous a way that I could.

"Yes that's what I will do my friend, good idea!" Miguel said, sitting down at the table opposite me and starting to pour coffee for us both. I waited patiently in silence for him to finish but it was too much for me when, as if he'd forgotten his important news, he proceeded to drink his!

"Are you going to *tell me* or are you going to keep me *guessing* all day!" I almost shouted. A look of surprise crossed his face quickly followed by one of sudden comprehension.

"Oh. Si! I'm sorry! The news from Rico is so good that it has put my mind out of gear!" he said, placing his cup on the table and picking up the coffee pot again. This was too much for me; already short on sleep, I was getting very dangerously close to being short on temper also.

"Rico? *Who the hell is Rico*?" I said in a fierce whisper.

Looking around as if to ensure no one else could hear; he leaned forward across the table before saying in a rush, "Rico is the son of Felipe, who is one of my men and he has entered the house of El Jefe. I have just received confirmation from him that his operation had gone well also and the bugs were in place and ready."... I banged the table with my hand to stop him.

"*Miguel*, please forgive me for any rudeness to you in your house, *but... you... are... making... No... Bloody... Sense!*" I enunciated slowly to ensure he understood me.

"Si Ben. You're right of course, I'm not making sense to myself either," he added apologetically. "Let me explain it to you as I should have done earlier."

We were interrupted by the maid, who placed plates of food in front of us. I felt her hand rub across my shoulder as she leaned around me and when I looked at her she gave me the sweetest smile. I watched her walking away across the courtyard and realised that Miguel was talking to me again.

"...... told you last night, they have been told to do certain tasks for me, on your behalf of course!" He hurriedly corrected himself. "We have already spoken of Manuel who entered El Jefe's house in Bogotá, now I am pleased to say that Rico has been able to plant electronic bugs in the house of El Jefe also!" He stopped and looked at me obviously waiting for me to comment.

"*Hey!* You've lost me again pal!" I said, patting his arm. "Are you telling me that they have both been into the *same* house?"

"No Ben!" Miguel said, as if talking to a young child. "Manuel entered the town house of El Jefe, which was empty! Rico was working at a children's party in the *country* house of El Jefe! *That* is where he planted the bugs!" His voice made it sound as if I should have known that all along.

"But," he added, in a worried tone, "Rico thinks we should perhaps move our plans forward a few days. He has heard a rumour that the Cartel is moving a big shipment in the next week or two!"

"Hey, that's great!" My eager response was sincere. "Just the sort of information we need, but will I be able to debrief these two guys myself, or do we have to rely on their reports only?"

"They will be joining us soon and will tell you everything you wish to know, now let's eat before the food spoils," Miguel stated wisely.

After the meal we went into the lounge where he had the big map still laid out on the table. He showed me the locations of the two houses in question; the country one didn't seem to be too far away from our suspected target area.

When he had completed his explanation, I put a bundle of money in front of him and said, "please give these two guys two thousand dollars each, they have done well and should be rewarded for their work. But I feel they should get out of their locality as soon as possible"......

"Have no fear," interrupted Miguel. "I shall give them the money willingly, but they are both coming to meet us as I said, so you could give them their reward yourself hey? He paused in thought. "Oh yes! They both want to be involved in any of the future action with us!"

"Now we have to start getting ready ourselves, because as you heard, the bugs are in place and we should be ready to move. The Cartel had their meeting and the drugs will be ready to go in a short while, so there is no time to waste!" He held out his hand and grasped mine in a fierce grip.

"*At last* Ben, thanks to *you* we have a chance to rid our countries of slime such as these. They are the biggest Cartel and he, this El Jefe, is the most powerful Drug Baron. I think it's time we went flying my friend!"

I pocketed the money again, while he collected the map, at the same time explaining that in view of the changes to the timings, he had taken the liberty to give instructions for the crates containing the weapons to be brought up to his workshop where we could prepare them.

"We should fly out to my friends old place in Riosucio so we can prepare it for the arrival of our 'soldiers', don't you think?" he asked anxiously.

"Yes of course, it is best that we get things moving as quickly as possible. But we will have plenty to do here as well," I added.

He was in agreement that we should not waste time and showed me the details of a flight plan - which I noted only covered a flight over Panamanian territory. Miguel then led me out of the back of the house to where Marguerite, dressed in jeans and a loose blouse, was waiting behind the wheel of a 4x4 vehicle.

Seeing our expressions she remarked, "Hey, I hope you two are not on drugs yourselves! You look pretty high to me." Fixing a bandanna to keep her hair from her eyes as we jumped into the vehicle, she then drove us off at speed. A fast journey of twenty minutes took us out of San Miguelito to speed along a good main road dodging the many heavy lorries and buses. Soon she turned off onto a smaller, less busy road sign posted to Pedregal. This road initially took us through several small clusters of houses and factories, before eventually running out into the countryside.

Half an hour later we pulled into what appeared to be a farm and without hesitation, Marguerite drove the vehicle across a dry, dusty field to a very large barn. She stopped the vehicle in a cloud of dust that drifted over us. A man appeared from a smaller building and waved as he went over and started to pull the barn doors open. As I beat the dust off my clothing I watched the doors move apart and was surprised to see that the barn was in fact a fully equipped hangar, with workbenches and machinery all around the walls. To my utter amazement, in the middle of all this stood two planes.

Miguel waved a hand casually towards them and proudly said, "These are the beginning of my air fleet; they are used for carrying passengers for the big businesses in this area."

Pointing to the newer one, which sported twin engines and a twin tail boom, he added, "This, my friend, is a Twin Beechcraft and is our transport to the Bogotá region." He lovingly patted the cowling of one of the engines as he continued. "She has been fitted with twin Turbine engines that will give us a cruising range more than we need to get to our target and back to our refuel point. She will carry up to seven passengers or a good cargo weight".

He carried out a pre-flight inspection as he spoke, walking around the airplane checking that every panel was clipped securely and the dust covers were removed from delicate instrument heads. It was obvious that he too was a Pilot. Showing me to the wide door on the left hand side of the plane, he indicated for me to climb aboard.

On entering, I saw that the seating was the comfortable Executive style, with small tables fitted to the floor between the seats and were of a type that could be removed or redesigned according to requirements. Both of the front seats each had a lightweight headset on which the passenger could talk to the pilot. Miguel demonstrated how to operate the rear toilet compartment and showed me the cargo nets in the adjacent baggage hold.

Moving to the front of the cabin, he explained the operation of the high-powered radio receiver that had been mounted on a table against the front bulkhead. Finally, he pointed out the repeater display, on which passengers could see the airspeed, altimeter and compass bearings in digital form. To my surprise, the plane started to move as it was towed out into the open as we were talking. No sooner had it come to a stop, than it started to vibrate with the noise of one of the engines starting up. Looking past Miguel into the cockpit, I saw that Marguerite was sat in the left hand Pilot's seat.

"Don't worry, she has a licence and is very good!" Miguel laughed seeing my look of surprise. With that remark he slapped me on the shoulder and told me to strap in, then went into the cockpit and sat in the co-pilot's seat. When both engines had been run up and she was satisfied they were operating properly, Marguerite gave a signal to the mechanic – the man who had opened the barn for us - to remove the wheel chocks. Taxiing for a short distance we came to a halt while the engines were wound up to full power. I could see the hands of both Miguel and Marguerite on the throttle levers as they boosted the power; a final check of the dials and the plane shot forward as the brakes were released.

With a quiet confidence that showed many years of experience, Marguerite handled the take-off smoothly, lifting the plane into the sky with practiced ease. Over the intercom she pointed out several large passenger aircraft circling in the distance.

"Getting ready to land at Tocumen, the main Panama City Airport," she advised. Then giving attention to her duties, she gave instruction to Miguel to retract the undercarriage and in rapid Spanish; she cleared the pre-planned flight with the local Air Traffic Control and settled the airplane on its main course.

We flew back over Panama City and out over the locks on the Canal, before turning towards the sea. From my window I had a panoramic view of the port area, with ships at the dockside and several of ocean-going size lying off at anchor. To my relief, I couldn't see the ship I had suffered on. Then, as if it were a finger pointing the way, we followed the long straight arm of the sea wall that runs out on the left hand side of the harbour approach.

I watched the clear blue waters getting rapidly darker, indicating increasing depth as we flew onwards out over the Gulf of Panama. The plane soon settled at an economical cruising speed of about 300kph. This gave me the chance to unstrap and step up to the cockpit where I stood between my two newfound friends, watching with admiration as they carried out their respective duties.

Having always enjoyed flying, I could not fail to be impressed with the quiet, professional way that Marguerite handled the aircraft. With light sure touches on the controls, she guided it out across the water, staying low enough for me to see the many ships of all sizes and the little islets that were dotted around this part of the Gulf. Soon, what started as a dark mass low on the horizon, gradually took the form of the Isla Del Rey, which she informed me, was about the halfway mark down the Darien Coast.

I listened as Marguerite talked to the local Air Traffic Controller as this larger island, with its small domestic airport and its myriad of smaller islands, passed under us. She altered course enough to put the plane on a heading for the spot where the border between Panama and Colombia lay. Asking Miguel to take over, she climbed out of her seat and following me into the cabin, she opened a compact hostess unit and poured coffee for each of us and opened a pack of sandwiches.

Spreading a chart on the small tabletop, she showed me where we were and the route we would be taking. My mind was not fully on what she was saying, as my eyes were drawn to the opening of her blouse as she bent toward the map.

"We will be landing at a private landing strip, on a Plantation owned by a Colombian friend of ours," she informed me, with a knowing look.

"The place is near a town called Riosucio, which is also where our friends will be waiting. I must warn you, the last part of the trip will be flown at sea level so that we can get under the Coastal Radar operated by the Military. It may get a bit 'hairy' as you English say. Then we fly low along the border." Pausing to take a quick look out of the cabin window, she continued.

"Perhaps you will like to sit up front then, eh?" she asked.

"Not on your *Nellie*!" I said with mock fear. "I want **both** drivers of this plane where they **should** be!" Laughing, she went back to the cockpit with food and drink for her husband.

As we were only halfway to the Colombian coast, I decided to have a nap; it only seemed like a few minutes later that I awoke to a sudden feeling of falling into an abyss. Looking out the window I saw that we were approaching a coastline but there was nothing wrong, the plane was flying straight and level. Getting up, I went to the cockpit, where Miguel greeted me with a laugh.

"Sorry about that air pocket, but unlike a hole in the road you can't see them!"

I noticed that Marguerite was intently staring at a spot on the horizon, then suddenly she exclaimed, "strap in quickly! We have a visitor coming our way fast." She pointed to the object that was closing with us so fast that it could only be a jet plane.

"Stay out of sight!" she told me. I went to the rear seats where I could look carefully out of the small window without being seen. The plane was indeed a jet fighter; it swept over us so close that its jet wash rocked us. Making a wide turn and slowing to match our speed, it came up alongside from the rear port side and the pilot could be seen making hand signals that indicated he wanted to speak to us.

Being sure that I had seen Marguerite wearing her head set all the time; I was surprised to see that she had now removed it. Not only that, but she had also removed her blouse and as she obviously had no need of a bra, the fighter pilot - and myself - were able to see her firm, proud breasts jiggling as she waved enthusiastically to him.

What a sight that must be, I thought, to come up to investigate an intruder and be welcomed by the sight of a beautiful, near naked woman waving at you!"

Craning my neck, I could see that Miguel had also removed his shirt and was in the act of calmly toasting the fighter pilot with what appeared to be a glass of Champagne!

Fumbling with the headset but only succeeding to get it tangled with her luxuriant hair, Marguerite made more displays for the benefit of the pilot. By now though, he was undoubtedly having some problems of his own. With such a distracting display going on, he had completely forgotten to watch his plane's airspeed and was about to stall. Rapidly dropping away in a desperate effort to regain flying speed and in an equally desperate attempt not to miss any of the highly delightful show going on in the Beechcraft, he made a very fast return to our port side. This time though, he was even closer, with the wing tips a few feet apart and nearly overlapping.

Marguerite stood up and started to slowly undo the belt of her jeans, while Manuel let out a sudden laugh and flipped a switch on the central radio consul. The cabin was filled with the sound of an excited voice, gabbling on in a rapid stream of unintelligible Spanish, which I took to be the fighter Pilot giving his report. Suddenly, he was interrupted by a stern voice that exuded authority, cutting off his excited chatter. Taking another quick peak out the window, I saw the Pilot blow a kiss to Marguerite and then he pulled his aircraft over into a sharp turn, lit his afterburner and was gone.

Marguerite untangled herself from the radio headset and collecting her blouse, she stepped out into the cabin where she dressed herself and tidied her hai but not before she had looked to see if I was impressed with her display.

Under the circumstances, all that this poor stricken man could do was to remain seated and mumble, "Well done, that was quick thinking! But what was it all about?"   With a secret smile on her lips, Marguerite replied.

"From its markings we realized that it was a Mirage 5S of the Colombian Air Force. Then we heard him on the radio saying he had been sent out to investigate us as a possible drug runner!" she said, pouring a coffee for herself.

"As we are nearly in Colombian air space he was under orders to either escort us to an airfield, or shoot us down! As I have no wish to have to put on a better and more personal *'display'* for the combined Chiefs of the Colombian Air Force Staff, I had to act as if Miguel and I were just up here having a good old time. I'm sorry if it offended you."........

"No," I cut in, perhaps too hurriedly. "I mean, I'm not offended, just *very* grateful to a very beautiful and courageous lady for perhaps saving my life!" With a broad smile and a wiggle of her slim hips, Marguerite resumed her seat in the cockpit.

Shortly after this Miguel joined me.

"Well my friend, we had best have our last cup of coffee now, as we are nearly at the point when we go hedge hopping." As I poured two cups, he continued.

"I hope that little incident did not upset you, but it was so funny listening to that pilot. He got so excited by Marguerite's antics that his boss ordered him to return to base and to report to the Medical Centre for a Drug Test!!" The cabin was filled with the sound of our laughter at the poor unfortunate pilot's expense. Nevertheless, it had been a close call. With the tension of the past half hour eased and fortified by more coffee, we settled down to the job in hand. Miguel acted as both the co-pilot and flight engineer, while Marguerite took the plane down to just above sea level.

From my viewpoint I thought it looked as if we were almost on the wave tops, but a look at the cabin altimeter showed me that we were flying at 50ft above them. While this knowledge neither actually caused concern nor gave me any comfort, I still wondered how we were going to find our landing site, particularly as it was now fast approaching dusk.

To pass the time I was quite content to listen on my headset to the idle chatter between the extraordinary husband and wife team up front, with just the occasional need to interrupt or add a remark myself. The plane sped on with an occasional variation in its height, caused according to Marguerite.

"Mainly by the need to fly *over* ships rather than *through* them!" She had hardly started to inform me that we had reached the coast of Colombia, just a little behind the planned time, when without warning, the plane seemed to shoot up in the air at what I termed to be a perilous angle with the twin engines screaming as they clawed for height.

"We've just climbed a cliff! Are you OK back there?" Marguerite queried in a casual voice.

"My God, but you really do take some beating," I managed to get out, as I struggled to get my stomach back in place.

From then on, the next half hour or so was packed full of such incidents, as Marguerite literally flew between the trees. All I could see was a blur as the treetops went by and at times we seemed to be below them. We passed over a small Indian village - or as I would put it, we passed *through* a small Indian village because I would swear I saw the TOPS of their huts going past the wing tips.

Later, when I spoke to Miguel about it he laughed and said, "You are right Ben; we *were* lower than the top of the huts. In this swamp, they build them on *stilts!*"

There was no relief greater than what I felt when at last we arrived at our destination. Riosucio was no more than a larger village surrounded by the swamps around the Atrato River. The planes wheels kicked up a small cloud of light dust as we landed on what must surely be the only bit of dry land in the region. Marguerite taxied the aircraft straight into a large barn, the doors of which were immediately closed by unseen hands. The back door of the aircraft was thrown open before we had hardly stopped and in jumped a very excited young man. Coming straight to me he announced in an excited voice.

"Senõr Carson, I am Rico!" he blurted. "It was *I* who planted the bugs in El Jefe's house and I want to go into the mountains with you Señor!" This was said with a fierce pride in his voice. Under this onslaught I gave up the struggle to get out of my seat while I thought how best to handle this unexpected request.

"Well Rico," I said. "I am indeed *very* pleased to meet you and I think you have done a wonderful job for us." I paused to gather my thoughts.

"Let me discuss this matter with Miguel, before we make any final decision, eh!" I said, rising and squeezing past him before he could respond.

Following the weak loom of light coming from an oil lamp on the verandah of the house I made my way indoors. Miguel had not told me that the owner had moved out and the place had not been lived in for some time. Cobwebs as thick as lace curtains hung across doorways and between objects. Dust was pretty thick everywhere. I was just finishing a quick look around the kitchen area when I became aware of several strange voices in another room, which I decided to investigate. On entering the large downstairs room where all the activity and noise seemed to be, I spotting Miguel in the middle of a small crowd of people, all of whom were dressed in paramilitary fashion which, with their dark swarthy skins and mainly unshaven faces, made them look mean. Seeing me as I made my way towards him, Miguel gave a piercing whistle to gain attention.

"My friends! This is the man of whom I have spoken, it is *he*," he said with emphasis, "who has started the war on the Cartel which *we* will help him win!" He looked at me with a sheepish grin on his face. "I am very pleased to introduce Señor Ben Carson to you!" With that he stepped back, leaving me standing on my own facing them.

Code Name SNOWBIRD

"Gentlemen," I said gathering my thoughts. "Please sit down and then we can have a quick talk." I waited for the last man to settle himself in some semblance of comfort on a packing case, before I continued.

"I understand that you all share the common urge to rid this country of these people. Your reasons for doing so may be the same as mine; I will explain that more fully at a later time." I paused to look at them; long-haired generally; their swarthy skins showing them to be of Native origins.

"Having come so far and achieved so much, I am sure that with your expert help we *will* be able to defeat them. Firstly, they will *not* be expecting an attack. Secondly, you are all veterans of the type of war we intend to wage. Thirdly and perhaps most important of all, you have a *need* to succeed!" I took the bottle of warm beer offered me by Marguerite who had just joined us, taking a swig before continuing.

"It is too dark to do anything here as yet, the place needs cleaning up and you are all tired after your journeys. So I will look forward to meeting you all properly at a better time. Now I hand you back to Miguel who will lay down the plan for the immediate future. Thank you!" As I stepped back, I was pleasantly surprised by a round of applause.

"Well my friends!" said Miguel in an authoritative voice. "First, this place has to be made decent enough to live in and Marguerite tells me she has made arrangements for a local family to come in and help do that tomorrow." He paused to indicate his wife and myself.

"We will be flying back to Panama to get our weapons etc. so all I want you to do is, make the place secure, check the area thoroughly out to a ten mile perimeter. Set up 'telltales' - a system of small 'invisible' indicators that would be disturbed by anyone passing - on any tracks you may find. We will rejoin you in two days time at the latest."

With that we trooped off to the kitchen, where Marguerite already had a young Indian girl making coffee and stew from what looked like 'Compo' rations. After a quick hot drink we returned to the plane, which had been refuelled and stood waiting. We had a hair-raising takeoff in the half light - I for one couldn't see a thing - but fervently hoped and prayed that Marguerite could!

Code Name SNOWBIRD

Chapter 16

A Romantic Interlude.

I must have dozed off during the return flight; it was so uneventful that it could be called boring. Anyway, unable to see nothing from the cabin window but the blackness of the night, lit only by the strobe light of the aircraft, I gave up.

"Ben, Ben, wake up!" A distant female voice called. Struggling from the depth of my slumber I recalled where we were and visions of us flying into cliffs snapped me wide awake.

"What's the matter?" I replied in alarm.

"Nothing's wrong Ben, it's just that we are approaching Panama City now, so you should strap yourself in for the landing!" Marguerite said.

Easing the kinks out of my neck and heaving a sigh of relief, I stepped up to the cockpit door. The lights of the docks and city were strung like fairy lights across the sky in the distance, so I returned to my seat content that another part of this 'adventure' was drawing to a close.

A few minutes later we landed without mishap, the plane was towed into the barn and Miguel drove us home. It was late when we arrived at the Lopez's house and there was no sign of anyone else about. A cold supper was laid on the table waiting for us - prepared by the maid I assumed - this was devoured by the three of us, as we had suddenly realised how hungry we were.

Just after midnight, I wished both my companions a good night and went to my room.

I took a quick warm shower to refresh and relax myself, then for the first time in my life; I stretched out naked on a waterbed and under the luxury of a silk sheet. The events of the day were turning over in my mind as I drifted off to sleep. Tired though I was; the active soldier's instinct for danger; instilled through the years of service alerted me some time later, when I sensed, rather than saw, the bedroom door open. Without moving or altering my breathing pattern, I slowly opened one eye and saw a vague shape - more a darker patch of the darkness - moving toward me. I tensed ready to roll away from the expected attack.

Is it an intruder? No. Not with those bloody great dogs on guard! I answered my own question. Then it can only be .....

I silenced my thoughts as my ears picked up the distinctive rustle of soft clothing as the figure unerringly approached my bed. The smell of a musky, sensuous perfume drifted down over me as my shadowy 'visitor' stopped beside the bed.

"Marguerite?" I thought. Then there was the faintest rustling sound as she dropped her robe to the floor. The top sheet was lifted and the bed moved gently as she eased herself in beside me. I felt her cool naked breasts brush against my arm, followed by the equally cool length of her body pressed eagerly against me. A hand slipped across my stomach and down to my groin; long cool fingers gently caressing. The tip of her tongue flicked at my ear, I turned my head and as she found my lips, I tasted her sweet breath as we kissed passionately.

Little moans of passion rose from within her throat as she fondled me, our tongues darting like fencer's swords. Pushing me back against the bed, she rose a shadow in the night above me, her hips straddled mine, her long hair falling over her face, then I too moaned as I felt the heat inside her as she guided herself down, down. Reaching up for her, I fondled her firm breasts; my fingers and thumbs teasing her already erect nipples. A deep sigh came from within her throat as she moved above me.

"Oh Señor Ben! I have waited too long for this moment," I heard Juanita say as she took command of me, riding me, squeezing me and drawing me deeper within her.

JUANITA! The name exploded in my head. My mind was in a whirl, I had guessed wrongly and was in no position, or condition to object to being made passionate love to by this beautiful 20 year old girl - or should I say young woman, because she was all that. I was lost!

The next hour or so passed in a mixture of pure lust, as I realised how long it had been since I had last enjoyed the company of a woman. After the first flush, our lovemaking turned to long deep explorations of each other's pleasure. Juanita was totally uninhibited and our bodies were bathed in sweat as we went from one climax to another. Finally as we saw that it would soon be dawn, we showered together and after a long parting kiss, she slipped away to her room. My mind in a whirl, I fell on the bed and immediately dropped into an exhausted sleep.

"Ah, Ben! I was wondering what had happened to you," Miguel chided me, when I finally made a *very* late appearance for breakfast. "I didn't realise you would be so tired!" he added, with a funny half smile on his face. The sound of a young female singing came from the passageway as Juanita came in with a jug of fresh coffee.

"What would you like to eat Señor Ben? You can have whatever you wish," she said, with a slight stress on the whatever - or was that just my imagination.

"Just a couple of poached eggs, please," I replied, feeling the heat of a blush in my cheeks when I looked at her. Her smile deepened and with more humming she returned to the kitchen.

"Good morning Ben!" Marguerite chirped as she came into the room. "I hope you had a very good night." Again, was it my imagination that she stressed very good?

"Yes. Yes I did thank you," I replied half-heartedly.

A burst of distant singing made Marguerite smile as she said, "Well, it seems that *someone* had a good night, don't you think?"

I squirmed as I realised that she definitely knew that Juanita had been with me last night. Seeing my growing discomfort, she reached across and squeezed my arm, and said, "Miguel has some more good news for you, Ben!" With that she took her coffee out onto the courtyard and to change the subject I gave Miguel a questioning look.

"Si! Ben, we have been informed that all your weapons are cleaned and assembled ready for use. Everything has been degreased and checked and my Foreman, who is himself an ex soldier, tells me that it is all in working order," he announced proudly, as he settled back into his chair. "I have instructed that it is all re-packed and loaded into the aircraft ready for immediate take off, I hope you agree," he added.

"Well, that's certainly good news," I replied, unable to argue with such logic. "So all we have to do is set the final plans, agree the timings and return to Riosucio?" Seeing Juanita bringing my breakfast in, I busied myself pouring more coffee for us both.

"Excuse me," Marguerite interrupted as she returned to the room. "I have to ground the planes for a full service and check over. If we are going to use them in this operation, they will have to be in top condition, no? They will not be available until tomorrow night at the earliest." She looked at her husband as she added, "we will both be very busy, but I think we could spare Juanita to show Ben the sights of the area and perhaps to take him swimming don't you think darling?"

"Good idea my love. I'm going to feed the fish!" he said before I could object.

Marguerite turned to me as her husband left the room.

"Don't be angry Ben. Juanita has a genuine crush on you and I feel that you need to relax a little don't you agree?" she asked, as she came to stand behind my chair and started running her hands over my shoulders in a massaging movement.

Pushing my plate away, I let myself relax under her ministrations, then, making up my mind I said, "Yes, I agree. We are all adults here and Juanita is as you say, a beautiful young woman and I feel privileged by her attentions. Now, I think I understand you a bit more, so will not feel so awkward about it."

"That's great!" Marguerite cried happily. "It will give you something to want to return home to after the attack!" With a parting laugh she went out to the kitchen - presumably to break the news and I finished my coffee before returning to my room. I was in the bathroom cleaning my teeth when I heard the door open and Juanita came in to the bedroom. She seemed unaware of my presence, so I watched her through the part open door as she remade the bed with fresh sheets. I admired her smooth slim hips and rounded firm buttocks under her flimsy dress as she bent over, her breasts moving seductively inside her blouse. I felt a stirring in my loins, as visions of last night's passion was rekindled. I could stand it no longer.

"Hello Juanita," I said as I opened the door and walked in to the room. She was bending over tucking the sheet in and her lovely dark hair was hanging over her face just as it had last night as she gave me pleasure. Hearing my voice she straightened up and turned towards me, her face was flushed and her breath came in short gasps - whether this was from her exertions, or from embarrassment I could not tell.

"I'm glad I've seen you, because I want to have a chat with you," I said gently taking her hand and leading her to a chair. I could see she was worried, so I didn't hesitate.

"Juanita, last night was one of the most magical moments in my life, please don't be afraid, I am not angry at you," I said as reassuringly as I could. "In fact, to be perfectly honest," I continued, "I am very pleased and honoured that you find me attractive enough for that!"

"Señor Ben, I was so happy last night, but this morning I thought you may be angry," she gasped. "It is my hope that we may become friends, yes?" The pleading look in her eyes tore at my heart.

"Juanita, I feel that we are already more than just friends and that you should take the day off as Marguerite suggests, then we could go swimming" ...... Before I could finish, she planted a kiss on my lips and dashed from the room, reappearing just as quickly to gather up the soiled bed linen before disappearing down the stairs. Twenty minutes later, we departed in one of the 4 x 4's, waved off by a jubilant Marguerite, as armed with a hastily filled picnic basket; we set off for our swim.

The rest of the day was spent at an isolated cove, where I helped Juanita undress, my hands wandering over her as I feasted my eyes on the beauty of her young body. The jutting breasts, flat stomach, rounded buttocks and long firm thighs with a thick thatch of hair in between. All of this had been denied me last night, as we had made love in the dark and now I made up for it as she stood there proudly with her feet slightly apart. I walked around her, drinking in every facet of her being, I could not deny that I was one hell of a lucky man.

Then it was her turn. Juanita slowly removed my clothing, teasing me with quick, feather-light touches of her hands. Trance-like, I reached for her, but every time I tried to lift her to her feet to caress her, she stopped me. I couldn't resist her, my whole body ached for her; I had to grab this dream before I woke up. Just as I felt I was about to explode, she rose quickly and turning, she ran for the water.

"That will make you want to come back to me after your swim!" She called over her shoulder as she went and both of us ran into the water, naked as the day we were born, splashing each other and making feeble efforts to escape each other's grasp. For the rest of the day, we divided our time between swimming and making love on the warm sand. It was very late that evening when we returned to the villa after having had a lovely meal in a hotel - Juanita's first experience of dinning out I learned - we crept up to my room.

I noticed that another pillow had been placed beside mine in our absence, a note on one of the pillows informed me that Miguel and Marguerite would be back the next afternoon, having gone out for the night. The rest of the night was passed as it would be by any lovers, and again, it was early the next morning before we finally went to sleep.

Chapter 17

<u>Riosucio, in the Atrato Swamps of Colombia.</u>

<u>The Team assemble</u>

Lacking interception by jet fighters, or the need to fly up cliffs, our return flight to Riosucio two days later was much less interesting than the first one. The only difference - or perhaps advantage - was that this time, we came in daylight, giving me the chance to see what would become our Training Area from the air. Shaped in an elongated triangular fashion, it ran out from close to the airstrip, stretching towards the Atrato River on one side and the huge coastal marshlands on the other. Roughly the equivalent size of the huge Salisbury Plain Training Area as used by the British Army, it varied from marshy lowland, to the heavily forested foothills of the not too distant Cordillera mountain range. The far distant boundary was formed by the Colombian / Panamanian border, unusable because of the mass of treacherous swamps.

As we did another over-flight at my request, I was interested to note the many tracks that crossed the area - both animal and vehicle tracks were evident. These would be used extensively in our training sessions. Satisfied with what I had seen, I asked Marguerite to take us down. The plane came to a standstill in its usual cloud of dust and a group of men crowded round to welcome us as we climbed out. My arm was grabbed as I was eagerly greeted by a small, wiry man of about 38 years of age, who stretched himself to his full height as he proudly introduced himself.

"I," - his chest grew a little larger as he pointed to himself with his index finger - "am Manuel Gonzales, Señor Carson. Like my Compadres, I too am from the US Rangers." It was strange, but as he spoke in a high-pitched voice with an obvious Mexican/Spanish accent, I had the impression he should have said, 'Speedy' Gonzales. If he'd noticed my puzzlement, it certainly didn't stop him.

"It was I who entered the town house of El Jefe and stole those documents Señor."

Then, with a conspiratorial wink he added, "I also left a Satchel Bomb hidden in the cellar area Señor!"

"Great! That's really great!" I mumbled, shaking him firmly by the hand. "I was very impressed when I heard what you had done and would like you to accept this as a bonus." I handed him one of the bundles of cash - thinking at the same time - *"What Satchel Bomb?"*

Before I could corner Miguel for an explanation, I was firmly confronted by two more men, the older of whom was offering me a very welcome overflowing beer glass and this time it was a cold one. This man, standing squarely in front of me with shoulders straight, announced.

"My name is Felipe, Ex US Rangers and this hombre, Señor," he spoke fondly and with obvious pride - indicating the tall youth who stood beside him - "is my son Rico. It was he who entered El Jefe's house and planted the bugs and a bomb!"

Once again I looked round for Miguel to ask about the bombs, but not seeing him, I firmly shook hands with both father and son, at the same time as congratulating Rico who I'd already met, on his initiative and technical skill in making the bugs and on his bravery in planting them. The whole group raised a cheer for the lad as I paid him the other cash bonus for a job well done; it was obvious that he had earned their respect already.

Turning to move on my way, I found myself confronted by yet another extremely fit looking man who favoured the Rambo style of sleeveless jacket with many pockets, as well as the black Bandanna to keep his long black hair out of his face. Not to be outdone by the others, he nervously and hurriedly introduced himself.

"Buenas tardes, Señor. I am called Ramon, I too am Ex US Rangers." Firmly shaking hands with me, he seemed to suddenly remember something and added, "Señor, we are happy that you have come to do this thing and will help in any way!" Turning abruptly, he walked quickly back into the small crowd.

"So, these are my team," I mused to myself as I looked them over. They were a mixed bunch indeed, all of whom - with the exception of Rico - I estimated to be in their late thirties or early forties and extremely fit, but most importantly, would all be able to play their part by instinct and training. Best of all, they were hand-picked volunteers to a man, which meant that they could be trusted and having served in the Rangers with Miguel and worked on Contract for him still, they would all be reliable. No one could have wished for a better team, which now numbered seven people in all.

With the introductions over, we moved inside to the room that was designated as the Briefing cum Mess room. Rapping on a table with my knuckles to gain their attention, I asked them to settle down so that they could be given a quick briefing.

I had to admit to being very pleased to find that the hard slog of instructing through an interpreter would not be required as they all spoke very reasonable English - though I felt they had far too many of the usual Americanisms in their dialogue. It also pleased me to learn from Miguel that there was no need to go into lengthy explanations for them, as they had already been advised about the mission in general, as well as the part I had already played since leaving England. Stirring myself from my reverie, I addressed them.

"First of all, I would like to thank you for becoming involved in what could, without doubt, become a *very* dangerous mission. Secondly, I would like you to know that regardless of the outcome, the sum of $100,000 will be deposited in each of your names in a Panama Bank; Marguerite will give you the details later. There will, I hope, also be generous bonuses when we have completed what we set out to do." I saw the genuine looks of pleasure on their faces at this news; money was always welcome in their lives. Taking a moment to collect my thoughts, I took a sip of my now warm beer before continuing.

"Although we are all equals in this 'army,' there is obviously a need to have some sort of control. I will be in overall command, with Miguel as my second in command, but I wish you to know now, right at the beginning, that we shall only issue and work to plans that have first of all been fully discussed, understood and accepted by all of you. This is a team event and every member of the team must be fully aware of what is happening." Their agreement to this was evident from their eager nods, so I continued.

"Rico, who has already undoubtedly proved his technical skills, will be put in charge of all of our Communications and Manuel; on the recommendation of Miguel; will take command and responsibility of the forward scouts. Any questions on that?" I looked at Manuel, who nodded to show he agreed, while the others, nodded acceptance.

"I understand from him, that we will have a party of six scouts, all of whom he has worked with before and all of them know the mountains well."

"As for that other all important matter of transport, it seems obvious," I watched their faces as I announced, "that as she has demonstrated her very exceptional skills as a Pilot, Marguerite should be responsible for the transport arrangements." There was a buzz of agreement, which showed they all knew and admired Marguerite's ability. "Now, before we get down to finer details, let's hear what Ramon has to tell us. He was detailed a few days ago by Manuel, to investigate El Jefe and his whole organization."

"Come on Ramon, tell us your news," I said, beckoning the shy, slim man forward. Typical of his type of person; though he may be a physically tough and very experienced man in the world of soldiering; Ramon proved to be a doer, rather than a thinker. His very real shyness was almost painful to see, when he stood in front of this group. Fiddling with his hands he hesitated and then slowly gaining courage, he launched into a full and very comprehensive report on his early part of the mission.

Keeping his eyes firmly fixed on his old friend Miguel, Ramon then explained that by mixing with the local Indians - he had been courting a girl in Amalfi for a long time - and from listening to the gossip of her family and friends, he had learned that the authorities had been mounting road blocks etc. to stop the trade. El Jefe and his Cartel had been defeating these half-hearted attempts to stop the cocaine leaving the country, by simply using the forces of nature for most of the long journey. Warming to his theme, he continued.

"The pure refined cocaine leaves the illegal factory by the lorry load. It is then driven through the night, to a secret distribution centre near the small town of Puerto Berrio on the banks of the Magdalena River." He indicated that location on the map that had been hurriedly pinned on the wall. "The Magdalena River is very fast flowing, as it rises on the eastern slopes of the Cordillera Central Mountains," - again his hand swept across a region filled with very tightly packed contour lines depicting extremely high and steep mountains. "It then flows north for over 950 miles until it reaches the Caribbean Sea near Barranquilla City, where there is a port for ocean going vessels. It is navigable for over 930 miles, so it is this river that does most of the work for the smugglers."

"Which shows he took the trouble to gen' up on this matter!" I thought, as he continued.

"They then load the cocaine - packed in thick plastic bags, each weighing about 25 kilo's - onto specially made pallets. Four of these pallets, each containing 10 such packs, are placed in the bottom of a large container and covered in sacks of coffee beans, rice or corn. The containers are then loaded by crane onto the barges that are used to carry the various local produce of the country. Several barges are used, so the amount of drugs shipped at any time could be as much as 2400 kilograms." Without looking at anyone, Ramon dashed back to his seat and sat down in a rush.

I waited for the buzz of astonishment at the news he'd just imparted to quieten down. It seemed that nobody including myself had realised just how much cocaine was being moved by these people.

Thanking Ramon for the very comprehensive report he had given and the sketches he had produced, which not only showed the places, but also named them, I once again addressed them all.

"It seems, from what we have just heard, that our original plans will have to be changed as we will now be making a two-stage attack, one on the factory - hopefully when the Cartel bosses are there - and our objective will be to completely destroy them and the factory at the same time. The other will be on the convoy, which must *not* be allowed to get through. This will stretch us a bit thin on the ground, unless we can find a way of catching the convoy later and before it completes its journey."

Before I could continue, Ramon leaped to his feet, all of his earlier nervousness forgotten.

"I know where we can do it, Señor Ben," he gasped. Moving quickly over to the map of the region, he grabbed at my arm and excitedly jabbed his finger onto a spot on the map.

"There it is, the Los Palmas Coffee Plantation." Pointing to where we believed the factory was sited, he traced the rough winding mountain road that the convoy would have to take with his finger.

"There!" he exclaimed, triumphantly jabbing the map again. "There is a narrow single lane bridge over a very deep canyon; it will take them maybe three hours to get there. If we can find a way to get there, we can do it!" He sat down again suddenly, as if he had worn himself out. Everyone was chattering excitedly about what had been disclosed and I called for order, thanking Ramon for his extra contribution,

"This," I said, "has shown he had used his initiative and this in turn, had possibly saved the whole of the operation." Even I had now come to admit, that given the extreme harshness of the territory and the location of the target, I could not have done it alone. Ramon wore a very satisfied smile for the rest of the evening.

Collectively going into more detail, we completed the outline of the plan, with Miguel finally repeating it all in Spanish to avoid any possible misunderstandings. Before going to their rooms to settle in before the evening meal, we discussed and agreed the stages as outlined by myself as being:-

Stage 1. Marguerite to over-fly the electronic bugs to gather the information. (Plan the next move when the information is known.)

Stage 2. Move to the DZ (drop zone)

Stage 3. Tab (walk) to a LUP (Lay Up Point) near the First Target area.

(The Factory)

Stage 4. The hit. Take out the factory and Cartel personnel.

Stage 5. Move to the Second Target area. (Bridge) To lay timed explosives if possible.

Stage 6. Hit the convoy.

Stage 7. Withdraw.

It was then, that I remembered about the bombs I had been hearing about, so I asked Miguel for an explanation.

"Ah! Those!" he said with obvious embarrassment. "They are remotely fired; I instructed them to do this, just in case we fail in the main task; it's a sort of Plan B we can hit them with!" I gave this information some thought for a few moments and had to agree it made sense.

To Miguel's obvious relief, I said, "OK! As they are already in place, we will use them as part of the overall plan. But!" I said emphatically. "They will ONLY be used on my say-so; I don't want any innocent people killed!"

Noticing the appetising smell of food coming from the kitchen, I waited until they had all nodded their agreement before saying, "now it's time we all had a meal and went to bed." In a chorus of agreement the group broke up, with everyone noisily chattering excitedly as they went off to collect their food. Following a hearty meal that had been prepared by some of the local Indians under Marguerite's supervision, most of them retired to their respective rooms. Tomorrow, we would start the 'shakedown' period of preparation.

Chapter 18

<u>Over the target.</u>

At first light the following morning- or so it seemed - I was dragged from a very deep sleep by the sound of an aircraft's engines being run up. Climbing groggily to my feet, I went to the window and looking out saw that Marguerite and Miguel were already working on the plane. Dressing quickly, I went down to the kitchen, where an Indian house servant gave me a cup of hot strong coffee.

"Why can't I get a civilised drink like a decent cup of tea?" I moaned to myself; rather than upset the 'hired help,' who probably wouldn't know what I was on about anyway. Grabbing a thick sandwich from a plate that she indicated, I went outside to where the plane was vibrating contentedly like a racehorse straining at the starting gate. Seeing me coming, Miguel signalled to his wife to cut the engines and turning to me he said with a laugh.

"We couldn't find a bugle to play Reveille on my friend, so we had to make do with this." He gave a vague wave toward the plane. "Oh! By the way, four more of my men have arrived overnight; I will introduce them to you when we get back, OK?" I nodded my agreement as I bit into my sandwich, at the same time as Marguerite joined us, enquiring if I had slept well.

"Still be there, I think, if I didn't have such noisy neighbours who like to play with motors at unearthly hours!" I remarked with a wink. "Everything OK?" I asked her, pointing to the plane and nearly spilling my coffee.

"Fuelled and ready to go and as Rico has shown his skills in electronics, I think we should let him operate the equipment don't you?" she replied. With my mouth full of food, all I could do was to nod my head enthusiastically to show my agreement and continue chewing at my breakfast.

That way, I can concentrate on taking photos and seeing the lay of the land, I thought.

My food finished, I rushed to follow the others. Awkwardly dragging on my jacket, while shouting final instructions for Manuel, Felipe and Ramon to check all the various weapons and kit with the help of the newcomers in our absence. With a final push from Rico I climbed aboard the plane. We had no sooner strapped ourselves in our seats and donned the headsets, when Marguerite restarted the engines and set the plane rolling towards the dusty runway.

Not waiting for anything, she once again demonstrated her skills as a pilot, by pulling the plane off the ground in what I thought was under half the length of a normal take off run. Keeping close to the ground, only rising to clear the tops of the trees, she flew us inland, over the marshy areas of the border on a course that took us towards the distant mountain range. As I watched the panorama unfold beneath us, the trees dropped away and we passed over a fast flowing river.

"That's the Atrato River below." Marguerite informed us over the intercom. Looking down, Rico and I could clearly see that this river, though smaller than the

Magdalena, was still a powerful river to have to cross. It would have added considerably to our logistical problems if there were no bridges. Climbing gradually now, the plane rose to a height of 5500 ft, that would allow it to pass over the smaller mountains that stood in a formidable and seemingly immovable line across our front. Rico, eager to display his knowledge of this wild and beautiful country, informed me.

"These high coastal mountains are called the Cordillera Occidental; they form part of the Andes that splits into three ranges in Colombia. We are also going to be flying over the Cordillera Central, which is the middle range. When we clear this first range, you will see the Cauca River, on the other side of which is Amalfi, the place we seek."

I could only marvel at the diversity of the landscape that unfolded as we flew onwards, constantly changing; what had originally been marshy wasteland and scrubby forest transformed to jungle, then back to the rolling foothills of the mountains. Then, quite abruptly, we were looking down on so many cultivated and lush fields, that I thought we could have been over England. This scene changed yet again, as the ground got higher. Once again, we flew over deep forest areas clinging precariously to the steep slopes of the mountains. The higher we flew; these forests became interspersed with scattered outcrops of sharp, wicked looking volcanic rock. To my utter surprise, as we reach the highest points I saw that this, in turn, gave way to wide open grass plains, some of which ended in areas of high arid desert.

Deep mountain valleys appeared, some very narrow, others very wide and all were splendid in their beauty. Here and there, mountain streams gently meandered through the landscape, a few of them suddenly taking a dive over the edge of vertiginous cliffs, thus creating magnificent water falls. In some of the smaller lush valleys, groups of dwellings and cultivated areas could be seen, where industrious Indians had scratched a living for generations.

"Ben? Can you hear me Ben?" I became aware that Marguerite was calling me over the intercom.

"Yes, sorry but I was miles away," I replied.

"Miles away?" Marguerite responded. "You were so quiet I thought you had got out!" she quipped. "Anyway, we are now following the main route to Amalfi and I will fly lower in order for you to see the ground more clearly."

"Hey amigo!" Manuel cut in. "If you like, we will follow roughly the same route over the mountains, so that you can see the ground we will have to *walk* on!" He spoke with relish.

"Why are *you* so cheerful about *it old man?*" I retorted, trying to even the score. "Don't forget, that *you* will have to walk it also!" His answering laugh made me sure there was a nasty surprise in store for me down there, so I went back to watching eagerly out the window. I was able to pick out rough, stony mountain tracks, all of which would be hard on any vehicle; likewise I could see some of the narrow twisting trails that we would follow on foot. To my great alarm, I saw that in some places these actually followed the cliff edge.

"It looks to be a right bastard!" I said, unaware that I had spoken my thoughts out loud. This correct summing up of mine, said with such conviction, brought whoops of laughter from my three companions.

"Rico!" Miguel called, bringing us all back to the job in hand. "Rico, get the receiver ready, we are over Amalfi and only a few minutes flying time from the target area!"

As Rico went efficiently about his duties, I felt the adrenaline build up in my body again. This is why I had come halfway across the world and it would be my first sight of the target area. I busied myself preparing the long-range camera that Miguel had 'borrowed' for my use. Looking at the numerous complexities of the focus dials and lens markings, I again spoke my thoughts aloud.

"Hey, am I glad this is an automatic camera! I have no skills in that direction!" I thought I heard a chuckle in the head set.

Marguerite brought the plane down to around one thousand feet, so that we would get a good view of the Hacienda Los Palmos. This was as Rico had described it; a very large house with stables and other extensive outbuildings, all of which stood in an isolated wooded area at the head of a wide valley. The grounds immediately surrounding the house were like those of a cattle ranch, with wooden stock fences. A large stock yard and stable area stood to one side of the main house; I could see the sun glinting off the many water troughs around it as we flew over.

"That's it!" Rico said excitedly when I asked him to take a quick look. "That's the place at which I placed those bugs!"

Over the intercom, he informed Marguerite that the small main transmitter was situated near the foot of the rocky outcrop we could see some way up the mountainside behind the house and in line with the swimming pool, that glittered in the clear sunlight.

"Great!" came her reply. "That swimming pool gives me a very clear marker to line up on, well done Rico!"

The plane flew down the valley at a height suitable for the photographic equipment. As I clicked away as fast as I could, I recalled Rico's words as he explained about the transmitters. As far as the radio was concerned, this would be the *only* chance. When he gave the signal to transmit, the equipment would empty its memory into the ether, ten minutes later it would quietly self-destruct. Heated internally by a small magnesium charge, it would simply melt into an unidentifiable blob, removing all evidence as to what it was and what it had contained. In case of low power on the transmitter's internal batteries, we had to over-fly at a low altitude, yet high enough not to cause alarm if anyone were at the Hacienda. Using the camera as a high power telescope, I informed them that I could see no sign of people or cars, so we decided to risk it. However, in order not to raise any immediate alarm at the house, we flew on out over the central mountains, turning right and heading towards the mountain range that backed onto the Hacienda.

As we circled, I noticed that the seemingly never ending trees and rocks abruptly gave way to a wide, deep valley that showed obvious signs of having been cultivated in the past, though now neglected. The heavily forested slopes gave way to thick, overgrown vegetation, on the lower edge of which was a clearing that had obviously been cut by man. My eyes were drawn back to it as we passed by and I could see that a small cleared track led off one side of this clearing, disappearing into the jungle at the foot of the mountainside.

"Cleared area in thick overgrowth. Cleared track leading from it!" My mind was racing to sort this out before it was lost out of sight. "That's IT!" The glaringly obvious fact that it was still in use, hit me like a thunderbolt as I clicked away with the camera.

"My God! I think we've found the factory!" I shouted over the intercom. Everyone craned their necks to see, as I gave Marguerite instructions to bring her back over the spot. As the plane banked onto a reciprocal course, we could see a large complex of old buildings, partly hidden by the close growing trees. With the aid of the camera lens, I could see they were constructed with sheets of rusty old corrugated tin. This then was the factory and therefore the secondary target. Snapping away as we passed overhead, I identified several possible positions for the required OP's that we would have to mount.

We also caught glimpses of a well-used track running from the factory, across the lower slopes and down into the thickness of what amounted to jungle at the bottom of the valley, where it turned to run parallel with a small river. Looking at my map, I saw that it showed this track met up with an unmade mountain road further on. This in turn led to the road and bridge Ramon had described in his briefing. This valley, in my estimation, was less than 30 kilometres from the Hacienda and in fact showed no other signs of being occupied or used, nor was there any other house or village nearby.

The air was full of the electric excitement in us all at this piece of luck and we were all on a 'high' as we continued our flight. Shortly after this discovery, we over-flew another wider valley created by the mighty river that still flowed through it. As soon as I saw it I recalled the words of Ramon, when he had said 'the Cartel uses the forces of Nature to transport the drugs.' This must be the river they used, though the water level was low at this time of year, we could clearly see just why the river had become the favoured transport route of the Cartel. Wide and powerful, this was the mighty Magdalena River.

Even from our height, I could tell from the bow wave pushed up by some of the barges we could see, that it was flowing fast enough to take a fully loaded barge along at what I judged to be about 12 knots. It reminded me of that other main transport route in Europe, the mighty Rhine, which services so many different countries in the same way.

Taking a slow turn over the large riverside town of Barrancabermeja, Marguerite set us on course for the Hacienda again. This time though, as we cleared the mountains, she took the aircraft down to about 500 ft and slowed the engines slightly. When we were in range Rico sent a signal to the transmitter and gave a whoop of delight when he received a return signal that told him it was ready to send. In the capable hands of our pilot, we made our approach at a constant height, flying obliquely across the valley. As Rico sent his signal ordering the transmitter to transmit, I was staring at the general view out of the window.

"Bloody Hell! Talk about Lady Luck being on or side!" I said, suddenly grabbing the camera again and clicking away before the angles changed too much.

"Turn slightly left as soon as you can!" I instructed Marguerite.

"All signals completely recorded!" Rico called a few moments later, with a note of relief in his voice. Only a split second after receiving Rico's announcement, the plane banked left onto a new heading and my comment of "Well done!" was lost in the loud cheering from up front at this news.

"OK Ben" Marguerite's voice sounded calmly in my ear. "What exactly was all that about?"

"I *think*, I may have seen a possible landing site!" I explained.....

"What? Where?" The two voices from up front were as one at this news. Keeping my eye fixed on the spot, I continued to pass verbal instructions to Marguerite, which allowed her to fly us over what I had seen. Miguel, full of curiosity, came back to see what it was.

"There!" I said, unable to keep the excitement out of my voice as I pointed out of the window. "At the top of that larger mountain is a level area or plateau that looked like a small area of desert. This could be used as a landing strip and if my judgment is correct it's about midway between the factory area and the Hacienda on the other side of the mountain!"

"It could be worth another look." Miguel informed his wife. Then he spoke to me.

"Shall we go around again to make sure Ben?"

"It looks deserted down there, you can never be sure though," I said hesitantly. "It's too good a chance to miss and the light is failing." I paused, torn between two factors, one the need to know and the other the need to ensure secrecy.

"OK! But don't make it too obvious that is what we are looking at." No sooner had I uttered the words, than the plane tilted on the opposite wing. Marguerite had quickly assessed that an approach from the opposite direction was required to avoid being seen from the Hacienda again. Although there was no apparent movement in the area, you could never be sure who was watching, besides which, the plane could be heard miles away.

"I would like to take a look in case it is of use. There is no need to worry; we can make a quick dash across from another angle, using the mountains to mask the sound of our approach," she advised as if reading my thoughts.

Having already experienced the way she could quite effectively 'pop' the plane up over the top of cliffs and trees, I was only too happy to give the go ahead for her to take a look and asked everyone else to be ready to scan the area. Down we flew into another smaller valley, completely out of sight from both factory and Hacienda, then to my utter amazement, the plane turned into a re-entrant that was, it seemed, not much wider than the span of the wings. Following the valley floor as it gently rose up to meet the top of the mountain, Marguerite kept the plane just above the long grass. Then, as the ground rose to where it sloped right to the rim of the mountain top, she flew it up into the air much the same as a ski jumper would have launched themselves off a rising ramp. Levelling quickly, we flew at about 200 ft above the ground and there before us, as I had described, was a level area of dry barren land. Marguerite made a quick, low-level appraisal of the area before turning the plane for home.

Eager to learn the result, I crowded into the cockpit doorway, where along with her husband, I stared at her, waiting for her to comment. She sat concentrating on her job, as serene and beautiful as any woman I had ever seen. Then, as if she had suddenly become aware of our gaze, she gave way to fits of laughter when she saw the expressions on our faces.

"Madre de Dios," she exclaimed. "You look like children waiting to be told if you can have an ice cream!" More laughter creased her up, and then relenting, she went on to say.

"It's only about 20 - 25 kilometres from the factory and yes, it could be used. I must warn you that it will be very bumpy and dangerous at night." She took a quick look at her husband and then added, "it would be more suitable for a helicopter!"

With that, she settled down to the details of the return flight and Miguel came back into the cabin to see if the recording was OK. In answer to his questioning look, Rico gave a smile and the thumbs up. Relief showed in Miguel's face, but I noticed that he seemed to have sagged a little at the same time.

"Is there something wrong my friend?" I enquired, but Miguel shook his head and busied himself pouring coffee for us all.

The return flight proved uneventful, that is, if you discount the sudden heavy rain and wind that we flew into over the coastal mountaintops. The plane was suddenly thrown about like a leaf in a storm; Marguerite and Miguel were both fully occupied in regaining and keeping control. I noticed the look of panic on Rico's face, he had gone completely white and his skin was clammy. Giving his arm a reassuring squeeze, I told him that everything would be OK. After what seemed ages, but in reality was less than five minutes, the plane suddenly broke out into clearer skies. When asked, Marguerite quietly explained that in that area, the warm air off the sea rising rapidly up the mountainside, suddenly meets up with the cold rarefied air and causes such turbulent conditions. Though it was over almost as soon as it began, I was aware how dangerous it could have been for any novice pilot. The plane could have been dashed to the ground.

Rico had just about regained his normal colour by the time we landed and he staggered off to the toilet as quickly as he could. I helped Miguel to unload the radio receiver and carry it into the house. Setting everything up on the table, Rico, when he joined us, found that he was the centre of attention. Everyone had stopped what they were doing and had gathered around the radio set.

"Here you are Ben," Rico said, passing me a headset that was plugged into the receiver; he then switched the tape on to play. I was pleased to hear voices so clear that they could have been in the room with us, but they were speaking in such rapid Spanish that it was no good for me to try to listen.

Handing the headset to Miguel, I said, "would you two guys do a transcription for me?" Then I left them to it and went looking for a beer. Some time later, while I was in the kitchen getting drinks for us, I got the message that they had finished and were waiting for my return.

"Well?" I asked rather impatiently as I entered the room.

"Ben, you'll never believe this!" Miguel said, taking a beer from the pack I offered them.

"It seems that the meeting had not lasted all that long, it was all over in about one hour, most of which had been spent on reviewing the past years activities; we've made notes for you. During their discussions, we heard several interesting names being mentioned, as well as those of several companies involved in laundering the money," Miguel said in a matter of fact voice. "Did you know that they made $100 million in profit last year?"

Through the time I'd spent with John Paul and his gang, I had become aware of the huge profits these people made out of causing death and misery across the world, but $100 million in one year? It was sickening! I sat down with them and took the transcript, which I noted was all in excellent English - for my benefit. Rico ran the tape again as I listened. Even though I could not understand most of it, I noticed right from the start that one voice seemed to dominate the discussions, in its deep resonant tones; it seemed to overpower the others. From listening, yet not understanding all the words, I knew this was El Jefe and I formed a picture in my mind of a large man, whose very presence was enough to control the other Cartel members.

It was this voice that informed the meeting, that a much larger shipment of drugs was being prepared, a shipment that would return them over $40 million clear profit on its own. All of this was destined to be moved via the usual routes, for shipment to his son Jose in Europe.

"Hear that?" I shouted excitedly. "That's the first really positive mention of him as a link in the chain to Europe!" Miguel and I slapped each other's backs in excitement. "Keep that tape safe for evidence, mind, Rico," I instructed. He nodded and put the tape to play again.

"Stop! Go back a bit..... There! Now run it again." My blood had frozen. I did not want to hear the words I was hearing. The enthusiasm cooled rapidly when I grasped the meaning of the next piece of the tape. When the recording started again my spirits were really dashed, for I heard El Jefe say, in clear demanding tones that even I understood, that he wanted to bring the shipment date *forward*. At this stage, my supposition as to the speaker's authority was born out, when one excited man butted in to the speaker's rhetoric.

"Silencio!" the deep voice snapped, accompanied by the sound of someone banging the table at the same time. There followed a long drawn out pause and I was there in the room with them; I could *see* El Jefe glaring at them all in turn. A few chairs were heard to scrape the floor, as nervous occupants adjusted their posture. Then in a stern, authoritative voice, the speaker continued, telling his audience; 'The river is still just manageable at the moment, but the rains are expected soon, so I have decided that the production and shipment of the next load of cocaine would be speeded up.'

'I insist,' the speaker continued in a cold, but firm voice, 'that it *will* be completed a week earlier than originally planned and packed ready for shipment in *ten* days time.' There was a slight pause during which I could *see* him looking around at all the faces, looking for dissent, then. 'No longer!' he added for effect. A scratching sound came from the speakers. Puzzled, I looked at Miguel and Rico, who made mime of striking a match and lighting a cigar. Then the voice of El Jefe continued.

'The packages will be loaded into the containers as before and the convoy will leave the old coffee plantation just before dawn on the eighth day!' There was the sound of papers being collected together, then, as there were no more arguments forthcoming, El Jefe declared the meeting closed, while finally reminding them. 'There is a lot to be done, in little time.'

We sat there stunned; I could not wrap my mind around the problem that this was causing us. We three looked at each other in despair.

"Ten days!" Miguel gasped. "We will never make it across those mountains on foot in that time!" I could see the anguish on my friend's face as he saw the plans we had lain falling apart.

"I think we can," I said, placing a reassuring hand on Miguel's arm. "If we bring every*thing* and every*body* in by air!" Then, making a quick decision, I announced.

"Get Marguerite in here! This is her problem now, we will discuss this with her when she has finished fuelling the plane; she will have the final say. If she says it can be done, we will move in at night in six days time. That will give us enough time to acclimatise ourselves, to work into position and set everything up."

Miguel gave a nod and returned to the larger mess room, where he explained what we had learned to the others. Deep in thought, I left the building and made a beeline for Marguerite. Waiting impatiently until she had finished instructing the mechanic to check and refuel the plane to its capacity, I grabbed her arm and pulled her round to face me.

"I must know now!" I said impatiently. "Do you think we have a chance to get everyone with their kit and all the weapons up there to that plateau by air? Can we do it in the Beechcraft? Have you got access to helicopters? ......

"Hey Ben STOP!" Marguerite broke my grip on her arm and angrily pushed me away. "One question at a time and don't forget, I *am* on your side you know!" she said firmly.

"I am sorry, I must have panicked and I hope I didn't hurt you," I said, realising I had overstepped the mark. I tried to calm down and apologetically rubbed the red mark on her arm.

"That's OK. Rico told me what El Jefe said, I can well imagine how you feel, after all you have gone through you could see it failing," she said, touching my cheek softly. "Now to answer all of your questions. You saw the roughness of the ground; I think it will be too much for the Beechcraft. We may be able to get everyone and all the kit up there, but because of the rarefied air reducing the lift; it will be better in two helicopters. I shall have to look at the relevant charts and get the equipment weighed first. If it is possible, I must warn you now, that we will fly without Navigation lights and at *low* level!"

Smiling at her in the fast approaching twilight and cheered by her answers, I responded by saying.

"Tell me something new! I was beginning to think you always fly your planes <u>on</u> the ground!" Laughing at this cheeky comment, Marguerite took my arm as we walked towards the house and a much needed supper.

As we went in the door she said, "Oh yes! There's one more thing. So that I can calculate the lift ability and fuel required, I shall have to have an idea of the weight of every man including his full equipment. We don't want any accidents do we?"

Code Name SNOWBIRD

Chapter 19

Decision Time.

That evening, even though we had been joined by four newcomers, the normally boisterous 'soldiers' ate their meal in an unusual and uncharacteristic silence; it seemed that the word had got out about a possible hitch in our plans. Toying with their food, rather than devouring it hungrily as they usually did, each of them sat deep within their own thoughts; there was also a complete lack of the usual friendly banter.

"Depression," I said to myself recognising it for what it was. After the 'high' of the recent excitement and the continual successes over the past few months; now with this news, I was feeling perhaps the most depressed myself. Finishing my meal - leaving most of it on the plate through loss of appetite - I asked that everyone be in the sitting room for a briefing in half an hour. I was stopped by Miguel as I made my way to my room.

"Ah! Ben, I was just coming to look for you," he said. "Marguerite and I have looked at the charts, we *think* there is one chance of doing this, but it will be *very* risky."

"That's *great*! I responded perking up a bit. "I have called a group briefing for eight o'clock. Can you bring your charts down with any plan you may have then?" Confirming that this would be OK, Miguel went off in search of his wife. I then collected all the large-scale maps I had and made my way to the sitting room, where I stood a folding table on end to act as a display board and attached my best weatherproofed map to it. While we waited for everyone to arrive and settle down, Miguel called me over to introduce the new men to me.

"These are the best scouts in Central America," he boasted as he named them as Juan, Julio, Louis and Ernesto. After shaking hands and asking a few questions of them, I told them to get settled in with the others for the briefing. Calling for their attention, I started outlining the events of the day.

"You will already have heard that things are about to go tits-up against us, but I am telling you now, that no decision has been made to call off the attack!" I paused to let that sink in and saw the spark of renewed interest in their eyes.

"With El Jefe's order to bring the delivery dates forward, my original plan of foot slogging it across the mountains went out the window and I've had to change my plans a bit. No doubt, as experienced soldiers, you will already be used to being mucked about by the 'Brass' eh?" I joked, to cheer them up a bit more. It worked and the nods and murmurs of agreement, accompanied by wide smiles, told me they'd all 'been there.' "There is possibly a way we could carry on," I added cautiously. "To be fair to you, I have to say it has an added risk factor." Holding my hand up to stem the rush of questions, I continued. "So first of all, I will ask Marguerite to give her appraisal of the situation."

Marguerite, dressed in combat fatigues as she was, still managed to look beautiful and very much a woman as she stepped boldly forward, completely in command of the situation. The silence of these men while they waited on her word, showed the respect in which they held her, not only as Miguel's wife, but also for her own professionalism as a pilot. Pinning a sheet of notes on the display board, she cleared her throat before commencing her briefing in a clear firm voice.

"Amigo's, we are lucky that although the two targets are miles apart for anyone on the ground, thanks to the sharp eyes of Ben, we have discovered one chance of getting in between them both, by air." An enthusiastic murmur arose from the men at that information. Waiting for it to subside and indicating one of the three spots on the map that she had outlined in red chinagraph, she continued.

"Here it is; we will have to make any insertion at night and of course without lights for landing." She paused for them to absorb this information and after the mutterings quietened down, she resumed her plan.

"Fixed wing is out, the *only* way will be by helicopter, but as it is at very high altitude their lift capability will be badly reduced. You are all taking a very heavy kit load, so we will have to make our move in two machines rather than one." Pausing for breath and checking her notes, she proceeded.

"I will fly our Alouette, Miguel will fly the other and we will make our approach at low level, across here," she indicated a largely uninhabited area of land with her hand. "Then," she paused to watch their faces as she continued, using her finger to trace the route on the map. "We will fly up this gully keeping very close to the ground for twenty miles, approach the LZ here!" She concluded by slapping the spot marked LZ on the map loud enough to make a couple of them jump slightly. There were a few more muttered comments from her audience, they had all been on 'chopper' insertions before, but most of them had not flown with her.

"Gentlemen!" I called, seeking to quieten and assure them.

"I hear your comments and know your fears, but I can assure you, that in my opinion, if *anyone* can fly us in there in the dark, *in safety*, then that person is Marguerite!" I paused a moment to judge reactions.

"If it is of any consolation, *I* shall be sat in front of the machine *she* will be flying!" Judging by the laughter and nods of approval, this seemed to satisfy the worriers, who were also being 'advised' by those who had already had experience of her flying skills. As the hubbub gradually subsided, Miguel and I then set about splitting the men into four Fire Teams with two men in each and then into two further groups for the action and for the 'ride' to the LZ.

When listing was complete and there was relative silence in the room, I said, "make no mistake, in regard to the 'training' side, the next two or three days are going to be very hard on you all. Although you are already skilled and experienced as individuals, you have not worked together as members of teams. SO!" I stressed, "we must mould you into effective fighting teams in a very short space of time. Luckily, with the exception of Rico, you have all experienced the same training in the past, so all we will do is refresh it!" Then as if an after thought, I added, "and to build up your fitness!"

The resulting rude comments about fitness and their ages were only to be expected. So, in answer to the one or two references to my being their *Abuelo* - their grandfather - I responded.

"*Chico's,*" - children - "come the morning, we will see what we will see! Possibly the tortoise will teach the hare!" A few shouts of laughter resulted from that piece of wisdom, but no further comments were forthcoming, so I asked them all to get an early night, as tomorrow and the next day, they would start work before dawn and go on into the night.

Leaving the map for them to study, I joined Miguel and Marguerite in a nightcap in their room.

"I have been in touch by phone with a friend, who has promised to bring another 'chopper' down." Miguel said as he handed me a glass half full of whisky. "He should arrive by early tomorrow afternoon." The aircraft is a twin engine Bell 222, which can carry up to seven people. It will be more than capable of doing the job we have planned on one fuel load. Another big bonus is that it's fitted with skids and he lives near Bogotá."

Looking across at Marguerite he paused and when she nodded, he continued. "I have to say this Ben; I *cannot* fly a chopper on this mission." Holding his hand up to stop my questions, he took a deep breath. "You see, I had a very bad night crash a few years ago, doing much the same thing. It seems I cannot judge distances and speed in poor light, as my eyes have weakened!" His voice betrayed his embarrassment as he explained, "I will not put the lives of you, my wife and my friends at risk!" His shoulders had slumped in a despairing fashion. "But my friend Zack, that's who is bringing the other chopper down, was a Marine Pilot in Vietnam and has said he will fly it for us!"

I looked at this man, who in so short a time had quickly become my trusted friend and who had already given so much. I could see he was breaking apart with the guilt of letting me down.

I grasped his arm as I said, "I appreciate your honesty Miguel. I thought there might be something, but it makes no difference as long as we can get in and out without difficulty. If you say your friend is good enough, that's fine by me." I patted his arm reassuringly. "So make the arrangements; you *are* my Second in Command after all!" I chided.

Giving his arm a squeeze and tossing a kiss to his wife, I stood up and wished them both a good night. Then as I opened the door, I paused and looked back at him to say.

"You are twice the man I thought you were and I'm proud to have you as my partner!" The look of relief that flashed across his face at my words was worth seeing. He was a happier man as I left the room.

Chapter 20

<u>Back to Basics.</u>

The earth shook at 4 am the following morning.

"Reveille! Reveille!" I shouted. True to my word, I was going to show them who was fit or not. Everyone was rudely awakened by my shouts, accompanied by Miguel beating a tin can with a metal bar. The unwelcome intrusion into the depths of sleep was also accompanied by us tipping their camp beds over. This rough treatment was designed to jerk them awake, while acting as a test to see who could take the pressure. Groping around on the floor in a heap of bedding, in what must feel like the middle of a very cold night, was not conducive to good temper. The expected grumbles were increased a thousand fold when I informed them that breakfast would be at 8am and it would not be served until they had all taken part in a cross-country run. For Miguel and myself, the object of the 'exercise' had been achieved; no one lost their temper

"Fall in outside in ten minutes!" Miguel instructed.

This then, was the start of the hard training they had been promised. When they were formed up in the chill, early morning mist, I answered their continuing but bantering complaints.

"I should not need to remind you, we are going into action. Each man will rely on the other as a part of the team and if you are not brought up to a certain level of fitness, then you won't make the grade! Now let's MOVE!"

With that, I turned and started to run up the track leading from the Plantation at a nice steady jog. We kept to the low ground, skirting the boundaries of the crop growing areas while picking the best ground to run on. When I sensed that they had all warmed up - myself included, I stepped up the pace a little, ensuring that no one was left behind or being outpaced. I kept this up for about a mile, then brought them to a sharp walking pace for half a mile. This formula was repeated for the next hour and a half and as we came within range of the Plantation again, I increased the speed to a steady run. To my amazement - and pleasure, we managed to keep in a tight group on the approach to the house and jogged on the spot for a few minutes before I called a halt.

"Well *Chicos*!" I chided them. "While I congratulate you on your *present* level of fitness, I think you still need some more training." It was Manuel who, entering into the spirit of cut and thrust stepped forward and said.

"Hey, *Padrastro! We* can take whatever you can hand out!" The others laughed when they heard him call me his *stepfather*.

The aim of every leader in such a group should be to show you can do it yourself, not just dish out the orders. Respect must be earned. I had challenged them, I had led them and I had stuck with them. *They*, it seemed, had accepted me as an equal and the teasing born by mutual respect had begun.

"Come, come children," I said in softer tones. "I accept with honour the promotion from yesterday's grandfather, but whoever thinks he can beat me, let him *beware*! Now off to the showers because you *stink*!" I chided, "then breakfast will be followed by work!" With the sporting challenge down on the table, I knew from the looks of glee on their faces that not only had I gained some more respect, but I would have to be on my toes from now on.

"Wow!" Miguel said as he came over to me, "I missed what you said to them, but it seems they are all going to prove to *you* who is best! Perhaps you have increased the team spirit, by adding a spirit of competition, eh?"

"That's exactly what I want to hear my friend," I averred, "because they will gel together quicker if they compete. Now, a shower and food I think." I left him shaking his head in wonder.

When the breakfast meal was over, I informed them that we would all be doing some intensive weapons training, which would include mock fire and movement exercises. Of course, once again it was the cheeky Manuel who was fast becoming the unit clown who stood up to ask the obvious question.

"Why *mock* fire and movement Ben, don't you *trust* us?" As this was said in a friendly way, I knew he understood, but wanted an explanation for those that perhaps didn't.

"Trust. Yes, that is the best word Manuel," I responded. "That is an item that has to be earned, especially where weapons are concerned. *We* have never worked together before. *You* are learning to trust *me* with your lives in this mission. I too, have to learn now, if I can trust *you* with these weapons. Too late after an accident, to find that a man has *not* got the skills he professed!" There were mutterings of I agree and *absolutamente* from the others. Mission achieved, Manuel sat down with a satisfied smile on his face.

Miguel handed out the training schedules, which showed the teams and their times of attendance at the training 'stands' he and Marguerite had set up while we were out for our run. We started on time at 9 am, continuing through to 12.30 pm, when we broke for a light lunch. Each team had to attend a 'stand,' and carry out a given task on a tight timetable such as:

Field strip and clean weapons against the clock. Carry out a first aid task correctly. Use of map and compass; select and approach fire positions stealthily; then finally, a combined effort in observation of the ground, in which each team was asked to identify and locate possible enemy positions. This was easy, as they would in fact be observing another team getting into a defensive position - of course, without an actual enemy, there is no need to be careful is there! Or is there?

After a fairly successful morning, the overall results of which were encouraging in that no 'dead wood' had been identified, we let them off for lunch. As they ate, again aiming to increase the competitive spirit, I let each team know who had observed who and left them to pick the bones.

Lunch was a special high calorie meal, the first of a kind designed not to be too heavy to work on for the next session, but to give the required energy input. We had to introduce these carefully over a period of days, for if they had them for every meal straight out, then we could expect severe complications of their digestive systems. Generally, to the relief of Miguel and myself, the training during the rest of the day went well, with each man proving that he was reliable and it was soon noticed that the Fire Teams had already started to compete against each other. They were handling the Browning Heavy Machine guns and other weapons with which they had been issued, with a familiarity bred by constant use.   When we compared notes at the end of the day, there was little doubt left in the minds of either Miguel or myself.

"They gave some excellent demonstrations of field craft Ben," he said casually.

"Yes I agree," I replied, "and in their turn, some of the over-confident squad members were surprised to have been 'put down' while acting as an enemy guard!"

"Ha! Yes!" he laughed. "There were one or two hard lessons learned." Our general consensus of opinion was that they were ready for the next stage!

Prior to the evening meal, we repeated the morning's run and I was greatly impressed when they said they wanted to do a *proper* forced march. Setting off at a good pace, I once again led them into the surrounding area; this time we jogged for a mile and marched for ten minutes, then jogged again. On this occasion, I chose a slightly different route, which took us onto rising ground and into the surrounding jungle where the footing gradually became tougher.

The clinging humid heat, rough ground and faster pace soon had everyone perspiring heavily. Shirts and trousers, though lightweight, were black and heavy with water by the time we returned to the Plantation. Not many moans were heard when I told them to shower and change and be outside ready for some night movement practice as soon as the meal was over. They were beginning to enjoy doing what they all enjoyed doing best! Being soldiers! Fitness training was one of the biggest factors in any army as it boosts confidence and welds men into teams quickly.

The fitness of each individual was all-important to us; it could win or lose a battle as easily as anything. In a normal War Theatre, soldiers were part of a group - small or large - the commander of which could radio back to his HQ and speak to some guy surrounded by radios, attack computers, map displays and so on. He could request extra rations or ammunition be dropped to him, or if they were up against a superior enemy force, he could call in Artillery fire or an Air Strike. In *our* type of action, we don't have the luxury of those choices; what you need you carry! Simple as that!

When they were all ready after the meal, Miguel issued the weapons we had chosen to use on the task ahead. Felipe and Rico, forming Fire Team 1 were issued with a belt fed Browning Heavy Machine gun along with the Heckler & Koch 9mm MP5 submachine guns they had both chosen as their personal weapon, this meant they were extremely well armed.

Fire Team 2 consisted of Manuel and Ramon - by their own choice - they were armed the same as the No. 1 team. In their turn, Juan and Julio in Fire Team 3 would act as scouts and if needed, together with Louis and Ernesto of Fire Team 4, would make up an Ambush section. They were similarly armed as the others, but each member had a cut-down Winchester and Remington Pump Action Shot gun for CQB - close quarter battle if needed.

Each man would carry a compass and a hand held satellite navigation kit to ensure they knew where they were. If that was not enough, they all had a Browning .9mm high power pistol in a belt holster for personal protection, or for use for a *'Final Sanction'* should they be in danger of being captured. Despite the humidity being uncomfortable, each man was issued with lightweight Kevlar Body Armour and the personal webbing I had designed. During the actual attack, my own weapons would be a 'Hochler'- as I called the beautiful Heckler & Koch .9 mm submachine gun - plus the very lethal and versatile cut down Pump Action Shot gun.

The overall plan was that Miguel and I would be acting independently of the others, each being armed with a rocket launcher and two rockets, plus a Heckler & Koch G3SG 7.62mm Sniper rifle, in addition to the same personal weapons as the remainder of the group. In the main attack I would use a rocket on the helicopter, while Miguel would use his to demolish the factory. Each team member was given night vision goggles; which used the ambient light to aid in any night movement as well as for observation.

By prearranged use of the Red Strobe Light on the goggles, they could also ensure that team members would not be mistaken for enemy in the likely event of a Fire Fight. Just for luck, I had issued each man with a couple of Fragmentation Grenades. With all this kit to be carried, as well as the weapons needing to be regularly cleaned owing to the dampness of the jungle, they knew they were in for a tough time.

Rico, being in charge of Communications, then issued each man with a small, but very efficient lightweight high-powered personal radio. These were fitted into a top pocket on the user's jacket and came complete with an earpiece for privacy. They would use the accompanying throat mike that was fitted on soft elastic around the throat, with the mike resting gently on the side of the man's Adam's apple. Even a whisper could be broadcast by these radios, but in the interest of security and safety, Rico and I had devised a code system that would be used. The wearer could, by simply clicking his send button for the required amount of clicks, send previously agreed messages and acknowledgement, without speech.

We wouldn't be sleeping in tents or 'basha' style shelters during the actual task, so bedding rolls were not issued. We did, however, issue four day's rations to each man of the MRE type - Meals Ready to Eat, as beloved by the American Troops, who promptly and efficiently 'salted' it away into their kit.

At around 10pm, when they had cleaned their weapons, ensuring that they were liberally oiled against the continual dampness, I sent them off on a simple manoeuvre that would involve each team avoiding the others, while crossing the same area of ground. The first team back two hours later, was Felipe and Rico of Fire Team 1. It turned out that they had not been spotted by the others, but had 'marked the cards' of two of the other teams during the exercise.

Weapons were cleaned again and satisfied that all was going pretty well, we sent them off to their beds, with a reminder that from then on, no more alcohol would be permitted, but ample supplies of C-Cola and 7Up were kept cold in the Plantation icebox.

5 am the following morning saw another rude and noisy awakening and I was pleased to note that each man was outside with his personal weapon and webbing on at the appointed time. We set off on our run with me in the lead; this time at every two mile interval I called a name. That man sprinted past the others to take 'point;' he was then responsible for leading us along the winding and poorly marked tracks that had been studied on maps and committed to memory the previous day. This method ensured that their sense of direction was honed to a sharper awareness and if the track took us away from our objective, they were forced to use their map and compasses to help regain their proper course. In a brief discussion during a rest period, Miguel and I both agreed that there would be no problem with their direction finding in daylight, so we hatched a plan for the same test to be conducted that night.

Soaked with perspiration, tired, but in good spirits, we returned to the Plantation in time for a good cooked breakfast. After their meal, I gave each Fire Team leader an envelope containing instructions for the day's training. Each team was given a task, in which they had to move across a pre-determined area of the land that had been selected for its close similarity to the jungle in the region of the targets.

Neither team knew the designated tasks of the others, nor would they be on the same area or course as another. They would possibly - if their powers of observation were good enough - see or hear the others at times. Team leaders were to record all such sightings, giving correct map co-ordinates and times. Complete with weapons and all their kit - filled with sand to assimilate the weight of their issue of rations and ammunition, they had four hours in which to cover a ten mile course, each setting off from a different drop point and at a set time. To this end, we had tasked Marguerite with driving an ex military lorry into the jungle.

Watching their progress from vantage points, Miguel and I were convinced that we had the right men. It became abundantly clear from the start that they knew their jobs. Not only were they all very experienced in their individual tasks, they had also 'knitted' together most effectively and more important still, they all knew the jungle and how to use it. Later, at the debrief, Marguerite reported that while she was driving around - acting the part of an 'enemy' patrol - she had stopped at the points where the teams would cross the muddy tracks. Santos, an old Mexican/Indian tracker who had gone with her and knew the area from birth, was tasked to look for any unwanted spoor.

"The good news is," she announced, "he has seen none!" This caused a few smug grins and handshakes.

After a late lunch, they were stood down for a few hours rest until at 7 pm, they once again gathered together in the house and while they ate their evening meal, Miguel briefed them on that night's exercise. Each man would draw his weapons - a supply of ammunition would be issued later - they were to conduct a Search and Destroy sweep in a remote, marshy area that was known to be devoid of humans. He also warned them that I would already be out there with Santos, ready to 'pick off 'any unwary squad member.

Miguel advised them that in the centre of the area was an old building standing on sour ground reclaimed by the swamps. This was their target for a co-ordinated attack that would be a simulation of the actual action against the Cartel's factory. Timings and communication details would be handed out with the ammunition.

With a grave voice, Miguel added, "I should not need to remind you that this will be your last chance to get it right; we have to move to the real target area the following evening and that will be a night move."

Shortly after 9 pm, the truck dropped the teams off at their respective Start Points. When all were ready, a series of four clicks on their radios signalled the start. Team leaders would respond with their team number in 'clicks,' in reply as acknowledgment. It was not long before they found themselves wading waist deep in swamps, or having to push through dense undergrowth and clamber over fallen trees. Felipe and Rico, who had been dropped at the second Start Point, found themselves on a small rise in the ground. Though it overlooked some of the easier terrain it was still just as wet, as they soon discovered. Within a few minutes of them starting, even with the use of the night vision goggles, Felipe found that he had difficulty in judging the depth of water, or firmness of ground. The weight of the Browning Heavy Machine gun made him sink into the mire, but he had to keep it dry if possible.

To ensure that water was kept out of the barrel, he, like the others, had placed a condom over it, but this was only of limited success. Completely soaked and cursing silently, he made a brave effort to keep his feet. Rico, being new to the game was getting on no better. Weighted down by sand to simulate belt fed ammunition for the gun, he was tiring after only going for an hour, so he had dropped behind and lost contact with Felipe. Realising the situation, he did the right thing in deciding to stand still and wait for his partner to retrace his steps. Placing his weapon and ammunition box on a log, he attempted to wipe the sweat and mud from his face and pull the numerous leeches from his skin.

Then to his complete horror, a nearby thick floating mat of twigs rose up from the water and launched itself at him. Hitting him full in the chest, the mass pushed him over and backwards down into the swamp. Desperately fighting to avoid swallowing the filthy water, Rico pushed the mass of twigs off and struggled to his feet. Gasping for breath, he wiped his eyes, only to find he was confronted with a dark human shape that was obviously not Felipe. The shape reached out a long arm and a hand grasped him by the front of his jacket. A fierce voice hissed in his ear.

"Don't get caught like that again, or you'll not come with us! Now Vámonos Amigo!"

"Ben? Is that you?" the shaken Rico gasped, only to find he was talking to himself. There was no one there; he had not even heard his attacker leave. Felipe, finding he was on his own, had retraced his steps and was surprised to find Rico apparently talking to himself. He asked what had happened and Rico could only gasp.

"I don't really know! I *think* Ben just attacked me!"

With a nervous laugh, Felipe said sharply, "well if that's right, you had better pull your finger out and keep up!" With that he passed Rico his weapon and set off, his head moving from right to left as he looked for danger. This time, Rico kept close to him. Later, as they approached the designated rendezvous position, they found the other squad members already there.

"Here's some hot soup," Miguel said, thrusting a mess tin into their hands. "Put your weapons over there," he added, indicating that they should stack their weapons around a good-sized bush in the centre of the clearing. Worn out, they both collapsed in soggy heaps on the ground. Each of the other team members were complaining of their various experiences. Felipe and Rico soon realised from the tales told by the others, that they too had suffered their own respective forms of hell.

Marguerite and Santos were kept busy handing out more hot soup to help them recover. In their turn, they were equally amused to hear of the variety of shapes of the Devils and huge Monsters that had risen from the marshy wastes, to throw the unwary down into the depths. Rico, when listening to these 'tales,' was secretly pleased to realise that he had not been singled out because of his newness. Each team was vying with the others in inventing new and not very complementary descriptions of myself and Santos, most of which were not very reverential. Some in fact were downright blasphemous.

"Friends!" Miguel called for their attention. "I have heard all you have to say. Now perhaps it would be best if you listen to Ben's own report on the exercise and on your efforts!"

"Hey Miguel! How can we listen to Ben? He isn't here!" Ramon cut in from his position flat on the ground with his feet in the air. This was greeted by noisy shouts of agreement from the others.

"Perhaps he's got lost in the swamp!" Manuel 'the clown' called with such glee that it resulted in another chorus of ribald comments. Each man amidst the laughter passed their own comments about where they thought I should be.

Suddenly, with an ear-shattering roar, the 'bush' they had all rested their weapons against rose into the air; the various weaponry falling like dead limbs alongside it. The few men who were standing fell back in shock - some actually ending up on their asses on the ground. Those already on the ground skittered away like frightened kittens, spilling mess tins and falling over each other. These brave, but irreverent 'soldiers' crossed themselves hastily as the 'bush' walked towards them.

Stopping in their midst, it emitted another loud bellow and with a sudden violent shaking, cast all the twigs off. It was some minutes later that all the nervous laughter from the now completely embarrassed 'soldiers' died away and they stood there with heads bowed in shame as they realised it was me standing there grinning at them. Ramon, who had nearly been trampled in the mad rush to escape this new Devil, stepped forward sheepishly.

"Señor Ben, forgive me, I was only joking and did not mean to be rude about you!" he said, in a very embarrassed voice.

Still having difficulty in controlling my own amusement, I wiped the tears from my eyes.

"Don't worry Ramon, I deserve it, I did treat some of you very harshly out there. But I feel you have all shown that you can take it and are ready for the task ahead. Stop worrying and join me in a drink!" So saying, amidst cheers from the men I passed a bottle of rum out for them to share.

"To ward off the early morning chill," I whispered to Miguel.

After a quick change of necessary clothing, I set them off once again on the final leg of the journey. As each team member passed me and slipped away into the night, they crossed themselves and appealed to the Virgin Mary for protection. I didn't know if they were serious, or mocking me still. Two hours later and only three miles further into the jungle, Felipe and Rico could hear the 'clicks' on the radio as the other teams reported their arrival in predetermined locations, forming an arc to one side of and on a slight tree-lined rise above the target. On arrival at their allotted position, they found that they had a reasonably clear view of the ramshackle building that was the 'target' for tonight's exercise. Their team task was to 'engage' a group of enemy guards - imaginary on this occasion - and to ensure that no interference with Miguel or myself was allowed.

As the actual attack on the Cartel's factory would take place just after dawn, we had the best part of an hour in which to rest, don dry underclothes, clean weapons and grab some cold rations. In the meantime, Juan and Julio in Fire Team 3 would scout the area and identify any previously unknown trouble spot.

The previous silence of the radios was broken as the scouts' reports came in. In whispers, they gave the grid references of the locations of the guards - sheets of silver foil hung in the trees by Santos - as well as their strength and alertness. Each man, though he knew this was just a practice, felt a tingle of apprehension as it heralded the start of the action. At fifteen minutes before the appointed time, I gave one code word over the radio, which was in turn acknowledged by each team leader. This brought them all to the highest state of readiness.

Precisely on the stroke of 5 am, just as the sun rose above the surrounding hills, they opened fire on their designated targets - on this occasion no return fire would be experienced. They steadily poured a concentrated hail of lead into the area; the heavy chatter of the Browning's sounding loud and clear above the sharper cracks of the lighter weapons. Smoke and debris obscured their vision; the strong acrid smell of cordite filled our noses. Then, above the constant rattle of machine gun fire, there came the sharp smack of grenades exploding; these threw up clouds of dirt and loose vegetation to add to the confusion.

To the left of the buildings - where El Jefe's aircraft would land - a separate, but equally ferocious battle was taking place. Marguerite had accompanied me and she was clearly enjoying herself as she laid down a withering stream of bullets at a small clump of bushes that we had designated as 'the helicopter.' These bushes, though some three hundred metres away, were already tattered and torn by flying lead and suddenly they disappeared in a bright orange explosion as my rocket found its target.

At almost the same instant, to our right and some distance away across the killing ground, the remains of the old building that had already taken on the look of a sieve, suddenly and in spectacular fashion, appeared to launch itself up into the air supported on the top of a mushroom cloud of flame, smoke and dirt. The rocket that Miguel had fired had successfully detonated the Fire Bomb that Santos had planted there. With a clattering and crashing of tin, the remains fell to the ground over a wide area.

Recovering quickly from the shock, Marguerite, eager not to be outdone by me - or anyone else for that matter - emptied her magazine as she directed her fire on to an old withered tree stump standing forlornly in the midst of this area of destruction.

"*That,*" she said, with a winning smile on her grubby face in answer to my questioning look, "was the fuel dump! That was!"

"Yes, well done!" I replied lamely as the last fragments fell to the ground. I realised that she could have been right - I had not considered that the Cartel may possibly keep fuel at the factory. "Well done," I repeated.

Giving the radio signal for a ceasefire and waiting for everyone to acknowledge, I helped Marguerite up off the ground. Apparently still dazed by the noise, she staggered a bit as she gathered her equipment. Then, with her leaning on my arm, we picked our way across the marshy ground and I found that I was enjoying the close intimate contact with this beautiful and constantly surprising woman. The pressure of the side of her breast against my bare forearm made my skin feel as if it had been burnt. Even then, with all the dust, dirt and the acrid smell of cordite in the air, I could still smell that most alluring perfume she wore.

As we passed into an area of heavily overgrown trees, I stopped, roughly turning her to face me and holding her by the shoulders, kissed her full on the lips. I felt her body sag against mine, alive and warm, her lips softened to return the kiss. Feeling a powerful surge deep within my loins, I suddenly broke off pushing her away.

"I'm sorry, I didn't know what I was doing."

Marguerite stood firmly in front of me, her breasts heaving - whether from the excitement of the recent action or the kiss, I did not know.

"Don't worry about it Ben, don't be sorry! I accept it as the just reward for my work so far." With a smile, she reached out to touch my arm. "I shall look forward to 'pay day' from now on and perhaps a bonus?" she said with a wicked grin on her face. With a light laugh at my surprised look, she turned and walked jauntily up the track to where the others were gathering.

Even a blind man could have located where our 'troops' had gathered, their excited chatter could be heard miles away. I paused on the edge of the clearing where they were busy cleaning their weapons - the sign of good soldiers. They had undoubtedly enjoyed the simulated battle; it had driven all thoughts of Devils and Monsters out of their minds.

"Wow! That was really something!" Miguel enthused, as he spotted us. "Did you enjoy yourself my love?" he asked his wife.

"Oh, yes. Very much indeed, especially the last part!" she replied happily. My stomach flipped at her words. Behind my back, I felt her hand squeeze my arm reassuringly.

"Well Miguel? Do you think they will be safe and can I trust them to bring me back safely from the task ahead?" I asked, hastily changing the subject and in a voice loud enough to be heard by the men. They turned in anticipation of his reply.

"Mmm?" Miguel mused, teasingly. "I think Ben, that good leadership by example is the way to gain trust." He let his gaze wander round their expectant faces. "I also feel that by your professional approach to the planning, training and conducting of this exercise, that you have shown yourself as a leader who could be followed to Hell and back!" A loud cheer and cries of 'I agree' came from the assembled group, who I felt, also deserved some praise. Holding up my hand for silence, I waited as the final comments died down.

"Amigos! Friends, for that is what I feel you are. You have shown in a very short time that not only can you be trusted and are efficient, but you are of the highest quality of soldier that I have ever been privileged to serve with!" The response to that was deafening, so I had to wait for it to subside before adding.

"As a reward for this hard work, you can all have the day off, but tonight ...... We Go To WAR!" Morale booster? No, it was the honest truth; these guys were good and we were off to fight a war.

When the excitement had died down, we cleared the area and returned to the Plantation for a well earned rest..

Chapter 21

Into Action.

Though the journey back to the Plantation was rough - Marguerite did not slow down for some of the rough patches on the track - the men were all in high spirits. Relief showed in some faces, but there was a palpable overall air of confidence. I was relieved to hear some of them openly admitting that they had made mistakes, thus leaving themselves open to unwanted attention. Everyone agreed that what had happened to them had been their own fault and they were the better for the lesson.

"I think we have cracked it now Ben," Miguel said after listening to some of the comments. "So are we moving up tonight?" I gave a nervous cough before replying.

"Yes, the men are ready and the clock is against us now, so we must press forward," I paused to collect my thoughts before adding, "if you agree, we use the same teams as today and I would like to have a final briefing after the evening meal. Then we draw weapons and ammunition and if the 'choppers' are there, we go!" Looks of approval flashed around the men on hearing this.

Immediately on arrival at base, we cleaned and returned weapons, then showered before enjoying a well-deserved and hearty breakfast. With everything seemingly well in hand, we were happy to stand the men down until 5 pm. They all went straight to bed, not only were they tired, but the move that night would mean they should grab as much rest as possible. Miguel, Marguerite and I sat pouring over the maps, making final decisions as to what, when and where things were to happen and most important of all, who was doing it. My two aviators mapped out the route for our incursion and gave me a copy.

As we parted outside their bedroom door, I asked to meet them for a last chat before the final briefing. Marguerite had arranged that as we slept, Indian servants would collect all of our dirty clothing and wash it ready for the next stage. To reduce the chance of casualties from broken footwear, they would also spend time rubbing a special mixture of beeswax and animal fat into all of our boots.

When we came down later, the wall of sound that greeted my arrival in the briefing room told me they were all there waiting for us. Each one was expounding on what they were going to do and how they would do it; the excitement was tangible with lots of kidding going on. This was their way of easing their mounting tension.

"Right then let's get on with it!" I called. I banged a table loudly and the buzz of chatter died away.

"First of all, Miguel and I have decided on a suitable code name for this operation. As we are going in to destroy the cocaine referred to as 'Snow' in the drug trade and our transport; being aircraft; are referred to as 'Birds,' this leaves us with 'Snow Bird.' Therefore the Ops Code will be SNOW BIRD and will be used as a password as well as in radio comm.'s." Murmurs of general approval went round the room at this. I then continued.

"I will repeat what I said earlier, I am *very* pleased with your progress and the way you have all pulled together in such a short time. BUT!" I emphasised this to bring them down another level. "This must not be allowed to go to your heads. You don't need me to tell you that they are *hungry out there!* Neither do you need me to remind you that they will EAT YOU!" I raised my voice again, before saying in almost a whisper. "You will get only *one* chance." I paused again, as this statement started an increasing murmur of agreement amongst them and I could see these strong men looking sheepish at this.

"Now!" I called above the raised voices. "While I'm aware of your high state of readiness, this is not matched by the standard of planning we have been able to achieve." Miguel held up his hand to stop any further questions. "Owing to the uncertainty of what we're up against, I can only say that things *may* change as we get further into the mission." Some very questioning looks were thrown at me at this revelation, but ignoring them I pressed on. "We are ready! El Jefe will not wait, so we will go with the minimum of planning and execute the mission with maximum skill!" A huge roar of consent broke out at this. They were proud. They were itching to go!

"Are you READY?" I yelled.

"YES!" they screamed, waving their fists in the air.

"Who will win?" I yelled, struggling to be heard above the noise.

"WE WILL!" Came the unanimous response and they broke into a chant of "Snow Birds! Snow Birds!

Snow Birds!" They'd already adopted the code as a badge or standard around which they would rally, which in the end is what all soldiers do. Waiting for them to calm down a bit, I banged the table with the butt of my pistol. Gradually the chanting faded away and gathering my thoughts, I spoke loudly.

"*I* am happy to hear that you won't let your mates down!" I paused as if to draw breath. "And so are THEY!"

There was a great roar of laughter at this and I took a quick gulp of beer while I waited for it to subside once again, then turning to Marguerite, I asked her to introduce the stranger who had come into the room with her.

"This is Zack an old friend of ours who we have known since Nam," she announced, "he is a very experienced 'chopper' pilot and he will fly Group 2 into position." She informed them in a clear voice, then with a cheeky grin she added.

"He is just as crazy as me hombre's!" Ignoring the ribald comments about that piece of useless information, she stepped back to let me continue with the proper briefing.

"With regard to air transport, I have decided that after dropping us in, the two choppers wll 'stand off' high up the mountainside so that they can be called in if we need to evacuate quickly!"

The wisdom of this was acknowledged by all. I then detailed the members of the two 'airlift' groups, while reminding them all of the team structures. Miguel was busy handing out written instructions - to be read and destroyed before their departure - which contained simple directions and map references, we then double checked that they all had the right co-ordinates. After the inevitable questions had been dealt with and Miguel and I were satisfied they all knew what they were doing, I let them go, knowing that they were as prepared as any one could be for the mission ahead. No matter what training they'd had, they would all agree that there is nothing like doing it for real.

There was a big rush to get the weapons and ammunition, plus all the other gear they would need such as food and changes of warm dry clothing. Then each man was left to pack his kit away in his own fashion and to use soft pieces of specially stained cloth to wrap around his chosen weapon - we could not afford rattles from equipment to give the game away. With this done, they collected together in their respective groups and made their way out to the now waiting aircraft.

The Alouette belonging to Miguel would carry Group 1 and myself, while Group 2 would go in the Bell 222 that Zack had flown in that day. It was just light enough for them to see that these machines had been stripped of all unnecessary items such as seats and doors. Though the absence of doors would make it very cold up there, this was very necessary, as we would be flying up into the higher altitudes where the air was thinner and lift from the rotors would be harder to obtain. From the way they were dressed, it seemed that no one needed to remind them that it would also be much colder in the higher mountains at night.

Once the engines had been 'run up' satisfactorily, the pilots gave the thumbs-up signal for the men to start loading. Settling themselves on the hard floor, they each used the tie-downs provided for both their kit and themselves.

"Snow Birds GO!" I called over the radio, giving the order to lift off. Fighting the ground effect created by the down wash of the rotors, the heavily laden 'choppers' rose as if tied together. Dropping their noses slightly to gain forward motion, they flew out across the swamps in the opposite direction from our objective. There was as usual, a thin mist rising from the swamps, which we all knew would eventually get much thicker over the watery areas. As we were not using navigation lights, Zack stayed behind and slightly to the right of Marguerite's aircraft; he also flew lower so that she was silhouetted against the darkening sky. I knew that later, when we were in the mountains, the pilots would use Radar only if required for safety reasons.

In a steady formation and maintaining a speed of 250 knots, we flew parallel to the coast for 15 minutes before gradually turning in towards the towering coastal mountain range. Leaving the lower swampy region behind and emerging as noisy dragons from the thickening mist, we flew up over the jungle canopy under which we had sweated so hard over the past days. The men sat in silence - conversation was impossible with the engine noise and pulsing beat of the rotors - so each man was locked in his own world, with his own thoughts on what lay ahead.

Marguerite flew us into a wide valley running into the heart of the mountain range. Pulling back gently on the cyclic at the same time as adjusting the collective, she gave us lift to match the rising ground. The moon was coming clear of the few clouds, but not enough to make us identifiable as we passed like shadows. The pass climbed ever higher while at the same time narrowing, causing the men to draw inwards from the side of the aircraft as they sensed the razor sharp rocks waiting to rip the spinning rotor blades into a million pieces, and us with it. With her uncanny skill, Marguerite brought us out between the peaks of two towering mountains without mishap; I could just make out their shape looming above us in the darkness. A quick glance at the compass to confirm her direction and she took the chopper down to fly as close to the ground as was safe. From my position in the co-pilot's seat, I felt as if I wanted to draw my feet and legs up in case they touched the unseen rocks that I could almost feel rushing past underneath us.

Now and again, intermittent streaks of white flashed past under us; these I realised were patches of white water from the rapids on the larger rivers. Suddenly, a wall of white would loom up seemingly just in front of us and we would be squashed back into our seats as Marguerite pulled back on her collective and the chopper swooped upwards to clear the massive waterfall we had just 'climbed'.

Equally as frightening was the way she would make the craft dive down with gut wrenching swoops into the blackness below after clearing a high ridge. With the old feeling of combat tension building up in me, I had been concentrating on straining my eyes for danger ever since take off, now my alarm grew. Just as my stomach 'bottomed out' after one particularly long drop, I tore my eyes from the impending doom in front of me and looked across at Marguerite for the first time.

"Jeez!" I said to myself. "Thank Christ for THAT!" To my relief I saw that she was wearing a set of night vision goggles. This then, accounted for our unhesitating progress so far.

"Bloody idiot!" I mentally kicked myself for being such a fool as not to have realised it earlier and I started to relax slightly. Some time later, the mighty Cauca River flashed past underneath us and I mentally logged us just over half way to the LZ - Landing Zone. We started to climb again, turning onto a heading that would take us into the selected landing spot without being seen in the area of either of the targets. In the distance, I caught a glimpse of an aircraft's lights, which, judging by the altitude and speed, was a passenger liner bound for the airport near Bogotá.

We continued to climb steadily, until without warning the mountainside suddenly flattened out. Bringing the 'chopper' to an abrupt hover, Marguerite looked around for the best place to set down.

"Christ! I hope the brake lights are working!" I gasped. The image of Zack's chopper standing on its nose behind us as we stopped flashed across my mind. The Alouette was not equipped with skids like the other craft, so she had to be sure of the surface. Skilfully handling the 'ground effect' - the down draught of the rotors against the ground, which builds up a cushion of air under the aircraft - she lowered the 'chopper' while watching Manuel, who was now sat in the open doorway wearing his night vision set also. He gave hand signals to guide her as she controlled our descent and I felt a slight bump as the one landing wheel touched the ground – or at least I hoped it was the ground, as visions of us perched in mid air with one wheel on a tall rock passed across my mind

    Looking back, I watched until Manuel gave the all clear, then when Marguerite nodded, at the same time as mouthing the word OUT, he gingerly stepped out onto the ground. Each man slid across the floor, carefully taking his cue from the pilot, so as not to upset the delicate balance she was playing with as she fought to keep the machine steady against the 'ground effect.' I followed on as the 'tail end Charlie,' squeezing her on the shoulder as I passed. Once on the ground and happy that all kit and bodies were clear and accounted for, I waved her off. Crouching to avoid the stinging cloud of dust and grit thrown up by the rotor wash, I found we had been dropped near the edge of the flat area that I had identified on our recce flight. A hundred metres or so away, we could see and hear the other machine, which had been able to land on its skids. A mark of the professionalism of these men - *my Chico's* - was that without spoken orders, they immediately prepared their personal weapons and went into all-round defence mode to secure the perimeter while we waited for the others to join us.

Soon after take off, I had switched myself into 'battle mode' and having given strict instructions at the briefing that all movement would be in silence, any routine orders coming from the team leaders would be given at RV's -rendezvous. I knew the others would have done the same as me and would now be ready for anything. As the other team closed on us, I waved my team forward and led off on a bearing, which would quickly take us off the high mountain. Each man's senses would be on full alert from now on. When I considered that we had moved far enough away from the LZ, I gathered them all into a group and told them in a whisper.

"From this moment on, we're in the front line. Move silently and remain alert!" I pulled my hand held Satellite Navigation kit out of my pocket and gave them all the position it showed. It would be the emergency RV; should anything go wrong and we got split up; each man would make his way back to this spot. This they committed to memory in order to preserve security in the event of capture. A final quick check of our kit for rattly bits, a synchronisation of watches and we split into our respective groups ready for the move.

In his own way, each man would be feeling the euphoric effect of being dropped behind enemy lines. Special Forces troops across the world have all felt the 'buzz' when senses suddenly sharpen and they come 'alive.'

After confirming the bearing and direction of travel with me, Juan and Julio assumed their role of forward scouts and moved out in advance. The plan being that they would scout the agreed route, at least one kilometre ahead, giving prearranged clicks on the send button of their radios in accordance with what they found. It was not long before the cold that had worked into us all during the flight began to ease. We moved reasonably quickly at the beginning; no one, not even the bandits that roamed the Colombian mountains lived up this high; so we followed animal trails down the mountainside. Care was taken not to slip, as the razor sharp rocks would be unforgiving. The thin rarefied air began to affect us before long; heads began to ache and breathing became laboured. Miguel called a halt so that we could rest briefly and some of the men popped Tylenol tablets to ease their headache.

Ten minutes later, thinking it was a good job that we were going downhill and not up, I set them off again; I did not want the scouts cut off in case of trouble. Suddenly two loud clicks in my earpiece made me jump - I scrabbled to turn the volume down as I acknowledged the 'all clear' signal. Within a short time, I heard three clicks which told me the scouts had reached their first objective, here they would lay-up and rest until the groups joined them.

I stopped my group to allow Miguel's to take over point section duties.

"The scouts are at RV 1," I whispered as he went past.

"They must have skateboards on!" he remarked quietly, as he looked at the luminous dial of his watch. "Speed is OK, as long as they're not passing anything that could be a problem for us!" He moved off to warn his men to be extra vigilant.

"Oh ye of little faith!" I murmured as I followed.

We all moved carefully onwards, ears alert for the slightest sound, eyes scanning side to side for signs of movement. Feet feeling their way on the rocky ground before settling, fingers poised on triggers in readiness for a sentry to rise from position and fill the air with the vicious crackle of bullets. Even with these seasoned soldiers, their imagination would play tricks on them, as low rocks and bushes became crouching enemy.

"No one who hasn't done this would believe how nerve wracking it is!" I thought as I moved forward. We moved, bent almost double, in order to reduce our own silhouettes and to reduce the chance of a person down below us seeing us against the skyline. This meant we would not be able to go very far if the pace was too slow, on the other hand, speed could kill!

Fifteen minutes later, we arrived at the first objective, a heap of rubble showing as the only remains of a shepherd's hut. There was just the rustle of clothing, when in near perfect silence, the men went into an automatic all round defence. Each man lay facing outward in a circle, with his legs apart and his left foot resting on top of the right ankle of the man on his left - this would give them the means of passing predetermined messages by tapping their legs together, without the need for verbal instructions.

"This is proof of the quality of these guys!" I thought as I sensed, rather than saw, the practised smoothness of the action in the half-light. Even the younger Rico had fitted in, having been well briefed by his father. After conferring with the scouts and confirming their next objective, I sent them off; the main body would rest for fifteen more minutes before following. Keeping their fitness in mind, I had to be careful not to let them chill down too much, as the low temperature this high in the mountains, would soon sap the heat from the body. Movement gave little warmth, but without body heat, we would soon become dangerously near exposure.

I was also well aware, that the scouts were now approaching the level of the mountainside that was heavily wooded and could therefore be inhabited which would not show on any map. They would have to use not only their sight and hearing, but also their sense of smell. Animals could be smelt on the pure clean air, long before they would be seen or heard. Likewise, man and the smells he unwittingly manufactures such as smoke from a cooking fire, or the smell of food itself, both would travel for miles around, drifting up the mountainside. But most important of all, they would now be alert for the very distinctive smell of man's weakness, tobacco. A sentry having a crafty smoke - even though the glow of the cigarette may be hidden - could be detected a long way away if the wind were right. Equal to this, there was also the acrid smell of human urine that would alert the wary soldier; many times this had been proven over the years.

"The Mountain Gods must be with us." I thought when once again I heard two clicks - the all clear from the Scouts - on my radio, followed sometime later by the three clicks informing me of their arrival at RV 2. With our nerves on edge and employing identical skills of detection, we made our own cautious progress down the mountainside, to eventually link up with the scouts again. As we approached their position, the men again silently peeled off into their positions and a shadowy figure detached itself from the rocks and came over to me.

"Señor Ben," a husky voice whispered. I recognised it as Juan the lead scout.

"Yes Juan, what's the matter?" I muttered, my voice betraying my feeling of something going to go wrong.

"Nothing's wrong, Señor Ben. But I am going to leave well in advance of the others. I think it's best if the scouts were spread out now." He paused, as talking in a whisper was effectively shortening his breathing. "There have been some old signs of a group of people up here," he stated with confidence. "They were probably bandits, chased up here by the Army." Another pause. "So if you agree, we will split to cover a five hundred metre front. OK?"

"Wait before you go Juan, because I remember the map showing a ravine around about here somewhere, so don't go before you look at the map again. Oh! And let me have any new signals you four agree on!" We sought Miguel to check on the map, then when fully satisfied we all knew what everyone was doing, Juan and his scouts left us. Miguel and I discussed the next move and agreed to proceed in a classic Infantry leap-frog type action - one section moving forward while the others covered them.

Going to ground after a given distance then covering the other section as it moved through their positions etc.

I gave the order to move and had gone only a few hundred yards when the whispered order *"FREEZE!"* came over the radio set. From my right flank, a strange and unidentifiable smell came faintly on the breeze. With my skin prickling and the sound of blood pounding in my ears, I tried to regulate my pounding heart as I slowly looked around me. I could see nothing! Carefully I raised myself from the half crouch I was in, eased my footing and sank equally slowly into a full crouch on the floor of the forest we had just entered.

"There to my right!" I could make out a line of bulky shapes moving across our flank. Unable to make them out myself, I had to wait for one of the men to identify them. I slowly eased my safety catch off my machine gun, at the same time as I checked all around my position for other intruders.

"Why hadn't the scouts reported them?" I thought angrily. But as I watched the shapes climb the slope of the mountain, I realised that they were appearing from out of a dip in the ground, so would not have been seen by the scouts. I crept forward, making sure that I made no noise. Inch by inch, foot by foot, until I was able to use the trunk of a very large tree to lean against. My knees, calf muscles and thighs were aching from the effort; it was a relief to stand up. I watched, as what I thought must be the twentieth shape pass upwards in the gloom. The silence with which the shapes moved was unnerving, no sound, not even a cough or a footstep. Then I realised that the smell had strengthened as the shapes crossed our upwind quarter. The tension eased as the signs of movement receded into the darkness higher up the mountain. A few minutes later, a voice - perhaps the most welcome one ever - whispered in my earpiece.

"All clear, no more problems! Señor Ben, I will explain when we stop again. OK?" I clicked my button once to acknowledge as I thought. "Yes Ernesto! You _will_ explain later!"

We moved on, for the next three hours we crept down the mountainside without any more alarms. Unexpectedly, we found our way barred by a fast flowing and icy cold stream, which we would have to cross. Here the men drank their fill of clear fresh water, topping up water bottles where needed. Miguel found his way to me and as he slumped down thankfully on the hard, unforgiving ground he gasped.

"We have a place to cross Ben, it's just above us and is just a matter of jumping across a few rocks." He paused to gulp some water before adding, "if we can find the energy!" I knew what he meant only too well. We had brought ourselves up to a high state of fitness, but that had not prepared our leg muscles for the tortuous job of walking partly bent, down a rough mountainside. Each man's leg and thigh muscles were surely screaming with agony, I knew mine were!

"Pass the order to make sure they keep their feet dry Miguel; if they get wet now, it will make matters worse." He nodded in agreement as he got up, staggering under his heavy load. Then I remembered the unknown 'shapes' that had caused the earlier panic.

"Ask Ernesto to step into the 'office' will you please." With a laugh and a wave he was gone, fading into the darkness and I was left to listen to the deafening sound of rushing water. I also offered a silent prayer to the 'Mountain Gods,' asking them for their continued protection.

"You want me Señor Ben?" An anxious Ernesto asked as he crashed down beside me. "I have done something wrong Señor?"

"No, Ernesto you've done nothing wrong," I assured him. "We haven't had a chance to speak with you since our scare up in the tree line, so all I wanted to know is exactly what, or who those people were?"

"People Señor?" he exclaimed, with obvious amusement. "There were only two people, the rest were pack mules and lamas! We could have dealt with them easily if you had wished it!"

"Pack mules! Llamas?" I blurted in disbelief. "There must have been twenty of them, whose were they?"

"Perhaps Señor, they were gun runners, or maybe they carried drugs." He retorted with a shrug, obviously puzzled as to why I should care.

Code Name SNOWBIRD

Chapter 22

<u>The Final Slog.</u>

After everyone had rested and being anxious that they didn't cool down too much while aware of the rapid passing of time, I gave the order to move out. We started to climb up the moss-covered rocks that bordered this river; the fact that the air was damp from the overnight mist didn't help. Slipping and sliding over boulders that must weigh 40 tons or more, our heavy loads making things harder, we inched our way up to the crossing point that Miguel's men had found. Juan and Julio had gone over while we rested and were scouting the way ahead already.

Thankfully the river was shallower here and some huge boulders that had fallen there perhaps thousands of years before had formed a sort of footbridge with moderate gaps between them. In the poor light, I could plainly see that these boulders had been smoothed off from the passage of storm water and they were also wet from the moisture-laden air. It did not look as if it was going to be easy and we had to remain dry at all costs, so careful rock hopping was the only way.

Team spirit took over with the younger, fitter men going first to establish a chain for passing the bundles of kit over. They took a couple of good ropes across and succeeded in fixing them to trees on the far side. One man established himself in the centre and the others passed the kit, then made their own way over. Ernesto volunteered to stay 'till last; he would release the ropes on this side. Still carrying our personal weapons in case of surprises, we all made a reasonably safe crossing with just a few heart-stopping moments, when feet slid on landing and bodies wavered precariously in the air.

Once we were all safely established on the other side, kit was redistributed and we started the harder job of climbing out. The side of the ravine was perhaps three hundred feet high and was virtually impossible to climb straight up. I chose to follow the numerous goat tracks that wandered in zigzag fashion across the face of the cliff. This method, though covering much more ground - approximately half a mile - helped to reduce the physical wear and tear on us as the resulting slopes were easier.

"Who said goats were daft animals?" I asked myself. Not me! A little whisper sounded in my ear.

Dawn was breaking as I reached the top of the cliff and I was dreading to find that we had another ravine or even a deep valley to cross. Time was now disappearing fast and with it the cover of darkness. To my great relief, Juan and Julio were sat waiting for us to arrive at the top and their news was good to say the least.

"Señor Ben," Julio whispered. "We have been forward for one kilometre and the ground is going in a long slope through the jungle. There is no more problem we think." This news was better than a shot in the arm; it meant that we could catch up a bit of lost time, while remaining under cover of the jungle. I passed it on to Miguel when he came up to me, we checked our bearings and agreed our estimated location.

"OK!" I said in a low voice. "We are approaching the area of the plantation; I would think we are perhaps five to six kilometres from it now. Recheck all kit for loose items, clean weapons now and change into dry lightweight clothing. We will need to work our way forward as quickly, but as quietly as possible, starting in twenty minutes."

"I agree Ben, the distance should be about right," Miguel replied. "Perhaps we will find our Lay Up Point soon." He moved off to issue the order for kit changes and weapon checks. As he moved away, I used the ground to air radio and checked with Marguerite that all was OK with them. Deliberately avoiding use of Service type language to avoid causing any chance listener to raise the alarm, I simply whispered one word into the mike.

"Snowbirds?"

"All OK. We have 'bedded' down for the night some 30k from you." Marguerite's voice came whispering through the air, indicating they were on the ground. "Do you wish us to move up?"

One click on the send button - confirming that I would like them closer to the action in case of need.

"Do the tourist thing and look around when you think you can." Two clicks confirmed she had heard. As I took my weapons apart and re-oiled them, I was content with knowing that one or the other would be flying a recce as the light improved. If we needed them, they would not be far away.

"Ready to go Ben?" Miguel's whispered question came out of the dawn gloom. Seeing my nod of agreement, he gave a low whistle and the members of his group started moving past me. I moved my group out after them and keeping in close contact, we made good time over the easier ground that now started to slope down gently to the tree line. We entered the trees where I was relieved to find that by pure luck, we had stumbled across a wide swathe of new growth. Going would be easier in this softer vegetation, no old twisted creepers to cut away, no gnarled old limbs fallen across our path. This, I realised, must be land that the jungle was reclaiming from the plantation.

After pushing our way through the soft undergrowth for an hour, we came across a dip in the ground similar to that of a bomb crater. Miguel's instincts must have been the same as mine, for within a minute he was at my side, eager to talk.

"Ben, this is as good a place as any to establish our forward base, don't you think?" he queried.

"Rest your group," I instructed. "My group will stand too. Meanwhile, I will send out the scouts to see what there is in the area first." He squeezed my shoulder in agreement and padded softly away.

I called the four scouts in, issued them their instructions and off they went. An hour passed before a slight, almost imperceptible stirring of movement to our right flank brought the men to readiness. A low bird call, followed by two clicks on the radio, signified that it was Louis and Ernesto of scout group two coming in. The men relaxed but still maintained their readiness.

"Señor Ben," Louis said as he approached. "We have been down the hill to our right and found the remains of the old workers' huts about two kilometres away. They are clear but with signs of recent movement in the area." I patted him on the shoulder and thanked him just as the radio clicked again for number one scout groups return.

"We have found the track to the old factory one kilometre from here Señor, it has been well used in the past few days," Julio informed me with confidence. "The main part of the factory buildings are a further three kilometres below this position and to the left about 5 degrees." I saw the flash of his smile as the first rays of sunlight found us.

Not a moment too soon, we had arrived in the right area and had no cause for concern for the moment. Leaving four men - one from each Fire Team - on guard at the cardinal points of the compass, I called the others in for an update briefing. After informing them of our lucky chance in finding this spot, I told them to eat and rest, then to brief their partners before relieving them to get their meal; the change of guards would then be on a two hourly basis. Turning to Miguel, I indicated that I would like a private word with him, so we moved away from the others.

"Miguel, I am going to call Marguerite in a minute, do you agree that she should come in closer to the target area?" I asked him, quickly adding, "Zack *could* manage on his own I suppose."

"Ben, you do not understand two things," Miguel declared firmly and with a sad smile. "First, you forget that the choppers can*not* carry much weight in the high mountains." Secondly and most important of all, you underestimate my wife! She will want to be in the thick of it if she can," he said, shaking his head. "No! Let her come in closer if they can find a spot, it will be best for us anyway!"

While he was talking, I had opened one of my self-heating cans of food and started to prepare a meal for myself. Seeing what I was doing, he rummaged in his pack for a tin and followed suit and we sat chatting quietly while the meals heated.

"Right my friend!" I said when we had finished. "Now we must decide the location of the Fire Teams around the target. As agreed, I will make for the landing place which is the other side of the plantation and you site the others where you think best, eh?"

"Of course I will my friend, but we cannot move in until tonight anyway, so we really should get some rest. The factory must be in use now if they are going to meet their deadline, we will have to carry out some careful patrols." Miguel paused, looking at me as if trying to read my mind, then he added, "If I may suggest, let the four scouts do their job in the entire area; they are very good you know."

"Of course!" I said, giving his arm a shake. "I entirely agree with you and the first pair can start out in an hour, so please brief them on their task." With a pleased grin on his face, he moved quietly back to the main group. When he had gone, I settled down to reflect on the situation. Seeing no obvious problems at that time, I called Marguerite on the radio.

"Snowbirds." Within a few seconds, her soft voice repeated the same word.

"We are in the square at Golf Hotel," I said, giving the two coordinates for the kilometre square on the map in which we had settled. "We have a splendid view from here and are expecting the family to be at 'home' when we go visiting." By this, I had indicated that we could see the target and we thought it was occupied, so would be doing recce patrols.

"I see," came the quick reply. "We will find other lodgings a bit closer, perhaps something more in the shade," Marguerite added. I understood this to mean she would relocate into, or nearer the wooded area for camouflage purposes. Satisfied that all was well in hand, I told Miguel that I was going to get my head down and have a sleep. A good rest was very important for me now, because having to work my way around to the other side of the target area, I would need to be moving out from this position fairly soon

"Ben! Ben! Wake up, the scouts are back." Miguel's insistent whisper dragged me back from a surprisingly deep sleep. "The scouts have reported a lot of activity in the old factory and some heavy vehicles were heard on the track into it," he advised, offering me a cup of tea.

"Who? ... How many people?" I mumbled, as I tried to clear my thoughts and looking around me I saw it was still daylight and the sun was high. My watch told me it was almost 11.30 am so I had slept for nearly four and a half hours.

"Juan and Julio watched the factory for over an hour," Miguel continued as he saw I was now alert. "They saw at least twenty people who looked like Campesino - peasants - and it seems that they sleep and eat in a separate building about two hundred metres away from the factory. This building is always under guard."

"Well," I replied, now wide awake after digesting this information. "If they are under guard, that means they are being kept against their will." My mind was racing, trying to sort out this new problem. Suddenly it came to me.

"Am I right when I say, that because of the excessive heat of the boilers and the sun on that tin roofing, that it will get *very hot* in there?" I asked.

"There will be a terrible heat and little air to move it," Miguel confirmed, looking at me with a puzzled frown.

"In that case, having a guard on that hut means it is likely that they work in two shifts!" I announced. I watched his face as I said this and as expected he looked grim. This would mean that the guards would be on duty all night as well, so we would not have the freedom of movement we would have liked. With no time for delay now, we had to make the right decision. A plan formed in my mind.

"Change the original orders, to allow for the early elimination of the guard. As they are in an area away from immediate danger during our attack, we will then ensure the release of the workers *after* we have made the hit! OK?" I queried.

Miguel didn't need to think about that for too long. He nodded, patted me on the shoulder and moved off to relay the new orders.

We are already fully committed and stretched to the limit; just how we are going to arrange that I don't know, I thought when he was gone.

I was just packing my kit when he returned and to my amazement saw he was accompanied by Santos our Indian tracker.

"Where the bloody hell did you come from?" I gasped, trying to retain my temper. This was not part of the original plan and I did *not* like surprises.

"Sorry, Señor Ben!" Santos whispered. He didn't look the least bit sorry, stood there with his head held defiantly high. "I came up in the big 'chopper,' the pilot didn't know I was on board!" he explained, with a pleased look on his face. "You will need me here, Señor!" This was said with such confidence, that I thought he may know something we didn't. Again, my brain was in a spin, he had no weapons, no rations or kit. He was going to be a liability. Then the answer hit me like a sledge hammer.

"Of course!" I said, so fiercely that it made them both jump. "Santos can deal with the guard and as he speaks Amerindian, he can let the workers go as we discussed!" I looked at Miguel half expecting him to argue. He nodded his head vigorously in agreement.

"It would be easier for him to do that, he can kill without a sound and the workers will accept his word far better that that of an armed Gringo!" he said, justifying the decision.

Turning to Santos, I said, "Santos, while your 'surprise visit' still annoys me, I think you couldn't have arrived at a better time. We have a task for you to carry out that we had not included in our planning and it will save the lives of all the 'workers' in the factory."

"Si Señor, anything to help will be my humble part in this war," he said proudly.

I then explained to Miguel roughly where I was going to be located, then after shaking his hand and wishing him luck and a quick 'good-bye' to the lads; I quietly left the area

Chapter 23

<u>The Factory.</u>

By my calculations, I would have to take an indirect route skirting the valley to get anywhere near the location of the landing site for *El Jefe's* helicopter, which meant my covering a distance of about 5 kilometres over some very rough ground. The harder part would be in the old, well established jungle area at the beginning, when I would have to be very quiet, not leave any tracks or slash marks from cutting my way through what would be thick entanglements of vines and branches. The rest, being in the area of the old plantation now in the throes of being reclaimed by nature and with softer, new vegetation should be easier. The only difficulty would be avoiding damaging the new growth and leaving clear marks of my passage, plus a possibility of encountering a few wild animals.

I hadn't gone very far, when the new area of growth I was pushing through suddenly appeared to swing around to the left across the face of the mountain and *away* from the factory area. Not only that, it was thinner vegetation and shorter in height, which meant I would be exposed to view for a considerable distance. I couldn't risk it; the only option open to me was to get into the old jungle again!

"Damn!" I silently cursed. "That's all I need. Now I suppose I am going to have to crawl the rest of the way!" I stopped at the edge of the old jungle to survey the area. At first glance, it seemed I was out of luck, then

I realized that the taller old trees, visible above the new stuff, actually gave me a good guiding line.

"Stick to the edge of the jungle. Idiot!" I silently admonished myself for nearly overlooking the obvious. Suddenly, I became aware of a very strong smell in the air. I couldn't identify it at first, but having been brought up in the countryside at home - and crossed the scent of a fox or badger on the evening air - I knew it was an animal I could smell. I moved slowly onwards, the hair at the nape of my neck squirming in alarm. The smell became quite strong as I crossed a well-worn animal track. I stopped to listen - I had to wait for the sound of my heartbeat to quieten before I could hear anything anyway. Nothing! Except the usual sounds of the smaller jungle animals.

Lion or tiger!" That's what it reminds me of! This alarming thought came hurtling at me when, from the deep dark recesses of my brain, I recalled myself as a child, standing by the lion's cages in Bristol Zoo. The smell was so strong there, that it had been imprinted on my brain. To counter this thought, I quickly reminded myself that there were no lions or tigers in this country.

Big cat then! My brain insisted. Could be, but I'm not too sure what sort, possibly puma or something!

My tired memory dredged back into the depths of my childhood and threw an echo of a school lesson at me. 'Jaguar, the largest member of the cat family is found on the American continents. Its average length is between 6 and 7 feet (about 2 metres).'

Cripes! If it's one of those I'm in trouble, my internal voice reminded me. They even take on crocodiles! No matter which it was, it posed a big problem, one that I could quite well do without. For safety's sake, I moved away from the immediate region of this unknown creature's favourite walk. Moving quietly, I crept down the tree line, all the time expecting the sudden pain of huge claws ripping my flesh. Following the slope on downwards, I crossed fainter 'scent tracks' that proved to me I was in the general hunting area of the unknown beast and these served to make me move quicker through the thickening undergrowth.

Without giving any warning, the land seemed to fall away from under my feet. Down I tumbled in a rush, collecting masses of undergrowth as I barged through. With a strange soggy sound, I came to rest upside down at the edge of an evil smelling jungle swamp. A quick, but careful wriggle of all my extremities proved that battered and bruised though they may be, nothing was broken thank God! The only injury I was not happy with was a growing lump on the side of my head that had come into contact with the rocket launcher tube during my tumble.

"Weapons!" The word smacked me between the eyes. "What if they are damaged, or lost!" With panic rising in me, I scrambled back to the bottom of the slope where an obvious 'trail' of broken vegetation showed the line of my decent. Checking my pouches and pockets I found nothing missing, but the carrier with two rockets in was no longer strapped to my pack. Cursing my luck, I scrambled my way back up the slippery slope, but not making very good headway because there were few footholds. Then I saw it, jammed in the lower branches of a large bush halfway up through the centre of which I had obviously travelled. I dragged it free and checked it for damage and to my great relief, other than a broken retaining strap, everything seemed OK, so I slid to the bottom of the slope again. Refitting the carrier to my pack and digging lumps of soil and vegetation out of my clothing, I prepared to move off up the lower slope of the crater I was in. I'd only gone about 200 metres, when I froze in my tracks.

"What the bloody hell was THAT!" I gasped out loud. A strange sound, half roar, half scream rent the air. I'd heard nothing like it in my life before and I admit that it sent deep shivers of cold fear down my spine. Standing stock still, I waited, hardly drawing breath in case the sound attracted whatever it was out there.

"There it is again! It can't be far from where I am by the sound of it!" With a distinct feeling of looseness in my bowels, I eased myself down into a sitting position and inched the pistol out of its holster. Slowly, I drew the silencer out of my pocket and fitted it, trying not to make any noise by hurrying. All the time, my nerves screamed at me to hurry, while the hairs on my body were running relay races all over the place. A sudden noise in the undergrowth above me on the opposite side of the swamp made my stomach squirm and my pulse race. Whatever it was, it was not being very quiet. In fact, it sounded as if it was dragging something through the thickness of the undergrowth.

"If that is right," I said half aloud. "The scream may have been from its victim and I am not the target!" I once again became aware of the awful smell coming up from the swamp and realized that I was soaking up the juices of it by sitting in it.

"Of course!" I exclaimed in a whisper. "If I soak myself all over, then my scent won't give me away. Not what I had bargained for, but, when in need as they say!" With that, I retraced my steps to a particularly watery patch, took off my equipment and retaining a firm grip on the pistol, I crawled over to a deeper part and lay myself in the dark brown, evil smelling mess. From this position, I could see that this swamp was in fact a deep bowl in the hillside. It appeared to be about fifty metres across and about fifteen at the deepest end. Exactly how deep the stinking mire in it was, I had no wish to discover.

Looking up from my vantage point, I scanned the area for any sign of the creature. It was then that I noticed that there seemed to be a deep groove in the forest floor that led into the swamp above the far end.

So! This hole was probably formed by the occasional flash floods caused by the heavy rain that lashed these parts from time to time. Over the years, loose dirt and vegetation had become trapped here, rotting away quietly waiting for me to arrive!

After about fifteen minutes had passed, I felt sure that not only would I smell less attractive to the creature, but more importantly that it had in fact gone on its way. Scraping thick mud from the bottom of the ooze, I plastered it on my blonde hair that I'd pulled back in a short pony tail, working it well in, then I moved carefully back to the side and started rubbing the thick muck into my exposed skin as well. Working quickly, I then gathered my kit together and inched my way up the lowest part of the bank. A quick survey of the area - no good sniffing the air, as my own stink now masked any other smells - I moved cautiously out of the area.

Half an hour later, I came across a well-worn track that looked as if it was used by men and horses. I dared not use it, so was forced to divert into the older and well-established jungle once again. Remembering Ernesto's words about pack horses, I realized that this could be a track used by the coca growers to deliver their supply to the factory. Taking out my compass, I found that it ran more or less in the right direction, so I would have to be extra careful from now on. I crept off into the denser growth again.

After a while, I stopped and switched the radio on. The rubber aerial had not been broken and a subdued hissing of static in my earpiece told me it was still receiving. I needed to know if it still transmitted and Miguel should know of this track. Turning the volume down I pressed the send button and spoke quietly.

"Snowbird two." And waited.

"Snowbird one." Though like me, he would be speaking in a whisper, Miguel's voice came clearly over the ether in reply. He automatically adopted the abbreviated radio procedure as used by the Services, to reduce any chance of any location finder - even Drug Barons have such things - and to reduce battery wear.

"Two. Pack animal track located at Golf Lima, running east to west. Still used. Will call again if family located."

"One. Understood. Family active in this close area. Going towards home. No contact yet. Our late comer heard that Uncle is expected in 26."

In this cryptic form, Miguel had conveyed to me that some of the guards or other gang members had been seen near to his location and going towards the factory; a patrol perhaps. His men had not been spotted. In using the words late comer, he meant Santos - who it seemed - had already crept in to the vicinity of the labour force, where he overheard that El Jefe – who we had coded as Uncle - was expected in 26 hours time. Thinking quickly, I decided that the best thing in both our cases would be to reduce the possibility of a radio being heard by the enemy.

"Two. Roger. Radio silence immediate unless urgent. When in location and ready, will send 2 x 3. Out." By this I meant that when I was in position, I would let him know by sending three clicks twice.

Two clicks came back as acknowledgment and from now on we would resort to radios only in dire emergency. Once the attack was started, then we could 'light up' again. If all this had in fact been heard by the enemy, we would soon know.

We had less than twenty-six hours in which to get our act together; I *had* to be in position well before then. Likewise, Miguel would be establishing his Fire Team's positions for the main assault. Moving as quietly as I could, I pushed on for the next two hours towards the side of the valley overlooking the landing ground. On eventually arriving there, I took stock of the lower surrounding area, which had been part of the cleared plantations cultivated land at some time.

The landing ground itself amounted to nothing but a cleared rough circle in the thicker new vegetation. Being round it would stand out from the air and act as a marker for the pilot. It was in fact this shape and the path leading off of it that had attracted my eye when we flew over. Moving up into the tree line and selecting the position for my OP was easy, the soft earth below the convenient trunk of a large fallen tree suited me.

The light was fading now, so I started digging, marking out the area of my 'hole in the ground', which would be my 'hide'. As I dug, I was investigated by birds, which took any grubs I unearthed and young inquisitive monkeys that saw me as a source of entertainment. Making good progress over the next hour or so, I fashioned the main hole, then as the light finally went, I decided to complete the task later and do a recce of the target first.

Seeing no one about, I hid my pack and equipment and crept down to the lower ground to learn as much about it as I could. The heavier vegetation was nearly shoulder height and the landing area - nearly the size of a football pitch - was more than large enough for one 'chopper' to get into without difficulty. Carefully, I moved off up the wide cleared path. A short distance from my start point, the unexpected and very unmistakable smell of Avgas assailed my nostrils and it didn't take me long to find the dump of four, fifty gallon aviation fuel barrels hidden to one side of the track.

Beside them stood a dozen or more sealed jerry cans and a hand pump.

"Just as Marguerite had said it would be," I muttered. "That will be useful to remember!" I moved on up the track, being careful not to leave any obvious tracks. As I approached the top of a slight rise, my nose once again alerted me to danger. The strong smell of tobacco smoke drifted down on the air and I went to ground. A slight movement against the denser green of the jungle to my front proved to be made by a man in green combat clothes with a rifle slung over his shoulder, standing in the middle of the track about fifty metres away. He had his back to me and was relieving his boredom by kicking a small stone around with his foot. Withdrawing slowly, I moved off into the thicker vegetation above and behind him. Then as silently as possible, I inched my way forward through the undergrowth. Only the years of training and the now instinctive skills honed to perfection in jungle fighting across the world, made it possible to move without advertising my presence with snapping twigs and rustling leaves. Finding a suitable spot, I settled down to watch.

A quarter of an hour passed during which I studied the man while he continued kicking small stones about and smoked heavily. From my vantage point, I could see he didn't have any webbing on. I breathed a sigh of relief as this meant he was not a professional soldier, what's more; his mates were probably of the same type. Time passed and still no relief came, nor did he call to any unseen person nearby or use a radio, so it seemed he was on a long spell of lonely duty. Having proved he was a solitary guard, the waiting had been worthwhile and if this was the standard of the average guard, then we would have no trouble, but it would be fatal to count on it. Easing my cramped limbs, I rose slowly and moved off across the hillside and into the trees, to continue along to a spot above the dimly lit factory itself.

    Partly hidden by the overhanging trees- I would never have seen it had we flown on the opposite course; it was ramshackle to say the least. The fact that it was in use by the Cartel, proved that it was still good on the inside at least - the Chemist they employed would have to have as near decent laboratory conditions in which to work as possible. The storage of the cocaine in its powder form would have to be good even if it was sealed in the usual plastic packs. Again I settled down to watch, keeping my ears and eyes open for sounds of roving guards or the changing of the work force. With the rising heat of the sun during the day, the humidity had risen during my foray into this part of the jungle and I was glad that it was not the middle of the summer. It soon became obvious that the centre of the old building - the largest part - was the area of activity. With the aid of my binoculars, I could see through a section of the walling that had collapsed and into the reasonably well lit main building. Rows of long benches were surrounded by what I took to be the labourers working by the light of a few storm lanterns as they sorted the coca leaves. What lay out of sight would have to wait for total darkness when I would get in as close as possible.

Maintaining my watchfulness I spotted a few guards wandering about. Bored out of their skulls by the look of them, I thought, but that would change when the Big Man arrives I'm sure.

In the meantime, I was dying to take advantage of their boredom and get in much closer. The sound of a generator starting up brought my attention back to the main building. Brighter lights appeared one by one as the circuit breakers were thrown and I was very relieved to see that no outside security lights came on.

"Well. Well! There's a golden opportunity if there ever was one," I mumbled to myself. "Shame *not* to take advantage of this." Buried in the jungle, far from anywhere, they were too sure of their own security to even bother about lights on the outside of the building. Besides which, I had not heard or seen any sign of aircraft flying over. It was just the chance I wanted, so taking my commando knife out of its sheath, I crept forward. Sweating like the proverbial pig from the humidity, which only enhanced the stink I must give off anyway, I moved down the hillside. Pausing by the track - which I noticed ran onto the hard rocky surface of the one and only 'road' into this place - seeing it was all clear I moved into the deeper shadows of the building itself.

The ground was littered with loose bits of tin and other debris that had collected over the years and I had to tread very carefully as I moved slowly along the edge of the track. The adrenaline coursing through my veins served to sharpen my senses - hearing and sight seemed improved. My sense of smell proved this, as clearly above my own malodorous scent, I could smell the cooking pots in which the cocaine was being rendered down. Taking advantage of a hole in the wall that presumably had been a window and which was not near to the brightly lit end where all the work was being done, I looked inside.

The first thing I noticed - could not escape in fact - was the heat coming out of the opening. Mixed with the awful smell of the coca being processed was the strong smell of dozens of unwashed bodies. The reason for this became clear when I adjusted my position slightly to see further in; several long rows of benches - that I had seen earlier - were surrounded by the peasant labourers. In a well-established production line I saw men and women of all ages in one row, who were busy emptying sacks of coca leaves and sorting them out. Others moved backwards and forwards between the area of the sorters and the Chemists, who in turn gave instructions as to which of the six huge cauldrons were to be filled. Under each cauldron, the flames of a fire could clearly be seen.

Fire without smoke? My little voice whispered. That can only mean Gas!

Craning my neck even further, I looked down the side of the building. Yes! There they were, about twelve large Propane Gas cylinders stood against the wall.

Now that's what I call organization, I thought. On the other side, I could make out a long row of people busily engaged in filling large plastic sacks with the white cocaine powder. Even more were packing these sacks into larger, heavy-duty plastic bags ready for shipment. I counted twelve guards - all of who were lazy and sure of their power - and estimated about twenty workers. In a stack against the back wall, I counted twenty of the larger packs, each of which was handled by one person with a bit of struggle - so I guessed they were of about 25 kilograms in weight.

My mathematics were not good enough to produce an accurate figure, but I knew that this innocuous looking powder was purchased by dealers who in turn in turn 'cut' it - mix it with flour, baking powder or talc to increase the quantity – then sell it for an on the street price of around £85 per gram or more. I felt utterly sick when I realized the supply that I could see in front of me represented MILLIONS of dollars to the Cartel already! I doubted if the poor peasants working there were paid more than a few Centavos for their work.

Sickened by what I was seeing, I felt like getting down in there right then and destroying everything. *That is what we were all here for after all.* But no! Firstly I had to get the innocent workers away, and then I could avenge Sophie by exterminating such people as El Jefe and his cronies. Having seen enough, I carefully withdrew from the side of the building and moved back across the track into the jungle. Once clear of the immediate area, I sat down with my back to a tree to ponder the situation.

While my mind was working on this problem, I took a piece of Pemmican - dried meat - out of my pocket and started to chew it. Slowly, as the saliva and my chewing softened the meat, the flavour flowed and the germ of an idea came to me, fertilized by the steady hum of the generator that I could hear.

"My first priority is to get the workers out of the building and that can be arranged by a power cut I'm sure. Quite how I can do it without raising their suspicions, I don't know." The nourishment from renewed chewing seemed to refresh my brain, which in turn gave birth to more thoughts. I reached for my water bottle.

"That's IT!" I nearly shouted for the world to hear. "Water! I can put some water in the generator's fuel tank!" Hastily, I secured my kit and withdrew further into the jungle, all thoughts of drinking forgotten. What I intended to do now forced an immediate change of my plans, so working my way around to the other side of the small slope out of sight of the factory, I sat down and called Miguel.

"One," came the prompt reply.

"Two. Have inspected property. Power cut expected late tonight. Be ready for release of the 'lambs.' Action will follow on my say!" I informed him, using shortened versions of speech I knew he'd understand. There was a pause, during which time I expect he was making sure from the others that they were ready. This would mean he had to ensure that Santos was in position to release the workers - or 'lambs' as I had referred to them.

"One. What about 'Uncle'?" Miguel said, referring to El Jefe.

"Two. Power failure in two hours. 'Uncle' will arrive to sort out power cut and loss of 'lambs.' We wait 'til then."

"One. Understood," Miguel acknowledged, with the accepted lack of sentiment as is normal in the Services. By setting the time for the power cut for a few hours hence, I had given him enough time to prepare both Santos and the Fire Teams. It also gave me the required time I estimated it would take me to get to the generator and add the water to its fuel and then withdraw. Looking at my watch, I saw the time was close to ten o'clock. That meant the action would start at, or near to midnight. My hasty plan relied on there not being a spare generator and that it would take a few hours to strip the faulty one down. To avoid any escapes, the guards would also herd the workers into their prison while they worked on it. Likewise, if they failed to restart the generator, they would then send a message to El Jefe.

"God help the messenger!" I thought. Because his deadline was almost expired, El Jefe would likely blow his head off at receiving the news. "Ah well! All is fair in love and war!"

I made my cautious way back across the slope, to the area where I had established my 'hide' and set-to weaving a latticework of the strong, thin branches I'd gathered from various parts of the undergrowth. This would form the 'lid' to my hole. When completed, I turned back to finish digging again. Working quickly but quietly by the light of a shaded hand torch, I dug a pit about five feet deep and six foot square. To my surprise, I found the soil was reasonably soft as if it had already been raked over. Perhaps animals have already been digging here, I thought. Then on reflection, I realized that the softness of the earth was possibly why the tree had fallen anyway. Making good headway, I had finished the digging in just over an hour. My next task was to slide the 'lid' into place and view it from all angles. Satisfied that there was little chance of discovery, I settled myself down into my temporary 'home.'

I was quite prepared for a long, lonely wait in this dark and near silent jungle with nothing to keep me company. My throat was dry from my exertions and I was taking a quick swig from my water bottle, when my blood froze!

CRACK!

There, to my right! The sound of stealthy movement in the deep blackness! I could feel my skin going cold and clammy. I could see *nothing*, yet my sixth sense told me there <u>was</u> something out there! Suddenly, the sound of my heartbeat and the blood rushing around my system seemed to clear! The rustle of undergrowth being moved aside and a faint panting sound had managed to penetrate my hearing.

I felt the adrenaline rushing around my system and my heartbeat sounded like a drum in my ears. My tongue had suddenly gone so dry that it was sticking to my palate!

"I can put up a good defence against an animal." I tried to kid myself with a distinct lack of conviction. "But <u>not</u> in the position I'm in now! Any sudden movement may trigger a panic attack, by whatever it was out there!"

"I won't go without a fight," I said to myself very unconvincingly. Careful not to make a noise, I slowly reached my hand out for the silenced automatic pistol that was on one of the earthen shelves nearby. Gripping it firmly despite a very sweaty palm, I eased the safety catch off, then slowly, *very* slowly, I moved my body enough to give me a chance of bringing the weapon out from under the woven lid of the hide.

The sounds drew nearer; a shape materialized from the surrounding darkness. Boom! Boom! Bumpety Bump! My heart was going so fast the sound of it was deafening me and that awful feeling of looseness in my bowels returned with a distinct urgency. I raised the pistol, my eyes straining to seek the shape in the darkness. Whatever it was had sense and cunning enough to work from shadow to shadow. It was not going to give itself away by passing through the patches of weak moonlight.

That's strange! The thought flashed across my mind. It's actually employing HUMAN tactics! My train of thought was suddenly cut off, as I noticed an increase in the density of the shadow a few yards to the right of me. It seemed to grow taller, with two long thin things sticking up in the air like horns! Not horns you bloody fool! Those are ARMS! My brain cleared at the same time as the object took on the shape of a man and I faintly heard a voice calling in a whisper.

"Señor Ben!" Then slightly louder. "Señor Ben, it's me Santos!"

"Santos!" It came out as a gasp, but I nearly screamed aloud with relief. Santos? Here in the darkness of the jungle, where only I should be. Why?" The question was on my lips as I clicked the safety catch on the pistol and lowering my hand I called softly.

"Santos, Santos over here!" I pushed the cover of my hide away and stood up. With an audible sigh of relief, Santos came slowly towards me.

"What are you doing here?" I whispered. "What's gone wrong? How did you find me?"

"Sorry, Señor Ben, Miguel thinks you should know that I listened to the workers in their shed. I hear them saying that the last lorries will be leaving here early in the morning." Before I could voice the questions that were forming on my lips, he went on. "I also heard the boss of the guards saying that El Jefe will meet it at the river and not at the factory. Miguel wants to know what you have planned and I am to say they are all in place ready."

"OK. Santos. You've done well to find me this far from the main group. I have a plan that I want you to tell Miguel." Offering him some of my fresh water, we sat down on the jungle floor as I outlined my plan for him. When he had repeated it to me and I was satisfied he had it right, I told him to get back to Miguel quickly. Then I suddenly remembered he had not answered my one question, so I asked him again.

"Santos, just *how* did you find me this far away?" I saw the flash of his white teeth as he grinned in the darkness.

"That was the *easy* part, Señor Ben! I knew roughly which part you would have to be in, so I made for it. You *stink* worse than the jungle itself; all I had to do was stay down wind of you!" With that he was gone, like a shadow in the night.

Code Name SNOWBIRD

With a quiet laugh of relief, I sat down in my hide and pulled the cover over again. A sudden feeling swept over me; my hands were shaking and I realized I was suffering from delayed shock! I can honestly say that was the worst psychological experience of my life and would not wish to go through it again. Throwing caution to the winds, which were in fact blowing gently toward me from the clearing and into the jungle, I opened my pack and took a self heating can of *whatever* out and set it cooking. I *had* to have *something* to settle me down.

Code Name SNOWBIRD

Chapter 24

<u>Initial Action!</u>

The meal helped calm me down and after resting for half an hour, I was ready to go and 'do' the generator. Placing all my kit and weapons in the hide - I would rely on the commando knife and speed only for this job - I pulled the cover over and set off.

Initially following the various animal trails and moving as quickly as they would allow, I made my way down the hillside. Once on the track leading to the factory area, I took greater care, stopping to sniff the wind and listen just like a wild animal would. If there was a guard out there, it was a safe bet he'd be bored like the earlier one so would be making a noise and probably smoking. Special Forces training had instilled a kind of second sense in me, like a heightened awareness based on survival instincts. Like my comrades, I trusted my instincts and senses implicitly and at this stage it'd be foolish to take chances. My nose gave warning when I was about three hundred yards from the last bend before the factory. I froze. When I sniffed the soft breeze an acrid smell assaulted my nostrils. *Someone*, in the last few minutes had urinated on the track close to where I now crouched.

"Is it a single guard, or was it a member of a patrol?" Two vital questions and I hoped it proved to be the former as he could be handled quietly. Remaining in the deeper shadow on the inside curve of the track, I moved slowly forward. The smell of rough tobacco reached me and grew stronger; then a scraping noise in the darkness alerted me to his whereabouts. He was walking in the same direction as me and had scuffed his shoes as he turned around for the return leg of his patrol. Though he was but a shadow in the deeper shadows, his position was confirmed to me by the glow of his cigarette as he drew deeply on it. There was another smell - faint on the night air, but identifiable all the same - he was smoking a drug-laced cigarette.

"Better be careful in that case!" I cautioned myself. "If he's high, he may feel he's a Rambo type, not so easy to handle and that could go for the others also!" A crowd of drug-crazed heroes is just what we could do without. Staying low, I waited for him to turn and come closer as I would 'deal' with him as far from the factory and help as possible. Out of the surrounding darkness a darker patch came nearer. I lowered myself almost to the prone position so that he was nicely silhouetted against the slightly lighter night sky as he approached, totally unaware of my presence.

"Good!" I silently sent a prayer of thanks to the God of Gods. Making no attempt to be quiet, the guard had his rifle slung over his back and had no idea that death awaited him. He was also on my side of the track. He drew closer, his face now visible, lit up by the cigarette as he continued to inhale deeply. Suddenly he stopped! Had he seen me? For a few long seconds I waited with bated breath, tensed and ready to cut off any cry of alarm. He shuffled his feet some more and his face glowed like an unearthly Halloween mask as he drew heavily on his smoke just before turning to retrace his steps.

"Bang goes his night vision!" I muttered. Moving silently in behind him I reached forward with my left hand and grabbed him round his mouth, viciously pulling his head up and backwards, at the same time as ramming my right knee into the small of his back. His cry of alarm remained as a muffled noise within his tightly stretched throat. He passed out when I hit his temple hard with the metal butt of the knife and quickly became a dead weight as I pulled him into the thickness of the undergrowth. Laying him face down on the ground, I knelt on his back and grabbed a handful of hair, pulled his head up while reversing my hold on my knife. There was a rushing, gurgling sound as his lungs exploded his last breath out through the deep slash in his neck as I ran my knife from ear to ear, his life ebbed away. Wiping my knife on his clothing, I slid it back into its sheath, listening to see if anyone else was about, then I regained the track and continued my cautious way toward the main factory building. As I approached the old Overseer's house, I could hear the discordant sound of men shouting and singing drunkenly, as well as the screams of several female voices.

"The off duty guards are having fun, by the sound of it. Great! Now all I have to do, is find that bloody 'genny'. The night shift were hard at work in the factory when I eventually regained my earlier vantage point by the window. I counted twenty workers and could see four armed guards just inside the building. Just as I ducked down from the window, a sudden noise behind me made me freeze. Slowly, I twisted my upper body and moved my head and eyes to see over my shoulder. There, on the track, stood a man with a rifle on his shoulder.

"What are you doing?" he demanded in a slurred voice. Fumbling with my clothing, I replied in the best way I could. On hearing the sound of a deep sigh and splashing water, he soon got the message and went on his way.

"Phew! That was too close for comfort. I'd best deal with him as well I think." I followed the sounds he made as he stumbled along the track towards the jungle. "Where is he off to out here, I wonder?" The shadowy figure continued to stagger along an indistinct footpath for about 300 metres, then the answer to my unspoken question came as the muffled, but distinctive sound of a generator came from the building my quarry was heading for. A quick glare of light shot across the open space in front of me, as he opened the door and went in.

"Well. Well! That's nice of him isn't it?" I almost felt grateful to him. He had led me to my objective and I would have wasted a lot of time trying to find it in this clearing away from the main complex. "Right, let's see what we can see then!" Closing one eye tightly to preserve my night vision, I moved forward, crossing the small shafts of light coming out of several small holes in the buildings walls. Looking through one of the gaps where bricks were missing, I saw the man, moving unsteadily on his feet as he checked dials and gauges on the only generator. After satisfying himself to the performance of this machine, he wobbled across the room, slumped against a wall and resumed drinking from a bottle.

Reaching the door and easing it slowly open; I stepped silently inside, where the heat and stink hit me like a sledge hammer. The guard hadn't heard me above the noise of the generator, so I walked quickly over to where he had put his AK 47 rifle and moved it well away from his reach. Relying on his well and truly 'pickled' state at this moment, I assumed a drunken act, weaving my way across the room to where he had now slid down in a heap on the floor, bottle still in hand. He stank of urine, vomit and sweat. His hair was thickly matted with filth.

"Gracias Amigo!" I said taking the bottle from his loose hand. Why don you like the women eh?" I queried, pretending to take a swig then thrusting the bottle back to his mouth and pouring the liquid in.

"Putas," (whores!) he slurred, "all of 'em." His reply came slowly. I poured the bottle again, his mouth opening automatically to receive the liquid. He was so far gone that he was having difficulty getting his brain in gear. "Genrat'r! Fuel low. Fill in minit!" His chin slumped further into his chest and deep snores filled the air.

"You sleep there, pal!" I said. "I'll fix the 'genny' for you!", I walked across the room to the fuel tank and one look at the indicator told me it would probably stall in less than an hour as it was so low. Still using one eye, I looked around and identified a US Army pattern jerry can full of oil. In a corner was another with petrol stencilled on it in faded white paint.

"Things are looking good," I said to myself, as I went to the door and half opened it. Sticking my head out and using my other eye - the one that I had already rested so that I would be able to pick up movements in the dark - I scanned the area. No cause for alarm so I closed the door and put a small metal bar across the latch to delay any chance visitor. Grabbing the jerry can with the oil in, I opened the fuel tank filler cap. Petrol fumes spilled out, so I knew I was on the right track. Finding a rusty old funnel, I poured half of the oil into the fuel tank and dropped the can on the floor to make it look like the drunken guard had made a mistake. For good measure, I emptied my water bottle contents into the fuel tank and used a piece of thin wooden batten to stir its contents around well.

After filling my water bottle from the wash basin tap, I closed one eye again and squinting through the other, inspected my work. Satisfied that there would be a complete generator failure in a short time, I dragged the drunken man over and propped him against the wall by the fuel tank. I poured a bit of the oil and petrol mix down his legs - to look like he had mixed it - then leaving the cans on their sides near him, with the fuel filler cap open and the now empty bottle on his lap, I left.

Stepping out into the darkness and closing the door behind me, I opened my eyes fully and did a quick scan of the area. No one was about so I headed back the way I had come. There was no sound of either the men or the women as I passed the Overseer's house, so I took it they had all gone to sleep after their revels. Regaining the cover of the jungle, and moving a few metres up the slope above the factory buildings, I settled down to wait while keeping my ears open for any sound of danger.

Suddenly, I became aware that I could no longer see the buildings; the lights had gone out in all of them. The now complete and abrupt darkness was shattered by the sounds of men shouting and cursing. Some minutes of confusion passed, with people falling over each other in the darkness. From near the other side of the main building, the light of a solitary hand torch appeared. It wavered its way along the track at such a speed that I guessed the carrier was running. Heading in the direction of the power plant, it shortly returned and met up with a group of people on the track below me. An argument broke out and the light carrier and at least one other person went back to the plant room, to return a while later dragging what I assumed was the drunk.

"Imbécil! (imbecile) Estúpido idiot!" - (Stupid idiot) these were but a few of the words I could pick out from the torrent of angry, voluble Spanish thrown at this unfortunate man. The sound of a single pistol shot was followed a second later by the unmistakable thud of a body hitting the track, I knew that punishment had been meted out. The remainder, still being harangued by the boss, moved off in the direction of the power plant. I waited. Twenty minutes passed by before two men came down the track, one carrying the now weakening torch. As they went by my position, I heard one clearly saying that El Jefe should be told about the stupidity of the mechanic.

"Madre de Dios! We will all pay for this." The other man's foul tempered reply was only to be expected.

They made their way to the Overseer's house, with me keeping station close behind them. They went inside and started kicking some more of the drunken guards awake, I went to a window at the side.

"Get up you useless drunken bastards!" The boss, now working himself into a real frenzy as the extent of this disaster sunk in, shouted at the top of his voice. "Get the Peons - workers - into their building and make sure they stay there!" He turned his attention and the weakened light onto a younger man, who lay with his arms and legs wrapped around a naked girl.

"Get up and get that bloody machine working again!" he screamed at him, without even bothering to explain what had happened.

Without another word, he went into a room at the back of the building. I moved along the outside until I was near the glassless window. By the wavering light of his torch, on a bench opposite me I could see a high-powered radio set that would not be effected by the power cut as it ran off batteries. He picked up the microphone and my blood ran cold through my veins. Was he going to call in extra guards to deal with an act of sabotage, or was he just informing El Jefe of the breakdown? Amidst all the shouting of the others, I strained my ears to hear what he was saying. Dropping the microphone, he lurched back into the front of the house and yelled at them all to be quiet. Some semblance of order then prevailed, as the guards hastily dressed and left the building. The boss returned to the radio and he informed whoever was at the other end that the mechanic had got drunk and mixed fuel and oil together, causing a breakdown of the power supply. The reply, though loud, was indistinct due to atmospherics, but it resulted in him shamefully admitting he could not get the machine working and production had been stopped until morning.

"Great! He doesn't suspect sabotage!" The relief flooded through me like a tidal wave; we could well do without extra guards to contend with. He started speaking again.

"Si, Señor! Si. I shall attend to it at once. I have already dealt with him myself - referring to the mechanic I suppose – Si, Señor. Gracias, Señor!" He was almost grovelling as he replied; whoever he was speaking to must have the power of life and death over him, but it wouldn't be El Jefe at this time of the night! No, it would more than likely be his top aid, who would now have the unenviable task of passing on the news. Taking a quick peak over the windowsill, I could make out the man, sitting slumped over the desk, his head in his hands.

"Praying for God's deliverance!" The irreverent thought came to my mind. "You'll get it all right mate! But not how you want it!"

"Sanchez!" A metallic, but nevertheless imposing voice demanded from the radio. The man sat up as if he'd been given an electric shock and grabbed for the microphone as if his life depended on it - well it did, didn't it?

"Si, Señor Cordoba?" he blurted, his voice now filled with unadulterated fear. Flipping a switch he donned the headset and listened again as the cold words came across the ether to him. "Lo Siento, Señor - I'm sorry - it was not my fault." He listened again, then, "si, Señor Cordoba, at seven o'clock."

His hand dropped the 'mike' and he sat there, a man condemned. Ripping the headset off, he dragged his way to the door and yelled for his assistant, shouting that El Jefe will be coming at seven o'clock! Everything had to be ready for him!

"That's what I want to hear, now let's get out of this place before the proverbial hits the fan!" Heeding my own advice, I made my way quickly back to my hide. Climbing up through the jungle, the words of the boss-man echoed in my mind. "Cordoba! That's El Jefe's name. Christ almighty, Hell will be let loose on this lot if they dragged him from his bed!"

Well content with the night's work so far, I was happy to drag the radio out of my pack and call Miguel as soon as I reached my 'hide.'

"One," came his quick reply; he must have been sat waiting for my call.

"Two. Job done, the bees are buzzing. Numbers 40 'lambs' and estimated 15 shepherds. Uncle arriving at seven."

"One. Understood, we have heard them! We are ready and Big Eagle will be in attendance too. Out."

"Big Eagle? What's he on about," I wondered. Better not call him back to explain in case of being overheard, so it remained as another of those mysteries, the answer to which I will find later. Looking at my watch, I saw there was a little over three hours in which to rest, feed and prepare for the coming battle. Reaching for some thick clothing to stop me shivering as my body cooled in the colder night air, I again marvelled at just how quickly the heat of the tropics can turn to a numbing cold.

Warmly wrapped and snuggled down into my hide, my mind wandered over the past events. The thought of all the mayhem around the factory made me smile to myself.

Not only is the drug trade paying for its own demise, but its members are also working towards it by killing themselves off! This happy thought passed through my mind as my eyes closed for a quick and in my estimation, well-earned catnap.

Code Name SNOWBIRD

Chapter 25

Sweet Revenge!

Tired out after the events of the previous long day, I slept reasonably well for a few hours. My peace was not to last, however, as noisy sounds of frantic activity down on the landing area jerked me into wakefulness early the following morning. At first, the sound of several human voices made me think they were searching the area for me. Armed and ready to defend myself, I crept out to investigate. From the clanging tins and the curses of the men carrying them I soon realised they were preparing to refuel the helicopter when it landed. They were using the jerry cans I'd found by the fuel drums, hence all the noise. With El Jefe due within an hour, the leader was making sure everything would be ready.

Better be ready myself, I suppose and boy, am I hungry! The little voice in my mind spoke, as a familiar feeling in my stomach gave warning. Quickly returning to my hide and taking heed of the age-old adage - 'an army marches on its stomach'- I prepared and ate as hearty a breakfast as my compo rations would allow, this was a cold meal in case the smell attracted attention. I buried my empty tins and packets deep in the bottom of my hide and set-to checking my weapons. First and most importantly, I cleaned and oiled the 'Hochler' 9 mm submachine gun and the pump action shotgun. Then filled the magazine of the shotgun to capacity and laid the two rocket launchers and projectiles out close to hand.

"Good! No damage done in my tumble," I muttered, as I paid extra special attention to the sniper's rifle, with its powerful 'scope.' Satisfied that I was as prepared as I would ever be, I concentrated on clearing my mind and on slowing my already racing heart. Suddenly, there was a shout from down in the valley. It was repeated by various members of the gang, who were strewn out across the area.

"El Jefe is coming! El Jefe is coming!" Their excitement was clear - but I was sure that some of them down there were wishing they were somewhere else. I doubted if El Jefe would waste time on enquiries; it would be enough that a breakdown in the production had been allowed. *That* was all the reason he would need to hand out dire punishment. The unexpected sound of heavy lorries revving their engines made me prick up my ears. Not having seen them during my visit to the factory, I could only imagine they'd been parked inside the building. The sound of at least two vehicles came from within the growing cloud of dust that appeared above the young vegetation between the factory and my own position.

"Well, well! It seems that they are keen to earn *some* Brownie points by sending at least part of the load out!" I muttered to myself. As the dust cloud went slowly past my position, I could just make out the dim shapes of two very large vehicles of the type used to carry rocks from a quarry. Loaded though they were, their metal sides resounded like drums to the bumps and humps of the track. Their protesting gearboxes crunching and grinding, they made their slow and noisy way out of sight, disappearing around the bend of the mountainside and into the cover of the jungle. With the ensuing silence, another noise caught my attention. Faint, but identifiable, it was the buzz of a helicopter. Though I couldn't see it from under the trees, I knew that it was approaching from the direction of the Hacienda Los Palmos.

"El Jefe! At last, he's coming into my trap," I breathed, as I switched on the radio and whispered into the 'mike.'

"Two. Uncle is coming."

"One. We're ready." The immediate reply, soft as a gentle breeze wafted over my ear.

"Two. Wait my signal for all action."

"One. Wilco." Manuel's calm and confident voice replied.

The high buzzing sound of El Jefe's helicopter approaching at speed in the dawn light heralded the closing act of this mission. If all went well in the next hour or so, Colombia's Drug Baron would be dead along with any of his fellow Cartel members who accompanied him. The sound grew louder and it was then that I started to worry. As well as the 'buzz,' of a fast moving machine, my ear had now picked up the distinctive 'whump, whump,' sound that a helicopter makes as the blades bite the air as it lifts its nose before coming to the hover or on turning. A second machine must have flown in fast and low, its sound masked by the thick jungle. I grabbed for my send button to warn Miguel.

"Two! Urgent!" I voiced anxiously. One 'click' told me he was listening. "Figures Two Birds!" Another 'click' told me he understood. He would now change any plan to follow what action transpired.

"Two choppers! Why two?" My tired brain started to react as it wrestled with this new problem. "Maybe he's sent in extra guards! It may be because he travels in one machine, while his main guard travel in another?" All sorts of worries started to crowd my mind. "What if he's not in it? Perhaps he has sent one of his top men instead! If that's the case, do we still continue the attack or not?" I had an awful vision of El Jefe sat in his home, laughing at me and saying 'What are you going to do now, sucker?'

"STOP IT!" I almost shouted aloud. "Pack it in! Of course he's coming, he won't trust this sort of cock-up to a minion!" I silently cursed myself for allowing pre-action nerves to get at me. Knowing that the others of my group, lying out there in the jungle, would be suffering the same sort of anxiety didn't help either. To calm my nerves, I rechecked that everything was ready. Pistol in my holster with one bullet chambered ready. The 'Hochler' with double magazine inserted and cocked with safety catch on. The first rocket launcher close by, ready with the sights up and set. I could find nothing I had missed.

A sudden movement in the thick vegetation below me drew my eye. I gripped the sniper rifle and through its powerful telescope, I could see a man crouching as if he was hiding. *He was hiding!* There was no doubt about it. His face filled the lens and I could see he was terrified, desperate to escape from El Jefe! He must know what's coming to him as part of the failure of the system. If he comes near to me, he will die anyway. If he doesn't, then he can make his way out of here.

These thoughts passed through my mind as I watched his progress. As soon as the first 'chopper' dipped into the small valley behind the trees, he got up and made a dash for the thicker jungle; in there he at least had a chance to put distance between himself and those he feared. The dust cloud created by the down draught from the machine's rotors told me that it was over the area of the track and approaching the landing site. Using my binoculars, I kept watch on the point at which I guessed it should emerge into my line of vision. There it was! The early morning sun, reflecting off of a large shimmering, parallel disc as it cut through the air, was the first part I saw. Then as the full sweep of the rotors came into view, I could see the whole machine very clearly.

The beautifully streamlined, shark-like shape of a Bell 230 Executive helicopter filled my lenses.

"Nice! If you're going to travel, do it in style!" I muttered, as I watched the pilot bring his machine to the hover and lower the retractable landing wheels. Without hesitation, the machine settled very gracefully to the ground. Before the turbojet had wound down, the doors opened and eight men jumped out with smooth, well-practised movements. Fanning out and facing outwards, they completed a circle of the aircraft. The leader, a well-built man clutching his Schmeisser machine pistol to his chest made a visual survey of the area.

Satisfied that nothing was wrong, he waved to his pilot who surfed his machine across the ground to the edge of the clearing. Then raising a radio to his mouth, the leader gave what I presumed as the all clear to the pilot of the second and as yet unseen machine. The gleam of another rotor disc followed as the twin of the first machine slid into view. Following a similar approach, it slid gracefully into the landing area. As the wheels touched the ground, the front door opened and a man clutching a Schmeisser at the ready stepped down. He also visually swept the area before unlocking the door of the main cabin.

Very slick; very slick indeed. Don't take any chances do they! They send in the cavalry to check the area before letting the boss come in. My private thoughts intruded on my trance-like concentration.

Keeping his head low, the man who I assumed was the head bodyguard moved out of the arc of the rotors to take up a position of readiness. Once again he let his gaze travel all around the area - the turn of his head revealing a short pony tail at the back of his neck - then in response to a small nod of his head, the cabin door swung wide to allow the other passengers to disembark.

" Slick operators this lot!" I counselled myself. "If it comes to a fight, we're going to have to be very careful of them." My admiration was genuine, no matter that they were the enemy as such, I had to give credit for what was a job professionally done. More movement inside the doorway brought my eye back to the 'chopper.' The first four people out were very well dressed and obviously not carrying arms. Even at this distance I could see the cut of their expensive suits. From the arrogant way they held themselves, I assumed they could only be Cartel leaders. When the rotor had finally stilled and not a moment before, another person approached the open door. In a concerted move, the others respectfully stepped back like a guard of honour and waited for this other passenger to join them on the ground. Again I took up the sniper rifle to use the powerful telescope. That amount of deference could only mean it was El Jefe himself who was about to disembark.

There he was! A shiver went up my spine and my stomach knotted as I saw him for the first time. Dressed in a light coloured tropical suit that must have cost a small fortune, El Jefe stepped carefully - almost daintily - down to the ground. His image hovered on my foresight as he carefully placed a white Panama hat on his head. Then with a typically English gesture, he tapped it into place. My finger itched as it settled on the trigger. This was my first sight of the man himself and I had him 'cold.' Through the 'scope' I could almost reach out and touch him, I was dying to blow him away there and then. With an effort, I regained control of my feelings of anger and deep revulsion as I watched this diminutive, but sturdily built man walk towards the track and momentarily walk straight towards my position. A trick of the light, or was it my imagination? As he came forward, I could have sworn that he looked directly at me! Our eyes seemed to meet across the intervening space, but did not lock.

Again in well-rehearsed moves, the waiting group of bodyguards split into two smaller groups and adopted a protective arc to the front and rear of El Jefe and the others as they walked across the landing ground. I had the chance to study his face again before they disappeared out of my sight behind a clump of bushes. Clean-shaven with swarthy skin, his pockmarked face was that of a hard man. No kindness showed in the deep-set eyes that glowered out from under thick eyebrows. No smile crossed his lips and his nose was flared like that of an angry bull. In fact he looked unhappy. It was an image that burnt itself onto my brain; one I would never forget!

"So that's him, the man who creates all this misery!" I whispered quietly to myself. Although I was still angry, I had to admit to a sense of slight disappointment. From his outward appearance, he did not give any indication that he was a man of such cruelty or power, whose ruthless principles viewed life - other people's - as merely an expendable commodity. Illegally may be, but ruling with an iron fist and through the threat of death, this diminutive man controlled the whole of Colombia. As they passed momentarily out of my sight, I swung my binoculars back to the two choppers, noting that both the pilots were carrying out routine checks to their engines and airframes in readiness for the next move. Once again I admired the machines, before bringing my gaze back to the main group.

"Pity to destroy such beautiful machines!" I thought as the final plan started to form in my mind. "But destroy them we must. El Jefe will be at his most vulnerable when they are just taking off so I will wait until they are about three hundred feet up and turning to make their exit from here!" The scene was already playing in my mind. "One rocket will take but a few seconds to reach them. Any possible survivors will die in the explosion when the chopper crashes! Then we have the problem of the super efficient guards. In my opinion it would be best to avoid a gunfight with them, so they will be better dealt with in the confines of their chopper and simply done with another rocket."

My thoughts were interrupted when my attention was drawn back to the group now walking up the track across my front. They had been met by the boss man from the factory, who I had seen shouting all the orders during last night's panic. Though I could hear no words, it was easy to guess from El Jefe's arm waving and gesticulations and the bowing and general servility of this unfortunate fellow, that all was not well. As the trees and thicker vegetation finally obscured my vision, I called Miguel, who would now be able to watch their approach from his position.

"Two. Uncle's here, figures nine top shepherds plus five." My message told him the numbers and composition of the group, plus that the guards were top quality.

"One. Contact." His short reply informed me that they were within his view.

"I bet he's got them balanced on the foresight of his rifle!" I chuckled silently to myself. I could see it now. Each member of that party were split seconds away from death - just the time it would take a hail of lead to reach them - as their progress was marked by Miguel and the Fire Teams. This was the testing time for the discipline of my team. Would they just let rip now, or would they wait as ordered? A nerve-wracking pause of a few minutes passed, during which time I could neither hear nor see anything. Turning my gaze back to the choppers, I noted that the pilot of the first was now apparently asleep in his seat; the other was sat in his reading a paper of some sort.

"Good! This must be a routine they're used to, no cause for alarm there!" I surveyed the track and landing area with the binoculars again. No undue activity, but wait! What was that movement down there on the lower slope? A man's head appeared, then another and as I watched their shapes grow in my lenses, I realized it was the refuelling party. As the group cleared the track and walked across the intervening ground to the choppers, I saw that each man was bowed under the weight of two full jerry cans.

The pilot of El Jefe's machine was watching their approach and let them walk right up to it, before getting out of his seat and coming round the nose of the chopper to speak to them. In deference to the already rising humidity, he had now removed his helmet. To my surprise when he removed his dark 'Aviator' style sunglasses, I was looking at an American. He'd deliberately waited for the men to struggle over to him with their heavy loads, then shook his head and waved them away. He laughed at their feeble efforts as he watched them stumbling back the way they had come.

"Bastard! In it for the money, no doubt! Ah well! You will have to go with the others my friend!" I felt no sympathy for such a man, who worked for people he knew were killing thousands of his young fellow Americans and others all over the world. A slow half an hour went by. I guessed that El Jefe and his group were all in the area of the powerhouse and factory. Then suddenly, the distinctive sound of a machine gun on rapid fire brought my attention whipping back to the job in hand. The sound of it told me that it was not one of ours.

"More like the ripping silk sound of a Shmeisser!" I said reaching for the radio 'mike' and calling Miguel for a situation report.

"Two. Sitrep"

"One. Cousins have dealt with five of our problems!" he responded briefly.

"So. They have just shot five guards. That reduces our odds nicely." From my original estimation of about fifteen guards, I had despatched one. Boss man had shot another and now five more had bitten the dust. Take out two possible guards for the lorries, plus the one who had 'legged it' meant that my mental arithmetic told me that we should now have perhaps five to deal with.

That is if you are right, my inner voice told me. Don't forget the newly arrived experts! It mocked me again. OK! OK! Don't keep on. I'll make it anything up to eighteen for safety! These words of wisdom of mine could still only be guesswork anyway! My radio sprang briefly to life.

"One. Business coming your way." Miguel alerted me that they were on the move back towards my position.

"Two. Standby, Standby!" I gave the order to get ready for action and drew the first rocket launcher towards me. I felt a frisson of electricity run up and down my back. My pulse started to sound in my ears again, as imminent action loomed.

THIS is what you came for, my little voice said with glee. Just as the group came back into my view, another soft voice whispered in my ear.

"One. Lambs gone to pasture!" I recognised the voice of Santos, as he informed me that he had dealt with the guard on the workers and sent them all on their way to the relative safety of the jungle. I had no doubt that he had also told them to quickly get well away from the factory area.

"Two. Great! Now for what they are about to receive, etc. etc.," I quipped irreverently. The group of bodyguards and their masters reappeared as they moved out onto the landing area; the guards still as alert as before. El Jefe's pilot donned his helmet and started setting his switches. The other was doing likewise in the distance. Without glancing back, El Jefe climbed into the main cabin of the chopper and strapped himself into his seat. The others followed in turn, each strapping in also.

"That's right, strap yourselves into your coffin, it won't save you!" I said, as I watched through the binoculars. The head bodyguard gave another demonstration of his expertise by searching the area visually, before climbing in himself. Once the doors were shut, the pilot then started the turbo engine, its slowly increasing whine clearly reaching my position, where I had now brought the rocket launcher up to my shoulder in anxious readiness.

The engines of both machines reached the required speed and as El Jefe's pilot released the rotor brake, the blades started to move. Faster and faster they turned, kicking up a small dust storm. With my cheek pressed firmly against the side of the rocket launcher, I watched the rotor's spinning disc through the sights. I saw it begin to flex upward slightly as the blades gained sufficient lift and the pilot increased the revolutions. The landing wheels on El Jefe's machine lifted off the ground; a momentary hover while the pilot rechecked his dials, then the machine lifted away gracefully, sending clouds of dust and loose vegetation swirling. Immediately, the other machine with the bodyguards on board once again surfed across the ground until it was clear of the trees. Then it too lifted until it was about eighty feet underneath and to one side of the other one.

I tracked them with the launcher, sighting carefully on El Jefe's machine as they climbed through 150 feet, then 200 feet. As they reached 250 feet, I could clearly see the whole underside of El Jefe's chopper and the landing wheels withdrawing into their housing. The pilot, satisfied that all was well, was now fully committed to flight. Squinting through the sights I found a clear view of the underneath of the nose. I waited. Patience in this game was a virtue, as I knew that the rocket would have to fly for a certain distance before it armed itself. Besides, I didn't exactly want to be just underneath an exploding aircraft; people get hurt like that! Still tracking the aircraft as it increased its height; I watched it turn as the tail rotor pushed the body of the machine around into its anticipated line of flight away from me towards Bogotá. Then I had a continuous view of the underside from front to rear.

Drawing in my breath I let the front part by the pilot's feet slide over the sights. Releasing my breath slowly, I gently caressed the trigger just as the main cabin started to come into view. Taking up pressure on the trigger, I followed the forward movement of the chopper, leading the shot into it. This meant that when I fired, the chopper would fly into the course of the rocket.

"Steady. Steady!" I cautioned myself as I felt the excitement of the moment grip me. "Nearly there!" I gave the trigger the final gentle squeeze as the front edge of the cockpit centred on my sights.

WHOOSH! With a great gout of flame and smoke, the projectile flew from the tube. My eyes followed it as I reached for, loaded and aimed the second rocket in case of need. I had no time to draw a second breath before the trail of smoke and the chopper became merged as one in a massive explosion. The blast hurled pieces of the aircraft out in a very wide arc, some falling close to me. The heat from the fireball reached down across the intervening distance to wash over me, bringing with it the stench of burnt fuel and the faint smell of marzipan from the rocket's explosives.

I had no chance to fire the second rocket, as the flaming remains of the fatally stricken craft continued briefly in a forward motion. Then as it fell, twisting and turning with the torque of the engine, it almost collided with the rotor blades of the second machine, whose pilot avoided an aerial disaster by swooping away across the treetops and out of my sight. His fast action and skilful flying robbed me of another shot with the rocket. The burning wreckage of El Jefe's machine spun into the ground close to the factory building, starting another fiery inferno as it struck the fuel storage for the generator. Diesel fuel ignited, and what sounded like small arms ammunition started to 'cook off' with the heat.

"Goodbye El Jefe! That's for you, Sophie!" I shouted at the top of my voice. I had carried out my promise to Mal and Julie and I didn't care; nobody would hear me above the noise of the other chopper that was now frantically circling the area searching for the spot where the rocket came from.

An alarm bell rang in my mind as I realised how exposed I was. "Those rockets leave one hell of a smoke trail! Had they seen where the shot had come from?" I wasn't going to wait to find out! Frantically collecting my kit and weapons, I ran through the low vegetation for cover, my ears still ringing from the sound of the explosions. Suddenly, all hell broke loose around me. Scrabbling at the earth and loose vegetation on the ground, I sharply altered my direction. Too busy saving my own skin, I gave little thought to the action the others were carrying out. The first indication that Miguel had fired his rockets at the factory was when, out of the corner of my eye, I saw large pieces of corrugated iron flying up through the air, followed moments later by the sound of the explosions.

Gradually, as I moved down towards the track, my hearing began to clear and the sound of one of our own heavy machine guns firing on sustained fire came to me.

"They'll be dealing with the remainder of the guards I hope!" I voiced. This short, sharp spate of gunfire had attracted the attention of the guard's chopper as it came swooping low over my head in its rush towards the fire fight. The sound of shooting was now coming from the air, as well as the ground, as they had assumed the role of air support for the Cartel members by the remains of the factory.

Don't forget to keep an eye open for stragglers! The thought passed across my mind.

Moving from cover to cover, I gained the track and was just about to step out onto it when I saw two men running up the slope towards me from the direction of the Overseer's house. Not stopping to see if their comrades needed any help, these two 'brave' unsoldierly fellows were legging it for safety. They came on towards me, as I eased the safety catch off the 'Hochler' and stepped out into the middle of the track and drew their attention to my presence by firing a short burst over their heads. I don't like killing just for the sake of it and had given them a chance to surrender first. By their own choice they threw it away. Without stopping to aim, they raised their own AK47's and in desperation loosed the contents of their magazines haphazardly in my direction. Too high, and too scattered, each round passed over my head as they forgot to compensate for the rising ground and I was now kneeling ready to fire.

"OK, fellows, I'll return the compliment," I said, firing the 'Hochler' in a double tap burst, catching the nearest square in the chest, and the other one in the head. The force of the impact flung them backwards, returning them partly the way they had come. Arms waving and heads lolling, they fell like rag dolls to lay lifeless on the track. I moved into cover at the side, fearful that others would appear. No other danger presented itself from the ground, but all of a sudden the air was filled with the infuriated buzzing of bees or hornets and large lumps of foliage started showering down close around me.

"That's not bloody bees!" I shouted. "That's fucking bullets!" I dived for cover behind a thick tree just as the guard's helicopter flew low over my head. The fierce down draught of its rotor effectively flattened the vegetation where I had been.

"This guy knows his stuff!" I muttered through clenched teeth as I struggled to my feet and prepared the other launcher for firing. "He must have flown in 'Nam, because he's using the choppers down draught to blow my cover away!" This made me angry now. Not only at this pilot but at myself for being caught out like that. "Should have taken you out before moving!" I cursed, as the sound of an engine approached me again.

Brrrrrrr. Brrrrrrr. Brrrrrrr. The chain-saw like noise of a heavy machine gun came from above me and the ripping sound of high velocity bullets rent the air.

"Above me! Am I going mad? How can it be above me when Miguel and the Fire Teams are on the ground!?"

There was no time to investigate *that* mental aberration, as some distance away the guard's chopper was turning to come down at me again. I aimed the launcher at the small dot in the sky. Not much chance of a hit in a nose on angle, my little voice counselled. "Hopefully I may scare him off though!" I argued aloud.

A rushing noise and movement to my right made me dive flat on the ground. Another machine suddenly appeared, coming from the direction of the now fiercely burning factory.

"Oh, Hell!" I gasped as I rolled over into what little cover there was. "This is all going wrong! Where the *hell* did they get *another* 'chopper' from?" With a roar, a dark shape swept over me and I was able to vaguely recognise Zack's machine as an excited, but distinctly female voice shouting 'Air Cavalry to the rescue!' sounded in my earpiece. Grabbing the radio and keying the 'mike' while ignoring normal radio procedure, I yelled.

"Marguerite! Is that you?" A tinkling laugh was the only reply I heard. The sky above me was ripped apart by the sound of a heavy machine gun in rapid fire just as the guard's chopper swooped down, with bullets spraying from the guns that were thrust out of its windows. A few bullets buried themselves in the ground close to me. Once again my feet churned the dirt as I hastily legged it to another clump of trees; spouts of dirt closely followed me accompanied by the distinct *wiiiiing* noise of ricochets.

Snowbird One. Indicate!" Marguerite called over the radio, instructing me to reveal my position to her. Not wanting to be killed by *'Friendly Fire,'* I was only too glad to. Struggling with my webbing, I turned my left shoulder strap inside out and flashed the small heliograph reflector that I'd taped there twice to mark my position for her.

"Big Eagle sees you. .... Stay put!" Came the rather strange and unwelcome instruction from that lady. I was being *shot* at for Christ's sake; I didn't *want* to stay put! Then I saw what she intended. With the panache of a veteran pilot, she threw her machine - or Zack's to be precise - after the now rapidly climbing guard's machine. Using her advantage of flying an empty machine, Marguerite quickly gained height behind her quarry. They must have spotted her as she closed the distance, because they started taking evasive action. Throwing his machine erratically around the sky, the guard's pilot strove to shake her off. Like the ace she had proven herself to be, she made her chopper twist and turn, soar and plummet in an attempt to out-manoeuvre and out-guess the other pilot. I couldn't drag my eyes away from this aerial ballet, graceful though it was; there was no escape from its deadly purpose. There would be only one victor, the first pilot to get their machine into a killing position.

Desperately, the other pilot endeavoured to escape by diving in a sharp twisting turn, using the increased speed in a bid to get clear. Marguerite anticipated this move beautifully by throwing her machine into a corkscrew turn in the reverse direction; she placed her machine neatly inside the turning circle that the guard's machine was making. From the ground, I saw the muzzle flash of the sustained burst of heavy machine gun fire that erupted from the open side door, as Zack engaged his target. He couldn't miss at that range; his victim took a lot of punishment. Thankfully, this meant that all of the guard's attention was now drawn away from me so I wasted no time.

"Once more into the breach dear friend!" I muttered, legging it from my very exposed position and making for friendlier regions of this jungle. With a distinct feeling of relief, I reached the canopy of trees and paused to look at the two duelling machines now high above me. There was no doubt that the American pilot was good and knew his stuff, but Marguerite made the most of her own machine's ability by tilting the nose down and dropping at full power. Pirouetting it like a ballerina, she swerved back up behind the other machine, emerging on its blind side. Drawing away from it slightly, she once again presented Zack with an almost perfect target. He couldn't miss!

Brrrrrrrrrrrrrrrrrrrrrrr! With little need to aim, the long drawn out burst that I could faintly hear, caught the guard's machine in a long stitching move from nose to tail. The pilot must have been hit, because the nose immediately swung with the torque of the engine indicating a sudden loss of control. The main cabin, packed as it was with all those bodies, must have been like a charnel house as it took the full force of the burst, the last few rounds of which must have found the full fuel tank. The machine seemed to pause momentarily, then, as if in slow motion, it silently blossomed outwards in a huge red and orange fireball as it exploded, the sound of which took a couple of seconds to reach me.

Marguerite turned her chopper away from the huge ball of superheated flame thrown up by the explosion, fighting to stabilise the machine as the hot air wafted towards her. Twisted pieces fell like confetti all over the place and I saw two burning bodies fall into the jungle. One was screaming as he fell, the sound was abruptly cut off in a soggy plop as he hit the hard ground in the centre of the clearing not very far from me. The main wreckage followed, burning fiercely as it fell into almost the same spot. The slight breeze stirred, carrying with it the roast pork-like smell of the bodies in the burning machine and a sound like melting fat crackling in the flames.

"No one's going to survive that, as well as a fall of a thousand feet!" I said to the trees. Turning my back on the carnage with a tired sigh, I once again gathered my kit together and set off in the direction of the landing strip. The sound of sporadic shooting came clearly from my right, which I assumed was where the Fire Teams were still hammering away at the last bit of resistance.

"Snowbird One, this is Big Eagle. Do you require a lift?" Once again, the welcome voice of Marguerite came calmly over the air as she brought her machine down over the area I had just left.

"You bet!" I replied, gladly retracing my steps. "That was spectacular work, well done," I gasped.

"Before you land, could you check the area for any other business?" She knew I meant any of the enemy we had missed.

"Wilco." The affirmative came back as the huge machine lifted and heeled over into a turn that took it over the area of the landing site and across the wide open ground below the factory. Sweeping in a long graceful arc upwards, its rotors dispersed the cloud of thick black smoke that now poured from the factory buildings. Completing her circle of the area, Marguerite then brought it back across the valley to touch down and wait for me. I was suddenly aware of a great feeling of tiredness, as I dragged myself across the intervening space and knew I was now feeling the effect of what is widely known as 'post action flop.'

It is not common knowledge, but in times of danger or stress, the human body saturates itself with great bursts of adrenaline that give rise to extra energy. Medical people say it is our way of preparing for *fight or flight*. Whatever it is called, it enhances your senses and makes you feel invincible and it can give rise to a normal person doing *superhuman* acts. The more unpleasant 'downside' is that as the adrenaline surge wears off at the end of the action, the excess energy charge it created will burn off, leaving a distinct 'floppy' feeling. My system was now feeling the effects of the action that my adrenaline surge had masked. It's no good sitting down feeling sorry for yourself, you've got to live with it and carry the action forward.

Nothing that a good hot bath and a long sleep wouldn't cure my friendly little voice told me wearily.

Just as I was about to reach the chopper, Miguel called me on the radio.

"Snowbird One. All accounted for, lambs all safe. We now have the lorries to deal with. Over." Yes, the lorries! I'd forgotten them in the heat of the action.

"Two Roger, I've just caught a taxi! See you shortly. Out!" Then, patting Zack on the shoulder and fervently congratulating him for his work, I picked my way gingerly across the hundreds of empty brass cases that still littered the cargo bay floor and clambered into the co-pilot's seat to speak to Marguerite. She looked at me with a distinct glint of excitement in her eyes as I donned the helmet and positioned the 'mike.' From the redness of her face she was on an adrenaline 'charge' too!

"That was the most brilliant flying display I've ever witnessed!" I said sincerely. "You saved me from getting a good chewing over and dispatched the 'heavy' team. But whose idea was this 'Big Eagle' thing?"

"Ah! Well Ben!" Zack broke in on the intercom with his leisurely southern drawl. "I had a spare machine gun in the back and it seemed a pity to stay away from the action." Before I could comment further he continued. "This little lady here," he waved his hand towards Marguerite, "was itching to get us involved, so I thought why not?" With a shrug he resumed his seat in the back. Turning to Marguerite and intending to have my say about consultation before action, I saw the happy smile on her lovely face and all thought of admonishment was forgotten.

"Well," I said, sheepishly trying to cover my own very embarrassed feelings. "I'm certainly glad you had the idea and shall be forever grateful to you both for your courage." Turning to look out of the front, I added in a sharper tone of voice.

"Now. We still have a war to finish! So let's get this show on the road, I want to have a good view of the area then link up with the others! .... Let's go shall we!" With a secret grin on her face, Marguerite lifted the chopper off the ground and flew us towards the factory. As we passed over it, I could see that though it was severely damaged, it was not fully destroyed.

"Before we leave, we will make damn sure that nothing can be salvaged from there," I informed my two companions over the intercom. We flew in an ever widening pattern for a thorough search of the area, until we were satisfied that it was clear. On one pass, we flew close to where a large group of people stood waving at us and I realised it was the workers from the factory. Reaching into my pocket, I dragged out a bundle of dollar bills; some of my 'War Chest'!

"There's about six thousand dollars there," I shouted to Marguerite above the sound of the rotor. "It's not much, but they had better have it." She nodded and turned the 'chopper' to fly back over them. I tied the bundle with a spare bootlace and Zack dropped it out of the door. The waving was resumed more enthusiastically as they started to share the money out.

"Take us back to the landing site please," I instructed Marguerite. We had to deal with the lorries as Miguel had reminded me and couldn't take too long about it. A plan began to form in my mind as we flew over the area.

Code Name SNOWBIRD

The moment we touched down, we were surrounded by the members of our group. Big grins split their dirty faces and the atmosphere was electric.

"Ben, we've done it!" shouted Miguel above the noise of the others. Hands clasped my arms or slapped me on the back as I climbed out of the chopper. I noticed that although I was filthy and stinking dirty, there was no holding back in their very enthusiastic welcome.

Leaving two men to guard the machine, the rest of us walked over to the factory for a quick inspection. Marguerite took my arm as we moved towards the track; I could feel the excitement in her. When Miguel came up on the other side of me, I put my arms around their shoulders.

"Without the help of you two, it could not have been done! So my friends," I called to the others, "how about a big cheer for Marguerite and Miguel?" Eagerly, our scruffy band of 'soldiers' took up the chant.

"Viva Ben! Viva Marguerite! Viva Miguel! Adios El Jefe! Viva........" and so it went on for a few minutes, as in the euphoria of a holiday mood we danced along the track.

In amidst the smoking debris of the factory, we found piles of plastic packs of the cocaine powder. A quick count showed us a total of 30, all waiting for the lorries to return. There was also a pile of sacks full of coca leaves, which were promptly dragged into the centre of the workspace and slit open. One man found a can of diesel fuel that he poured over the heap. A further search proved that with a little bit of work, the place could be put into operation again. I was determined that would not happen.

"We will destroy this place my friends," I announced. "Santos, bring in any of the explosives you can spare. The rest of you search for anything that will burn and pile it around the cocaine packs. Nothing of this filth will be allowed to survive."

"Miguel, would you get as much debris from the two choppers brought to this area and scatter it about please." Ignoring the puzzled look he gave me I turned to Zack. "Would you be able to 'lift' the bulk of El Jefe's machine and drop it in there?" I asked.

"Aaaah! I understand now," Miguel said as he saw my reasoning. "An air crash! Brilliant!" Happily, he moved off to start organising his 'troops.'

With the help of a few men, Zack and Marguerite pulled some heavy tow chains from inside the partly ruined workshop and attaching them to the cargo hook under the chopper, they flew off on their salvage mission. We watched with interest as with practised ease, Zack swung the long length of chain like a pendulum into the wreck of El Jefe's machine. After a couple of failed attempts, he managed to get the hook to bight and very gently started to lift the still smouldering wreckage of the smaller machine. With it suspended below him, Zack lifted the wreckage into the position I had indicated. Satisfied with the results and trying to ignore the sickly sweet smell of burning flesh coming from the downed chopper, I placed a few pounds of explosives around it when Santos returned with his load. He'd also fashioned several explosive charges, two of which I inserted into the pile of cocaine packs. Others were placed in strategic points in the walls of the main building and between the Gas bottles. After stowing the remainder in my pack and handing it to Santos, I set the timers for an hour and a half and we cleared the building. Two men did a quick, but cautious search of the other buildings to ensure that no one was left alive.

"Right then, I have a nice little job for you that I think you will enjoy," I said, turning to Marguerite. "After you have recovered your machine and topped the tanks from the fuel dump here"........

"Me? I have fun just *being* here," she interrupted cheekily. "But what are you planning Ben?"

"Zack can fly his 'chopper' with you as load master and when the explosions are over, *you* can bomb this disgusting place with jerry cans of fuel!" I said watching her face for her reaction.

"Can I? Oh, that's great!" she exclaimed, doing a dance of glee and the crowd around her cheered as they also felt she was worth it. Nothing else could be done here so we moved out and returned to the landing site. Zack flew Marguerite back to where they had hidden her chopper. On their return a short while later, they topped the two machine's tanks off and we all had a quick brew and something to eat while Miguel and I held a Post Action Debrief.

"Well my friend! It seems we have done what we set out to do and have been very lucky." I watched his face as I spoke; he looked worn out.

"Si, Ben. We have taken no injuries, so perhaps we were lucky. Eh?" He nudged my shoulder with his fist, as he tried to hide his exhaustion.

"Surprise, my friend! That's what it's all about. We were not expected, so we caught them napping! But you seemed to be engaged for a long time after the choppers went down, who was it? I queried. I took a big swig of the scalding, sweet tea Santos had handed us both, while I waited for his reply.

"Them?" he responded. "Oh, they must have been out on a patrol. Silly fools thought they were the Cavalry; came charging in not knowing what they were up against. It was nothing!"

Patting him on the shoulder, I walked off to chat with the lads. They were all tired, but very happy. They had seen action before, but as several of them said, this had been personal; not someone else's war. This time, they had dealt a blow for their own families and country. Before I moved off to check my weapons and draw more ammunition, I reminded them that we had not finished here yet and time was ticking away with only 45 minutes to go.

🕊 Code Name SNOWBIRD 🕊

Chapter 26

<u>A Fiery Farewell!</u>

Marguerite supervised the loading of the spare fuel cans, seeing them safely placed into a cargo net that would be slung below the helicopter. Zack took his place in the pilot's seat and complying with her signals, gently lifted the machine off the ground. Two men dashed underneath to attach the hook and when the rope had tightened enough to lift the cans; she gave a signal for one of them to lift their lids off. With the open cans dangling well below the machine and she was laying flat in the open doorway - knife in hand, ready to cut the cord holding the net closed, they lifted straight up. Discretion being the better part of valour, while not wishing to miss the spectacle, we withdrew to a depression some three hundred metres from the burning building. Manuel in the meantime had gone into the jungle to answer the call of nature.

"Five hundred feet!" Zack's voice came over the radio.

"OK Zack! You have just about five minutes left, over!" I advised him; the explosions were now imminent as the clock was ticking inexorably away. Still steadily climbing, he moved the machine across until he was high above the factory, then held it in the hover directly over the smouldering ruins and waited.

"Seven hun ....! His words were cut off by an almighty noise. BBOOM-BBBOOM! The multiple explosions that seemed to run into one another made us all jump. The earth shook as the factory building erupted anew. Black dots fell through the air above it; the cans released by Marguerite pirouetted gracefully as they fell into the centre of the fiery explosion.

WHUMP! With an almighty flash and a gigantic gout of flame, the place became a raging inferno. The flames, now fuelled by Avgas, spread outward in a huge wall that devoured everything in its path. To my alarm, the conflagration seemed to leap across the open spaces as it spread rapidly towards our own position.

"DOWN!" I yelled, and we threw ourselves down behind the scant protection of the earthen bank around the rim of what looked like a dried out pond. No sooner had I tasted the flavour of the dried mud in the bottom of our hole, than an almighty heat wave swept over us. Leaves on the trees exploded with a hissing sound and small twigs burst into flame. My back was protected by my combat kit and still full backpack but all exposed skin felt as if a hot iron had been passed over it and the air was dragged from my lungs. Smoke curled thickly down into the depression, seeking us out with its oily tendrils.

Realizing that it was not safe to stay there, I struggled to my feet, coughing and choking, I kicked the man next to me to make him follow and the others soon followed suit. Running in a bent posture, with our hands across our mouths, we dashed through the smoke and smouldering ashes, stumbling and almost crashing into the burning remains of trees. Hot sparks scorched my skin and I could feel my hair burning as I scrambled madly to escape this death trap.

At last! After what seemed ages, we broke out into the clear, clean air - even the smell of burning helicopters and their cargo smelt better than the inside of that fire! Coughing and spluttering, my companions took stock of each other, knocking the still smouldering fragments off and checking for serious burns.

"Madre de Dios, Ben!" One black faced, sweaty man gasped, "what happened eh?" He broke off to cough up phlegm from deep within his throat.

"Droplets," I announced shakily, my own throat burning from the heat and smoke. "Droplets of fuel, blown out of the open cans as they fell and spread across the area by the down draught from the chopper..... .... I should have known! .... Nothing we could do about it, especially when the cans exploded and the vapour met the flames."

"Muchas gracias, Ben!" Another equally blackened character chipped in. "If you hadn't shouted when you did, we would all be cooked like the Tamales!" There was general laughter at his reference to being cooked like the Indians favourite spicy maize pancakes. It seemed that our brush with death had not broken their spirits.

"Hey hombre!" A voice behind me shouted. "With all those holes, your clothes look more like a fishing net".

I left them joking and insulting each other like true friends do. They had shared the dangers of battle and had survived being almost burnt to death - the worst kind of way to go I'm sure. They deserved to let the delayed shock come out as they saw fit. The unmistakable whump! whump! sound of a helicopter in the distance brought me back to reality. Apparently, the rapid spread of the fire and our near demise had not lasted as long as it seemed. Minutes! That's all it had been, but it sure felt like hours to me.

"The chopper!" I gasped as I came out into the open and scanned the sky, anxiously looking for the machine; the fear of it having been damaged in the blast was in the back of my mind. No! There it was, coming down in a swooping turn; Zack must have anticipated the upsurge of superheated air and was in the middle of a hasty spiralling turn to the windward side of the buildings. We could hear Marguerite's whoops of joy quite clearly over the radio. She was ecstatic. The sound of running feet broke into my thoughts and a strong hand clasped my shoulder. Turning I looked into Manuel's eyes.

"What happened Ben?" he gasped, out of breath after his mad dash across the landing ground to reach us.

"My fault!" I grunted, as I reached for the water bottle that hung at his waist. "It was obvious, and I should have known!"

"What should you have known? How did you all get so blackened like that? Tell me what happened!"

To stop his insistent questions - I was not feeling in the mood for an inquisition - I explained the events in simple terms, ending by saying, "all I wanted was for Marguerite to have a bit of fun in return for her hard work!" I emptied the remains of his water over my head; it felt as if all my hair had been scorched off. "It didn't bloody well work out as I planned though did it!" I muttered sheepishly as I tossed his empty water bottle back to him.

"No matter. You're all alive at least. You thought of her; *that* was good of you Ben. She deserved a little glory for herself I think." He was obviously very proud of his lovely wife's skills and actions, as we all were. I nodded dumbly.

Then gathering myself together I replied, "I owe her my life and we all owe her a big debt of gratitude that can never be repaid, my friend. It's hoped that the wasting of about eighty gallons of aviation fuel will keep her happy for a while, eh?" We both laughed together and as the chopper landed, we crowded round and when the Viva Marguerite's started again, I drew him aside to outline the plan for the lorries.

"Miguel my friend, I know that we are close to losing the lorries," I said, pushing some of my wet hair away from my face. Looking at my watch, I saw it was now nearly 10.30 am, which meant we had been in action for the best part of three hours.

"So! As we have no chance to catch them by going overland like we planned, with your agreement, I am going to ask our two pilots to become 'hunters.' You, along with half of the men, could be dropped on the road they are using. If you can spot them early enough to get in front of them, you could set up an ambush and we will run interference on them by slowing them down while you get into position. How does that strike you, my friend?" With a noncommittal grunt, he looked at the map he had taken from his pocket, tracing the narrow route the lorries had to take with his finger.

"It is well over 250 kilometres to the river. I doubt if they could have driven very fast on that track, the twists and turns as well as the steep valleys would hold them back," he said half aloud. "Bueno! OK! It is good. It's worth a try at least and I think they will be about here by now." He jabbed his finger on a section of the map, which showed the contours as almost blending together in some parts, thus indicating some extremely steep hills.

"*That* will be a very steep climb for them, so, we will possibly find them cooling the engines in that area there." He indicated another section and I saw the sense in his reasoning. The lorries would have to travel in low gear most of the time for over 30 kilometres and their engines would be overheating. At the point Miguel had indicated, there was a stream in the bottom of a *very* deep valley. It would be here that the drivers would rest themselves while the engines cooled. That would be followed by a long steep climb, which could only be done in low gear and meant they'd have to rest at the top as well. Knowing the poor standard of maintenance these lorries enjoyed - run until they fall apart - we could be pretty sure that they would have to top up the radiators from the stream as well!

"Then we still have to attack Señor Cordoba's home, don't forget!" He advised, giving me a big grin at the same time.

"Right then!" I slapped him on the back as I moved off towards the waiting chopper. "Let's pick us a few good *volunteers!*"

There was a stirring of interest among our soldiers when they heard the word volunteer. Most servicemen and women normally shied away from becoming one, but these men were different. They knew that volunteers would be called for to undertake a difficult or risky task. I had no need to call for their attention; they crowded around eagerly waiting the next detail.

"Right lads! This is what we have to do now. You are aware that the lorries are on the road already and we *have* to stop them and destroy their cargo." I paused to see their reaction. They were all nodding in agreement; some were muttering *bueno, bueno.* "Miguel thinks they are no further away than here," I said placing my finger on the map that he was holding up. We will split into two teams, one to ride with me in one of the machines, the other with Miguel. My team will ride interference and cause them to slow up, if they have passed that point. Miguel's team will fly unseen to a point in the road where an ambush can be set up."

Keen interest and excitement was shown at the chance of more action. It was then that I noticed that what I had taken as a jostling for a place to hear what was being said was in fact a subtle dividing into two teams! They had made their own decisions! Smiling to myself I turned to Zack.

"Zack, you will fly my team as your machine looks more military in case we come across anyone else." He nodded his agreement, his white teeth flashing a pleased smile.

"Marguerite, you take Miguel and his team across here." I indicated a course that would keep them out of the sight of the lorry drivers and any other travellers we may chance on. "When we spot them, I will radio the coordinates and you choose your landing spot. Miguel, you can then select an ambush point in conjunction with that. OK?" I looked at each in turn; all I saw was their dirty, smiling faces and an eagerness to get on with the job. As I walked to Zack's machine, I saw that Felipe, Rico, Ernesto and Santos were already busily engaged at the side of the chopper. When I joined them, I saw that they were tying down one of the heavy machine guns on the opposite side to the one Zack had already used to shoot the guards machine down with. We now had a gun-ship that could pack a mighty punch.

"Well done my friends!" I said as I watched them loading the spare belts of ammunition into each gun. Such a demonstration of initiative was only to be expected from such people. After all, the survival of each man relied on teamwork and that meant being able to anticipate what needed to be done next. As soon as preparations were complete, I gave the signal for the lift off. Up we went, the blackened ruin of the factory fell away below us and the extent of the damage became clear as we clawed our way into the sky giving us a clear view of the total devastation we had wreaked on this place. A shudder went up my spine when I saw how wide our fire had spread, just a few tendrils of smoke here and there, but over 2 square miles of undergrowth and trees had been badly scorched or burnt away. We were lucky not to have been barbecued, but we had achieved what we had set out to do, we'd liquidated the Cartel bosses, then destroyed their factory along with a huge amount of drugs. That destruction alone would set them back millions of dollars.

With the Cartel leaders dead, there would be others with ambition to take their place. The news of his father's death would, I felt sure, cause Jose to fly home from France and he would hold an enquiry of sorts. Outwardly, it must be seen as an accident caused by pilot error. Any bullet holes in the machines or bodies could be explained as being caused when the ammunition 'cooked off,' the likelihood of this happening was common knowledge to anyone who'd ever used a gun.

The last thing we wanted was a 'witch hunt,' so it was my hope that it would appear that both the Cartel's machines had collided and one had caused the destruction of the factory. I couldn't help myself thinking that somewhere behind us, hidden in the jungle; there were a crowd of local peasant labourers, whose salvation we had firmly established. It was now our duty to ensure that retribution would not be visited on them, by completing the destruction of the entire Cartel.

Following the course of the track, I watched keenly as Marguerite's machine disappeared over the top of a small mountain and out of sight.

It wasn't long before Zack brought me out of my trance like state by saying, "there it is Ben; the road those lorries would be on." Looking down through the blur of the trees, I could see the junction of the track and the seemingly rougher road it joined.

"Follow that lorry!" I quipped. Zack gave one of his Yeeeha! cowboy yells as he dropped the nose of the chopper and we clawed our way across a seemingly never-ending carpet of tree tops. Apart from the occasional flock of colourful birds that scattered at our approach, we saw no other signs of life. The trees were only broken by odd flashes of white water as we crossed fast running rivers or streams. Some brief glimpses of hard granite cliffs flashed under us as we hurtled across ravines, the noise of the machine echoing briefly down those forbidding places. Nearer the bottom of some small valleys, the blur of trees was broken by the odd, rough Indian dwellings that were marked only by their small clearings and smoke from cooking fires. Their herds of goats and other animals scattered in panic at the suddenness of our passing. The miles melted away from underneath us, as I reflected that it was best we had not tried this chase on foot after all. There below me was plenty of evidence that the maps were far less than accurate, it was a lesson learnt. We flew on, the aircraft effortlessly, if noisily, eating up the miles.

We swerved sharply around the side of one huge mountain outcrop, scattering an unsuspecting airborne flock of wild geese as we abruptly came into a wider valley with a fast flowing river running through it. On the other side, we could see the road clinging to the rock face as it climbed steeply up the mountainside. Zack slowed our forward motion so that I could check the road; even with my binoculars I could see no movement.

"We must be getting close to them by now!" I said to Zack over the intercom. With a nod to acknowledge my statement, he flew us on to the next vantage point. A smaller valley presented itself for our inspection. We could see the ribbon of the road clinging to its steep sides but no sign of vehicles. On we flew crossing above a razor sharp ridge of bare volcanic rock that divided this valley from the next, we again saw the road on the other side. It was climbing at an almost impossible angle.

"Hold it there!" I instructed Zack, who flared us into the hover so sharply, that the blades made a noisy whumping sound that I was sure could be heard for miles. Using my binoculars, I peered at the distant hillside. Yes! There was a vehicle moving slowly up the gradient. *Only one!* There *had* to be two. Following the line of the road, I anxiously searched for the other.

"May not be one of ours!" Zack muttered as he saw what I was looking at. "We'll have to move closer to make sure. Don't want to ambush a lorry load of chickens do we!" With a grin, he threw the chopper down into the valley. Flying just above tree level and using the contours and 'dead ground' to avoid being seen, we accelerated rapidly, the echo of the screaming engines flung back at us as we passed over scattered outcrops of rocks. I tore my eyes away from watching the chopper's shadow rise and fall on the blur of trees below us as we turned our back to the sun. Zack took us across and up the mountainside so that we emerged above the road, but behind the vehicle.

"What d'you think, boss?" he asked, as he held the machine on the blind side of the lorry.

"Not sure!" I said with a sense of despair. "All these damn vehicles look the same to me!"

"What?" Zack replied. "Are you telling me you didn't take the licence number?" I looked at him sharply, only to see from his wide grin that he was teasing me.

"Sorry. Never thought of that!" I threw back at him. "Let's get in front and see if we can spot the other.

Once again, like a lift, we climbed straight up and turned over the top of the mountain keeping out of sight of the lorry driver.

"There it is!" An excited shout came from the back. Rico, who had been leaning out of the open doorway, was excitedly pointing some way in front of us. Looking down, I could just see the shape of a large lorry in the shade of some isolated trees; it was stopped in the middle of the road. Both Zack and I saw the driver at the same instant. He was walking back to the top of the incline, presumably to wait for his mate. In answer to Zack's questioning look, I pointed straight on. The driver could not identify us from our height and to suddenly swerve off course may serve to make him suspicious. We flew on a few kilometres and I called the other machine.

"Snowbird Two." ..... No reply. "Damn it, the high mountains are shielding our radio's." Throwing a switch, Zack indicated that I could use the chopper's radio, so I tried again.

"Snowbird Two. Target spotted."

"Snowbird One. Roger, state position over." The reply came back crystal clear on the more powerful set. I hurriedly consulted the map, having to improvise as there were no grid lines to give coordinates from.

"Two. Target static just above and two inches to the right of the rest stop you indicated. We are observing and will advise, over."

"One. Roger that." Miguel indicated he understood. "We will recce the forward route for a picnic spot out." I had to laugh at his use of the word picnic as the ambush spot. Perhaps he thought it was going to be a picnic. By circling back across the high mountains and emerging on a parallel course, we maintained our watch. I hoped that from the ground we would look like several different machines flying the same course. A quarter of an hour went by as we circled back and forth.

At last, with the aid of the binoculars - that were marginally slower than Rico's sharper eyes - I spotted the second lorry wearily cresting the top of the climb. The driver was clearly having problems, a distinct cloud of steam was emitting from around the engine. This then had been the cause of its slow progress. I radioed Miguel and gave him the news.

"Two. The second lorry is now at the top; it has been feeling the heat. Over.

"One. If that's the case, we will have an hour or more to wait at least. Not found any good picnic spot so far, so will move further forward. Over" The sound of relief was clear in Miguel's voice as he acknowledged. Looking at the map, I could see what he was up against. Suitable ambush points would be no problem. There were just no landing areas at which he could drop his troops! Perhaps the enforced wait for the lorry's engine to cool would be to our benefit in the end.

"Damn!" The unexpected curse sprang from Zack's lips as we came back in sight of our quarry. I was on the blind side so could not see what he was excited about.

"What's the matter Zack? What can you see?" The anxiety was obvious in my voice.

"The clever little bastard obviously has a brain!" The vehemence in Zack's voice was hard to miss. "He's gotten a fire going! That's what!"

"So what?" I gasped as he swung the chopper round in a gut wrenching turn.

"If he heats the water, he won't have to wait so long for the engine to cool so's to fill it!" Zack spat out. "I think it's time our boys did their bit with the machine guns don't you?" He asked.

"Wait!" I snapped, as the stationary vehicles came into my view again. We can't chase them on until Miguel is good and ready." Turning to the men in the back, I instructed, "get everything ready, but *don't* shoot until I say so and remember, *all* we are doing is to wake them up a bit. OK?" They showed their understanding with the thumbs up and set to work checking their weapons, the rasp of them being armed carried clearly over the intercom. The gunners would lay flat on the unforgiving metal decking, anchored by cargo straps round their waist. These were fixed by quick release clips to cargo tie down points in the deck itself. As I keyed my 'mike' to call Miguel with the news, memories of my own uncomfortable van journey in France flashed across my mind. They would not be very comfortable.

"Two, Sitrep. Over." I was in need of his situation report in order to know what he planned.

"One. We are over the bridge. This will have to do! Over." It seemed that there was no other place then, but how were they going to off load the troops and weapons? I wasn't going to ask.

🕊 Code Name SNOWBIRD 🕊

"Two. Hot water being brewed for thirsty machine, they will move soon and we are ready to give chase. Over."

"That hombre must have seen service!" Marguerite came back bright and chirpy. "Perhaps you could get them to speed up a bit as we are now in place!" The invitation to action was welcomed by a collective cheer from my own men.

"Right Zack. Let's give them a taste of lead!" He gave me a big grin and another cowboy yell, as he dropped the nose of the machine into another stomach churning swoop in which I was pressed down into my seat and the gunners were flattened to the floor as he lined us up with the lorries some distance away across the valley. Down we flew, airspeed building up and the excitement of imminent action with it. We would pass about three hundred yards from them, making our approach from their rear. Our port side gunner would then have a few moments in which to play with them. Looking over my left shoulder, I was pleased to see that Rico was being given the chance to fire on this pass and on the other side Santos had been given the honour.

Team work brings respect! The satisfactory thought flashed across my mind.

"Yeeee-Haaa!" The sound of Zack's battle cry nearly deafened us as we started our first pass. I could see the two drivers busily engaged in pouring steaming water into the radiator of the nearest wagon. Brrrrrrrrrrrrrrrrrrrrr-Brrrrrrrrr-Brrrr. Even though we were wearing headsets, the sound of an inexperienced man on the gun was almost deafening. I saw puffs of dust from where the heavy rounds were hitting the cliff face *above* the two vehicles. At the same time I registered the complete and utter shock on the faces of the two drivers. They dropped the water container and ran for cover behind some rocks.

  We were pressed back in our seats as Zack threw the chopper into a sharp climb, narrowly missing the volcanic peaks of a rocky outcrop. Then, with another yell that sent a chill up my spine, he twisted the chopper on its axis and we were travelling back through the airspace we had just vacated! This time, Santos the starboard gunner would have a chance to chivvy the hidden drivers up.

  Partly hidden by the trees from above, the two lorries presented a splendid target from the side. Rounding a bend in the mountainside, we hurtled towards them at breakneck speed. Brrrrrr-Brrrrrrr-Brrrrrr; the sound of a more controlled burst of firing came from behind me and I watched for the strikes and saw dust flying from the rocks as we went by. Zack flew us out into the valley again, turning us equally as fiercely in readiness for another port side pass. Struggling against the fierce pull of gravity created by our sharp manoeuvres, I held up my hand and he pulled the machine into the hover. We hovered there.... menacing ...waiting. The sight of the chopper sitting there, with its machine gun aimed at them must have horrified the drivers as they dashed out and literally threw themselves into their cabs. In my imagination, I could almost hear the clashing, grinding noise of the gears being engaged without the benefit of the clutch.

"Give them the chance to really get moving, then do a tailing job on them, OK?" I whispered into the 'mike.'

"Yep! But we won't have clear vision of them for long with those overhanging trees," Zack replied. I had seen the same thing when we flew over, so I accepted his statement.

"OK. You can show us your skill at playing leap frog then!" He looked at me in surprise.

"You mean that?" he gasped in surprise. "Better warn the passengers back there then!" He adjusted his position in his seat in readiness for the manoeuvring he would soon have to do. Turning to the back, I called Felipe over the radio and explained what we were going to do. He nodded his understanding and went to brief the gunners. We circled over the stretch of road where the lorries would emerge from the trees. Suddenly, they virtually shot out into the open with only about fifty metres between them. Zack quickly checked their ground speed, as he took us down into their dust cloud.

Skimming the treetops and dodging the overhanging rocks, Zack brought us up behind the first lorry. We could see the driver's face in his large rear view mirror, as he anxiously scanned the sky for us. His jaw dropped as we slowly emerged from his own dust cloud just above and to the right of him. Zack swung the body of the chopper to the right, while maintaining the same direction of travel as the lorries. The port machine gun opened up in a long burst and we could see spouts of dust chasing the tail of the vehicle. Some were seen to strike the metal of the tailboard and raise a few sparks; the sound of this would be clearly heard in the cab.

Lifting, then dropping like a car on a roller coaster, we shot forward to carry out a similar exercise on the leading lorry, but this time Zack presented the starboard side machine gun. Clouds of dust and sparks flew up from beside the cab as Santos once again proved he could handle a weapon. Heavy trees rushed towards us, at the last moment we broke off as with the touch of an expert, Zack flew us over them, arcing back up into the air and clearly indicating to the drivers that more was to come. Both vehicles were now travelling at a dangerous speed, the twist and turns of the road and its rough condition forgotten in their anxiety to escape us. From the air, we could see there was no shelter for them, so we repeated the performance once more.

"Snowbird One. You are now visual at five clicks." Marguerite's calm warning came over the air, telling me she could see us five kilometres away. She must have dropped the troops and was acting as an aerial spotter.

"Two Roger. We will drive them on once more, then they are all yours. Any help required?" Not knowing the situation at their end, I was keen to know if their plans included us.

"One. Negative, we are ready and would require you as 'back stop' over!" Miguel broke in on my personal radio from on the ground. "We are on the far side of the crossing, keep clear of the arches as you may get your head knocked off!" His chuckle and the cryptic message made me wonder what he had planned. Zack and I looked at each other. He shrugged his shoulders and prepared for a final hop over the dust cloud containing the fleeing lorries. He pointed ahead with a jerk of his chin and dragging my eyes from the blur of the road and trees I saw that they were approaching a long clear stretch that swept down to the bridge across the river.

"Of course!" I gasped aloud, as understanding dawned on me. "Miguel is on the far side of the bridge and he has mined it in some way!" Zack gave me another of his wide grins and let out a whoopee! The other members of my group in the back would have heard Manuel's transmission as well, so there was no need to explain any further.

"HOLY MACKEREL!" Zack's loud exclamation of surprise, tempered with admiration, brought my head snapping back to the front. He was holding us in a 'stand off' position well out from the mountainside, waiting for the lorries to appear on the open stretch of road. There, up the valley to our right we had a clear view of the bridge across the river.

"Straight out of Isambard Brunnell's own catalogue!" I gasped. An unusual sight in this part of the world to say the least, neither of us expected to see the graceful arches of a metal bridge in such a god forsaken area. In the distance, two seemingly tall, thin towers supported the two arches across which the bridge was laid. The ends of the metal beams rested on manmade supports, part of which had been carved out of the living rock. The remainder was built to the specification of the engineers. The thick twin support cables stretched up either side into the mountain, where they were undoubtedly anchored into the rock. Aged and grimy from lack of paint, this edifice was at least two hundred feet above the fast flowing river by my reckoning.

"Here we go guys! Left then right, fire as you bear," Zack warned as he dived the chopper once more into action and my stomach suddenly lurched up into my chest cavity again. Snatching a quick glance across the cabin, I could see that Zack was concentrating on matching our forward speed to that of the vehicles. In testament to his flying skill and judgment, we cleared the top of their cover precisely at the same moment that the lorries appeared from under the trees. Down we went, Zack holding the chopper level at about 100yds behind the lorries and to my alarm we were speeding along no more than a metre above the track. With a twist of his hand on the collective and pressure of his foot on the tail rotor pedal, he spun the chopper into a sideways skid and the port gun instantaneously burst into action.

Brrrrr-Brrrrr-Brrrrr. Then we spun to the other side giving that weapon the chance to repeat the message. I didn't bother to watch for bullet strikes! I was too busy watching for oncoming traffic! My heart was in my mouth as we sidled along at speed, swaying and twisting like a couple dancing the waltz.

Probably be the LAST Waltz if we go on like this, my little internal voice said - and I was pleased to note that it was as scared as I was. I *knew* I was scared, I was nearly squeezing the metal frame of my seat to death! After what seemed like ages - but in reality could only be a few seconds - we zoomed up and away with another stomach churning swoop. The pilot yanked on the cyclic at the same time as he twisted and raised the collective, causing us to swoop up into a steep climbing turn in which the 'G' forces caused me to grey-out - the prelude to loosing consciousness. Seemingly unaffected by the fierce gravitational pull, Zack, just to prove how sadistic he could be, spun us around at the top and ramming the cyclic forward to send us into a near vertical dive straight at the hard, unforgiving ground hundreds of feet below.

"HOLD IT THERE ZACK!" Ignoring all radio procedure, Marguerite's crisp instruction invaded our ears in a loud and clear order. It was just as well she did, because as the blood mist cleared from my vision, I could see he had intended to fly us *under* the bridge. Like the professional he was, he had reacted to her command immediately by bringing us to the hover. In such circumstances, if a fellow warrior gives such a clear order, you don't argue. You just obey!

My earpiece crackled into life again, as Marguerite advised us that the lorries were approaching the turn onto the bridge and a fireworks display would now take place. Backing off, we climbed to a safe height above and well clear of the bridge to watch. The driver of the first lorry took the turning as fast as he dared; sliding on the loose surface his vehicle fishtailed and sent out a huge flare of sparks as he dragged it along the iron stanchions at the side. The second was close behind him, but managed to steer clear of that unforgiving ironwork. I began to get anxious as they drove onto the bridge, I could see the drivers eyeing us warily as we hovered above them. They coaxed their engines onwards, knowing that once they were across the other side we could not get near them. There the road, while still clinging to the precipitous mountainside, was completely obscured by thick, overhanging trees. We *had* to finish the job now! Nothing was happening! Where was the ambush? I was just about to call Miguel, when my radio crackled in my ear and his voice called out.

"Jose! This is for YOU my son!" The rock face opposite suddenly burst into flame, the sound of the heavy machine gun coming clearly to us as a blizzard of tracer arced gracefully towards the lorries. Small arms fire mixed with machine gun fire to lay down a deadly hail of lead. The first lorry slid to a halt, its cab literally chewed apart by the bullets. The driver was just a shredded carcass that slumped over the wheel. I shall never know what happened to the second driver, because what happened next took us all by surprise.

"Jose, my son, this is also for YOU!" Marguerite's voice choked as she added her own benediction to the memory of their son who had died at the hands of drug dealers. The world seemed to change colour, as the bridge blossomed in a brilliant flash of flame and flying pieces of iron that cart-wheeled crazily away into the void. The first lorry was thrown up into the air, its lethal cargo blasted mist-like to the four winds. Slowly, the remainder of the bridge sagged and buckled. The remaining vehicle toppled off the side, spilling many plastic bags of cocaine into the emptiness below. I watched mesmerized as slowly at first, they tumbled over and over, bursting apart as they hit the water or rocks far below.

"There will be a lot of happy fish in that river!" I said, shaking my head in disbelief at what I had just witnessed. Zack and I slapped our raised hands together and we all shouted with glee - and relief.

It seemed that the show was not over for us yet. We watched in amazement as Miguel and his men nimbly scaled the cliff, to stand on one of the massive blocks into which the support cables were set. Then in another brilliant display of flying skills, Marguerite sidled her chopper in so that they could all simply step aboard. From where we sat, we could see that the shimmering disc of her rotor tips were not many inches away from the branches and rocks above and my heart was in my mouth.

"WOW! That's some flying, that is!" Zack said in tribute to what we were witnessing. Me? I could only nod my agreement, as I prayed that the mountain Gods would be appeased by our offerings of huge quantities of cocaine and would spare this most beautiful and amazing woman.

"Hey amigo!" Miguel's voice, when he called me on my personal radio, was almost drowned out by the excited chatter of his troops. "How about that then?" he asked, the excitement of the recent action clear in his voice. I also noticed an underlying tiredness, almost as if he was exhausted.

"Excelencia! Maravilloso!" I replied. "I love you all! ...." I was cut off by Marguerite's sudden cry of alarm.

"Lookout Ben! On your right!" Her fear could be heard quite clearly in her voice, but I wasn't the pilot so why had she called me I wondered. A flash of silver across our front was accompanied by a rattling sound as a roaring, hurricane force wind took hold of our chopper. We were pushed bodily down into the valley, twisting and turning, our rotor flailing against the opposing forces. Zack fought the controls as we were bounced around by the unseen turbulence and I couldn't tell up from down. Then, with sudden clarity, I saw the cliff face looming above us.

This is IT! This is where I say good-bye to these brave people! The thought flashed across my mind as we raced toward certain death. Then, without warning, we were thrown in the opposite direction as the whirling wind literally bounced back off the hard rock face, taking us with it.

"Christ Almighty! Where the hell did *that* Son of a Bitch come from?" Zack's curse brought me back to reality.

"Never mind *where* it came from! What the bloody hell *was it*?" I managed to gasp, as I looked into the back to see if the men were all OK. Thankfully, these seasoned 'soldiers' had remained strapped in. I would not have given much for their chances otherwise since there were no doors on this machine. Sickly grins and a couple of silent thumbs up greeted me.

"HOLD ON! The bastards coming back!" Zack's warning cry came just as Miguel called out.

"Break left, Zack and climb when I say!" He gave us no chance to ask why. We weren't going to ask anyway! An experienced pilot like Zack knew that when told to break by a colleague, you did it without question. Once again we dropped into a left-handed twisting turn, falling like a stone towards the river below.

"Ready! .... Climb .... Now!" The single order came. With equal suddenness we shot upwards, the rotors whumping loudly as they clawed at the air and my stomach was in my boots. Again I heard the rattling sound. Looking down I could see sparks coming off the cliff face at about the position we had just vacated. I spun round to Zack.

"Did you see that?" The grim look of determination on his face as he nodded his reply, told me he already knew we were up against a jet fighter and we were being strafed. As we gained the altitude stipulated by Miguel, I saw a quick flash of sunlight reflected off a shiny surface high above us as the jet turned for another pass.

"Zack. A quarter kilometre on your right is a large overhang, get under it if you can and I will act as bait to draw him past your guns." Marguerite's voice was calm and collected, even in the face of such a drama.

"Right on!" Zack's reply was tinged with anger as he made the longest speech I ever heard him make. "That bastard used his jet wash to try to smash us into the cliff face, while he had a go at you with his cannon. He's no amateur, so be careful little lady!" I took the hint from his glance at me and turning to the boys in the back; I asked if they had heard.

"You bet!" Ernesto said with conviction. He and Felipe were busily changing places with Santos and Rico. This action had to be in the hands of skilled gunners. They were busily feeding new belts of ammunition into the guns, which were now both on the port side and they knew that with the speed of the jet, they had perhaps one chance to get it right. By leading the fire in front of the jet, they would let it fly into its own destruction. I watched as they secured both guns into position by the doorway. Working quickly, they anchored the guns and themselves down securely. Santos and Rico would feed the ammunition belts to them.

Teamwork! Again they have formed a plan and acted on it in a very short time, I thought as I watched with admiration.

"Ready when you are Zack, we have both of the guns on the port side," I advised him as he manoeuvred the chopper into place as instructed; turning us to face the guns outward. I noticed that the gunners had placed ear defenders over their headsets; just as well, it was going to get noisy back there.

"Ready little lady! Lead him in, but take care!" he said to Marguerite. We could see the sun glinting off the rotor disc on her machine below us across the valley; it was out in the open and moving across our front in a slow zigzag, seemingly unaware of any danger.

"She's making sure he sees her," Zack said. "He was above and behind us, so he will come down at an angle, then fly up from our left. He will try to stick to the middle of the valley for manoeuvrability." Getting a thumbs-up from Felipe, I saw that they had followed that information and would be ready.

I craned my neck to spot the fighter through the side window. "Nothing! Where was he? Had he run low on fuel and returned to base? No! There he was." A bright momentary flash of sunlight as he levelled off over a thousand feet above and behind us.

Code Name SNOWBIRD

"Here he comes," I called. Stealing a quick glance at the altimeter I saw our altitude was 1500ft, so he must be at 2500ft.

"About 2500 at your 10 o'clock." My mouth was dry as I called the warning to Marguerite. "He's dropped his nose and slowed down with his air brakes, I think he's stalking you!"

"OK! I think he will let me get higher before he makes a move. He can't risk diving down here at full speed, so let's see what he's made of!" Fearful for their safety though I was, I had to admit that Marguerite sounded perfectly in control of the situation.

"Right on!" was Zack's grunted agreement to this assessment of the situation. He was watching our position like a hawk, his eyes screwed against the reflected glare of the sun. "Hey little lady! He's going to over fly you and come up the valley instead. His racks are empty - meaning he had no air to air missiles on board - so he'll have to get into cannon range. You'll have to lead him away a little for our fire to bear." He looked at me as he gave this warning to the other chopper, and nodded his head towards the expected line of flight. "There Ben. We have a chance in this, 'cos he'll have to do two things to survive." There was a hard edge to his voice as he explained.

"One. Because his target is small and *slow,* he'll *have* to reduce his speed to keep it well in his fire cone and avoid overshooting it. Two. He'll have to maintain manoeuvring room for himself, so he'll fly up the centre of the valley, pop off at the chopper, and then, to clear the hanging wreckage of the bridge he'll lift up past us about level with that copper coloured outcrop over there." As he was busy maintaining the hover of our machine with both hands, he used his chin to indicate the direction I should look. I could clearly see the outcrop that he meant, which I estimated to be roughly half a kilometre away across the other side of the valley.

"D'you copy little lady?" I hadn't realized that Zack had left his radio 'mike' open, so the others could hear his summing up of the situation.

"Copy," Marguerite replied. "I'll draw him up the centre and hope to put him in line with your marker."

She sounds as if she is planning an afternoon tea party, <u>not</u> risking her pretty neck in front of a shower of red hot lead, my internal voice nagged at me. In an attempt to cover my growing concern, I turned to the others in the back.

"Do you see the indicator?" I asked the gunners.

Felipe nodded and put up a thumb.

"Well, I'll be damned! You'd think she was a combat Vet by what she's doing now." Zack said quietly as if to himself. I tried to see what Marguerite was up to, but I was unable to look down at the right angle.

"So what *is* she up to?" I demanded, my voice betraying my fear for her I'm sure.

"She's climbing in a slow spiral as if unaware of his presence, yet she is slowly drawing closer to the middle of the valley." Felipe filled me in as he strained to watch from the open doorway.

"Here he comes!" The voice of Miguel sounded strained as he advised his wife over the open radio link. "He's in a shallow dive now and is following the river to come in behind us." A few long agonizing moments of silence from the others. I wanted to scream out but I knew I had to leave the radio unblocked.

"Steady." A voice whispered in my ear. "Steady, he's at the river bend and climbing." I almost lost my stomach contents with the agony of waiting and being unable to see. I turned to Zack whose head was moving continually as he held us firmly in the hover under this overhang.

"NOW!" The shout came across the air and nearly split my eardrum. Miguel had given an instruction to his wife, the result of which I could not see.

"She's done it!" Zack gasped exuberantly. "She waited until he was lined up ready to fire, then did what no jet could possibly do!" He was so excited that he failed to remember that I could not see, let alone know what had happened.

"For Christ's sake!" I yelled at him. "what has she done, are they OK!"

"Just as he would have been about to fire, she dropped her chopper right down to the deck, at the same time as turning back *underneath* him! No way could he follow *that* sort of move!" The admiration in Zack's voice was so evident. His mouth moved as he continued his explanation, but I did not hear it.

Brrrrrrrrr. Brrrrrrrrrrrrrrrr. Brrrrrrrrrrrrrr. I jumped out of my skin as first one, then both of our heavy machine guns poured a deadly stream of lead across the valley. Turning in my seat, I could see both gunners, their clothing whipping in the wind from the rotors, oblivious to the red hot, shiny brass cases flying all round them as they poured hundreds of rounds out across the intervening space. Shrouded in gun smoke beside them, the other two were feverishly feeding long, heavy belts of the deadly ammunition. The colourful arcs of tracer and armoured shells seemed to float out into the empty void to strike the rocks on the opposite side.

Empty? It wasn't empty! Above Zack's shoulder I saw a sudden bright flash of movement. The jet! There it was, only about three hundred yards from us as large as life. A huge streak of flame belching out from behind it, as the pilot tried to use his afterburner in a desperate attempt to climb out of this valley that had suddenly become a death trap for him.

He was hopelessly trying to escape the continual stream of lead that was ripping pieces off of his aircraft, at the same time as avoiding a fatal collision with the still dangling remains of the bridge. The sustained fire from Felipe and Ernesto's guns had found him and held him as he struggled for altitude. Suddenly one of the gunners - I don't know which - altered his point of aim just enough to send something like 500 rounds per minute into the engine. Under such a hammering something had to give!

It did! The heavy shells ripped the engine into shreds, shattered pieces seemed to fall confetti like in slow motion from the plane. Then, some of the tracer shells found their way to the fuel tank! WHOOMPH! A blossoming ball of orange flame spread out and in a millionth of a second, the jet was no more. Gone! The pilot and other flammable parts had been vaporized. The wreckage; still burning fiercely continued on its way for a short distance before forming part of an obscene aerial ballet as it tumbled over and over into the valley below. A nauseating smell of burnt aviation fuel washed over us as the heat wave from the explosion blossomed around us. I felt the hair on my arms singing in the superheated air, but figured that we were lucky that its heat had been drastically reduced by the down wash from our rotor.

Death was no stranger, but I was shaking like a leaf. I'd never witnessed that sort of thing before. As if in a dream, I felt the chopper move away from under the cliff, spinning to face the open valley as Zack took us to join with Marguerite's machine.

"Are you OK? Have you taken any shots? How's your fuel situation?" These questions and more poured from Zack as he showed his concern.

"Hey! Stop worrying will you. We are all OK! No injuries and our fuel is good. How about you?" Miguel replied.

"Ready for my breakfast!" Zack joked. His casual comment resulted in a gust of laughter across the airwaves, as the tension relaxed in us all.

"Marguerite, that was an incredible piece of flying back there," I interrupted. "I don't want to be a wet blanket, but as we've been jumped once already, I think it would be best if we stayed off the air now."

"You're right Ben." Miguel's voice came in reply. "We will head for the next target, but must maintain a good watch!" With this sobering thought, the men in the back of both machines resumed their watchfulness as we wove our way between the mountains.

"Lead on ACE!" Zack said in a subdued voice, as he positioned us in formation to the right and slightly behind the other machine.

ACE! Yes, that was the right word; the *only* word that could be used to describe the way Marguerite had handled the situation. When I took a quick glance at my watch I was shocked to realize that the whole of that action, from the first attack by the jet to its final destruction, had amazingly taken less than ten minutes! Tired out from the recent action, each person was deep within his own secret thoughts as we flew on in silence. Staying at low altitude for as long as possible to reduce the chance of Radar detection, we headed back over the mountains for the Hacienda Los Palmos, home of the Late Señor Cordoba. There could be no rest for us yet; we had to act quickly before the death of El Jefe became public knowledge. Other, more ambitious and unscrupulous people, would try to profit from the day's events by taking over the Cartel's work. Now we had the advantage, we had to ensure the complete destruction of the organization. The next step in that direction was to destroy the Hacienda in which El Jefe had lived, and from which he had ruled his evil empire.

My eyes suddenly felt heavy, but before I sneaked a catnap, I stole a quick look at Zack. He was so preoccupied in keeping station with the other chopper that he wasn't paying any attention to me. A quick glance over my shoulder into the rear cargo space proved that as with veterans everywhere, my lot were no different. All four were obeying the Soldiers Commandments which said *'grab your sleep while you can!'* Without effort, I followed their example.

Code Name SNOWBIRD

🕊 Code Name SNOWBIRD 🕊

Chapter 27

<u>Return to Los Palmos!</u>

A sudden lurch as we hit air turbulence snapped me back to wide awake. My watch told me I'd only dozed for fifteen minutes, but that had served its purpose and refreshed me. Though I was worn ragged by the extraordinary combination of fear, extreme physical effort and the intense concentration needed in battle conditions, my mind remained very active as we flew onward. There were a million and one things to think about. Most important to me was the fact that together with these amazing people, I had achieved what I had set out to do. By killing El Jefe and his Cartel leaders, I had at last avenged the death of young Sophie!

"Thank you Uncle Ben! Thank you!" Her image seemed to float in front of my eyes and her soft voice once again echoed in my ears.

For the finale we were on our way to destroy El Jefe's home. It was our intention that no trace of this evil man would be left standing either at the Hacienda, or in Bogotá. We had already agreed that any items worth salvaging would be sold to raise money for the Clinics that were struggling against the drug trade. His family members would be cast out on the street - they had lived off the proceeds after all and any cash found would be donated to the Clinics after payments had been made to my valiant band of warriors. Any bank accounts we could find and gain access to would be treated the same.

Why should you hand over any money to the authorities? It all came from the drugs, so it should go to fight against it! My little internal voice had asked me that simple question on several occasions. Who was I to question such wisdom as this!

"Ben!" The sound of Miguel's voice over my personal radio brought me back to the task in hand.

"Uh! Sorry, what did you say?"

"We are now only about twenty kilometres from the Hacienda. How do you want to play it? Over."

"Let's see what we can see from above first," I replied. "If it seems all clear - meaning not too many guards - we go in fast and low. They saw two machines go out early this morning, so two coming back shouldn't cause any initial alarm and by the time they realize it's not El Jefe, it'll be too late. What d'you think? Over."

"Si. I expect they will not be on their toes anyway, so lets do it." Again, I had noticed a note of tiredness in Miguel's voice. We were all tired, but this was something different! I made a mental note to ask him about it later; over the radio was neither the time nor the place to discuss such a matter.

"Good. If you agree, we deplane in two groups without touchdown; you go right, we'll go left. Guards are targets. Family and staff, unless armed, can go into the garage or some other place as a holding facility. Over." I reeled this off, as my mind flashed over the plan I had been formulating.

"Agreed!" His reply was quick. "It's my guess the Cartel leader's cars would have gone back home, or he would meet them later at another place. So we should have only a few armed men to deal with. Out." He sounded quite sure of this statement as he ended the conversation. I hoped he was right.

A few minutes later, Zack pulled us up into the hover behind the other machine just below a ridge. Miguel climbed out and staying low, he dashed forward enough to be able to look over the top. I checked my map and saw that he would be looking down at the back of the main house that lay perhaps a kilometre away.

Crawling the last few yards, he settled himself down and raised a pair of powerful binoculars. A few moment's pause as he swept the area; then his whisper came over the radio. "All clear! Only two cars there!" He moved back to his machine and we edged back into the shallow valley that ran off to our right.

"Ben, do you think 'Big Eagle' will be needed down there?" Marguerite's question brought me up with a jerk while my little voice concurred. *She's right! There may be strong opposition.*

"Yes, that's a good idea. It'll give you a chance to get some more target practice in," I teased.

"Fantástico! D'you copy Zack?" The excitement could be heard in her voice.

"I copy Ace." His continued use of her new honorific pleased me.

"OK!" The fearless lady returned. "When we are Green - meaning all troops off loaded - we'll withdraw to the polo field and I join you as gunner, OK?" Two rapid clicks on the radio signified that he not only understood, but that he didn't mind taking instructions from her either and such cooperation was essential in our task.

Looking over my shoulder, I could see my erstwhile 'gunners' were already preparing the weapon for her and as they completed their task; I called the signal to start the action.

"Snowbirds. Bearing 145 degrees..... GO!"

Turning in unison, the two machines flew very low in echelon as the pilots concentrated on following the contours of the ground. We broke the skyline as one, rushing forward and swooping down the opposite slope. I hoped that anyone at the Hacienda would automatically look skyward as they heard the sound of our approach - the hill behind us would act as a baffle board and send the sound in all directions. Skimming the earth as we closed on our target, cattle scattered in panic in front of us, sheep ran crazily and I saw a horseman unseated as his horse reared in fright.

I clearly heard the sound of automatic weapons being loaded behind me as we flashed across the intervening distance. No need to issue orders, my team was ready; all we had to do was get there. We hovered a couple of feet above the front lawn in a cloud of dust and loose leaves from the nearby trees,. Men spilled from either side of the machine, dropping to the ground and running forward to take up defensive positions ready to return 'fire' if we should draw any. None came, so keeping low and zigzagging in true Rambo style, we headed for the left side of the main building. Above the strained sound of my breathing, I was vaguely aware of the noise of Marguerite's machine closing in on the other side.

Brrr. Brrr. A short controlled burst, fired by one of my men ripped into a man who ran around a corner waving a shotgun. He fell backwards, a gaping hole where his chest had been. We ran on.

Brrrrrrrrr. The sound of shooting came from the house and a few puffs of dust around our feet told me we were taking fire! I looked around for cover and spotting a huge concrete urn I headed for it, Felipe close behind me.

"On the right! Open window!" Brrrrr. Brrrrr. The target was indicated to me by Felipe, at the same time as he sent a stream of bullets in that direction.

"Damn it! I thought we wouldn't meet much organised resistance!" I cursed aloud. "Felipe! Where are you?" My radioed query ended abruptly as the wind was knocked out of me when I hit the deck behind the earth filled urn. I knew he wouldn't be far away.

"Behind an ugly statue!" This strange reply made me wonder what he meant. Turning my body carefully so as not to become a target, I took a look behind me. Indeed, there was a statue of a man there.

Perhaps it had been a good-looking one once! Whoever just shot its face away sure made it very ugly! My little voice whispered with a chuckle.

"OK! Give me covering fire," I said over the open channel while fumbling for a grenade and pulling the pin. Holding the grenade away from me so that Felipe could see what I intended. I prepared to move. Brrrr. Brrrr. Brrrrr. His burst of fire shattered the window and made bits of stonework fly off the building, and at the same instant I got up and ran the half dozen yards to the house wall. Flattening myself against it, struggling to regain my breath, I crouched ready to lob the grenade through the window. More shots were fired at Felipe from inside the room, but they only served to make the statue uglier. Inching forward as he sent another short burst in, I reached a point close to the window. Releasing the clip on the grenade and counting to three, I lobbed it through the opening and flattened myself against the wall at the same time.

CRUMP! The explosion deafened me momentarily and a cloud of dust choked me as chunks of masonry, wood and glass flew outwards. The building seemed to punch me in the back at the same time. I carefully stepped in front of the aperture and emptied my magazine into the room in a spraying motion. Silence! There would be no more fire from *that* direction. Quickly reloading as I moved on along the wall towards the corner, the sound of shooting at the rear of the building became louder.

Sounds like Miguel's boys are busy too, my little voice advised me. That shooting is by the outbuildings and means that he may not have cleared the main building yet! I reached for my radio.

"Two. Sitrep Over!" I called.

"One. We have four men in the servant's building; they are all armed. Over." The sound of shooting coming over the radio nearly drowned Miguel's voice out.

"Two. Roger, we're going to clear the main building now. Out!" My mind vaguely registered the two clicks as Miguel acknowledged and I turned and beckoned Felipe and the others over to me. It was then that I noticed Rico was limping and blood was showing on his trouser leg. His face was pale as he leaned against the wall, sweating heavily.

"You're hit?" I asked him.

"Si! Señor Ben. I'm sorry," he stuttered." It ... it is only my lower leg." His face contorted as pain surged through him, but he gritted his teeth and waved me on.

"OK! Rico you stay here and cover our backs." He nodded and settled himself against the wall of a doorway, weapon at the ready. "Felipe, put a wound dressing on that for him." My instruction was met with a wide grin as Felipe, who had anticipated my command bent to tie a small dressing pad on the wound.

The stuff of heroes, I thought as I tapped Ernesto and Santos on the shoulder.

"In through here Ernesto!" I pointed to the window out of which clouds of smoke still drifted. "Felipe and I will go in through the other one along there." Ernesto nodded his full understanding as he moved off. Scuttling along the verandah, we crouched beside the now shattered window as for safety sake; I lobbed in a grenade as Felipe rejoined me.

Again the building shook and debris flew; we both stood and sprayed the room with automatic fire before diving through the aperture. Landing in a forward roll, closely followed by Felipe, I felt, as well as heard, broken plaster and glass crunching under us. In perfect unison that would have pleased any Depot Instructor, we rolled into the crouch position with weapons at the ready and facing opposite corners of the room. The strong, unmistakable smell of blood hit us even though it was mixed with the smell of burnt flesh. There on the floor, partially concealed by the bed lay the remains of a man, his chest cavity still smoking from the grenade explosion.

Must have taken the full force of the grenade, a decidedly dispassionate voice whispered inside my head. Turning, I noticed the lower part of another body draped across the remains of another bed; its upper torso was on the floor, a gun still clutched uselessly in one hand.

"Looks like he got sawed in half Ben!" Felipe muttered as he crouched beside me.

"Yeh! He shouldn't have got in the way then should he?" I retorted, indicating that he should check the next room.

Moving fast and staying low, Felipe kicked the door open, firing as he did so. Brr. Brr. Another controlled short burst of fire as he double tapped his trigger was followed by a muffled scream and the sound of a body hitting the floor, proving he was on target. Moving into the room behind him - at the same time as covering our rear - I saw a half dressed man slumped against the wall he too clutched a rifle. Felipe was busily checking the pockets of his expensive jacket.

"Here you are Ben," he said, handing me a wad of paper. A quick look showed me that it was a couple of sheets of notes containing a few names and addresses in Bogotá, Medellin and Quibdo. I shoved the list in my pocket. They were probably taken at a briefing with El Jefe, so would come in useful in tracing any other Cartel members.

"This guy must have been the head hon ......" I started to say.

"*Shhhh!*" The sudden hiss of warning came from Felipe at the same time as the sound of glass being crushed under someone's foot reached my ears. We froze. Using two fingers angled at his eyes, he indicated that he could see movement outside the room in the passageway. We waited!

Scrunch! There it was again, closer this time. Partly concealed by a large easy chair, Felipe sank silently into a crouch, his weapon pointed at the doorway. I stayed where I was, Right Opposite the Door!

Scrruunch! Scrruunch! The distinctive barrel of an AK47 rifle edged its way around the corner. Not one of ours, my little voice sagely advised. The weapon was followed by first the arm, then the head and shoulders of a very large man and what little light there was in the passage was blocked, as his body filled the doorway. His eyes widened in shock when he saw me stood there. His arms seemed to move in slow motion as he swung the weapon up. My arms felt like lead as I tried to bring my weapon to bear. My blood ran cold when I realised that he was going to beat me to it!

Brrrrr! A blast of high velocity lead from Felipe's gun took the man full in the chest, flinging him backwards against the wall of the passage. Brr. Brrrrrrrrrrrrrrr. His finger tightened in a reflex action on his trigger as he died, his weapon spraying bullets at random. Training and instinct made both Felipe and I hit the floor, encouraged by the angry buzzing of hot lead zipping past our ears. Showers of plaster fell from the walls and ceiling until the man's weapon was empty.

"Are you OK, Ben?" Felipe's voice sounded muffled and distant; the close proximity of the muzzle blast was still ringing in my ears as I scrambled to my feet.

"Yes, I'm OK. Thanks, how about you?" I dusted him off and helped him up.

"I'll live!" he replied shortly. "We were lucky he was walking on glass, or I may not have heard him." Nodding my agreement, I cautiously moved out into the passage and followed it into the main hall of the building. As we gained the centre of the hallway, a noise at the top of the stairs made us both spin around, weapons at the ready, fingers already tightening on the triggers.

"Who are *you*?" I demanded of the young lady who stood there clutching two wide-eyed children to her.

"I," she replied, in good English, "am Rosita Cordoba Señor!" Then with a haughty jerk of her head, she continued. "I ask who are *you*, to come and blow up my home and kill my servants."

"There'll be time for questions later," my reply was sharp. Taken aback by her self-assured stance though I was, we didn't have time to debate rights or wrongs with stuck-up females. "For now, you must move yourself and anyone else out of this house and into the servant's quarters!" I ordered her brusquely as she moved down the stairs towards me, keeping herself erect while moving with a feline grace. Her two young children were obviously very traumatized and clung firmly to her dress with vacant expressions on their faces.

"Damn! Why did they have to be here? We could do without any such complications." I blamed myself for putting the children at risk.

At that moment, Ernesto and Santos joined us in the hallway and their silent thumbs-up sign told me they had checked the other rooms. Signing for them and Felipe to check the upper part of the building, I admired the professional way they moved quietly up the staircase. Beckoning the still pale-faced Rico in from his place in the passageway, I indicated for him to take the rear while I led the woman and her children outside. She only paused momentarily at the sight of a body in the kitchen as we passed through and I had to admire her stoic courage.

"Hold it there!" My outstretched hand stopped them as we reached the back door. Even though we could hear no shooting, I wanted to be sure that it was safe to cross the yard.

"Two, Sitrep. Over."

"One. We are in the servant's quarters, four down its all clear."

"Roger. Three troops clearing the upper floor. Two of us are coming out of the back door, one female and two children in company!" I wanted Miguel to know our disposition and for his group to cover us as we stepped outside. We could not see the roof area - best be safe than sorry was my motto. Looking across the yard, I could see some movement in two windows as weapons were placed to cover us.

A hand waved from the shadows of the opposite entrance. Moving slowly, I edged my way out first, turning to scan the building and yard as I moved. All clear. I signed for the Cordoba woman to bring her children out. Moving as quickly as the injured Rico could manage, we crossed without incident. As my eyes adjusted to the shadows inside the building, I found we were in the communal room of the servant's building. Slumped around the room in various groups, were eight or nine people. One of them, a young woman, suddenly jumped up with a cry and dashed toward us. I swung my weapon to cover her and Miguel grabbed her in a bear hug nearly stifling her torrent of voluble Spanish.

"It's OK, Ben. She's a servant girl, probably wants to be with her Mistress," he said. This comment resulted in a further rapid stream of Spanish that I could not follow. Seeing my querying look, Miguel translated that she had recognized Rico and was eager to see to his injury.

"Well, Rico my friend. It seems you have your own private nurse!" I said, and we all laughed at his obvious embarrassment as the girl fussed over him.

"No, Señor Ben!" he whispered, so that her Mistress could not hear. "This is Juanita Arroyo, she is the maid I met at the party."

"Ah! I see," I replied, recalling that he'd told us about a maid helping him plant the bugs in the Hacienda.

Turning to her and with a reassuring smile I said. "Bienvenido ...." My intended speech of welcome was suddenly cut short as the sound of a helicopter alerted us all to the real purpose of why we were here. Our radio earpieces were filled with the sound of Marguerite's voice.

"One. You are compromised!" There was a break, while she obviously struggled with the G-force of an erratic turn of the machine she was in. Then....

"Two off-road vehicles, with what looks like armed men in each, coming down the road. We are going to deal with them and there are several people on horses coming from higher up the valley!"

"Where did they come from?" I didn't have any answer to my own question, so I turned to the lady of the house.

"Two jeeps with men in and men on horseback. Who are they?" I demanded.

"Before I answer you Señor, please answer my earlier question. Who are you?" She said with a defiant toss of her head.

Angry but unable to harm such a courageous woman as this, I replied, "We are avenging the deaths of countless people caused by your husband who was supplying drugs across the world!" She went to say something, but I held my hand up. "No argument! It is a proven fact and one that you should have surely known." Her face gave no indication of her thoughts as she took this in.

Then without emotion, I added, "I must tell you, Señora Cordoba that your husband is dead!" Callous maybe, but we didn't have time for polite conversation and gentle explanation. She hesitated a moment, then made the sign of the Cross and took a glance at her children before she spoke.

"The men in the trucks will be fresh guards coming from the town. Those on horseback will be our ranch hands. My children do not speak your language Señor, so please tell me how you know my husband is dead." If I had expected any hysterical display of grief from this woman, I wasn't going to get it. She remained cool, almost detached while I gave her a quick and accurate outline of how he had died. A moment's pause, a deep intake of breath and she seemed to have made up her mind.

"Señor, I cannot pretend to be shocked at this, the death of my husband. I have known how he made his money; it is true. We have, what you call, an arranged marriage. My father was very rich and powerful and Señor Cordoba; I will no longer refer to him as my husband; was ambitious. I never loved him and feel no loss." This simple, bold statement was delivered without any sign of emotion. I believed her, simple as that! It changed things slightly, but not our main objective.

Looking around for Miguel, I found him watching me from a few feet away. Beckoning him to join me, I moved out of her earshot.

"What d'you think, my friend? Is she telling the truth?" I needed to know if he believed her as well.

"Ben. It may seem strange to you, but such marriages are normal in this country. She shows no emotion, so I believe her. *But!*" he stressed, tapping the side of his nose. "Perhaps we should leave such a decision to one of her own kind to decide on, eh?"

Seeing my puzzled expression, he explained, "Marguerite! She will find the truth in this, trust me."

Without another word, he turned back to checking his weapon.

"I'm going outside to see what is happening, keep everyone here, Miguel." He waved his acknowledgment as followed by Felipe, I moved out of the door. Crossing the yard quickly, we entered the kitchen door and moved down the passage. A voice called from the main hallway.

"Señor Ben! This way." It was Ernesto calling from the first floor landing. His face showed his excitement as he greeted us at the top of the stairs. "Quick Señor, we have spotted some visitors outside." Felipe and I followed him into one of the front rooms and as we crossed the thick carpet to the window, I vaguely realised from the faint, but obvious smell of perfume that it must be Señora Cordoba's room. We pressed ourselves flat to the wall on either side of the large window and took a careful look outside. There, about half a kilometre away and kicking up a cloud of dust as they approached the buildings at a gallop, were eight or nine horsemen.

Just like a scene from Bonanza, that old TV series! The thought flipped across my mind as Felipe turned to me.

"Vaquero's! - Cowboys and they will be well-armed, Señor." I moved over to his side of the window to kneel down beside him as he pointed out that they would have to make the final approach up the long driveway. As this was enclosed by high stock railings on both sides, they would have to follow it until it opened out into the stockyard at the side of the Hacienda. Seeing that I understood, he nodded. "OK, Señor. We can manage this quite easily!" Turning to the others, he issued rapid instructions and they moved out onto the upper balcony.

The riders, perhaps thinking they would have the upper hand, kept galloping right up to the first of the many long water troughs. Halting in a cloud of dust, they jumped from their mounts and dashed forward to the first fence line, clasping their rifles.

Ben Cartwright would be proud of them, my little voice said. Seeing no movement, their leader waved them on and in a loose group they ran across the open stock yard to seek cover behind the last of the water troughs. A few metres from me, I heard Ernesto click his tongue twice - no words of command would be needed in *this* team. Thumbs came up and pushed safety catches forward. I heard another almost inaudible click, as the fire selector switches were pushed to Automatic.

These cowboys are in for a surprise, I thought. A shout, muffled by the distance, heralded their final move. As one, they stood up and began indiscriminately firing their rifles as they walked toward the outhouses.

They don't know we're here! God! This is going to be nothing short of a cold-blooded slaughter, I thought as realization dawned. Sporadic return fire from Miguel's men in the lower building made the Vaquero's hesitate, then Ernesto deliberately stood and fired a burst at the ground in front of them. Spinning sharply to face this new and unexpected challenge, the nearest ones returned haphazard shots in the direction of the main building. Ernesto made one slicing motion with his hand.

Brrrrr.Brrrrr.Brrrrr.Brrrrr. A long stream of automatic rifle fire 'walked' along the line of them. They went down like ninepins and lay still in the dust of the yard. Silence reigned again, as the sound of shooting faded. I grabbed Ernesto by the shoulder and spun him round to face me.

"Why didn't you give them a chance to surrender?" I shouted angrily. "Why just shoot them down like that?"

"As I said, Señor! Those were Vaquero's! They are scum who would not think of surrender. If they had gone to ground, we would have a long job to finish them off! Besides Señor, it would mean we would fight on two fronts as we have other visitors in vehicles eh?" This was said with such conviction, that his voice was shaking. I paused, angry with myself for missing the obvious.

"Yes. You're right, my friend. I'm sorry, I didn't think!" I patted him on the shoulder and turned to walk away. A hand held my arm firmly, pulling me back round.

"Ben!" Ernesto said quietly. "Believe me, it was the *only* way! These are not people you can take prisoner, nor talk to. They enjoy killing for killing's sake. They *had* to die!" I could hear the sincerity in his voice. Placing my arm around his shoulder, I nodded my agreement as we retraced our steps along the balcony. An urgent shout from Santos made us hurry. Turning the corner onto the eastern side, we saw the helicopter as it swooped down behind a rapidly moving dust cloud less than a kilometre away.

"One of the Jeeps, Señor Ben." With a jerk of his head, Santos indicated a fast moving vehicle that was attempting to outrun the helicopter. "He is a good driver, so he may make it to the trees." I followed his gaze. There, three hundred metres from the Hacienda, the track dived into a long avenue of thick trees that led the way almost to the buildings.

"Maybe he thinks he will be safe there!" Ernesto's voice came from behind me as he jostled for a look. "There again, he may have a surprise coming to him yet!" I heard two heavy clicks as catches were released. It was a sound I recognised and one that I had made myself, not so many hours ago. Spinning round, I saw that Ernesto was busy preparing the last of our rocket launchers. We moved aside to give him space in which to operate, besides, none of us wanted to be stood behind *that* when it was fired!

"I wonder why Marguerite is not shooting at him." My whispered question was meant for me, more than the men with me. "Better find out I suppose." I had hardly finished thinking, when Zack's voice burst over the radio.

"Snowbird. Are you able to deal with this?" He jinked the machine quickly aside even as he spoke. The popping sound of someone shooting at him came clearly to us.

"Big Eagle! We have a hot tailed welcome waiting." I hoped he would understand that by 'hot tailed' I referred to a rocket. "I would suggest you just shepherd him into the trees. Over."

"Right on!" Zack replied as he once again swung his machine across the tail of the vehicle. "Our little lady has dealt with the other wagon, and then the gun a jammed!"

"Roger, Big Eagle. Get ready to Bug Out!" It was unfortunate that Marguerite's weapon had jammed, but she had reduced the odds by fifty percent. Now I could see the bouncing and madly weaving jeep was almost at the far end of the trees. It was doubtful if the occupants could see us, or even if they knew we were there.

"I will shoot as he comes out of the trees, Ben!" Ernesto informed me. Looking down, I could see he was already kneeling in the firing position, using one of the balcony pillars to steady his aim. The vehicle cleared the final one hundred metres of open road, disappearing into the shelter of the trees. The driver was probably thinking they were safe now, because they would soon be inside the shelter of the Hacienda yard. He was wrong!

WHOOSH! At the same instant that the vehicle leaped out of the tree line, so the rocket leapt out of its launcher. I stood with my mouth open, not only to absorb the air-blast of the explosion, but in amazement. The jeep hurtled along the last bit of road, as the rocket, followed by its fiery tail flew unerringly towards it.

Surely he can see it! My little voice sounded really surprised.

In the space of a few short seconds, the rocket crossed the intervening space and smashed straight through the front windscreen of the Jeep. A loud bang was followed by a fireball as the rocket exploded. The body of the vehicle simply disintegrated; bits and pieces flying all around. Some larger than others, could have been pieces of the occupants. No one would live through that! We watched transfixed, as the remains of the chassis rolled onwards, spreading fire as it went by and out of sight. A loud crunch indicated that it had hit against the side of one of the buildings.

"Ernesto. That was some shooting!" I managed to get out, as I gathered myself together and indicated they should follow me down the stairs. They were laughing and joking, mercilessly teasing Ernesto about his prowess with the rocket. Nevertheless, there was still the sobering thought that we had just seen four or more men blown to bits. Snapping out of it, I turned and chivvied them up.

"Come on! We can't stay around here slapping each others' backs all day, there is still a long way to go." We crossed the yard in relative silence to be greeted as heroes by Miguel's group. A quick explanation of what had happened meant another round of back slapping for Ernesto complete with his replay of events. Miguel came to me and we watched the post action stress being relieved in the time-honoured fashion. Tales of 'I did this and I did that,' were only surpassed by the story of Ernesto's 'hot shot' as it became known.

"Well, Ben. That's another target cleared!" He sounded relieved. I think we all were. "Now what are we going to do with 'Madam' and her brood?" I was about to reply, when the young girl Juanita thrust a mug of hot, sweet tea into my hands along with a thick wedge of bread and cheese. My stomach lurched! It seemed so long ago since we last ate. Taking a swig of the tea and revelling in the feeling of the hot liquid rushing down my gullet, I thought about my answer.

"Good question, pal! Perhaps it will be best to do as you suggest and let Marguerite have a 'chat' with her." He nodded his agreement. "If her story is genuine, we will have to offer some sort of compromise," I said bluntly before filling my mouth with delicious fresh bread and cheese. He let me chew my food in peace as he left to supervise the others.

A few minutes later, we heard Zack's chopper coming to land at the side of the Hacienda. Unbidden, two of the 'troops' went out to escort Zack and Marguerite in. I watched with quiet amusement as Juanita, ably helped by the apparently recovered Rico, started to make fresh supplies of food and drink. My mind wandered to that other beautiful young lady by the same name, who I hoped was awaiting my safe return.

We all - with the exception of the Cordoba woman and her retainers - gathered round our two fearless air warriors, eager to hear their story. Zack explained that he had set up his chopper in a position to surprise the two advancing Jeeps. He had flown out to the ambush area via a dry riverbed. Then he'd simply 'popped' up over a low hill, slewing the machine to one side to give Marguerite a good target.

"Jeeze Man!" he gasped. "Our little lady here simply blew the first one away. I've never seen shooting like it, we could have done with her in Nam', boys!" The troops patted the embarrassed Marguerite on the back, muttering congratulations etc. I could clearly see that once again she had risen in their estimation.

"What happened to the second one?" Miguel managed to make his question heard above the general din of excited voices. "How did that get by you?"

"Ah, well, that was entirely my fault," Marguerite announced with a slightly embarrassed smile. "You see, though I can fire that weapon, no one has *ever* thought to teach me to change the belt. So when I fired the first long burst at the leading Jeep, I had only a part belt left. Enough to put the fear of God up the second one though!" She shrugged. "Then it stopped firing. When I tried to reload, I just couldn't manage. .... Sorry!" She hung her head in mock shame.

"Hey! Hombres! Cut out this crap." The indignant voice of Ernesto stopped all other conversation in the room. "If that hadn't happened, I wouldn't have been able to do my Audy Murphy act!" This was answered by a burst of laughter and the comment that perhaps Señora Lopez should make a special 'appointment' for an interview, when Señor 'Hot Shot' could tell her all about it. More genuine laughter ensued as the crowd broke up to tend to their own weapons and kit. Joining Miguel and Marguerite, I put my arms around their shoulders.

"Well my friends, I think we're all learning something about ourselves, don't you?" Before they could respond to that rhetorical question, I reminded them that it was time we moved out, but there were things to be done first. I quickly explained about the Cordoba woman to Marguerite and asked her to check her out.

"Once again, Lady Luck is with us my friend," I remarked turning to Miguel as she moved off. "I hope she stays that way, because now we have to move on the town house and it could be that word has got out and a reception awaits us." He gave a quick wave of dismissal.

"Ben, while you were outside, I have already been on the phone from here. My contact says the house is still empty, so don't worry!" His hand patted my arm as he gave this assurance, but I still couldn't shake off the feeling of doubt.

"OK! That's good thinking. We now have to very quickly remove the items of interest and value from here. So could you deal with that while I look for the safe?" There was a dreamy look in his eyes as he nodded his agreement. "What's the matter? What did I say, eh?" His reply was cut of by the return of Marguerite.

"She is OK, Ben, I am sure of this. I checked with her staff and they say she was afraid of El Jefe. They all were!"

"Right then! We will have to let her salvage something of value and give her transport out." ......

"Why does she have to leave?" Marguerite interrupted.

"Because my dear, we are blowing this place up. Removing the stain from the landscape!" I explained firmly. Turning away to avoid the expected argument, I went to find Rico.

"How's the leg now Rico? Can you use it?" The young man's face was still etched with pain and from the angry mess on the side of his leg, I could understand why. Having been the recipient of a bullet myself, I know that such flesh wounds are painful enough. This one however, had caught him in a part of his leg that is full of nerves and blood vessels. It looked clean, the bleeding had stopped and the edges were taped together. His reply to my question showed he still had the fighting spirit.

"Si, Señor Ben. It is sore, but I am ready to move when you are." I watched as the young Juanita carefully applied some antiseptic cream and a bandage.

"It seems you have got quite a catch there my young friend," I said when she had finished. He blushed and muttered something I didn't catch. "Anyway, down to business. I seem to recall that you planted a bomb here, where is it and how is it operated?"

"It is in the cellar," he replied enthusiastically. "I have a small remote device in my pocket; this will set the timer going. We will then have fifteen minutes to clear the area." He paused and then added, "can I blow it, Ben?" There was a certain pleading in his voice, that couldn't be ignored.

"Why not? .... Of course you can, you deserve it but you will have to allow me to reposition this device first." Meaning I wanted to make sure it did the most possible damage by being in the right place. He couldn't reply as he had a mouth full of thermometer, so he nodded his agreement through clenched teeth. "Find me when you are ready," I said, and moved away.

Chapter 28

<u>Farewell to Los Palmos!</u>

"Come ON! Get a bloody move on!" I was beginning to lose my patience with the wrangling over the articles that should be 'rescued' from the house. I had only claimed a couple of boxes of personal papers from El Jefe's study, which I thought the Courts may find interesting. The men however, were being choosy over some paintings, each of them having suddenly become an Art Expert!

The Cordoba woman, when I asked her if she wanted to take anything, simply shrugged and said, "do what you have to do, Señor. I have a family to go to, they will help me. ….. Besides!" She suddenly snapped her voice full of feeling. "I HATE this place. I never want to see it again!"

Well, so far so good, I thought. No hysterics about losing her home, so we can get on with the job.

"Are we all set now?" I said turning to Rico, who was sat on a chair nearby.

"Si, Ben. I set the timer after you placed the satchel; it will take the building right down." He gave me a smile when he said that, as he knew I didn't want to leave any stone standing.

"Don't forget that we have placed some cans of petrol around it also!" Miguel said, as he stepped up onto the verandah beside us.

"Great!" I exclaimed. "Now get those servants away from here." He moved off with Santos to supervise the small convoy of two cars and an old lorry. Crammed with the servants and the household objects strapped on the roof that Señora Cordoba had allowed them to take from the Hacienda, these were ready to move off.

"Rico. Get yourself and your young lady - we had allowed her to accompany us as Nurse for the wounded - onto Zack's chopper quickly," I instructed as I walked across the yard to the first car. Leaning in the back window, I spoke to Señora Cordoba, who sat there looking as cool as if preparing to leave on a picnic.

"Leave now, Señora and I wish you well. Please don't think too harshly of us." A quick smile was all I got in reply and an instruction to the driver and they were off. The other car followed close behind, the servants staring out at us with blank expressions on their faces. At least she is taking them with her! My little voice whispered above the rattling and groaning of the overloaded lorry as it too pulled away.

Spinning on my heels, I moved quickly back to the yard to collect my pack and weapons. Taking a last look around, I waved the troops back to the two choppers that were already waiting with engines running. Taking off, they flew out in different directions. Their task was to have one final look over the property in case we had left anything undone and to make sure nobody was in the area for what was to happen next.

At my command - after I had cleared the area myself - Rico would blow the Hacienda up. Marguerite would then return to pick me up from the stockyard, after I had tossed a few grenades into any remaining structure left standing. At least, that was the plan!

"This is for you Sophie and for your mum and dad," I whispered to myself as I moved away from the main building. Reaching a corner of the stockyard where I could observe the explosion and hopefully be safe, I called Rico on the radio to let him know the area was clear.

"I am ready Señor Ben." His eager voice came to me above the roar of the rotors.

"All clear on this side!" Zack informed me.

"Same here!" Marguerite's call proved she was also monitoring my transmissions.

"OK. Rico. The stage is yours!" I could see their faces lining the doors of both choppers as they circled well out of the danger area. I fiddled with my pack, extracting a few grenades in preparation. Then I sat down on the edge of a water trough to wait. Both machines continued to circle in opposite directions, the sound of their engines fading and rising as they came and went. I started to feel sleepy, my eyes burned and I realised how long we had been going without proper rest. I was vaguely aware of Rico's voice counting down from ten.

"It'll soon be over and then I can sleep for a week!" That was the last clear thought I had before.

B-BOOOOM! An earsplitting explosion shook the earth beneath me; it seemed to ripple upwards like a carpet being shaken. I felt myself fly through the air as the force of the explosion knocked me across the yard. I landed with a crash against a wall at the same time as having a strange feeling of drowning. The prolonged rumbling noise gradually stopped and in the sudden silence I realised there was a great weight pressing down on me. Water was dripping all over me as well and I couldn't breathe! My mouth and throat were full of a thick, sticky muck. Panic started to override my rational thoughts. Coughing and spitting I cleared my mouth to call for help.

Sit up! That way you'll make a small chamber when you draw your legs up, my little voice said, reminding me of some training in the snowfields of Norway. "I wonder if the same thing applies to bricks and mortar, as it does for avalanches?" I asked myself as I tried to move.

"Oh shit!" I heard myself croak. I couldn't feel my legs! The blood was pounding in my ears and my head ached terribly. My lungs heaved with short gasping breaths. No air! I was beginning to pant like a dog and the temperature in my 'prison' had shot up. My brain was in such a whirl that I didn't know up from down. I felt at peace with the world. There was no need to get up from under all the rubble I knew was covering me.

Someone may find me someday. This strange thought crossed my mind as I drifted into unconsciousness.

Chapter 29.

<u>Rescue!</u>

"Ben! Ben!" I heard a distant, soft female voice calling my name. I couldn't reply so it faded away.

"Ben! Can you hear me? Oh! Madre de Dios! I have killed him!" A man's voice sobbed in my ear and at the same time my shoulder was being fiercely shaken.

"Come *ON* you guys! We've got to get him away from here before that damned wall buries him again!" A new firmer voice broke in; I vaguely identified it as Zack's from his slow drawl.

He sounds distinctly anxious; I don't know why, my little voice counselled me. The sound of voices was fading as the darkness crept over me again. Through the mist, I heard grunts and swear words accompanied by rumbling sounds and I felt dust falling onto my face.

"Careful! His legs may be broken." The same female voice ordered sharply.

What's Marguerite talking about? What's happened? Has someone been hurt? These thoughts slipped slowly across my mind and I tried to open my eyes to see who it was they were talking about. It was hard work; my eyelids were so heavy.

"He's waking up!" The excited squeal of a female voice sounded nearer, and then I caught a whiff of Marguerite's perfume cutting through the cloying dust and dirt that seemed to be blocking my nose. A soft hand caressed my cheek, gently smoothing away the dirt from my eyes. I felt a sudden lightening of my lower limbs, as if a weight had been lifted off me.

"He's free! Now you can move him." Miguel's voice sounded close to my head. As if in a dream, I felt hands gripping me firmly by my shoulders, then I was pulled roughly backwards and more hands gripped my legs. Once again I felt as if I was floating.

I'm comfortable, why do they want to disturb me? My mind was busy trying to make sense of what was happening. "I don't want to get up!" I tried to say. The words wouldn't come, my mouth was gritty and my throat was dry. Uneven jerky movements followed a sensation of floating up into the air.

"That's what it was like when I acted as the unconscious accident victim on an Exercise!" The realization suddenly came to me. I was being carried on a stretcher! It was *me* that was hurt! More excited voices sounded around me and I felt myself being lowered onto something solid. Hands scrabbled at my clothing.

"Let me do *that!*" the female voice demanded. I felt firm, but gentle hands rubbing around my head. "There's a large bruise, it could be a severe head injury!" she said and then her hands were running up and down my arms and legs, moving them gently but firmly before declaring that I had no broken bones.

"What the hell!" I was just drifting off into the comfort of the darkness again, when I felt the cold blade of a knife against my skin. A ripping sound registered as my trousers were cut up through the legs. The person doing the cutting continued right up to my crotch. Cool air caressed my skin as the cloth was folded back. Fingers prodded gently.

"Ouch!" I winced inwardly as a finger found a sore spot; they didn't hear me so they carried on prodding and poking. A sudden coldness hit my inner thigh and something cold ran down my leg.

Water! They've found some water to wash me with. Oh that's nice! I started to enjoy the attention; the water was soothing my thighs that were becoming distinctly painful. Just as well go to sleep, my little voice whispered in my ear. Soldier's motto: sleep while you can. I could not argue with that logic. The sounds around me faded away to soft whispers as I gave in to the feeling of sinking into deep cotton wool. The voices drifted further away and I had no sense of feeling. The probing hands felt lighter.

Peace, beautiful peace! I could smell the perfume of beautiful flowers as I entered into a sort of tunnel in the darkness through which I could see a bright, yet soft light in front of me. I knew that if I made it into the light, I would be OK. Sophie was waiting for me there.

A massive blow in the middle of my chest snapped me back to the surface again. Hands pushed down on me, trying to push me through the floor. My head was dragged backwards by my hair, fingers delved inside my mouth and lips closed over mine!

Whoosh! Whoosh! Air was being breathed into me! Urgent hands pumped at my chest again!

Another thump! More air! More pumping! My heart fluttered feebly and I took a choking breath of air for myself.

"He's breathing! Now **keep** him awake!" I heard Marguerite's voice gasp near my ear and the smell of her perfume was even stronger. It had been that, not flowers that I'd smelt. "Ben can you hear me?" She shook my shoulder firmly. I tried to open my eyes. They felt as if they were glued together. Try again!

A dull, grey misty light seemed to hover in front of me. A vague movement in the middle of it as something came closer. Not something! Somebody! It was a face, so distorted by the poor light that I couldn't see whose.

"It's OK, Ben. You had a knock on the head and are concussed," Marguerite said softly, as she used a damp cloth to carefully wipe my forehead and bathe my eyes.

"Wh...What happened?" I managed to get out; my head was starting to hurt as much as my legs.

"My Legs! What happened to my legs?" I tried to sit up and look. Dizziness and a feeling of the need to be violently sick forced me back again. Hands pressed me firmly down.

"It's OK Ben! A water trough landed on top of you when the house blew up........" She was interrupted by the sound of someone running.

"Ben! You're OK! My god, I thought I had killed you!" Rico gabbled, as he slid to a stop almost on top of me. "Please forgive me Ben!"

"That's enough Rico! He will be OK now, but will need rest, so leave him alone." My self appointed nurse instructed firmly. "Oh, by the way! Would you ask my husband to come here please?" she added as Rico backed reluctantly away. Busying herself in tidying me up, Marguerite fussed around making soft clucking noises to herself when she found some small cut or bruise. I found I could stay awake quite easily if I watched her at work.

"How is he, my love?" The unexpected sound of Miguel's voice behind me made me start; I didn't know he was there.

"He's all right at the moment. There is a very large bruise on his head." she replied, gently parting my hair with her fingers. "That makes me think he may slip back into unconsciousness again if we don't watch him. He really needs to be seen by a Doctor." The concern in her voice was genuine. I reached out to touch her arm but couldn't get the strength.

"I'll be OK. I've only got a head ache!" I managed to croak before my throat clamped up again. I didn't sound very convinced of this myself though. Marguerite lifted my head gently as she held a cup of water to my lips and I sipped thankfully. The next thing I knew was four of my band of warriors came and lifted the canvas stretcher gently up. Working together, they carried me out into the bright sunlight and across the yard to the waiting helicopter. Zack's face encased in his 'Bone Dome' helmet suddenly appeared in front of me as he clasped my hand.

"Great to see you're alive old buddy!" He turned to hawk into the dust at his feet. "I'll drive you home eh!" he quipped, before climbing into the pilot's seat and my stretcher was manoeuvred into the cargo bay. Eager hands busied themselves strapping me down. A ring of filthy, sweaty faces grinned down at me. As they finished, they all muttered their 'get well's' and disappeared.

"Zack!" Marguerite called, "keep low as much as you can and please, no rapid climbs either, we don't want suddenly increased pressure on his head wound!"

"Yes ma'am!" came the reply and I heard the generator whine as the engine 'spooled' up.

A soft hand touched my face; I looked round into the large brown eyes of Juanita. So it seems that our nurse now had two patients to tend to, for I saw Rico sat beside her.

The floor shook and the machine wobbled slightly as it overcame gravity and left the ground. I closed my eyes, not because I was tired, but trying to look out of the side of them hurt like blazes!

The vibrations of the machine, the roar of its engines and the clatter of its rotor made it very uncomfortable for me. I drifted in and out of a fitful sleep during the journey back to our temporary base. I was looking forward to the dubious, but nevertheless welcome comforts awaiting us at Riosucio. It wasn't 'till we landed that I realised the other machine was not with us.

"Where is Marguerite and the others?" I shouted weakly as the sound of the engine died away.

"They've gone to Bogota to sort out the town house." Zack's disembodied voice replied from the dust cloud created by the rotors. "We are going to join them there later on. In the meantime, there's someone here to sort you out my friend!" he added, as he came to stand at the foot of the stretcher with a big grin on his face.

🕊 Code Name SNOWBIRD 🕊

"What's with the monkey face?" I asked him as I struggled to rise against the retaining straps. A grinning Rico pushed me back down as he slid out to take his place behind me.

"Just be patient, let's get you off loaded and into the house." He waved his hands in a placating gesture and his grin seemed to widen. Unseen hands released the straps at my head, while he and Juanita dealt with those at my feet. Freed at last, they slid me away from them and scrambled through the cargo bay to grab the stretcher at the other side where Zack took one handle and Juanita the other.

"Hey! D'you think that Juanita can manage?" I queried, meaning her ability to carry me all the way to the house. Zack's face, still partly hidden by his large 'Bone Dome' helmet seemed to light up at my question.

"Oh! I'm sure that *one* Juanita is quite capable," he giggled. "Just as I'm sure that TWO Juanita's would be more than capable!" His voice spluttered off into another fit of giggles at this.

"What's the matter with you, Bozo?" I snapped wearily. "Can't you see there's only one Juanita here or have you lost your marbles or something?"

"No, Ben, he has not lost his marbles and there are *two* Juanita's!" A soft, unforgettable female voice said from behind my head.

JUANITA? That's the second time she's done this to me, I thought.

"What! Where... How...?" I couldn't get the words out properly; I was struck dumb. They stopped marching forward and I craned my neck backwards to see if I was dreaming again. No! The vision of loveliness stood grinning down at me was definitely no dream and she was also helping to carry the stretcher.

"Juanita you're.... Oh God! **I STINK!**" I gasped in embarrassment before collapsing back onto the stretcher. My obvious surprise - and discomfort - resulted in a great deal of laughter from my stretcher bearers, so much so in fact, that I was scared they would drop me as they started off again. I was thankful when they finally placed the stretcher on the large kitchen table and removed the carrying poles that had been digging mercilessly into my shoulders and hips.

"How did you get here?" I asked Juanita as they fussed around me.

"Senor Miguel telephoned me and told me what had happened," she replied. "Then he sent a friend of his to fly me in the helicopter to this place, now we must get the things we need, so you lay still. OK?" With a squeeze of my hand she turned away and the girls went into a whispered huddle before disappearing, while Rico and Zack started to fix blankets to the rafters so that they hung down as a screen. Finally satisfied with their handiwork, they gave me a cheerful wave and were gone. I heard the sound of the chopper taking off a few minutes later.

"Ah well!" I muttered. "It seems I'm being left to clean myself up, so I'd best get on with it." I started undoing what remained of my combat kit. Trying not to aggravate the now constant pains in my legs, I levered myself up into a half sitting position and had just succeeded in undoing the jacket when the sound of my heart pounded in my ears. A sudden clammy, nauseous feeling swept over me and I felt faint. I tried shaking my head to clear it.

The room started to spin and my eyes wouldn't focus. In front of me, the largest of the brightly patterned blankets became a blur. Then as blackness came over me, I felt myself falling into a deep pit. As if in a dream, I felt hands lifting me; then something warm and wet covered my face. I faintly heard Juanita's voice calling me.

"What did you think you were doing, Ben?" she said, as she mopped my face with a damp cloth. The feeling of sickness gradually receded and my eyes focused again.

"Getting ready to wash this muck off!" My whispered reply was a bit sharp, but I thought it was obvious what I was doing.

"Oh! Is that so?" said my Juanita, with a knowing look at her namesake who stood on the other side of me. "So you think you are fit enough to do it yourself, do you? Don't you realise you have concussion and are still in shock?!" This was accompanied by a stern look that would have done any Ward Sister proud. I wasn't about to be bullied by this young lady, I would make *that* quite clear.

"How else do you think I'm going to get clean?" I declared. Then I stopped as I saw the look on their faces and realisation dawned on me.

"Oh NO!" The shock in my voice was real. "You can't, you mustn't ...... My objections were ignored, as one on either side; they gently but firmly pulled me up enough to remove my jacket and vest. Holding these at arms length by her fingertips, the younger Juanita consigned them to the floor. Expecting them to start washing me then, I was even more shocked when, after removing my boots and socks, they raised me by the hips and dragged the remains of my trousers off.

"Thank goodness I've got pants on!" I thought, fully expecting to be handed a washcloth then, but no.

"Hey! You can't do THAT!" My voice rose to a higher croak, as Rico's girl friend calmly produced a pair of scissors and quickly cut the sides of my pants, and then with a deft flick of her wrist, my Juanita flipped the filthy remains off my body. Stark naked I lay there; too weak to move away - the pain in my legs had also worsened because of my struggles.

"Look at the state of you, Ben!" Juanita's voice conveyed her horror at the sight of me. Her concern was genuine. Looking down at what I could see of my body, I saw that it seemed as if I were wearing a close fitting undergarment of some sort. In reality, I knew it was a coating of swamp mud that had dyed my skin as well. I could also smell myself now. It was awful!

Working with a cloth and soap in their hands, both girls started washing me. Neither of them seemed to notice my nakedness as they worked, softening the dirt with a wet cloth before working soap into my skin. Working quickly and gently, they soaped my upper body until it was clean, drying me with warm towels. Then they worked their way down to my groin and upper legs, I couldn't watch them - I was busy making a close study of the roof of this ancient place and praying that their administrations would not result in me embarrassing them. I felt hands moving my private parts - whose hands they were I don't know - I daren't look as warm water and soap was worked well in and a cloth was used to wipe the muck away. Just as I thought they had finished, they started all over again with clean water and more handling as soap was lathered on me.

During the next hour or so, I 'suffered' them working in this way and then they rubbed some sort of sweet smelling oils into my skin. When fully satisfied with their handiwork, they gently rolled me onto my tummy and commenced work on my back. Even though my thighs were apparently extensively bruised - plus other small areas of damage elsewhere - this 'treatment' caused me no undue discomfort. In fact the opposite seemed to be the norm, as I actually dozed off during this session. Satisfied that they had at last cleaned me as much as they could, they dried me thoroughly dressed me in a shirt and pants then helped me to climb down and stretch out on an old sofa near the fire.

The last thing I remembered was both girls curling up in sleeping bags on the floor near my bed.

They aren't going to let you escape Ben Carson! A weary little voice sounded faintly in my ear, as the mist of sleep overtook me.

Code Name SNOWBIRD

Chapter 30

<u>Recovery</u>

Roaring noises sounded in my head; I was in a steam bath and couldn't get out. The heat was stifling. I couldn't breath! The sounds faded into the distance and I vaguely became aware of being shaken to pieces. Voices, mumbling like run down gramophones sounded in my head. I couldn't see who it was, or to whom they were talking. One voice, which sounded like someone shouting down a drainpipe, kept on calling. 'When? When?

"*Go awaaayayaya!*" I shouted at them silently, my voice echoing into the distance. Something was crawling up my nose! I couldn't stop it, I couldn't see what it was and more were trying to get into my eyes as well! I opened my mouth to scream, but more unseen things crawled inside it. I lashed out with my hands, trying to sweep them off my face. My hands came away wet and sticky!

Blood! My mind screamed at me. I'm being eaten alive! I sensed I was lying down in what felt like a swamp. I tried to get up but couldn't! Long slimy tendrils were wrapped around my arms and legs, holding me down! I wrestled with them and something cold and wet hit me in the face, smothering me. I felt it moving in a circular motion around my face. It flew off only to return colder and wetter than before. I fought it, but couldn't win so I sank back into the depth of the swamp as blackness overtook me once again. More faint sounds came into my head and I could hear female voices.

Are they Angels waiting for me now I'm dead? I thought. My eyes are open, why can't I see them? I shook my head and tried to wipe my eyes, but couldn't. There was something on them! It felt like wet cloth.

"What's that doing there?" I mumbled through cracked lips. My voice sounded cracked, like an old man's.

"I think I heard him speak!" A female voice spoke close to my ear. "Ben! It is me, Juanita! Can you hear me?"

I tried to answer, but my throat was so dry and my mouth felt gritty like the bottom of the proverbial parrot's cage. I turned my head towards the sound of her voice. It wouldn't move very far, something was holding it. All I could do was to make puffing noises with my lips.

"I'm going to take the cloth off your eyes Ben." Another voice sounded close to me as the heavy wetness slowly lifted away. At first I couldn't see anything more than shadows, then gradually, like the sunrise chasing away the darkness of the night, I began to see things moving in front of me as if through the morning mist.

Am I going blind?" I asked myself as I felt panic rising in me. What's wrong? I can't speak, I can't see! Somebody help me, PLEASE! The last word came out as a feeble scream. I didn't recognise the voice, yet I knew it was mine.

"It's OK Ben! You've had a fever and are in quite a mess, but you'll be all right now it's broken." Juanita's voice was soft and reassuring in my ear. I tried to turn towards her but could not. Then I felt her hand sliding under my neck and something hard touched my lips as she lifted me.

Water! Blessed Water! My little voice cried out as the precious liquid slipped between my lips and slid down my throat. I sipped again and let it trickle around inside my mouth, quenching the burning dryness there.

"That's enough for a minute my love, now I will remove the pads." My angel of mercy whispered to me as she gently eased the objects that had been around my head.

"Creatures!" I croaked. "In my eyes and mouth."

"Oh, they were just flies Ben!" Juanita explained with a little laugh. "I'd gone out to get some fresh water and they covered you as soon as I left." She continued to mop my face and chest gently with the damp cloth.

Fool! I admonished myself as I recalled some of the sensations of my waking. Fancy not knowing it was flies, but what was holding me down?

I shivered as I recalled the wet, slippery tendrils clinging to me like some deep-sea monster. I accepted some more water as Juanita held the cup to my lips again. Cool and sweet, it certainly refreshed the parts that nothing else had reached for a very long time.

"Now you are awake, I want to get you out of that wet bed and cleaned up." Those few words brought realisation to me as my befuddled brain suddenly cleared. Fever! .... Sweat ... not blood! Wet sheets ... not a sea monster. With a sigh of relief, I submitted to being lifted by several strong hands and gently laid down onto a soft, dry surface. I felt, rather than saw, the wet sheets pulled off me; followed by a cool feeling as what clothing I had on was also removed. Gentle hands started washing me, while more hands dried me with what felt like a warm towel.

"This is where I came in!" I thought.

"Can I see him yet?" I heard Miguel's anxious voice through the thickness of the towel as my hair was dried. "Is he going to be OK?"

"Yes he's OK! Just wait a few more minutes while we get him back to bed, *then* you can see him, Señor." Juanita's stern reply came from somewhere above me, or was it behind me? I could not tell if I was up or down.

"There you are Ben. Now you will feel better!" she said, as she finished drying me.

"Uh-huh!" I managed to grunt, as the towel was removed from around my head. I stretched my arms and legs, wriggling my fingers and toes at the same time.

"Yep! Seems to be all in working order," I whispered weakly. Then as my vision cleared, I saw Juanita smiling at me. Then, another smiling Juanita joined her as they helped me down off the table they had used to work on me.

"It's a bit like having double vision with you two in here," I joked feebly. "Looks a bit like an operating theatre too," I remarked as I saw piles of clothing, sheets and some blood soaked cloths on the floor. My knees wobbled and my legs felt like jelly as they helped me across the room. Thankfully, I sank down - or more like collapsed - on another bed; the dryness of its soft mattress was welcome after the other one. A welcome cup of tea was placed beside me as Miguel and the others came and clustered around the bed. With shaking hands, I grasped the cup and sipped the warm sweet tea.

Magic! Pure Magic, my little voice said in my ear. Strange, I thought. He sounds just as tired as I am!

"Ben. Are you able to talk now? I want to tell you what has been happening." An anxious Miguel asked as he drew a chair up beside me. I nodded weakly, thinking it may help concentrate my mind if he did update me. I noticed Juanita still hovering in the background as Miguel cleared his throat ready to start talking - a sure sign he had something to say.

"Before you start, tell me how long I've been unconscious," I demanded, gripping his forearm as tightly as I could.

"Well my friend, you were injured in the explosion, something hit your head and you've been in a fever for three days now..."

"Fever?" I interrupted. "What are you talking about? You don't get a fever from a knock on the head!" I exploded weakly.

"It was something you were bitten by in the swamp! Well that's what the old Indian lady said!" he replied, then before I could ask he explained.

"You were very ill! Delirious and burning with the fever for which we had neither Doctor nor any medicine available. I had no choice but to call in the local, how do you say?" He fumbled for words.

"A Witch Doctor. That is what she is," Marguerite said as she came into the room. She kissed me on the forehead and stood beside her husband.

"Yes! That's right," he exclaimed. "She cures all things for the swamp Indians, even acts as Midwife to them as well." Giving me a funny smile, he paused to raise the cup to my lips before continuing. "We have done it Ben! Everything you set out to do and more." He gripped my hand. "While you were ill, we have completed the task. All the Cartel leaders have been killed and those people named in the various notes have been arrested." Seeing my increasing agitated state, he stopped. "What? Oh! Of course, I should tell it as it happened. Sorry!" He raised my cup once more, while Juanita plumped up my pillows. I had a strange feeling that this tale was going to be some time in the telling!

"OK! Lets have a bedtime story Miguel," I said. His face was puzzled, then a big grin split it as he realised what I meant.

"Well, after digging you out of the rubble and sending you back here, we flew to a small village outside Bogotá. We refuelled and rested until dark, and then in a borrowed lorry we made our way to the Cordoba's town house." He looked around to see if we were all still listening. "When it was all quiet, we made our move, but to my surprise we were met at the gate by Señora Cordoba herself. She demanded to speak to you, but when I explained what had happened, she asked why you wanted to kill her husband and destroy his property. So!" he said with a shrug, "I told her the whole story, of Mal's daughter Sophie, my own son and the countless others that have died, or are dying from drugs." She thought it over for a few minutes, then went back to speak to someone in her car." He paused to study me.

"Am I tiring you Ben? Shall I come back later?" His anxious voice brought me back to the present.

"What? No, I was just visualising the action, that's why my eyes were closed!" I said hurriedly. My eyes had closed, but from the soporific effect of the dim light, tiredness and the sound of his voice. Wide-awake now, I urged him to continue.

"Well," he said, she called me to the car and introduced a man she called Juan-Fernando Lopez. He is a big time lawyer from Bogotá and he was acting for her own family."........

"Hey! Hold on," I interrupted. "You've lost me again. What d'you mean, he was acting for her family? Is she going to sue us?"

"Sorry Ben, I'm not good at telling this!" He sounded so disheartened that I had to apologise and told him to continue.

"She, Señora Cordoba had been thinking about what you had told her and what I confirmed. She does not want the property in Bogotá, but she does not want it destroyed as we planned. So!" he said, with a theatrical gesture. "She has come up with a plan herself!" This was too much for me; I could feel my blood begin to boil.

"A plan... SHE has come up with a plan! Who the hell does she think she is?" Exhausted, I collapsed back onto the pillows and my nurses rushed to calm me down. Damp cold cloth was wiped across my brow; I was heating up again and Miguel was looking very alarmed. "Give me five minutes Miguel, let me calm down." His wife firmly ushering him out the door along with the others drowned out his apologies.

"That's enough for tonight I think," Juanita whispered as she mopped the perspiration from my face and neck. The smell of her perfume was as a breath of fresh air to me, the nearness of her body was like sitting too close to a fire. Sensing my predicament, Marguerite took over and asked her to prepare a small snack for me. After a small bowl of soup, I had short nap and awakened eager for the rest of the story. In fact, I couldn't wait to find out what the Cordoba woman had plotted.

"My apologies for upsetting you earlier Ben," Miguel muttered shamefacedly when he returned. I waved his apology aside with a dismissive.

"No problem, please continue." Still uncertain of himself, he hesitated. Marguerite told him to get on with it.

"Well, as I said, Señora Cordoba has come up with a plan." His eyes stared at mine, watching for my reaction. Getting none, he continued.

"She has decided that the house would be more use as a Clinic to treat the drug addicts rather than being blown up. She gave me this!" With a truly dramatic flourish, he held out a sheet of paper that was covered in a lot of neat writing and a stiff official looking envelope. He hurried to explain.

"She'd overheard our plan to blow the house up and as you know, she was not the least bit interested in what had happened to her husband. In fact, she hated him. The long journey into town gave her plenty of time to think over what you had said and about what her husband had been doing. I believe her when she said she had no control over things, she wouldn't even dare mention the subject to him." When I nodded my acceptance of this statement, he continued his narrative.

"Having given a lot of thought to this matter, she called her lawyer and gave him instructions to immediately draw up this document." Fumbling in his haste, he opened the envelope and withdrew what looked like a Title Deed.

Taking it from him, I could see it was in fact a Deed of Transfer and even though it was written in Spanish, I could clearly see the name and address of the property on one line, followed by a lot of legal mumbo jumbo. The most important part of which, according to Juanita's softly whispered translation, clearly conveyed the property into the ownership of a company called Carson and Lopez. This was on the understanding that the property would be used as a Clinic and Rehabilitation Centre in the fight against drug abuse. Likewise, a sum equivalent to $5 million dollars US would be set aside in a Trust Fund to provide income for its daily needs. The Trust was to be managed jointly by Señor's B Carson and M Lopez.

My mind was in a whirl. Not only had we beaten the Devil himself in the form of El Jefe, but we now had the means to set up a remedial Clinic as well! In addition to which, we also had sufficient money to fund it. I became aware that Juanita was nudging me and pointing to a Codicil of the Deed. In the neatly written letter, presumably added in her own hand, Señora Cordoba had given clear instructions that translated as, 'ownership under this Deed of Transfer shall include all existing fixtures fittings and any valuables presently contained within the said property. All of such could be disposed of as the Trustees should see fit to provide further funding as and when required.'

By that generous act alone, she had effectively quadrupled the value of the Trust at least; we could sell the many valuable paintings, etc. and this meant we could raise more cash.

"WOW!" I breathed. "How wrong can you be about a person? She sure has come up trumps in that." The next minute, we were all laughing - or crying - with joy, the realisation that the action was not only over, but had paid off in such a magnificent way suddenly swept over us.

"Now all I have to do is get better!" I thought as I slipped back onto the pillows and closed my eyes.

"THE SATCHEL BOMB!" They all jumped when the words exploded from me. "What about the bloody bomb Manuel planted?" There was a long silence, broken only by the pounding of my heart it seemed. Then Miguel spoke.

"The bomb? Yes. .... Um. Well!"...... Fidgeting with the hat in his hands, he paused and looked slowly around the group. To my alarm, each of them had a sheepish look on his face.

They've forgotten it, my little voice said gleefully.

"What if it gets triggered?" I cried in desperation. "We will lose everything!" Weakened as I was, I was not prepared to see it all blown sky high just because some idiot forgot there was a bomb there.

"It's got to be deactivated!" I said, panicking and struggling to get off the bed. Firm hands held me down.

"The bomb!" Miguel repeated, as he turned to face me again. Then his face split into a wide grin. "We. ... We took it out!" He spluttered, trying to stifle a giggle. Loud laughter burst from the assembled 'troops,' when they saw the panic-stricken look on my face. Their laughter thankfully drowned my expletive.

"Bastard! Don't wind me up like that!" Then I joined in the merriment - what better way is there to release pent up feelings? After the hubbub had subsided, I called Miguel over.

"All right clever clogs!" I said, as I feebly jabbed him in the chest with my finger. "Tell me. Why was I almost killed by the bomb at Los Palmos? Before he could respond, I threw the next question at him.

"How big was the charge and how come it completely blew the bloody place apart?" Slumping back onto the pillows, I enjoyed his obvious discomfort as we waited for his reply.

"Rico placed the satchel bomb as instructed," Miguel said hurriedly, showing more signs of discomfort - he had put me 'on the spot,' now it was his turn. "The charge was small, but we didn't know that in a room behind the main house cellar, was another room!" His voice tailed off as he looked around for help from his friends.

"Si. Señor Ben!" Manuel said, from the back of the group. "Miguel is right. After the explosion we landed and cleared the rubble from you.".....

"Yeah! I'm only too aware of that!" I interrupted impatiently. "What I want to know is, how come there was another cellar that we didn't know of and why such a large explosion if only a small charge had been used?"

"Señor," Manuel continued. "While we were digging you out, we found an old underground passage that ran from the Hacienda, to the big crater where the second explosion happened."

"Second explosion?" I queried incredulously. "Are you telling me there was another one?"

"Si, Señor Ben! We saw it from the 'chopper.' it was almost how you say....... at the same time?" Manuel paused, searching for the right words.

"Simultaneous!" I offered.

"Si! That is right. Simultaneous." He paused shortly, as if to savour this new word before continuing. "It was at the same time, but not at the same place!"

"He's right Ben, I saw it too," Marguerite offered. "I think there must have been a disused cellar under where the water trough was. That is where the crater is anyway!" She fumbled in her pocket for something while we digested this information. "Ah! Here it is. This is a sketch one of the Cordoba's old servants drew for me." She passed a piece of crumpled paper to me. It showed an outline of the main buildings on both sides of the yard. Picked out in a dotted line, was a short passage from the Hacienda, that lead to a room under the yard, right under where I waited!

"Yes Ben, it is perhaps as you suspect. The old man said it was never used as it was too small, but there were some racks along a wall and in <u>this</u> corner," she indicated a wall backing on to what was the cellar where Rico had planted the satchel bomb. "He said he remembered some small boxes with a drawing on them." I looked at Miguel in alarm. From the look on his face, he too had realised what the sketch his wife had offered actually meant.

"DYNAMITE!" I gasped. "A disused underground room with racks on one wall can only mean an armoury! Boxes with a drawing on can only mean Dynamite!" There was a long drawn out silence as they digested this news.

"I think I'd best explain in case anyone doesn't know," I said. "If dynamite is not stored properly it becomes unstable and sweats little beads of clear moisture that appear all over it. If this moisture just trickles to the ground, it is reasonably safe. On the other hand, if just the tiniest drop just happened to **fall** onto a hard surface, then there would be an explosion. Dynamite sweats nitro-glycerine when unstable and nitro-glycerine is a devastating explosive!" I watched as realisation dawned on their faces

"It was set off in a sympathetic explosion!"

"Sympathy, Ben?" Miguel queried. "What d'you mean, how can sympathy cause an explosion?"

"A sym-path-etic explosion is one set of by another one in close proximity," I explained and was relieved to see nods of understanding around the room; I did not feel like explaining much more anyway.

"Aha!" Marguerite cried. "Dynamite! Not candles!" Seeing our exasperated looks, she hastened to clarify her statement. "The old man, you know, the one who saw the boxes?" Seeing my nod of understanding, she continued. "Well, he said there were only four dirty old candles in one box, the rest were empty!"

"Pity El Jefe didn't try to light one of his 'old candles'; it would have saved me a job!" I declared. Their loud laughter was genuine, but it still did not alter how lucky I had been.

"Right then!" Marguerite called. "Everyone out now please, I think Ben feels the need to rest!" I nodded in agreement and grunted in reply as they left me in peace. A few minutes later, I felt sleep overtaking me at last and gave in without a fight.

Chapter 31

<u>The Parting.</u>

There was little doubt that I needed some time to recover from my injuries and I also needed to be looked at by a Doctor. Although I was being tended to by the 'girls' as I had started calling them, there were a few worrying episodes when I tried to get out of bed that forced me to admit to being far from fit. While I rested, the troops spent the next couple of days just winding down.

I could hear them outside, playing football, laughing and joking or just generally larking about and they deserved it. When they came in to sit around my bed and chat, I sensed a reluctance to accept the inevitable. In our hearts, we all knew it had to end; yet we didn't want it to. We had met as strangers, trained and worked as a team and gone through hell together! We were now closer than brothers! You can't bring a group such as this together then simply pack them off home at the end of the action.

They'd been away from their homes and families long enough, so Miguel and I agreed to turn the Saturday night into a party. Beer and a good supply of cigarettes were shipped in by Zack, who never seemed to tire of flying his machine. Food was brought in by Marguerite, who also called in at a Bank and withdrew their money, plus bonuses.

On Saturday, two of the troops dragged my bed out onto the veranda and this seemed to signal the start of the proceedings. Local Indians were employed as cooks, waiters and bar tenders. All we had to do was eat, drink and be merry! A wonderful feast was placed in front of us and suitably demolished. Beer flowed liberally - but with these guys, drunkenness was no problem. After the remains of the meal had been cleared away, it fell to Marguerite to play the Paymaster. Calling each man by name; she handed him a bundle of bank notes. Each received the same amount and they would all go home rich men.

Suddenly there was a hush, as if the act of taking payment signalled the end. No sign of embarrassment showed on any of them as tears rolled down their cheeks. These hard men, who had killed and would no doubt kill again, were just as soft under the surface. I turned my head into my pillow as I felt the first tear trickle down my face.

The following morning, when they'd all gathered in the main room after breakfast, I spoke from my heart as I gave my farewell speech.

"Together, you and I have achieved what we set out to do. At first, I thought it would be impossible, but here in Colombia we have crushed the biggest Drug Cartel and by doing so, we have opened the way for the Government to follow in our steps. Miguel has been contacted by a Senior Government official - we suspected the Cordoba woman's influence there - who has told us that the army has been instructed to set up a Special Force that will be responsible for continuing what we have started." Pausing to sip some water, I watched their faces as they took this in. Surprise was quickly followed by delight, as the meaning of my words struck home. Cutting short the rising buzz of questions and exclamations, I continued.

"Now for the best part!" I waited for them to quieten down. "An offer has been made; for any of you who are interested; to help train this Special Force. If you do, you will have officer rank and pay for the duration of the contract." The sheer volume of questions defeated me, so I gave up trying. Thankfully, Miguel took over and started to calm them down.

"Yes, it is true!" He shouted over the general hubbub, then waited silent until he had their full attention. "I *know* and *trust* the General who will head this force; he feels the same as you and I about drug dealers. So! Go to your homes now. Greet your families and think about what you have started. If you want to see it continued, then contact me and I will do the rest."

With that, the men queued up excitedly as they waited to say their farewells. Firm handshakes, a quick pat on the back and they were gone! I heard the two choppers take off. Only one would return. Zack had muttered his farewells and stated his intention of keeping in touch, then left without fuss or ceremony. I heard a sound behind me and turning; I saw Rico and his Juanita standing there.

"Señor Ben," he said, fumbling with something in his hands. "I. .... We." He paused as he indicated Juanita. "We want you to know that we are getting married!" There was an excited squeal from behind me - I'd forgotten that *my* Juanita was stood there. She rushed forward to shower kisses on the now more flustered Rico and Juanita.

"Would you be able to attend the wedding Señor?" he mumbled between kisses.

"On two conditions Rico," I replied, flattered that they had asked. In answer to his questioning look, I continued. "Condition one is, that you stop calling me Señor, we are friends and my friends call me Ben. OK?"

"Si! S...." He stopped just in time, then with a big smile he blurted, "Si! Ben, but what was condition number two?"

"Ah Well!" Trying to sound serious I said, "I will attend, but *only* if you allow me to pay for it; you have deserved it more than any other. Besides, the others are already married!" I joined them in their laughter, *and then* Rico dropped his bombshell!

"Gracias, Ben. That is very generous of you, but perhaps you had better know where the wedding will be!" I saw his Juanita nervously take his hand as he said this.

"Perhaps I had," I agreed warily, suspecting I had dropped myself in it.

"Juanita comes from a small village outside of a town called Zipaquira and this town has a special Cathedral in it." Nervously wiping his face with his hand, he searched for words. I nodded my encouragement to him. "Well you see, the Cathedral is very special and will cost a lot of money, Se... Ben. It is so special; it can only be used on certain days in the year." His voice tailed off into a mumble. Here was the young man, who had never been trained as a soldier, yet had kept up with experts on a dangerous mission and been wounded to boot. Yet he was tongue-tied with embarrassment while discussing his own wedding plans!

"So what is so difficult about that?" I asked. He shuffled forward, avoiding my gaze.

"Next Sunday will be the last day we can use it and we cannot contact any high official in the church to make the arrangements in time without your help, Ben!" He gulped in much needed oxygen.

Before he could start again, I said, "I have no contacts within your church - or anywhere come to that - so I can't see how I can help you!" The crestfallen look on his face made me feel guilty. "Maybe, just maybe I know someone who does though!" I muttered thoughtfully to myself as an idea came to me. "Take me through to the radio please." With their willing help, I staggered more than walked into the next room where I collapsed in a chair by the high power radio that was Rico's 'baby.' Switching it on he looked at me for instructions.

"Get me Miguel!" I said brusquely. Rico twiddled some of the controls and called Miguel who was flying with Marguerite as they dropped off some of the 'troops.' When he replied, I grabbed the 'mike' from Rico and asked for a Sitrep - Situation Report.

"Snowbird One." he said still using the Snowbird radio codes. "We are just clearing Bogotá with a Doctor on board! Why, is anything wrong? Over." He sounded anxious.

"Two. No! No problem, but I have a little job I'd like you to do for me. Can you contact the Señora

Cordoba quickly from where you are? Over." I could imagine the puzzled look on his face when I asked this.

"One. Yes and I take it that you mean right now?" He had caught my sense of urgency.

"Two. Yes if you can, I want you to tell her that Rico and Juanita ...." I relayed the gist of the matter to him, plus explaining the problem over the Church.

"One. I've got all that and am landing again now, we will go back to the Doctors house to make the call. We will call you later. Over." I handed the 'mike' back to Rico who signed us off.

"Well people!" I exclaimed with a smile. "It seems we have acted just in time, now all we have to do is hope that your ex mistress," I said looking at Juanita, "thinks enough of you to help. That will also depend on what contacts she has, I suspect. Now, how about some food, I'm starving!" The two girls departed for the kitchen amid excited chatter and I looked at Rico who was now nervously chewing his nails.

"Right! I think it's about time you explained what's so special about this Cathedral, don't you?" I murmured.

"Mmm? Oh! Si, Ben." He replied absently, his mind had obviously been elsewhere. "Zipaquira is about 35 kilometres north of Bogotá; it is a mining town where they have mined rock salt out of the mountains for years. In the 1950's, the miners built a full size Cathedral." Seeing my incredulous look at this statement, he paused. "It is true!" he almost shouted.

"OK! I believe you, so calm down. Now let's settle some of the details like guest lists and such shall we?" I was grateful for the return of the girls and the sight of the cold cuts and hot steaming bread made my mouth water. We sat in a huddle as needless to say, the girls set to planning the great event. Even my half-hearted reminder that no decision had been reached about the Church had little effect on them. Two hours later, they were still nattering as I drifted fitfully in and out of sleep, their voices a soothing buzz in the distance.

"Snowbird One over." The voice of Miguel boomed across the room. I nearly fell out of my chair as Rico scrabbled to turn the volume of the radio down.

"Two over," I replied hastily, grabbing the 'mike' that Rico offered me.

"One. Message passed to the lady. She is delighted to be of help and has contacted her cousin who is secretary to the Bishop of Bogotá. They; Rico and Juanita don't know how lucky they are to have such friends......." I was distracted as both these young people almost climbed into the radio in their eagerness to hear the news, so I missed part of Miguel's transmission. Then I realised that he was silent, which meant he was waiting for a reply.

"Two. That's great news, thanks. You had better ask your Doctor to prescribe two lots of tranquillisers. Over."

"What? ..... Oh! Yes, I expect they're excited eh!" he replied as the 'penny dropped.' "Well, the rest of the news will probably blow their minds, so we will administer it under proper Medical supervision on our arrival OK? Over."

"Two. Roger that. Out." Miguel had obviously cottoned on to my meaning pretty well, as he now played them along too.

The chopper landed two hours later to be greeted by the eager couple. Miguel stuck to his word refusing to comment until after the Doctor had examined me. When they were all gathered in the house, Marguerite and the girls went into an immediate huddle, while I succumbed to a rigorous examination by the elderly, but efficient Doctor they had brought. He prodded, poked and peered at me as if I was a specimen in his Lab. Shining lights into my eyes, looking into my ears and taking my blood pressure. When he was sounding my heart and chest he grunted something, and then wired me up to a portable cardiac monitor. He was getting me worried! What had he found? Half an hour later, he pronounced his verdict.

"Mr Carson, you have a mild concussion, the remnants of Swamp Fever, some minor lacerations that are healing well, the bruising on your head and in your ribs and thighs will also heal, given time. Other than that, you are quite healthy, so I shall give you an injection and some tablets to take. Oh yes, I congratulate your 'nurses' on their achievements, especially in breaking the fever," he quietly pronounced in a brisk Oxford English that took me completely by surprise.

"Well? Doctor......?" I posed the question, as nobody had actually introduced him.

"What? Oh yes, of course!" he said as he caught my meaning. "My name is Mendoza and yes, I did train in England as you probably guessed." He smiled, as he'd read my thoughts. "You are, by all accounts, a very lucky man, by which I mean not only to have survived such an explosion, but to have had such nursing abilities close to hand as well. Indeed, I will say *that* is what saved your life!" I couldn't help noticing that Marguerite had a delightful blush on her face at this comment.

"Yes, I am indeed fortunate Doc,' now, how soon can I be moved out of here?"

"Mmm! Well, you ought to be able to fly tomorrow, but! I warn you that there should be no untoward excitement," he paused, turned to my Juanita with a meaningful look over the top of his glasses before completing his reply. "Or any undue physical exertions!" That poor unfortunate girl turned bright red and hid behind a giggling Marguerite.

"Doctor," Miguel said, coming to the rescue. "We will be having dinner soon and as you are staying overnight, perhaps I should show you to your room?" Taking the Doctor's bag, he guided him from the room.

"How *did* he know? The obvious question exploded from Juanita's lips. The answer hit her at almost the same time as she posed the question.

"How *could* he, Señora?" she gasped, turning to follow Marguerite as she headed towards the kitchen. It seemed that Miguel was in trouble again. His saving grace was when he later called for Rico and Juanita to join him by my bed so that he could brief us on what Señora Cordoba had said.

Surrounded by the five others positioned strategically around my bed, I felt as if they had come to visit me in hospital - well perhaps they had. Once they were all settled, Miguel took the floor, clearing his throat as he did so.

"It seems Juanita, that the Señora Cordoba was very fond of you." Pausing, he placed his hand on Marguerite's shoulder as he said, "much the same as *we* are very fond of *our* Juanita!" There were smiles all round as he reminded us of this unusual coincidence of names. "She is so pleased to hear that you have become attached to people who she sees as sensible and worthy." He looked at us all in turn as he said this. "Her choice of words, not mine," he said with a shrug. "She is pleased enough, that she has called her cousin, who I remind you is Secretary to the Bishop of Bogotá under whose control the Salt Cathedral at Zipaquira comes. Now!" he added dramatically, "as she comes from a family who have supported the Church financially for many years, the Bishop did not hesitate to agree to conduct your wedding *himself!*" With a contented smile on his face, he sat down. It would have been no use continuing anyway; he would have been drowned out by the excited chatter of the females.

"That great event will take place next Sunday!" he announced in a short lull in the excitement, which only served to refresh the clamour.

Rico and his bride-to-be didn't join us for diner that evening; they preferred their own company it seemed. So the meal was a much quieter event than last night's - I was already missing our crowd of boisterous troopers but Doctor Mendoza entertained us by telling us about his time spent in England - all the time dropping tempting bits of information deliberately aimed at

Juanita, who I could see was not exactly disinterested. Finally, after a good meal followed by an equally good brandy - I was allowed one for medicinal purposes too - we turned in for the night. Tomorrow would be a busy day.

The following morning, after a lazy breakfast that lasted for two hours - Rico and Juanita both said their final farewells. They were flying back to Bogotá with Miguel when he took Doctor Mendoza home. I knew I would see them again at the Cathedral, yet I was unusually sad at their departure. Perhaps it was because their leaving heralded another closing chapter in this adventure. Miguel would also pick up Marguerite in the Beechcraft after she had delivered the chopper to a friend who would, in turn, fly it back to Panama.

As Juanita and I waved them off, I realised that we had the place to ourselves for the day. My arm was around her waist; not just for support; but to keep her near me.

Returning to the lounger they had placed outside for me, I felt strange emotions sweeping over me. Suddenly, I realised that I wanted this woman near me always. She had affected me in a way no other female had. I couldn't explain it.....

Yes you can! That little voice was back! You love her! That's what it is!

"Oh shut up! Don't be so stupid!" I exclaimed to myself, as I adjusted my position in the lounger.

"What did you say Ben?" Juanita asked from the doorway.

"Nothing, my love, just talking to myself!" I replied, relieved she had not heard properly. I closed my eyes and lay back on the deep cushions. Within minutes I was asleep. A noise beside me brought me back to awareness; the smell of food invaded my senses.

"How long have I slept?" I asked Juanita, as she squatted down on a stool she had pushed alongside me - that had been the noise I'd heard.

"About two hours, darling," she murmured, a soft smile on her lips.

"What are you smiling about, my love?"

"You were talking in your sleep, darling," she replied. There it was again! Not just the smile; but *that* word! She'd called me darling! Oh, I know that Julie called me darling and so did most of her friends, but that was just the way they talked. *This* was different!

"Nothing rude I hope, my love?" There! Now I'm at it myself! That's about the fourth time you've called her that! My little voice laughed in my ear. You've got it bad you have mate! You'll be proposing to her next! I tried to ignore the voice. You can't ignore yourself can you? It shouted in my ear. Myself? What do I mean myself? Realisation dawned. I had been talking to myself, trying to ignore the obvious. Is this how love affects you? I took Juanita's hand as she handed me my tablets and a glass.

"Thanks, darling," I said, as I tossed the tablets into my mouth and swallowed some water to swill them down. My mind was made up.

"Juanita, I love you!" I whispered.

"I know Ben and I love you!" Her reply was almost lost in a long lingering kiss.

She curled up contentedly beside me, her head resting in my lap. As I studied her, the thought crossed my mind that I hadn't known her very long, just a few weeks. I knew nothing about her, other than she was some sort of distant relative of Marguerite and who had no other family. Yet I *knew* she was the girl for me.

"She's uncomplicated and sincere. She has no false exterior like the English girls I've known," I said to myself, as if to justify what I was about to say. Go ON then! Say it! That voice seemed to shout in my ear.

"Will you marry me?" I whispered in her ear, my voice choking as I put the question. I realised I was willing her to say yes.

"Ben, darling!" she whispered, as she uncurled herself and we sank into another deep kiss. After what seemed ages, she broke away gasping for breath and knelt up beside me.

"You know that is all I want in this world. I know we won't be able to marry in church but I don't care!" She lapsed into a thoughtful silence, and then with a newly found determination in her voice, she declared, "we can go to the Civil Registry Office in Panama, Señor Miguel will be able to fix it for us he has one of his co*usins* there, I believe." She paused, and then jumping up excitedly, she said. "I. ...... We," she smiled as she corrected herself, "can ask them when they come back!"

Now you've done it, my little voice said, with certain smugness.

It was starting to get dark when we heard the engines of the returning plane and Juanita dashed off to the kitchen to put the meal she had prepared on to heat. With a sudden roar and rush of wind, the plane swooped low as it skimmed the rooftop. Dropping dramatically down onto the prepared runway, it rolled out of sight behind some trees, only to reappear as Marguerite taxied it back to the fuelling point by the barn. An old Indian man hobbled out and started to assemble the hand pump ready for fuelling. He was greeted by Marguerite as she climbed out; a few words and a quick laugh and she ran up the path towards us.

"Where's Miguel?" I queried as she flopped into a chair.

"Oh, he's sorting out some papers, flight plans and things," she replied. "He'll be along in a minute." Juanita came out and placed a tray of coffee on the table for us all as I was about to ask how the trip went. I didn't get a chance, Marguerite; her feminine instincts working at full stretch took one look at Juanita and squealed in delight.

"Oh Juanita! I'm so pleased! When?" She paused to grab the girl in a hug, both of then dancing up and down as if in a sack race.

"How the *hell* did you know?" My utter astonishment was clear in my voice. "Neither of you spoke! So how do you *know*?" I repeated my question to Marguerite.

"Know what? What's all the excitement?" A puzzled Miguel asked as he joined us.

"I don't know mate!" I exclaimed with exasperation. "It's beyond me; you'd better ask your wife." Grabbing a cup off the tray, I concentrated on what I could relate to. My mind was in a whirl. According to some, feminine intuition was a force to be reckoned with and I wasn't about to argue having just seen clear proof of it, so I stayed with my thoughts. I was vaguely aware of their voices in the background, as the secret that wasn't a secret, was explained to Miguel. A heavy hand slapped me on the shoulder, nearly causing me to add scalds to my list of injuries.

"That's great!" I heard Miguel's voice saying. "I am so very pleased to hear this news, Ben." Then he was energetically pumping my hand and Marguerite was plastering me with kisses. Gradually, they calmed down and we stared discussing the 'nitty-gritty' of organising a wedding. Suddenly, Miguel held his hand up for silence.

"Ben. There is perhaps one thing you have forgotten!" he said, looking me straight in the eye.

"What?" I asked rather vaguely, not having the faintest idea what he was on about.

"I think perhaps Mal and his wife would be unable to attend if you marry in Panama!" he stated. "There is also his brother?"

"Yes you're right," I muttered dejectedly. By stating the obvious, he had just poured cold water on my plans. He was right though, I would feel awful if I hadn't included Mal and all his family. I looked at Juanita, fully expecting to see disappointment in her face. But no, she was smiling.

"It doesn't matter where we marry, my love, as long as we do! But I would like you to give me away," she said turning to Miguel. His face lit up in the biggest smile I'd seen on him at that.

"Well! That's it then!" he expounded with dramatic gestures. "You will marry in England and we will come with you!" He looked at his wife questioningly; she just nodded in reply.

"Oh! Madre de Dios!" Juanita suddenly shouted as she dashed for the kitchen door. "The dinner!" It was then that we noticed a faint burning smell. Marguerite hurried after her and Miguel shook my hand once again - thankfully, this time he was not so over enthusiastic.

"Well Ben, I am truly happy that we welcome you into our family." He paused as a thought struck him, then with another broad grin he said, "of course! You will be like another *cousin*!" Our loud roars of laughter were interrupted by the meal - which was not entirely ruined - being placed before us. During the remainder of the evening, my future and that of Juanita was planned. Our main priorities, of course, were for me to recover, followed by our attendance at the wedding of Rico and his Juanita in one week's time then to return to Panama - it seemed we'd been here on the edge of the swamps for ages.

To my relief, with the topic exhausted - for now at least - we went to bed. Juanita quietly helped me up to her room where we cuddled close together for the night.

Chapter 32

<u>The Clinic</u>

We finally left the swamps of Riosucio the following morning with sadness in our hearts. I stared out of the window as the plane lifted above the old building that had been our temporary home for so long, yet I knew that I would be returning here in the future. The Colombian Army were going to take on the task of crushing the drug production so would need training. Where better to do that than where we had trained ourselves?

Images of burning lorries, exploding buildings and planes flashed across my mind. Sweating, filthy men, their teeth gleaming white against their dark skins as they grimaced with the pain of extreme physical exertion. Gasping for breath, they ran with their equipment weighing them down. They disappeared into the smoke and flames of explosions, only to reappear with triumphant grins on their faces. Miguel, Felipe, Ramon, Rico..... they all ran towards me. I felt proud to have known and led such men.

"Ben! Ben, we are landing now, so wake up!" Juanita's soft voice brought me back to reality. I had been dreaming.

"Mmmm?" I said as I stretched in the limited space of the Beechcraft cabin, a cabin in which the beautiful, brave Marguerite had saved our lives. When? It all seemed so long ago. Then the softest of bumps told me we had touched down at a place near Bogotá.

Another *'cousin'* or was it a business contact of Miguel's? No matter, whoever he was, we had been given the use of his ranch for the duration, so here we were.

As soon as the plane stopped I was assisted into a Jeep and driven with Juanita in attendance to the main house. Servants fussed round us like we were royalty. Juanita was quite understandably a bit embarrassed by it all.

Doctor Mendoza was waiting to greet me and he wasted no time before checking me over. Satisfied with his findings, he prescribed a long hot bath to ease my aches and pains followed by at least a couple of days of bed rest. I agreed and was promptly whisked away to the bathroom by Juanita who claimed that department as her privilege. Feigning a sudden weakness, I could not resist - I didn't want to anyway!

While Marguerite and Miguel liaised with Rico and his fiancée - who had come to welcome us - about the wedding, I spent the next two whole days doing nothing, with the exception that is, of carrying out some prescribed physiotherapy exercises. My body was recovering well, I felt fairly good and was benefiting from the hot baths and gentle massages as various healing oils were rubbed in. Enough strength was returning to my limbs for me to ask Miguel, during our evening get together, to take us to see the Clinic.

"A great idea!" he replied, enthusiastically. "But you must be prepared for a big surprise." I like surprises, but no amount of questioning would make him expand on the matter. Marguerite, when asked simply replied mysteriously.

"I am sworn to secrecy by my Lord and Master!" Then as if to change the subject, she started to tell us about their visit to the Bishop, who it seemed, was very excited by the chance to hold a wedding in the Cathedral at Zipaquira.

"Well then! If you won't tell me about the Clinic, at least tell me what's so wonderfully special about this Cathedral!" I exclaimed in exasperation.

"No! I think it best not to spoil your undoubted surprise by giving you what can only be, unsatisfactory descriptions," she said smugly. It seemed I had to wait, as Juanita and Miguel both nodded in agreement. The only consolation being that Juanita kissed me when she said sorry!

The following morning we piled into a car for the drive to Bogotá. For my sins, I had thought of it as being just a large township, with unpretentious buildings. As we drove through the outskirts into the old colonial quarter, I realised how wrong I'd been. Here was a beautiful gracious city, laid out in a grid pattern with spacious green parks and open spaces, wide sweeping boulevards and fountains. The Old Quarter still boasted the attractive traditional buildings, which having been built for the extremely rich merchants and Princes, were of grand designs, standing securely behind high walls and surrounded by shady trees. The homes of the normal citizens were in direct contrast with their low red pan tile roofed houses whose eaves stretched out to each other over the streets and with some modern architecture seemingly dropped in between. The main city, which spread for miles proved to be ultra modern with high-rise buildings and wide sweeping modern road systems. The noise from the extremely heavy traffic was almost overpowering, with cars hooting as they dodged the buses and lorries that vied for space on the bustling streets.

To the eastern side of the city, two high mountain peaks loomed like sentinels standing guard over this bustle. Seeing me eyeing them, Miguel felt he should impart his knowledge of the area.

"Those two mountains," waving his hand in their direction he continued before I could reply, "if you were fit, I would recommend you to go up the smaller one. It is called Monserrate and has a cable car and funicular railway that will take you to one of the finest views you could ever see." He paused, as he concentrated on dodging a large open top lorry loaded with bellowing cattle. "There are restaurants, amusement parks and a reconstruction of the street called the Calle de Candelero as it was in 1887!" There was a pride in his voice as he continued, that made me wonder if he came from this country, but I refrained from asking. It did serve to remind me just how little I did know of him though.

"Sounds great, but I'll skip it this time round," I stated firmly. The car slowed, then to my surprise turned towards a double gateway that was protected by ornate wrought iron gates. An old man stepped out of a small lodge that was hidden behind the high wall and limping slightly, he pulled the gates open for us and raised his hat as we drove in. I didn't say anything; I was too busy admiring the well-maintained gardens we were driving through. The wide manicured lawns and gorgeous flowerbeds formed a suitable setting for the magnificent traditional style building we were approaching. The car tyres crunched on the gravel driveway, birds were singing in the trees, yet I could no longer hear the bustle of the sprawling city we had just left behind.

"Whose house is this? Is it another of your friends?" I asked Miguel, who, having stopped the car was now sat smiling at me.

"This, my friend!" he announced with an expansive sweep of his hand, "is our Clinic!" My gasp of disbelief was lost in the squeals of delight from the two females sat behind us.

"You're joking aren't you?" I queried. "Come on, stop messing about!"

"It is no joke my friend," Miguel assured me. "Until recently, this was the town house of the Cordoba family. Come, let me show you around." Climbing out, he helped me up the steps to the huge front door. I was barely able to believe my eyes and ears, as during the next hour, we were conducted on a tour of this magnificent place. There was no nook or cranny left unexplored by Marguerite and Juanita, who continually gave vent to oooh's! and aah's! at what they found.

"Now for the real Piece de Resistance!" Miguel announced proudly, as we entered the ground floor study. Sitting me in the swivel chair, he reached under the desk edge and pressed a switch.

"What the.....!" I gasped, as the floor opened and I sank down into the void, desk and all. I suddenly realised that this was the vault that our man Manuel had discovered. The lift stopped and I got off.

"Ben. Have a look around, and then come back up," Miguel called down to me. "It is empty as we have everything up here now." I spent a while poking around the various cupboards; it was an impressive place and definitely secure. Having exhausted my curiosity, I sat in the chair and marvelled at the construction of such a secret place that must have been used to store the drug money.

"That's it!" I gasped aloud. "Hey Miguel," I called as my head reappeared above the study floor. "If this is our Clinic, we are bound to have some drugs here, yes?" Miguel nodded, but was clearly unsure of my reasoning. "Well, I think that down there," I said, indicating the vault, "is the safest place to keep it and this room can be the office!" Pleased with myself, I stared at the faces of my friends. Then Marguerite spoke.

"Oh! You heard what we said then?" It seemed that my idea was not so new after all.

A light knocking on the door made us all jump. Juanita pulled it open and a young girl dressed as a maid entered nervously.

"Pardon Señor," she said, nervously addressing Miguel. "Your lunch is ready."

"Lunch?" I thought. "Of course! Why not, we do own the place after all!" I followed the others out of the house and onto a patio at the side. Under the shade of some large umbrellas, we found a table full of food and bottles of wine. Seating ourselves at the other table, we started planning the running of the Clinic as we set into a wonderful meal. Miguel informed us that domestic staff had already been retained, mainly from the Cordoba household anyway. Nursing and office staff had been advertised for and an experienced Doctor was very keen to join the project. All we had to do was to sign contracts.

"What are we going to call it?" Marguerite queried. We looked at each other for inspiration. The ensuing long silence as we thought proved that we had no ideas. Suddenly, Juanita jumped up, a big grin on her lovely face.

"I have a name!" she exclaimed excitedly. "We can call it 'THE SNOWBIRD CLINIC!' " It was a wonderful idea; I was so pleased and proud for her. She stood there looking a bit embarrassed at the general clamour of agreement.

"That's a wonderful idea Juanita, well done!" I grabbed her in my arms and kissed her firmly. "Now, if you don't mind, I am feeling very tired." With that, we left that magnificent building and returned through the hustle and bustle of the city to our temporary home.

Late the following morning, I was awakened by Juanita shaking me gently by the shoulder.

"Ben darling, you have a visitor coming in an hour."

"What?" I mumbled sleepily. "Who's that then?"

"It is Señor Juan-Fernando Lopez, the lawyer from the Señora Cordoba and he has the documents for you to sign."

"Damn!" My first reaction to this was to immediately dive under the sheets, but then I realised that by coming to us with the papers, Señor Lopez was saving me the bother of chasing him to complete the deal. I was after all, now very keen to return to England and fully brief Mal, with whom I'd only spoken a few times by telephone.

"OK. I'll be ready when he comes," I mumbled, stretching my limbs. As I washed and dried myself, I suddenly realised that my aches and pains were not bothering me so much.

"Great, I'm on the mend!" I told my reflection in the mirror as I dressed. Feeling a lot happier, I went down to grab a bit of breakfast.

Three hours later, I was feeling very thankful that I had Spanish-speaking people with me; I had become the legal partner in 'The Snowbird Clinic' of Bogotá. The lawyer, Señor Juan-Fernando Lopez, had produced such a thick wad of papers that I thought we'd still be reading through them in a year's time. With Miguel's help, along with that of Marguerite and Juanita, we condensed the reading to three hours. With a loud snap, Señor Juan-Fernando Lopez finally closed his briefcase and expressed his full and I thought, sincere satisfaction. He even willingly agreed to become the Clinic's Legal Representative with a seat on the Board. I rang for the servant girl to bring us some wine and they all raised their glasses to my toast.

"'The Snowbird's!' "Without them we couldn't have done it."

After all the formalities were over, I booked a call to England and briefed Mal on the events to date. Needless to say, he was ecstatic when he learned that I had achieved the goal and El Jefe and all his crew were dead. He threw numerous questions at me and his voice broke when I told him how it had been done.

"Thank you Ben," he whispered between sobs. Julie took the phone from him and asked when I would be back. I took the opportunity to tell her about Juanita and was strangely relieved to hear her reaction.

"Ben darling! That's wonderful news. I'm so happy for you. You must bring her to stay here. We've been so worried about you and can't wait to hear all about it."

Half an hour of questions later, I had to call an end to it. Promising to tell her my travel plans soon, I hung up. We retired to bed early that night, tomorrow was going to be a busy day and I would at last see this mysterious Cathedral!

🕊 Code Name SNOWBIRD 🕊

Chapter 33

<u>Zipaquira and a Surprise of a different kind!</u>

Excited voices and the sound of frantic activity greeted me on the Sunday morning. I'd not even felt Juanita slip quietly out of bed at the crack of dawn. That was one habit I was determined to stop when we were married.

"Marriage!" The realisation hit me. "That's what all this excitement is about! Of course, today is the day of the marriage of Rico and his young lady." A tepid shower brought me to full awareness. As I dried myself, I inspected my body in the long bathroom mirror. The scars were less livid and the bruises had lost their colour.

"Mmm! Not doing too badly I suppose," I said to my image.

"I would say that you are in good condition again, my darling," Juanita said from the doorway where she had obviously been watching me.

"How long have you been there?" I gasped, spinning round to face her.

"Long enough to agree with your findings," she replied, with a smile. Reaching for her, I dropped the towel and drew her close against my naked body and kissed her. Her body relaxed against mine as she put her arms around me. My hands wandered over her breasts and buttocks and she whimpered deep in her throat.

"Not now, Ben!" she said, suddenly pushing me away. "There is not much time for you to have breakfast and dress." Ignoring my protests, she turned and disappeared into the bedroom, where I heard her pouring coffee into two cups. Joining her, I gratefully took the cup she offered me and sat on the bed. I watched as she dropped her dress to the floor, removed her underclothes and sat naked on a stool as she brushed her lustrous black hair. Her firm breasts quivered gently with each stroke of the brush, sending electric shocks coursing through my body. Her light coffee coloured skin shone in the morning sunlight, a sure sign of her health and vitality.

"God! She's beautiful. I'm a very lucky man." I let my thoughts of Juanita wander as I ate my breakfast. Gone was the subservient housemaid and in her place was a cool, calm and completely composed young lady, whose posture and way of speaking gave the impression that this new way of life in which she found herself was perhaps not so new after all. She had adapted completely and demonstrated a kind and understanding way of dealing with any member of staff.

"I am so lucky," I once again reminded myself as I grabbed the suit she'd put out for me to wear and I left the room before I started something I knew I wouldn't be allowed to finish. Half an hour later I was pacing the hallway, when a light cough from the stairs made me turn. There, at the top stood a vision of loveliness. Juanita dressed in a low cut, pale cream body-hugging dress that was itself complimented by a neat, wide rimmed, matching hat with a half veil. Her gleaming black hair framed her lovely face. I stood mouth agape as she descended the stairs to stand in front of me. A smile played across her full lips on which I noticed she had applied a touch of red lipstick for the first time ever. She knew what she was doing to me, she knew that my insides were churning over and over and my hands ached to hold her. From the look she gave me, she *knew* all right!

"Coffee and cream!" I whispered. "You look good enough to eat!"

"Behave yourself, Ben!" she mouthed in mock horror. "Now take me out to the car please." Taking her arm in mine, I walked her out onto the wide verandah. A chorus of loud wolf whistles and applause greeted our appearance. There on the lawn, looking completely out of character as I knew them was every member of our troop, each with a lady on his arm. They were not as I last saw them though, in fact I hardly recognized them. This time they were dressed in the best quality suits, but wore the same happy smiles. It was great to see them all again. Quick introductions were made before we were ushered into the fleet of limousines that stood waiting on the driveway.

We were joined in our car by Marguerite and Miguel; both he and I sitting with our backs to the driver and facing our ladies. Marguerite also looked beautiful in a pale blue, figure-hugging outfit with a matching hat. Looking at them both as we moved off, I was sure I was in the company of the two most beautiful women in the world.

"Well, my friend!" Miguel said, as he struggled with an over-tight collar. "Today you will see the famous Salt Cathedral of Zipaquira."

"After all the mystery you've made of it, it had better be worth it," I replied with mock indignation. Looking out of the window, I saw the last of the city vanish behind us as we sped along the busy main road. Gradually, the houses gave way to an area of lush green fields, with herds of fat healthy cattle. Fleeting glimpses of large ranches flashed by at intervals, each surrounded by neat wooden fences. Then after we had travelled about 15 kilometres, the hills abruptly closed around us until they towered above the road on both sides, as they became the foothills of a mountain range. Miguel tapped me on the shoulder and pointed to our front. A road sign flashed past that showed we had entered Zipaquira itself. I turned in my seat, eager to catch my first glimpse of the Cathedral.

Our convoy of limo's swept through the outskirts of this sizable town and into the main square, not even pausing to avoid a flock of chickens that scratched the dry ground in search of food. Scattering them in squawking protest, we passed the small church that stood to one side. I turned to Miguel.

"Patience," he whispered, as we sped onward. I realised that we couldn't go much further as the high, wooded hills now formed an unbroken barrier across our path.

"So! It's got to be here in the woods," I reasoned silently. The vehicle slowed then turned into a small car park in the shade of the trees. I noticed several more cars already there, along with a dozen Police Cars. As we got out and stretched our limbs, one of the Policemen approached us. Saluting the ladies, he introduced himself to me.

"Señor Carson? Buenas Dias. I am Colonel Mendoza, Chief of Police in Bogotá," he announced proudly. "It is an honour to welcome you and your companions to Zipaquira Señor."

"Muchas Gracias, Colonel," I replied cautiously. Having spotted at least two dozen uniformed officers, I was curious as to their duties. "Why so many men may I ask?"

"Ah. Señor. The word is that there has been a tragic plane crash that killed the Señor Cordoba and his business partners. As their business was drugs Señor, this means there may be a war between different families if you get my meaning?" the Colonel explained. "You, Señor Carson, are an important guest in our country, so we wish to ensure you are not, how d'you say?.... disturbed?" He finished with an expansive gesture.

"Colonel, I am very grateful for your concern and protection of course," I hastened to add. "But such matters would not effect me would they?" I was curious as to how much he knew? Was he aware of my involvement and been ordered to give protection? I wanted him to put his cards on the table. "Surely you don't think I or my friends are at risk, do you?" I pushed.

Taking me by the arm, he steered me away from the others, then looking me in the eye he quietly announced, "Señor Carson. I need to speak as we say Mana-a-Mano - man to man - is that OK?" His face was all serious as he awaited my reply.

"Yes. Yes of course, please explain." This guy was getting me worried. Here I was, having entered this country *illegally*, killed people, damaged property and now here was the Chief of Police telling me I'm an important guest in his country. It just didn't add up!

"Lo Siento! I'm sorry Señor, allow me to introduce myself properly," he said, offering me an official ID card and a business card.

"Brigadier Juan Mendoza? But you said you're a Police Colon......!'" My voice tailed off as he held up his hand to stop my questions.

"Si Señor, that is my real name. My men and I, are how you call 'Special Forces,' we have been ordered to protect you until you leave the country." Seeing my look of surprise, he held up his hands in a placating gesture. "No Señor. You are not being escorted out; we have to protect you as long as you stay." I was just about to reply, when Miguel called me to join the procession that had formed ready to enter the Cathedral that I still hadn't seen yet! Handing him his ID card and pocketing the business card, I asked the Colonel / Brigadier; whatever he was, to excuse me and to join us later when he could enlighten me more fully.

"What is wrong, darling?" Juanita asked, as I took her arm and followed the others towards a well-worn path in the trees. I told her I'd explain later as we stepped onto a hardened track that was, I noticed, wide enough for cars to run on. We walked for about 15 minutes, the path rising all the time. As we rounded a corner, I saw that the track disappeared into a tunnel in the side of the hill. Soft lighting at ground level ensured we did not lose

Code Name SNOWBIRD

our footing as we walked on. Even to my untrained eye, the tunnel walls showed obvious signs of having been carved by hand. As we moved deeper into the hillside, I noticed that what had been the rock of the walls and roof, had gradually given way to a black shiny material.

"Salt. Rock salt," Juanita whispered when she saw my puzzled look. It was then that I realised we were entering a mine. After walking for about four minutes, the tunnel roof dramatically gave way to a huge, seemingly empty space that drew my eyes upwards to seek the roof. My eyes slowly adjusted to the strange lighting and I saw we were in a cavern of huge proportions. The walls gleamed blackly, reflecting the lights like the facets of a diamond. I could only stand and stare. In the far reaches of this place, I could make out intricate curving shapes, with rounded edges. There were mock high arched windows lining the walls, in between them were exquisitely carved figures in niches. We were stood inside a carving! *THIS* was the Cathedral!

Being from the West Country, I had seen Goff's Cave in the beautiful Cheddar Gorge. If I was expecting to see something similar here in Zipaquira today, then I was in for a shock.

"Wow!" My gasp of astonishment drew amused glances from my friends. Too busy staring at where the ceiling should be; I nearly tripped over a lighting cable. "It must be at *least* 20 metres high!" I voiced in a loud whisper. Juanita took my arm and firmly led me to a pew. "It's like diamonds! I've never seen anything like this, its wonder..." My comment was cut off as Juanita dug here elbow in my ribs. I became aware that the others were watching me with an air of amused interest and Juanita, who had been studying me as I stared around me, smiled gently as she took my hand to show me to my seat. I was spellbound by my surroundings. My brain was having difficulty in grasping the immensity of the task the miners of Zipaquira had taken on.

I became aware that someone was speaking to me. Looking down I saw a youth dressed as an altar boy offering me a board the shape of a hand paddle. On which was a description of the Cathedral.

' Rock Salt has been mined here for centuries, but over the years the cavern structure had become more unsafe and would eventually be closed. Work has been suspended even though there was still a supply big enough to last the <u>whole world</u> another 100 years. The ancient miners have created a huge chambe,r which their descendants had decided to transform into this beautiful and unique Cathedral. Over a period of 10 years, the miners completed the task and in 1954, the Cathedral was dedicated to **Nuestra Señora del Rosario** the patron Saint of miners. The roof is 23 metres high and the Altar is a solid block of salt weighing some 18 ton. The pews and other parts were fitted with Eucalyptus wood that helped avoid corrosion. Throughout the Cathedral, one could find designs such as the Nativity scene complete with a cow sitting in the position adopted by dogs! The font contained no water, as it would melt the salt. The whole thing is now a grand tourist attraction that can be visited by appointment only. Services are conducted by the Bishop on a preset, limited calendar and they are of short duration as the humidity created by lights and human bodies, tended to build rapidly.'

🕊 Code Name SNOWBIRD 🕊

The sound of voices singing brought me back to the present, I rose along with Juanita and the others to greet the Church procession as it entered from a hidden gap in the black wall - obviously there was a smaller chamber there. Lead by a procession of about thirty young choir boys the Bishop - a fat man who looked as if he hadn't walked under his own steam in years - waddled his painful way past us, closely followed by his numerous acolytes. Once they were all in place, the wedding ceremony began with Rico and his Best Man walking down the aisle to take their place at the front. Then, someone switched on a tape player that played the Wedding March. Although I first found this amusing, I soon realised that the metal in a proper organ would have been attacked by the corrosive salt in no time.

Down the centre aisle came a vision in white. Juanita, Rico's fiancée made her way forward on the arm of a man I took to be her father. She was a picture, even I, who was never impressed by weddings, had to admit that! She took her place by a smiling, calm Rico as the Bishop moved to greet them.

Needless to say, the ceremony was conducted in Spanish with a strong Catholic flavouring and was over sooner than I expected - the clerics had their eyes on the time, I suppose. With a final flourish, the newly weds were whisked off to sign for each other, then to reappear arm in arm to lead the congregation out. I was amazed how many people were there. It seemed, that everyone's *cousins and their cousins* were there! As she passed us, the happy bride blew us a kiss and gave me a big wink. We followed on and from the urgings of my Juanita; I gathered I had to hurry in order to preserve the 'pecking order.'

Once out in the open air again, as is usual at all weddings, we lined up for innumerable photo's and to what I refer to as *'meet and greet'* the relatives and everyone else's aunt! Not my scene. I feigned tiredness – well, I was still recovering from being blown up, after all! I told Juanita to enjoy herself while I slipped off to the car.

Moments after I sank gratefully into the soft leather seat, a tapping at the window made me jump.

Getting edgy aren't we, my little voice said. It's only Colonel Juan Mendoza, or whatever he calls himself! I pressed the button to lower the window.

"What's the matter Colonel?" I asked, using his Police rank as he was in uniform still.

"Is it convenient to talk?" he queried, leaning down to the window. In reply, I simply opened the door for him and waited for him to settle before throwing my 6 million dollar question at him.

"Right!" I snapped, all feeling of tiredness gone. "Who are you, why are you here and who sent you?"

"Señor. If I answer your questions, I must know you will not pass the information to anyone, is that agreed?"

"No! It's damn well not agreed," I replied indignantly. "I'm here with a partner, a man whom I trust with my life. What I know, *he* knows! OK?" My anger was genuine; he looked taken aback by my attitude and paused deep in thought.

"Señor Lopez?" he queried, after a few minutes. In reply to the slight inclination of my head, he made up his mind quickly.

"Only him, Señor! It will endanger my life, the lives of my men and worse still, it will put my Principal at risk also." There was such genuine concern in his voice, that I believed he was sincere. I signified my agreement with a grunt.

"You have recently been advised of my government's intention to establish a special anti-drug unit?" I nodded and he continued. "Well, Señor, in Colombia a lot of people get rich, *very* rich from the drugs."

He paused briefly before adding dramatically. "They are at all levels, even at the top of the government and military. So there is a lot of resistance to this move. We, my squad and I, along with others, are tasked in seeing that you succeed and to maintain your safety. I am also keen on learning what we can of your methods." I sat deep in silent thought myself at this revelation. He continued.

"We have the backing of some very influential businessmen, who are prepared to 'fix' next month's elections in order to cut out some of the opposition," he explained. Being no stranger to the twilight world where politics, big business and personal interests meet, I was not surprised at this statement. This country was no different from most others in that respect. Politics could be read as meaning Corruption!

"OK Colonel. I'll go with it for now, but you must know that our involvement is nearly over?"

"Si, Señor. We have been aware of your movements for a long time. As a professional, I must say I admire your abilities; it is these we are interested in. Of course, we have a small elite force the same as everyone else." He shrugged as he said this. "But they are no match for the British SAS! *You* have started something *we* will have to finish, so we will need to be trained eh?"

Reaching into his pocket, he took out a piece of paper and handed it to me. It was a cutting from a recent newspaper that reported on the death of the much-respected businessman Señor Cordoba of Bogotá. Indignant though I was at this statement, my interest was caught by the paragraph that claimed the deceased had been responsible for funding several initiatives to stop drug production. He had ploughed millions from his own pocket into rehabilitation projects and a hospital.

"That!" I said, slapping the paper angrily. "Is the biggest load of bull I've ever heard!"

"You now see, Señor, what we are up against. That," he said, pointing to the clipping as if it were a dead rat. "is from the most influential newspaper in the country." He paused to collect his thoughts before continuing. "It is also why we will need the help of you and your men to keep this thing going. You see, the Air Force General who sent that jet to shoot you down is the brother of the owner of that paper!" He lapsed into silence with a dejected look on his face,.

I asked him to excuse me for a while. I got out of the car, called Miguel over and briefed him on what the Colonel had said and who he really was. Then, after a quick discussion, we made a decision based on the fact that we had nothing to lose, but everything to gain. Miguel departed to keep the ladies company.

"Before I give any commitment," I told the Colonel when I rejoined him, "I must know the conditions under which my men will work. I would want to pick the training area, the equipment and to draw up the SOP's - meaning the Standard Operating Procedures the force would work under. Manpower would be left to you, but I insist that we set up a selection centre, where each man will be tested for his mental and physical suitability by members of my team." Before he could reply to all that, I continued. "*We* will set the training program. The duration and content must not be interfered with. Finally, I reserve the right to conduct 'live tests' on my own conditions."

"How do you mean, live tests?" he asked, his face showing a puzzled look.

"Simply, that when I feel a squad is ready for action, we select a live target to test them on!" A look of horror came over his face and I hastened to add, "by which I mean, we select some individual or group dealing in drugs. Each 'hit' would be designed to look as if a rival gang had carried it out, this will keep them from combining against us and at the same time, it will divide them further and be good 'training' for the men." His face became animated; what had earlier shown as horror, now showed eager understanding.

"Si, Señor. That is OK. I first thought you meant kill people!" he announced.

"Ah, but I *do* mean kill people Colonel. Do you have a problem with that?" I demanded.

"No!" ...... He paused momentarily as if listening to his conscience. "I have no problem, Señor. You are going to kill drug dealers; *they* are not people! *They* are like animals!" He spoke fervently, giving me what I called the right answer.

I noticed the others had gathered near the cars, from where they were watching us rather nervously. It seemed the photo session was over and as I climbed out, I turned to the man behind me saying in a friendly fashion.

"Thank you for your time Colonel, I enjoyed our little chat and would like to invite you to join us for dinner this evening." He nodded his acceptance as he stepped back to make way for the ladies to enter the car.

The next few hours were taken up with the reception and enjoyably chatting with the troops, who I noted, were only too pleased to loosen their collars. I found myself thoroughly relaxed in their company, answering questions about England, but mainly about why my Juanita and I didn't get married today. Trapped in a corner from which I could not easily escape, I was relieved when this happy gathering immediately broke up when Rico's bride said she was going to get changed. Amidst whoops of joy and catcalls, she was 'escorted' out of the room by an excited and noisy crowd of females. I took this sudden opportunity to ask the troops if they wanted to take up the offer made by the military. They all accepted to a man, so it seemed that the Colonel could report a successful mission to his masters. For myself, though I knew I would be involved indirectly, I still had the rest of my mission in Europe to complete. "Or could the two be combined?" I wondered.

Later that evening, with the Bride and Groom safely dispatched on their honeymoon journey and the others returned to their homes, the four of us enjoyed a modest meal in the company of Colonel Mendoza and his small, but very pretty wife, herself an ex officer of his force. Juan, as he insisted we call him, proved to be a very experienced man, with good sound knowledge of the Colombian Army as well as the political arena. He enlarged on how the Government was anxious to follow up on our success and how it was to be financed. We were amazed when we realised just how much actual detail of our operation had been known to Juan and his mysterious 'Principal', but he wouldn't divulge how.

We talked well into the early hours, coming to some tentative agreements with him - apparently he had full authority to do so, but would have to obtain the final sanction - regarding the training program, the anticipated pay and conditions of our 'troops' and equipment levels. As far as the latter was concerned, Juan assured us there would be no problems with anything for this force. With these encouraging factors amicably agreed, I took a chance and threw a question at him.

"Juan, while we are in agreement generally, I must ask if there would be any objections for some selected squads working overseas?" I noted the interest in the others at this, Miguel in particular, shifting forward on his seat.

"Before I could answer that, Ben," he replied cautiously. "I would have to know what you have in mind!"

"Yes! Me too!" Miguel interrupted rather sharply. "Do you think it will be necessary, Ben?"

"Sure I do! You are all aware that these Cartels operate abroad," I offered quietly. "So we must follow through or it will be like pulling the tail off a lizard; it would just grow back again!" I waited for the buzz of conversation to die down before continuing.

"We must ensure that all of the Cartel's interests are wiped out. It won't be any good just knocking them off here in Colombia, there are others waiting to climb the ladder of succession!" ....

"Ah! You are thinking of Jose Cordoba!" Miguel gasped. "Yes I agree, he will simply rebuild the empire after taking his fathers place! It is important to deal with him also."

"Gentlemen!" Juan interrupted the growing excitement. "Knowing this man personally, I also accept that he will have to be treated the same as his father. But!" He paused, holding up his hand in warning. "He will not be so easy, how you say in England?" He looked at me as he struggled with the language. Catching his meaning Marguerite came to his rescue.

"Not an easy nut to crack?" she murmured.

"Si. That is it!" Juan said, smacking his fist into his palm. "Not an easy nut to crack!" A long silence followed while he thought about his response.

"I can understand this and I am sure that when I put it to my Principal, he will agree!" Looking at his watch, he jumped up and held out his hand. "Well Ben. I look forward to reporting back to you and then hopefully working with you and Miguel. For now I will say good bye, duty calls I'm afraid." We shook hands all round and watched as he drove off to wherever he lived - he'd cleverly avoided answering any personal questions.

Two days later, I had good cause to celebrate. First the Doctor gave me the good news that my blood tests showed I was clear of the fever, so he gave his all clear for me to leave the country. On top of this, Juanita received the visa she had applied for from the British Consulate and I received - courtesy of the good Colonel - a Colombian Passport showing me as a resident of the country. With my medical clearance, there was no reason for us to stay so we prepared to leave. That evening, we were visited by Colonel Mendoza, who, I noted, had a very large grin on his face when he was shown into the lounge by the maid.

"There's a happy man if ever I saw one," I declared.

"Señor Ben! I have every reason to be happy I assure you," he said, accepting the large Scotch I poured for him.

"Sit down, man! Sit and tell us all about it." My eagerness to hear his news made him look at me questioningly. I gave him time to settle in a deep leather armchair and take a swig of his whisky.

"Well my friends!" he announced, looking around at us all in turn. "My Principal has given his fullest authority for the establishment of this Special Anti Drug Force," he paused for reaction. "But this has been partly achieved already, you understand?" he added, to confirm what we already knew. Clearing his throat he continued. "All of your men will be made Senior Lieutenants with good seniority. You two," he indicated Miguel and myself, "will hold the full rank of Major!" Having made this announcement, he sank back into the depth of the chair and attacked his drink.

A long silence followed as we took it all in, then with a laugh, Miguel turned to me and said, "I bet you didn't think you'd end up being enlisted into the army of the country you'd entered illegally, did you Ben?" Seeing the funny side of it, I joined into the general laughter and banter that his comment created.

"No I certainly didn't," I replied, looking at the Colonel. "But I feel there is something else Juan hasn't told us yet."

"You're right," he said with a typical Latin shrug and wave of his hands. "I have saved the best part to the last. You are also permitted to target people and groups overseas." A loud whoop of joy made me jump, as Miguel showed his excitement at this news.

"Brilliant! Absolutely brilliant!" he enthused. "We can now tackle the drug problem from all angles and d'you know what, Ben?" he asked, continuing with his excited speech before I could respond. "I think perhaps I have the answer to your prayers." He lapsed into silence, staring at me with an eager, encouraging look on his face. I was puzzled and he was willing me to guess what he had in mind

"I give in Miguel, I haven't the faintest idea what you're on about." To avoid this pantomime, I turned to the drinks trolley and poured myself another Scotch.

"My ship!" Miguel blurted with a cackling laugh. "Don't you see? We can use my ship!" He was almost dancing with excitement; he couldn't contain himself.

"Your ship?" I queried and then it dawned on me. "Yes, of course we can use it as cover!" It must have been the Scotch, but I was being very slow on the uptake here. "That means we have the troops, a cover that they could use to work and travel abroad under, plus the backing of the government! What more could we want?" I raised my glass in a toast.

"To the Snow Birds!"

"The Snow Birds!" They responded as one. Juan then advised us that he had other business to attend to and begged our leave, I saw him to the door and watched as his chauffer driven car whisked him away.

I returned to the lounge to find the others were still buzzing with the excitement of it all. We had achieved everything we had hoped for and more Marguerite pointed out the time and suggested we should be turning in, as tomorrow I wanted to fly back to Panama. I kissed her goodnight, once again savouring her perfume as she pressed herself against me.

Patting Miguel on the shoulder as I passed him, I said, "I can't wait to see you in uniform too!" The sound of his laughter followed Juanita and I up the stairs. A couple of hours later, as I watched Juanita drift off to sleep with a contented smile on her face, I reflected on the past few months.

Code Name SNOWBIRD

I had travelled halfway across the globe and met these wonderful people, achieving my prime aim of wiping out the Drug Cartel leaders and gained a wonderful bonus in the form of the Clinic. Then adding the icing to the cake by being offered the backing of the Colombian Government to train and use their Special Anti Drug Force.

On top of all that, I had the love of the beautiful young lady who was cuddled up to me.

There was no doubt in my mind as I too drifted into the depth; I would return home a happy man.

ISBN 1412026458